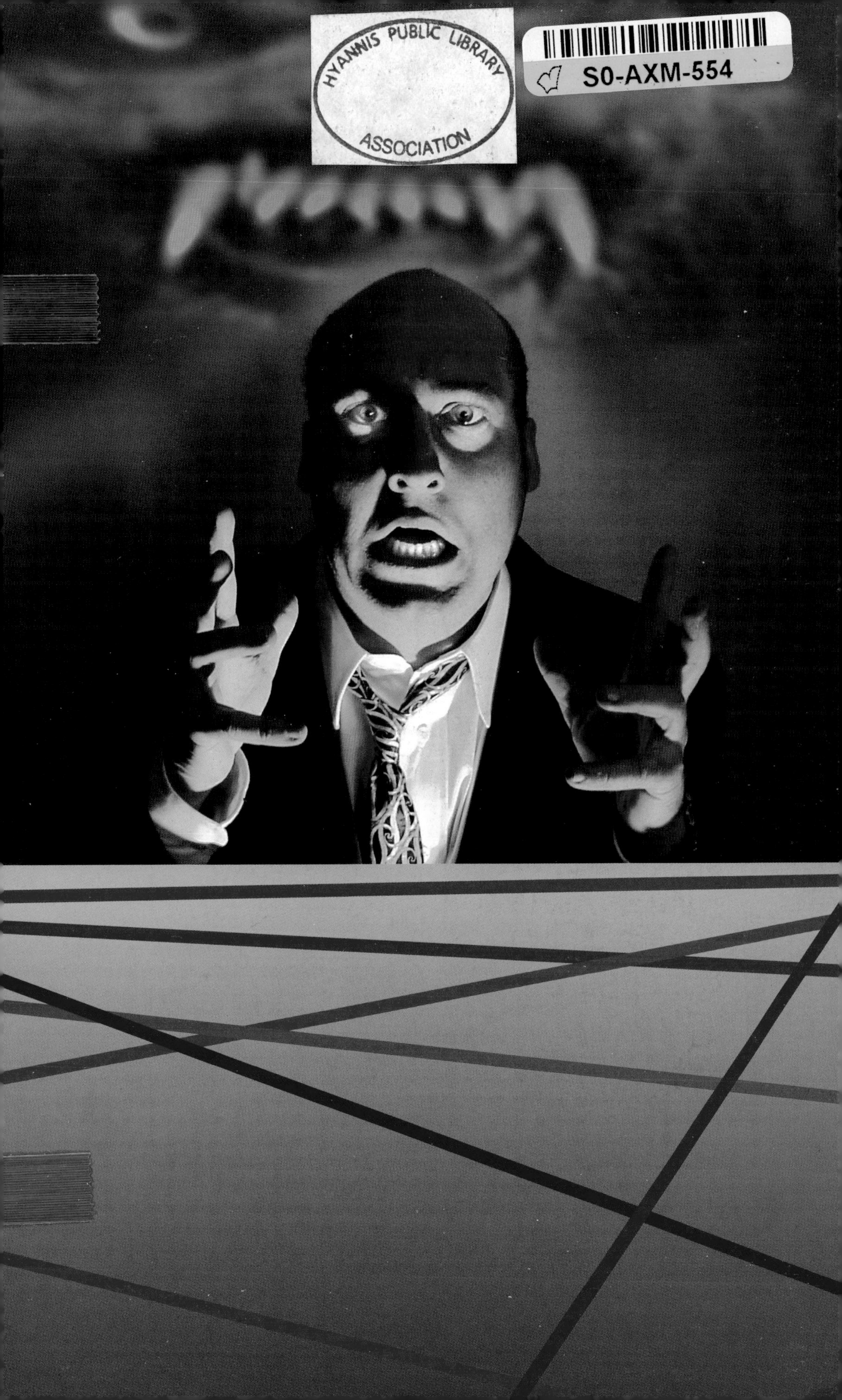

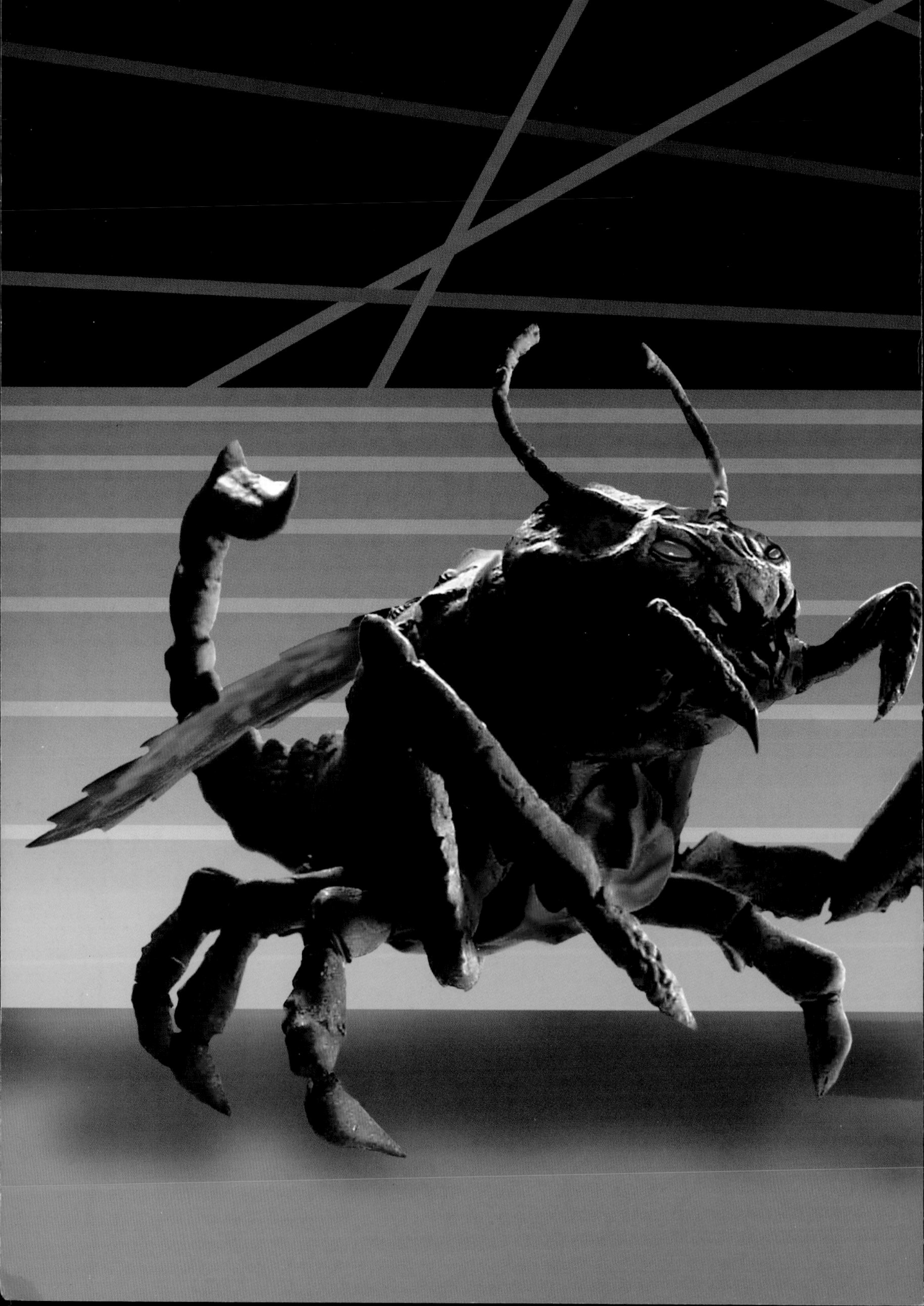

PETE VON SHOLLY'S
MORBID™

by Pete Von Sholly

DARK HORSE BOOKS™

Publisher: Mike Richardson

Editor: Dave Land

Assistant Editor: Philip W. Simon

Designer: Amy Arendts

Art Director: Mark Cox

PETE VON SHOLLY'S MORBID

Dark Horse Comics, Inc.
10956 SE Main Street
Milwaukie, OR 97222

www.darkhorse.com

To find a comics shop in your area call the Comic Shop Locator Service toll-free at (888) 266-4226

First edition: September 2003
ISBN: 1-59307-028-4

1 3 5 7 9 10 8 6 4 2
Printed in China

TABLE OF (MAL)CONTENTS

REPTITAN- THE PROBLEM FROM THE PAST 7
A rousing tale of a man-in-a-suit monster attacking Las Vegas brings back the shameless Captain Harry Hauser (last seen in Dark Horse Presents #152)
     Starring the indomitable Tim Flattery and the lovely Sarah Whiteaker Guest-starring the late great Vine Smith as Doctor Charles Crane

KUNG FI 21
Matrix Shmatrix! Let the fists and bullets fly in the metaphysical realm! It just has to look cool and be confusing.
     Showcasing the one and only Michael Anthony Jackson

THE ASTOUNDING SHEHEMOTH 29
Several key moments they always missed in the GIANT WOMAN movies. Plus an overgrown lizard with stuff glued on it! What more could you ask?
     Presenting the formidable Rich McGinis and an amalgam of Sarah Whiteaker and Kat Lester

CURSE OF THE WEREWIG 39
What happens when you seek to be more than you are? A cautionary tale of a terrifying transformation.
     Featuring the irrespressible (I tried to repress him, believe me) Mike Mitchell as P. Don Sheets

JUDGEMENT ON PLANET EX 43
Space travel and alien encounters from a pragmatist's point of view. Why should what's out there be any different from what's down here anyway?
     Bringing you the feisty Danny Jahnke as Vip Spang and the delightful Heather Whiteaker as Cosma

UNDEAD, MY ASS! 53
Fun with walking corpses! The undead can be very entertaining if you're careful.
     Dragging forth the unusual Bill Boes as Ed Weird and introducing Anthony Zierhut as the zombie who loses his head in a graphic scene. But loses it well!

DOCTOR TRICLOPS 57
A mad doctor made madder and monstrous by MUTANIUM! See him try to dominate the world, (what else?) by reducing his human foes to the size of mice! But will his tiny victims turn the (lab) tables?
     Barely containing the Astounding Richard Milner who always wanted to be a Mad Scientist. A man of many talents, just ask him!

YUGGOTH CALLING 65
Eldritch noisome fun at at a comics convention. Loosely adapted from THE OUTSIDER by H.P. Lovecraft.
Arkham if they can't take a joke.
     Reanimating Howard Phillips Lovecraft. Filmed at the Shrine Auditorium at Bruce Schwatz's fabulous monthly convention.

CATCHING HELL 69
Sea monsters from outer space and a hot girl in a bikini. Need I say more?
     Foisting upon you James Carson and the talented Melissa Spalding.

OUT OF PRINT 79
Books! Reading! Yeah, that's the stuff- the hell with video games. Sure.
     Shamelessly forcing Peter Von Sholly Junior into the 4 color spotlight as the dedicated Tuxford Noodlefactor.

MEDUSA 83
Mythological mayhem as the snaky she-demon gets the best of Testicles!
     Coaxing the once nimble Steve Duffy out of the back row and into the sandals of the Mighty Testicles! (That's TESS ti cleez, if you don't mind)

SCORPAMANTULA 85
Captain Hauser again (last seen on pp 7-20 of this book- ed.) in a battle against the ultimate "giant bug monster". Don't reveal the sickening ending to your friends.
     Re-presenting Tim Flattery and Heather Whiteaker. Scorpamantula sculpted by Andrea Von Sholly.
The great Vine Smith's last performance (sniff).

My sincere thanks and appreciation (in lieu of money) to all those who appeared, named and unnamed. Give it up for the Von Sholly Players!

When my dad was trying to explain something he would often say "do I have to draw you a picture?" Sarcasm aside, I knew what he meant. I liked drawing pictures from as far back as I can remember.

As a boy I dreamed of being a comic book artist, telling stories in pictures like Jack Kirby, Carl Barks, John Stanley and the guys in MAD magazine. I also loved moving pictures, especially if they had monsters in them. I was nurtured, inspired and forever warped by the horror and science fiction movies of the 50's and 60's and the great comic books of my youth. Fast forward and it wasn't long until I had relocated from New York to California and was working on the notorious "underground" comics of the late 60's / early 70's. Some were self-published, some for Last Gasp, one was even done in collaboration with Timothy Leary! In the mid-70's I also found opportunities to apply my skills in the animation field and, as luck would have it, motion pictures.

I have made a living drawing pictures for almost 30 years, for movies and television (THE CAT IN THE HAT, THE MASK, DARKMAN, MARS ATTACKS, THE SHAWSHANK REDEMPTION, THE GREEN MILE etc. and numerous cartoon shows). But they're called storyboards and the final medium of presentation is not print, but film. Storyboards relate strongly to comics and cartooning skills apply. But film is different, the drawn pictures being a blueprint, a means to an end, a way to get a director's vision on paper. And the artist is working in a highly collaborative medium, which can lead to a certain amount of frustration sometimes. Even when I managed to get some of my own movies made (such as the PREHYSTERIA series and PET SHOP) I was very unhappy with the way the stories were handled. It was a bittersweet experience but not one I regret as I functioned as a second unit director and learned a great deal.

More recently, during a stint at Disney Feature Animation, I was introduced to the computer, along with digital photography, which renewed my interest in comics. I discovered that I could bring photographic images into the comic format and manipulate them far more extensively than in the traditional "fumetti" I had seen. (Fumetti is a form of comics combining photos with word balloons.) And I now had the added fun of directing real actors, shooting my own scenes, background plates, etc. Even creating "special effects" without the complications of real movies and the tons of money they require. I could bring my movie making experience back to comics. And when you finish a comic story you at least have a finished product which you created the way you wanted it, without all the constraints of a huge studio and a million voices pulling the story every which way. I had begun to craft stories which refelct my own approach to the kind of material and subjects that appealed to me so much.

But, they always ask, why "Morbid"? I was always told I had a morbid sense of humor, but it's really "morbid with a wink".

Do I have to draw you a picture?

Pete Von Sholly
The Plateau
Early 21st Century

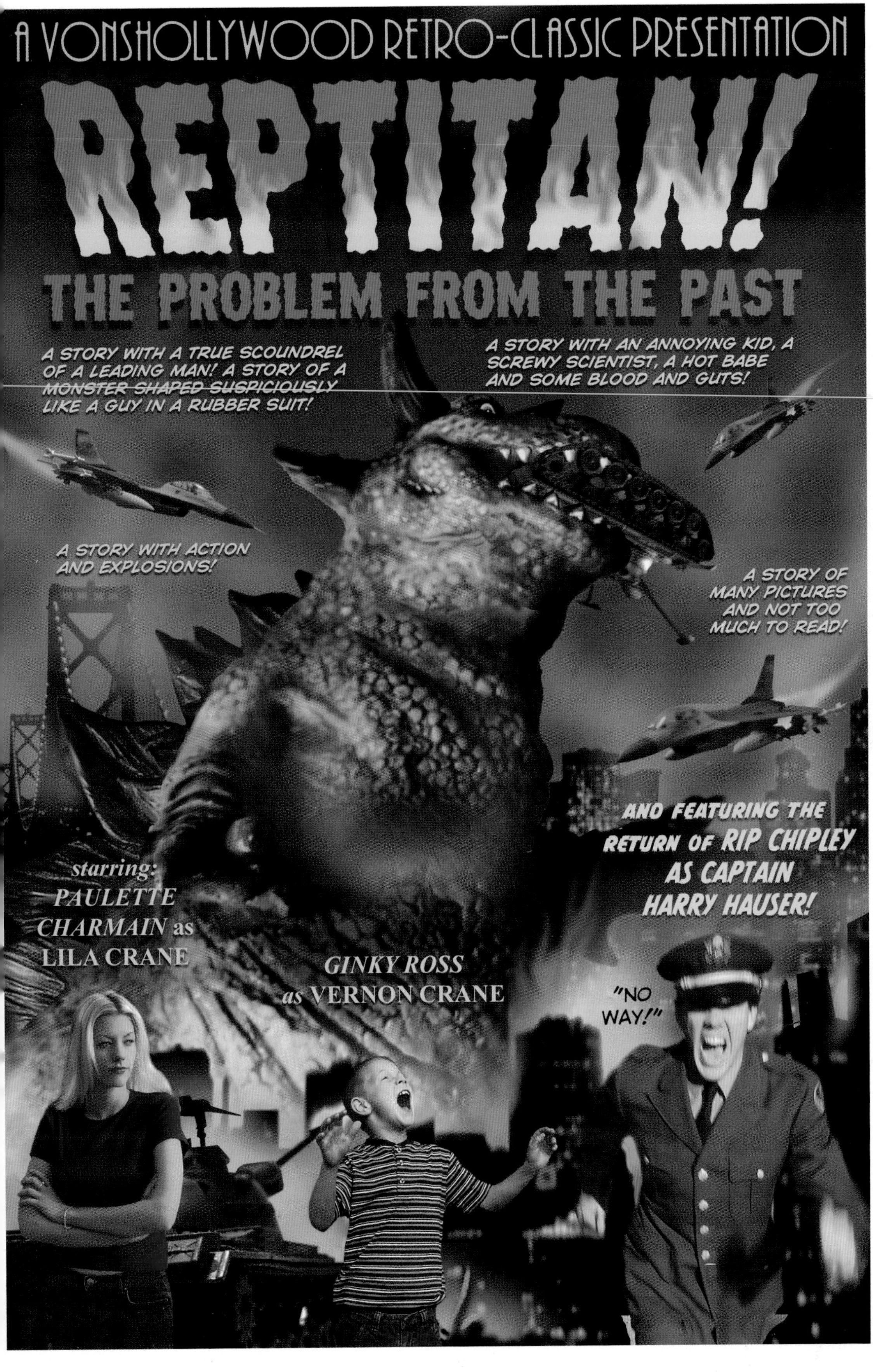

A VONSHOLLYWOOD RETRO-CLASSIC PRESENTATION
REPTITAN!
THE PROBLEM FROM THE PAST
A STORY WITH A TRUE SCOUNDREL OF A LEADING MAN! A STORY OF A MONSTER SHAPED SUSPICIOUSLY LIKE A GUY IN A RUBBER SUIT!
A STORY WITH AN ANNOYING KID, A SCREWY SCIENTIST, A HOT BABE AND SOME BLOOD AND GUTS!
A STORY WITH ACTION AND EXPLOSIONS!
A STORY OF MANY PICTURES AND NOT TOO MUCH TO READ!
AND FEATURING THE RETURN OF RIP CHIPLEY AS CAPTAIN HARRY HAUSER!
starring: PAULETTE CHARMAIN as LILA CRANE
GINKY ROSS as VERNON CRANE
"NO WAY!"

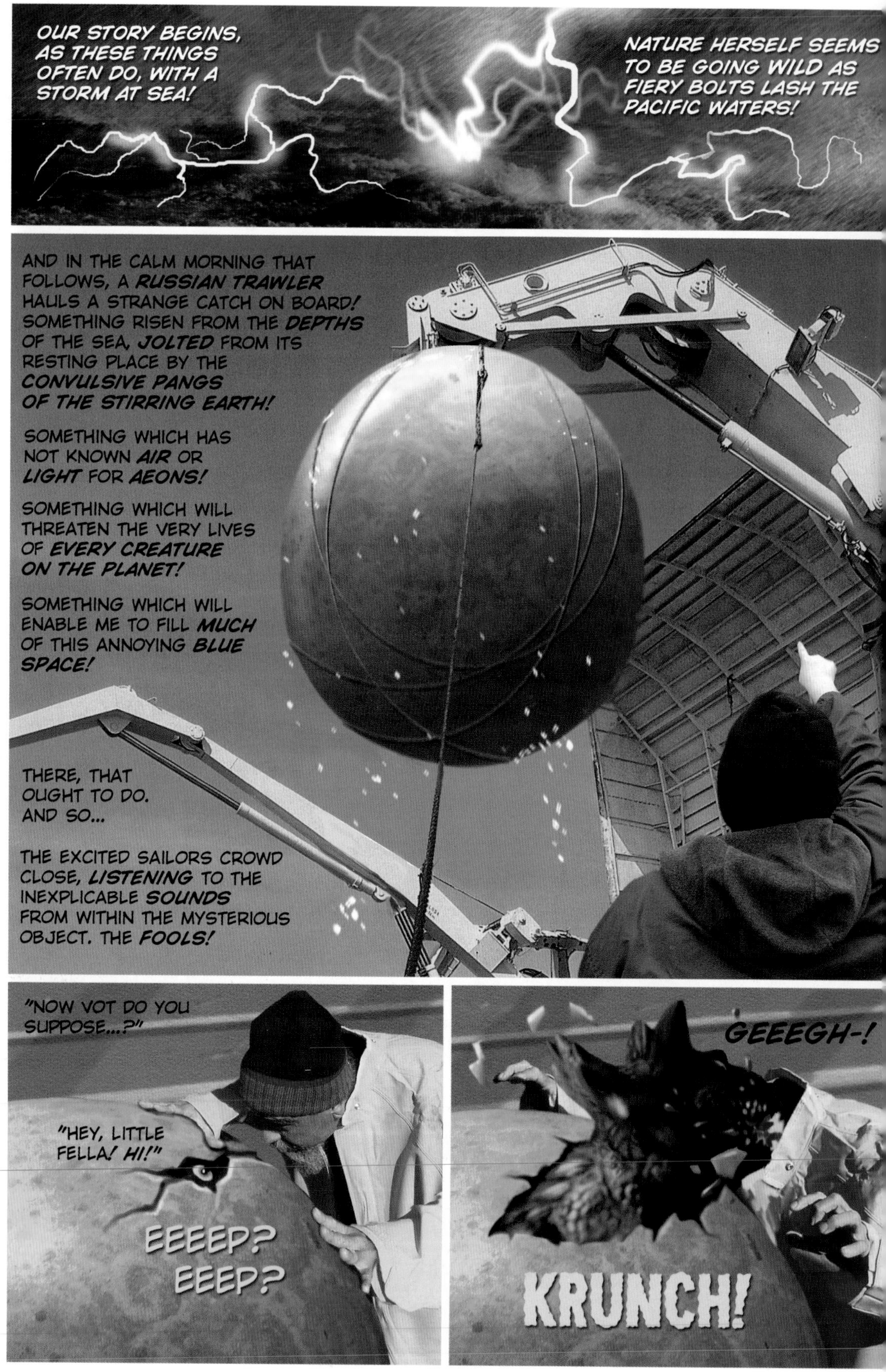
OUR STORY BEGINS, AS THESE THINGS OFTEN DO, WITH A STORM AT SEA!
NATURE HERSELF SEEMS TO BE GOING WILD AS FIERY BOLTS LASH THE PACIFIC WATERS!
AND IN THE CALM MORNING THAT FOLLOWS, A RUSSIAN TRAWLER HAULS A STRANGE CATCH ON BOARD! SOMETHING RISEN FROM THE DEPTHS OF THE SEA, JOLTED FROM ITS RESTING PLACE BY THE CONVULSIVE PANGS OF THE STIRRING EARTH!
SOMETHING WHICH HAS NOT KNOWN AIR OR LIGHT FOR AEONS!
SOMETHING WHICH WILL THREATEN THE VERY LIVES OF EVERY CREATURE ON THE PLANET!
SOMETHING WHICH WILL ENABLE ME TO FILL MUCH OF THIS ANNOYING BLUE SPACE!
THERE, THAT OUGHT TO DO. AND SO...
THE EXCITED SAILORS CROWD CLOSE, LISTENING TO THE INEXPLICABLE SOUNDS FROM WITHIN THE MYSTERIOUS OBJECT. THE FOOLS!
"NOW VOT DO YOU SUPPOSE...?"
"HEY, LITTLE FELLA! HI!"
EEEEP? EEEP?
GEEEGH-!
KRUNCH!

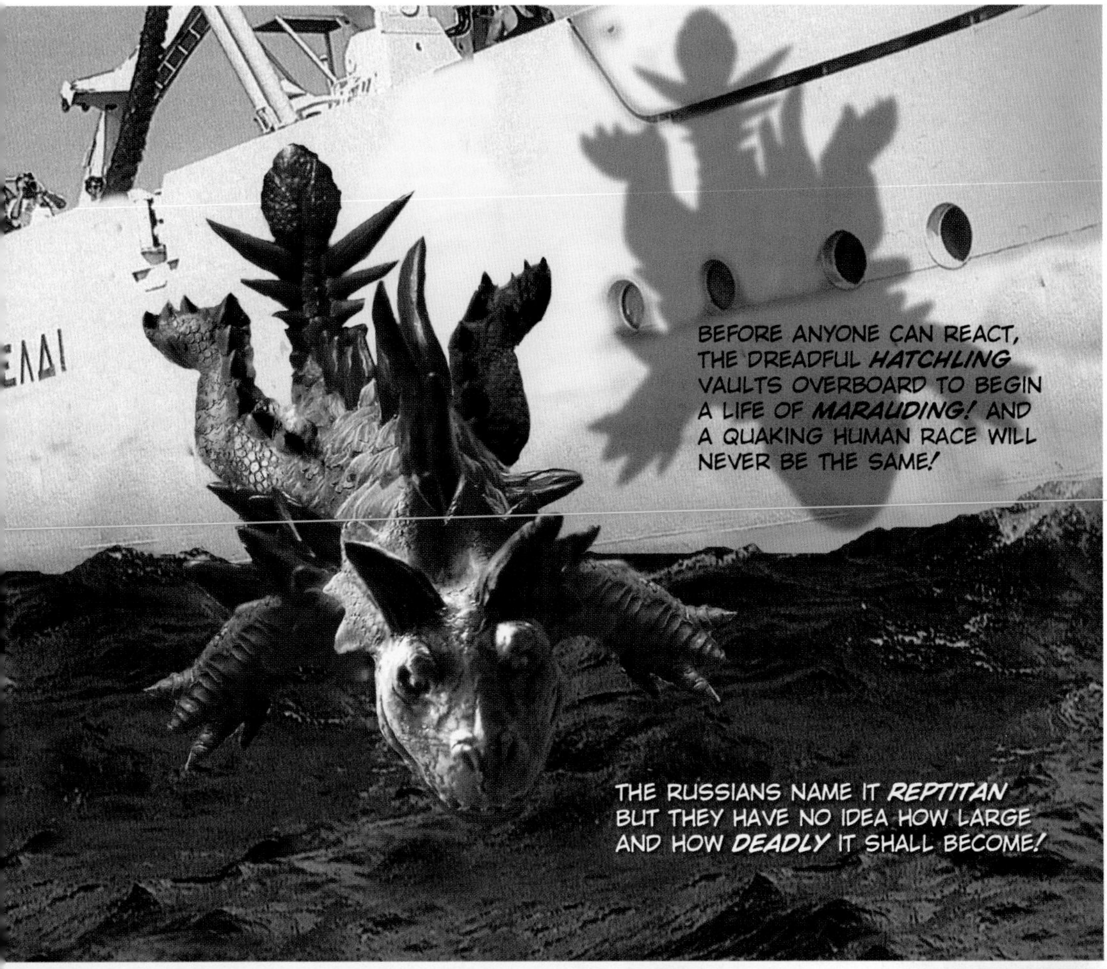
ΕΛΛΑΙ
BEFORE ANYONE CAN REACT, THE DREADFUL *HATCHLING* VAULTS OVERBOARD TO BEGIN A LIFE OF *MARAUDING!* AND A QUAKING HUMAN RACE WILL NEVER BE THE SAME!
THE RUSSIANS NAME IT *REPTITAN* BUT THEY HAVE NO IDEA HOW LARGE AND HOW *DEADLY* IT SHALL BECOME!

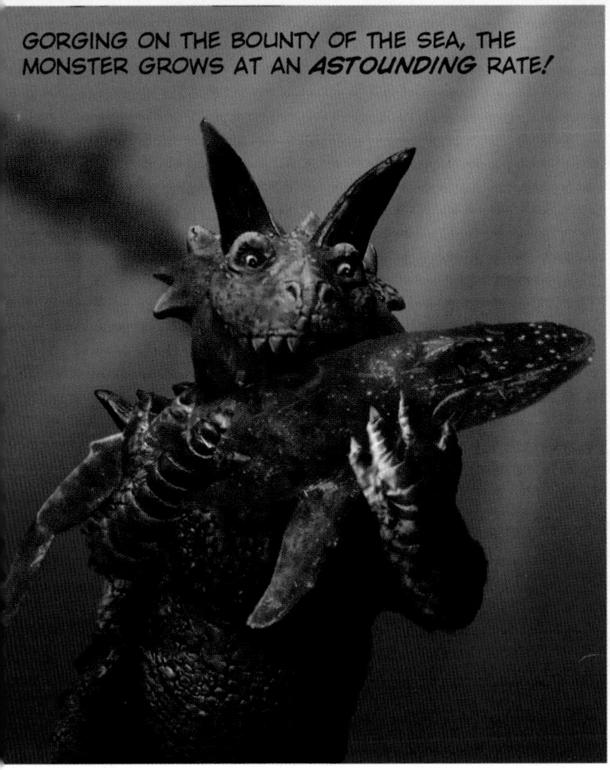
GORGING ON THE BOUNTY OF THE SEA, THE MONSTER GROWS AT AN *ASTOUNDING* RATE!

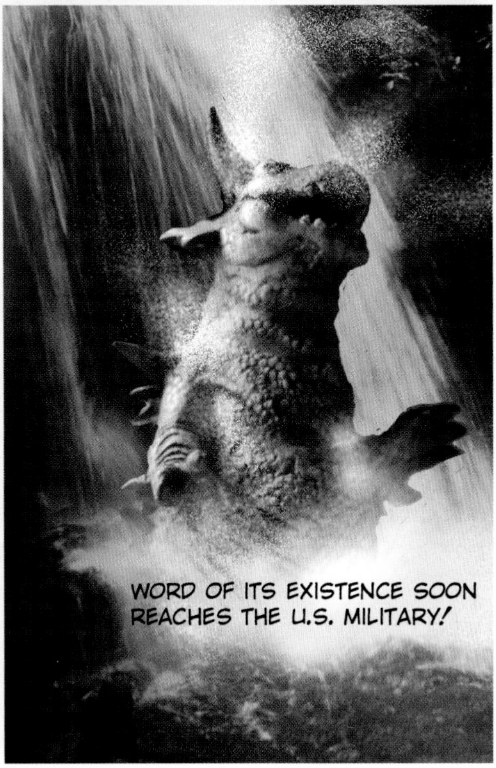
WORD OF ITS EXISTENCE SOON REACHES THE U.S. MILITARY!

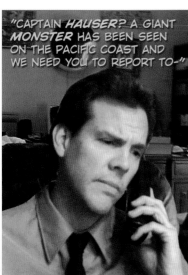

"CAPTAIN *HAUSER?* A GIANT *MONSTER* HAS BEEN SEEN ON THE PACIFIC COAST AND WE NEED YOU TO REPORT TO—"

"COUGH! SNIFF! I'B *SIG!* I HAB TO STAY ID *BED* FOR A WHOLE *WEEG!* COUGH. CAN'D *HELB* YOU, SNIFF. GA-*BYE!*"

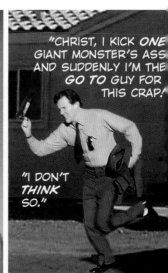

"CHRIST, I KICK *ONE* GIANT MONSTER'S ASS AND SUDDENLY I'M THE *GO TO* GUY FOR THIS CRAP!"

"I DON'T *THINK* SO."

"CAPTAIN HAUSER? PLEASE COME WITH US , SIR."

YES, HAUSER'S SUPERIORS ARE *WISE* TO HIS WILY WAYS! IN MINUTES, OUR RELUCTANT HERO IS EN ROUTE TO THE HIDDEN LAB OF DOCTOR *CHARLES CRANE*, THE GENETICS PIONEER!

WUP WUP WUP WUP WUP WUP!

BAWWWK!

GREAT.

BUCK-ACK

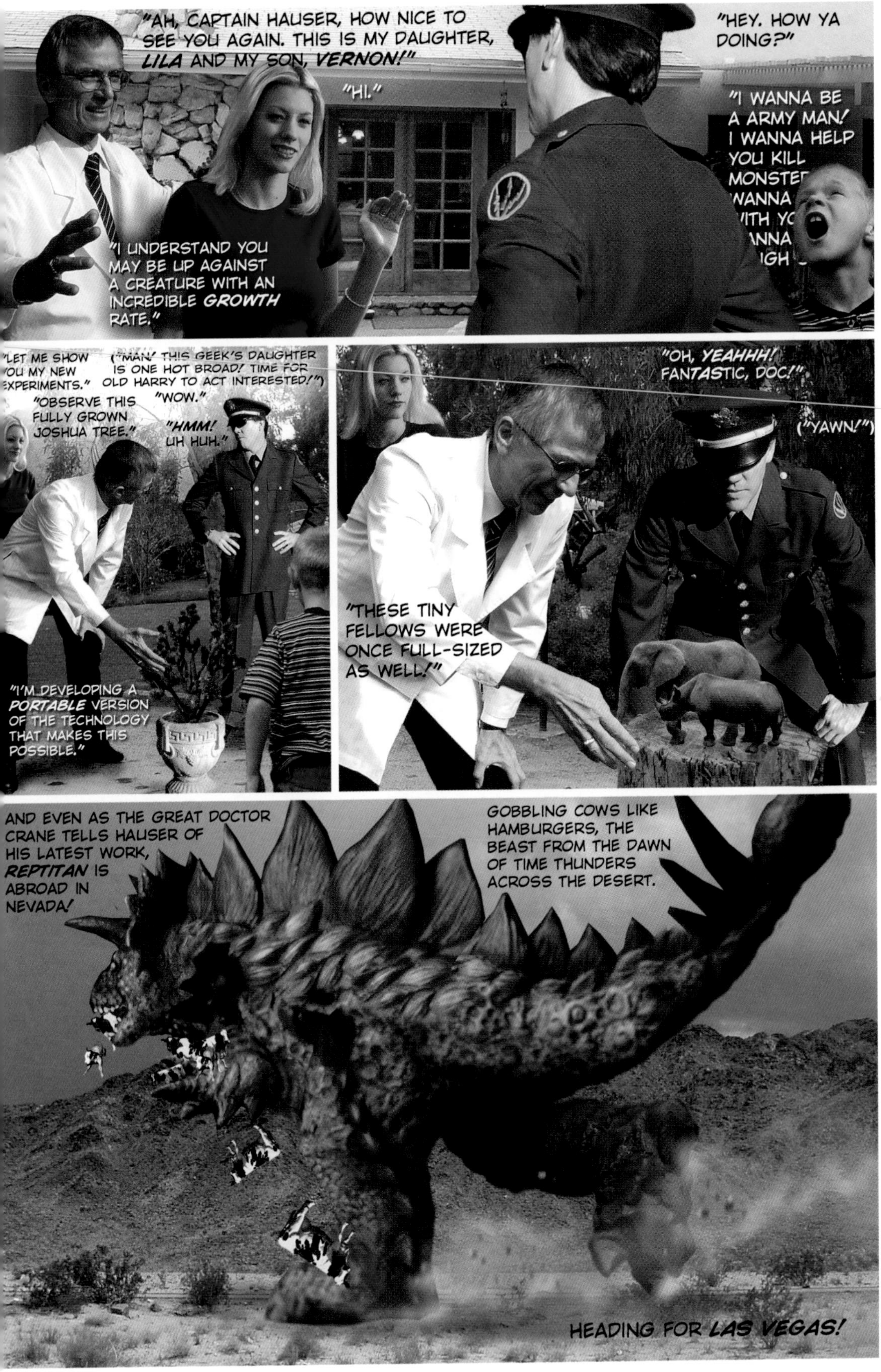
"AH, CAPTAIN HAUSER, HOW NICE TO SEE YOU AGAIN. THIS IS MY DAUGHTER, LILA AND MY SON, VERNON!"
"HEY. HOW YA DOING?"
"HI."
"I WANNA BE A ARMY MAN! I WANNA HELP YOU KILL MONSTE
"I UNDERSTAND YOU MAY BE UP AGAINST A CREATURE WITH AN INCREDIBLE GROWTH RATE."
"LET ME SHOW YOU MY NEW EXPERIMENTS."
("MAN! THIS GEEK'S DAUGHTER IS ONE HOT BROAD! TIME FOR OLD HARRY TO ACT INTERESTED!")
"OBSERVE THIS FULLY GROWN JOSHUA TREE."
"WOW."
"HMM! UH HUH."
"I'M DEVELOPING A PORTABLE VERSION OF THE TECHNOLOGY THAT MAKES THIS POSSIBLE."
"OH, YEAHHH! FANTASTIC, DOC!"
("YAWN!")
"THESE TINY FELLOWS WERE ONCE FULL-SIZED AS WELL!"
AND EVEN AS THE GREAT DOCTOR CRANE TELLS HAUSER OF HIS LATEST WORK, REPTITAN IS ABROAD IN NEVADA!
GOBBLING COWS LIKE HAMBURGERS, THE BEAST FROM THE DAWN OF TIME THUNDERS ACROSS THE DESERT.
HEADING FOR LAS VEGAS!

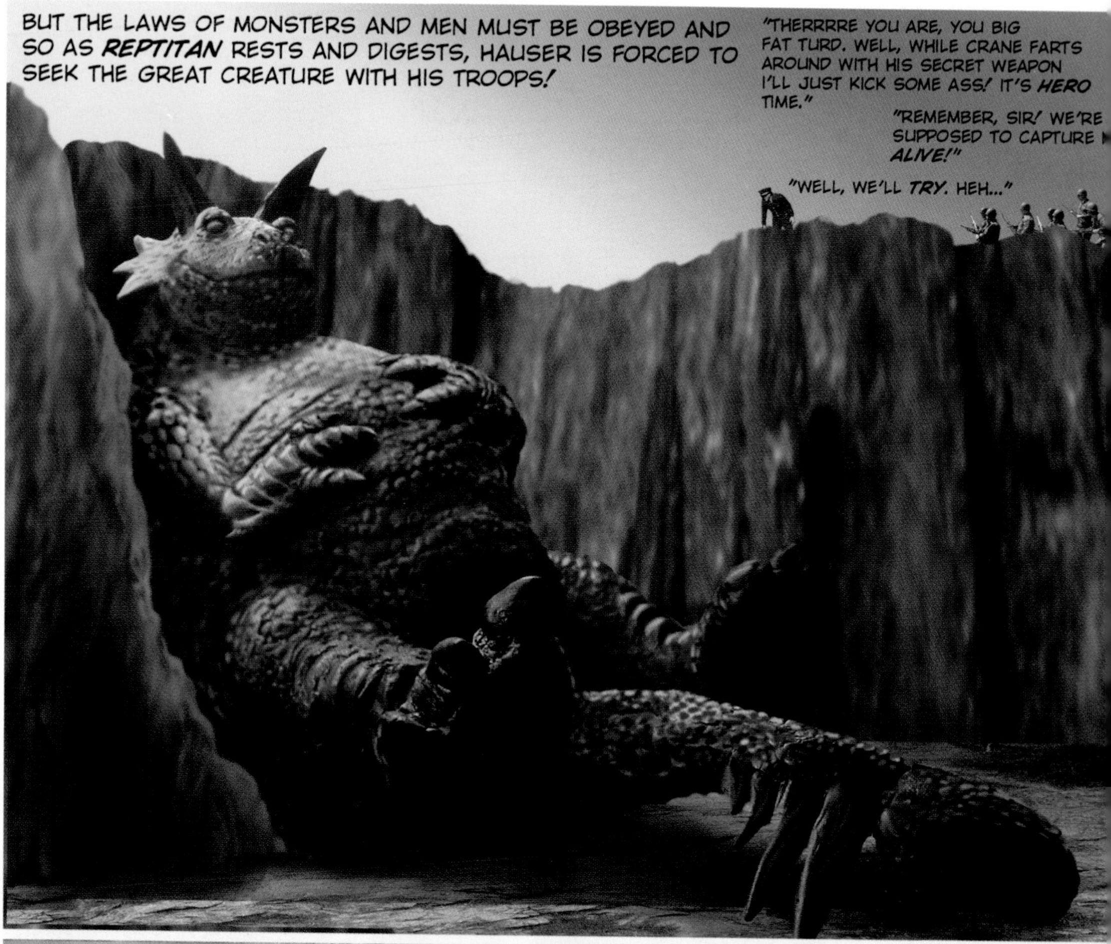
BUT THE LAWS OF MONSTERS AND MEN MUST BE OBEYED AND SO AS ***REPTITAN*** RESTS AND DIGESTS, HAUSER IS FORCED TO SEEK THE GREAT CREATURE WITH HIS TROOPS!
"THERRRRE YOU ARE, YOU BIG FAT TURD. WELL, WHILE CRANE FARTS AROUND WITH HIS SECRET WEAPON I'LL JUST KICK SOME ASS! IT'S ***HERO*** TIME."
"REMEMBER, SIR! WE'RE SUPPOSED TO CAPTURE ***ALIVE!***"
"WELL, WE'LL ***TRY***. HEH..."

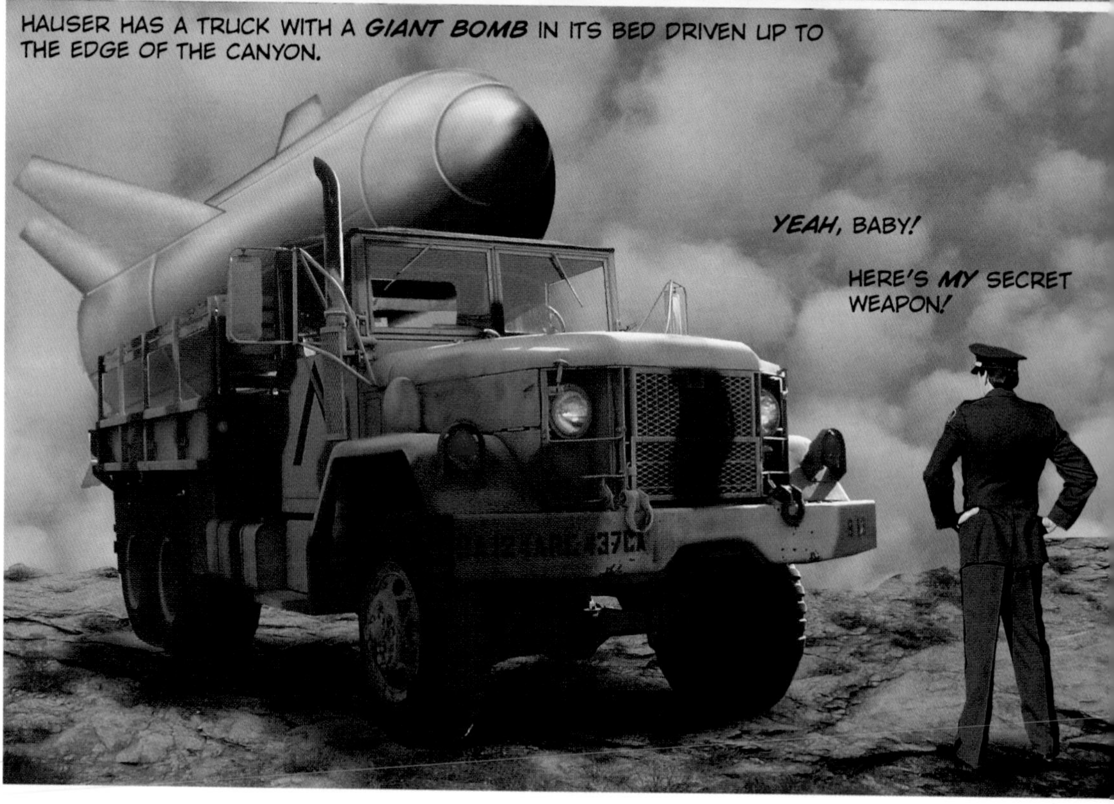
HAUSER HAS A TRUCK WITH A ***GIANT BOMB*** IN ITS BED DRIVEN UP TO THE EDGE OF THE CANYON.
YEAH, BABY!
HERE'S ***MY*** SECRET WEAPON!

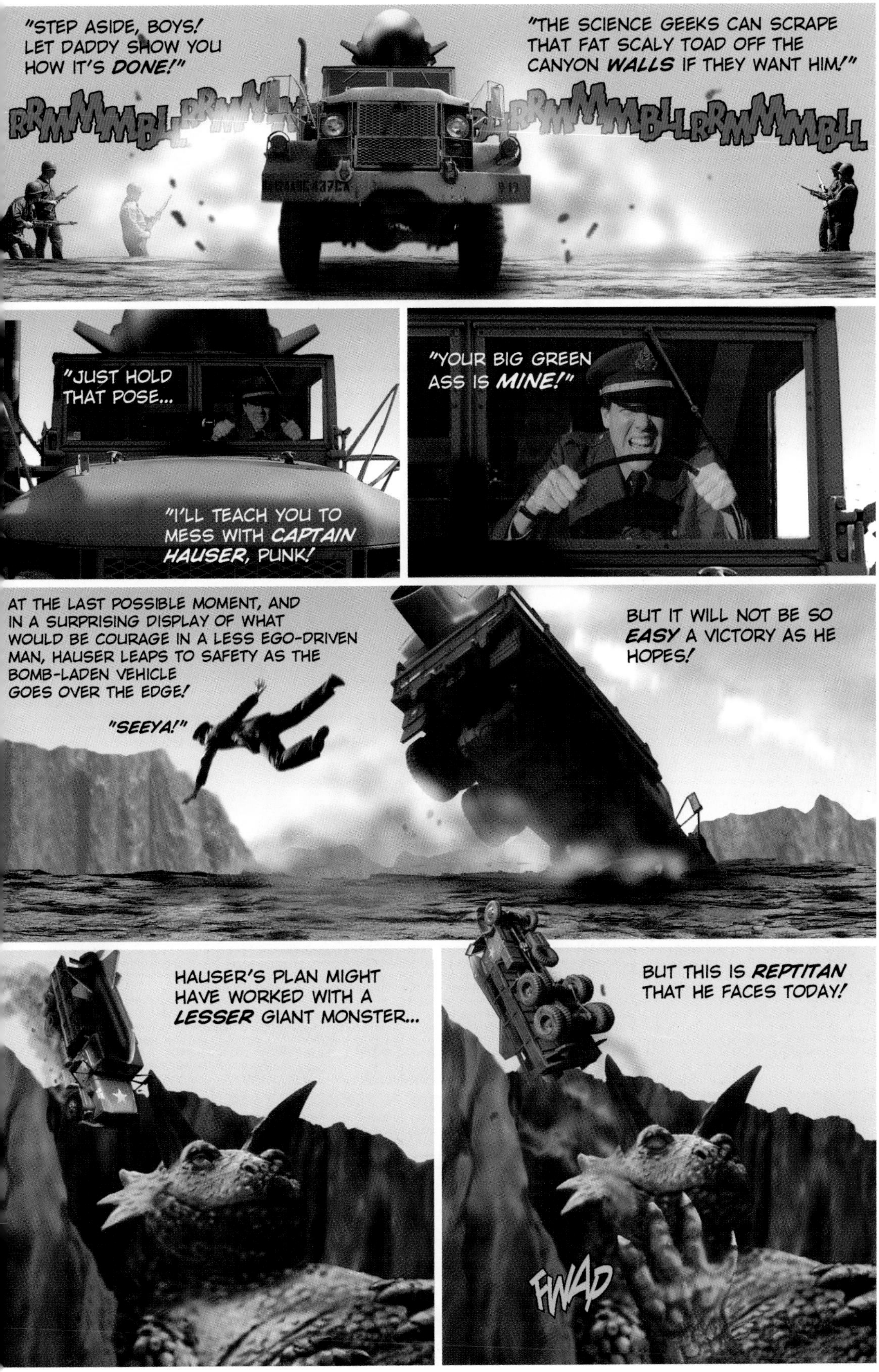
"STEP ASIDE, BOYS! LET DADDY SHOW YOU HOW IT'S DONE!"
"THE SCIENCE GEEKS CAN SCRAPE THAT FAT SCALY TOAD OFF THE CANYON WALLS IF THEY WANT HIM!"
RRMMMMBLLRRMMMMBLLRRMMMMBLLRRMMMMBLL
"JUST HOLD THAT POSE...
"I'LL TEACH YOU TO MESS WITH CAPTAIN HAUSER, PUNK!
"YOUR BIG GREEN ASS IS MINE!"
AT THE LAST POSSIBLE MOMENT, AND IN A SURPRISING DISPLAY OF WHAT WOULD BE COURAGE IN A LESS EGO-DRIVEN MAN, HAUSER LEAPS TO SAFETY AS THE BOMB-LADEN VEHICLE GOES OVER THE EDGE!
"SEEYA!"
BUT IT WILL NOT BE SO EASY A VICTORY AS HE HOPES!
HAUSER'S PLAN MIGHT HAVE WORKED WITH A LESSER GIANT MONSTER...
BUT THIS IS REPTITAN THAT HE FACES TODAY!
FWAP

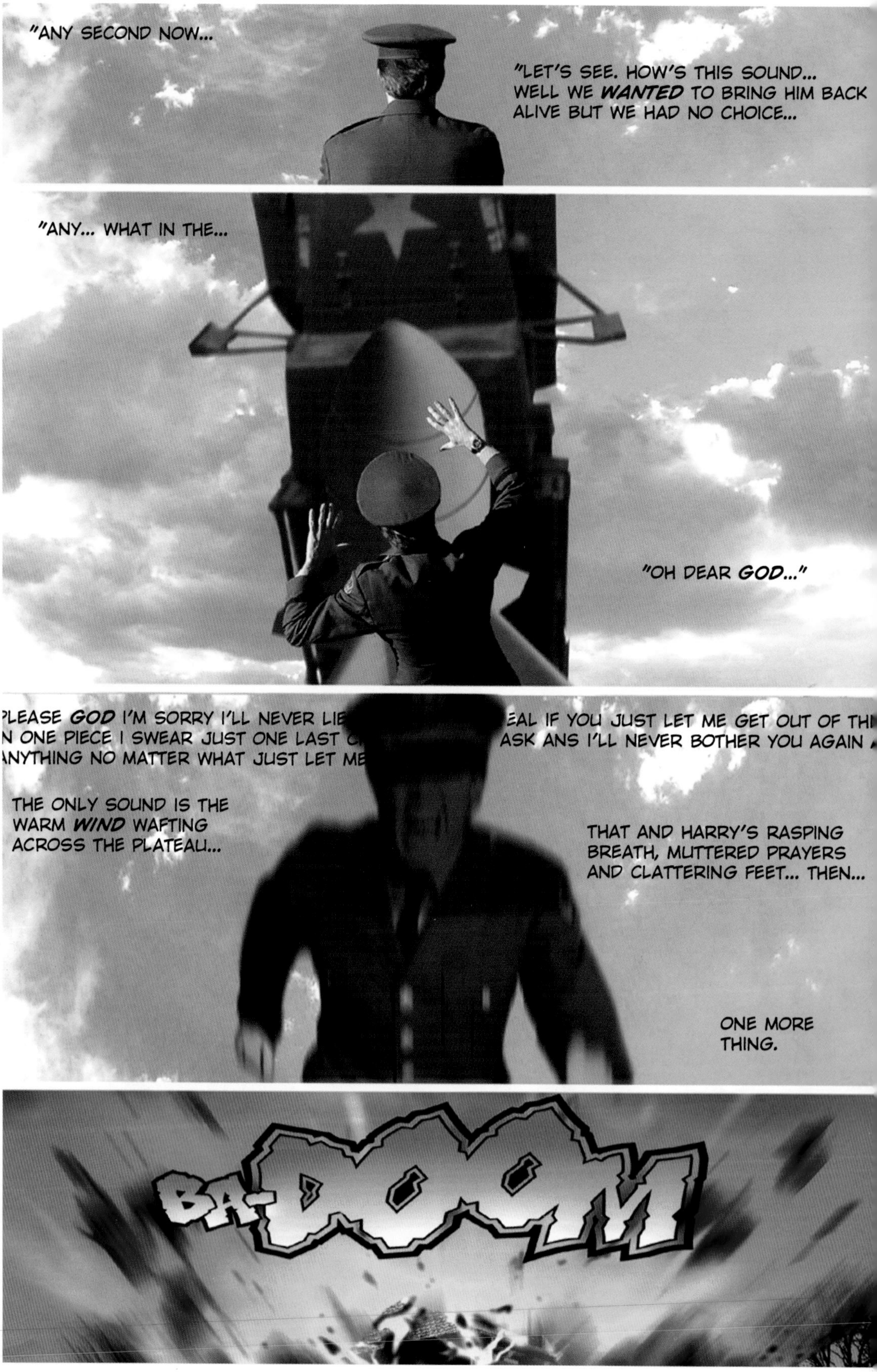

"ANY SECOND NOW...
"LET'S SEE. HOW'S THIS SOUND... WELL WE WANTED TO BRING HIM BACK ALIVE BUT WE HAD NO CHOICE...
"ANY... WHAT IN THE...
"OH DEAR GOD..."
PLEASE GOD I'M SORRY I'LL NEVER LIE
N ONE PIECE I SWEAR JUST ONE LAST C
NYTHING NO MATTER WHAT JUST LET ME
EAL IF YOU JUST LET ME GET OUT OF TH
ASK ANS I'LL NEVER BOTHER YOU AGAIN
THE ONLY SOUND IS THE WARM WIND WAFTING ACROSS THE PLATEAU...
THAT AND HARRY'S RASPING BREATH, MUTTERED PRAYERS AND CLATTERING FEET... THEN...
ONE MORE THING.
BA-DOOM

EVERYTHING HURTING, INCLUDING HIS PRIDE, HAUSER HAS SOMEHOW SURVIVED HIS OWN STUPID PLAN!

"WELL, THAT STINKING REPTILE KNOWS HE'S BEEN IN A FIGHT!"

"ALL THAT'S LEFT IS TO FINISH HIM OFF!"

MILES AWAY, REPTITAN, DASHES INTO A LAKE TO COOL OFF.

AND HE SEEMS TO BE *CHUCKLING*, IN HIS GIANT MONSTERISH WAY!

HAUSER'S DREAMS ARE ALL FIRE AND RAGE...

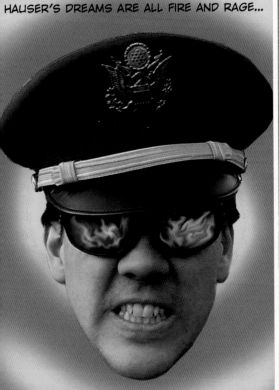

AND THEN THE DAMN *PHONE* RINGS AGAIN.

"*HAUSER!* THIS IS THE PRESIDENT! *REPTITAN* IS APPROACHING LAS VEGAS AND WE CAN'T STOP IT! DOCTOR CRANE HAS A WEAPON THAT HE THINKS MAY DO THE JOB! YOUR COUNTRY NEEDS YOU, HARRY! DON'T LET US DOWN!"

"THIS CAN'T BE HAPPENING..."

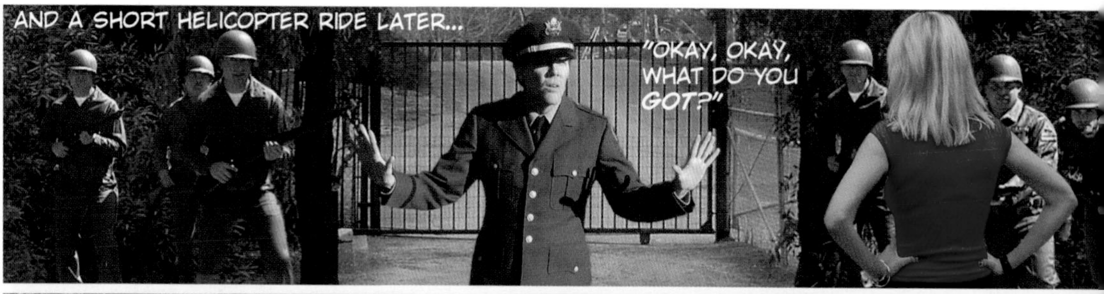
AND A SHORT HELICOPTER RIDE LATER...
"OKAY, OKAY, WHAT DO YOU GOT?"

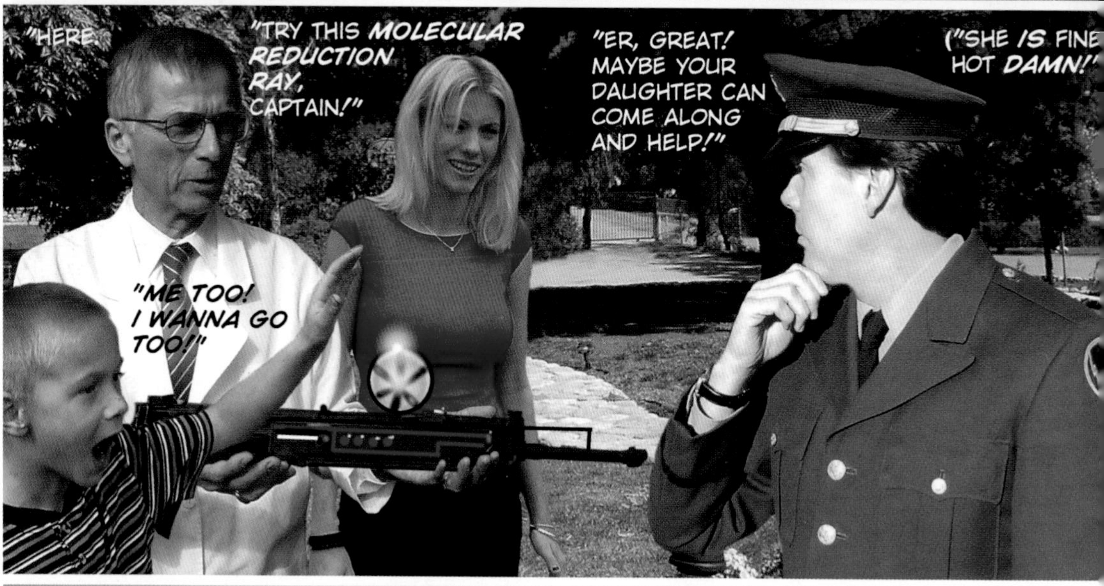
"HERE.
"TRY THIS MOLECULAR REDUCTION RAY, CAPTAIN!"
"ER, GREAT! MAYBE YOUR DAUGHTER CAN COME ALONG AND HELP!"
("SHE IS FINE HOT DAMN!"
"ME TOO! I WANNA GO TOO!"

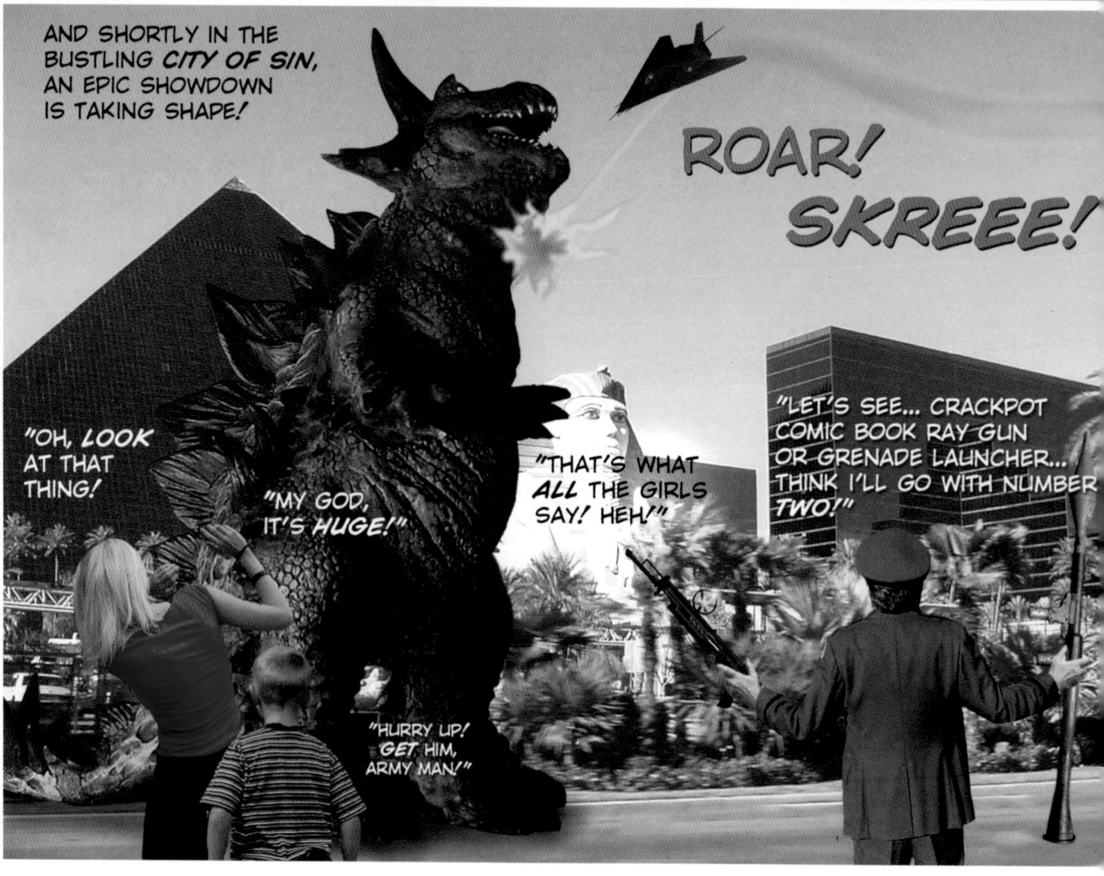
AND SHORTLY IN THE BUSTLING CITY OF SIN, AN EPIC SHOWDOWN IS TAKING SHAPE!
ROAR!
SKREEE!
"OH, LOOK AT THAT THING!
"MY GOD, IT'S HUGE!"
"THAT'S WHAT ALL THE GIRLS SAY! HEH!"
"LET'S SEE... CRACKPOT COMIC BOOK RAY GUN OR GRENADE LAUNCHER... THINK I'LL GO WITH NUMBER TWO!"
"HURRY UP! GET HIM, ARMY MAN!"

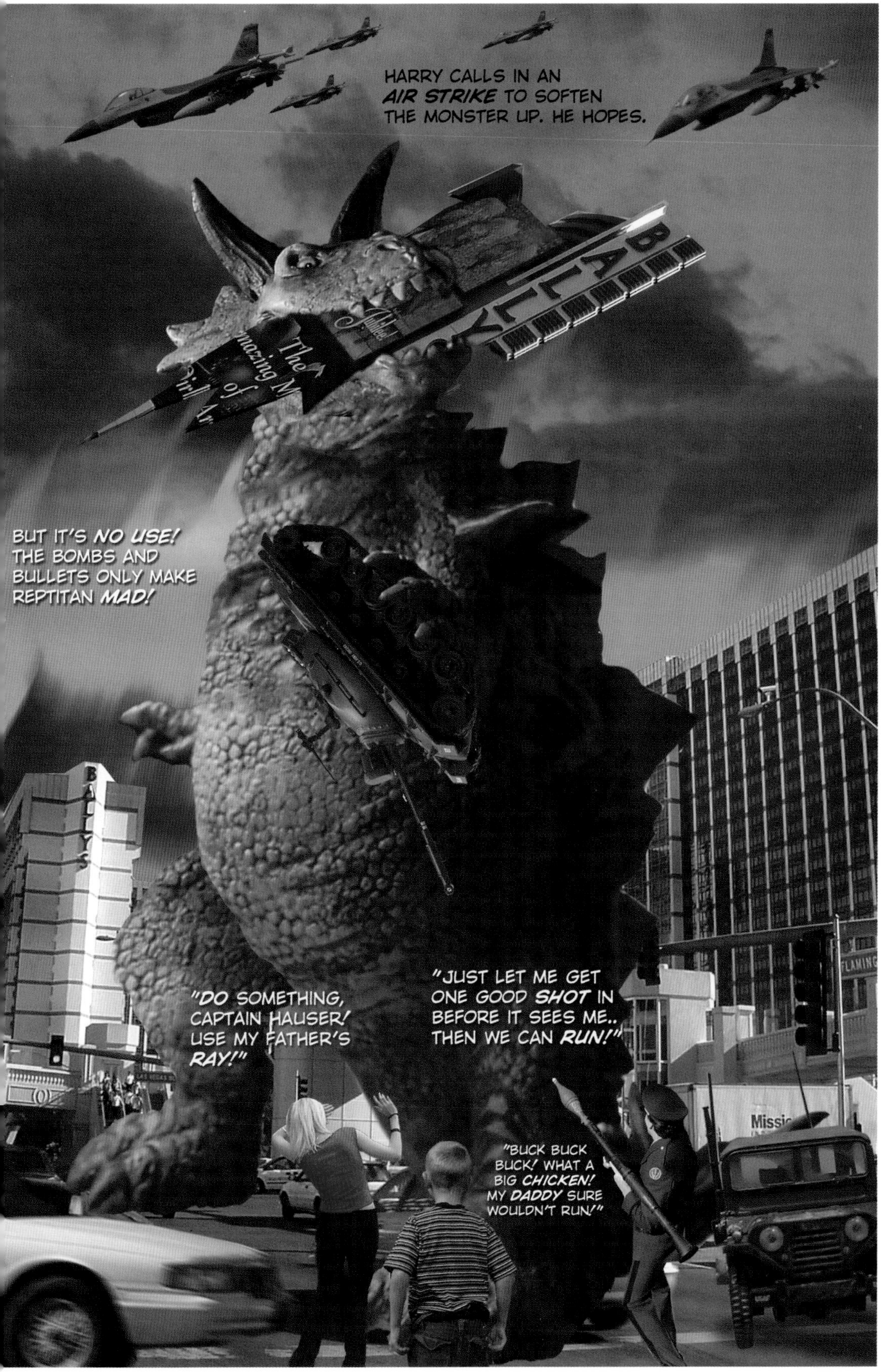
HARRY CALLS IN AN *AIR STRIKE* TO SOFTEN THE MONSTER UP. HE HOPES.
BUT IT'S *NO USE!* THE BOMBS AND BULLETS ONLY MAKE REPTITAN *MAD!*
"*DO* SOMETHING, CAPTAIN HAUSER! USE MY FATHER'S *RAY!*"
"JUST LET ME GET ONE GOOD *SHOT* IN BEFORE IT SEES ME.. THEN WE CAN *RUN!*"
"BUCK BUCK BUCK! WHAT A BIG *CHICKEN!* MY *DADDY* SURE WOULDN'T RUN!"

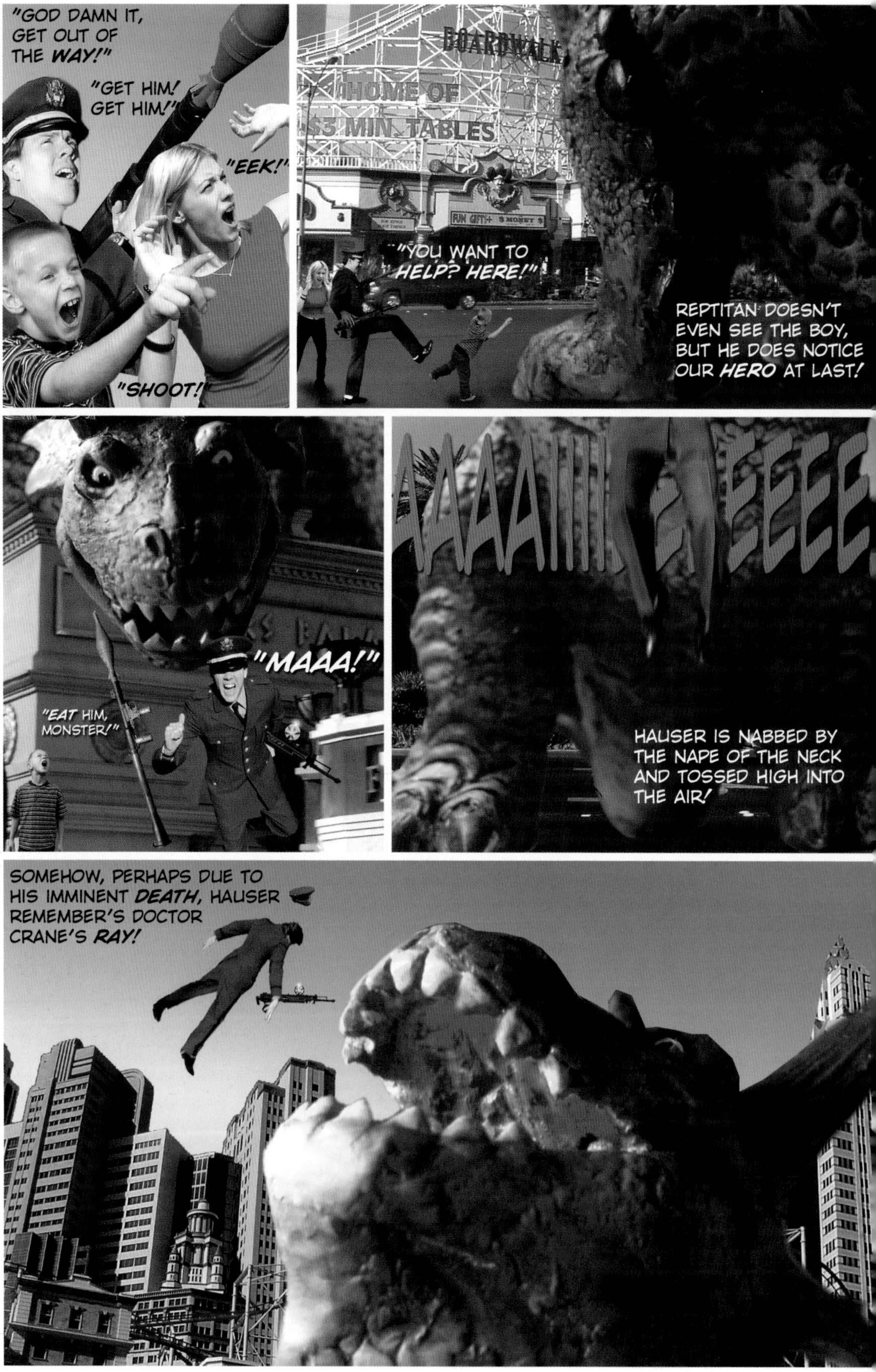
"GOD DAMN IT, GET OUT OF THE *WAY!*"
"GET HIM! GET HIM!"
"EEK!"
"SHOOT!"
BOARDWALK
HOME OF
$3 MIN. TABLES
"YOU WANT TO *HELP?* HERE!"
REPTITAN DOESN'T EVEN SEE THE BOY, BUT HE DOES NOTICE OUR *HERO* AT LAST!
"MAAA!"
"*EAT* HIM, MONSTER!"
AAAAIIII
EEEE
HAUSER IS NABBED BY THE NAPE OF THE NECK AND TOSSED HIGH INTO THE AIR!
SOMEHOW, PERHAPS DUE TO HIS IMMINENT *DEATH*, HAUSER REMEMBER'S DOCTOR CRANE'S *RAY!*

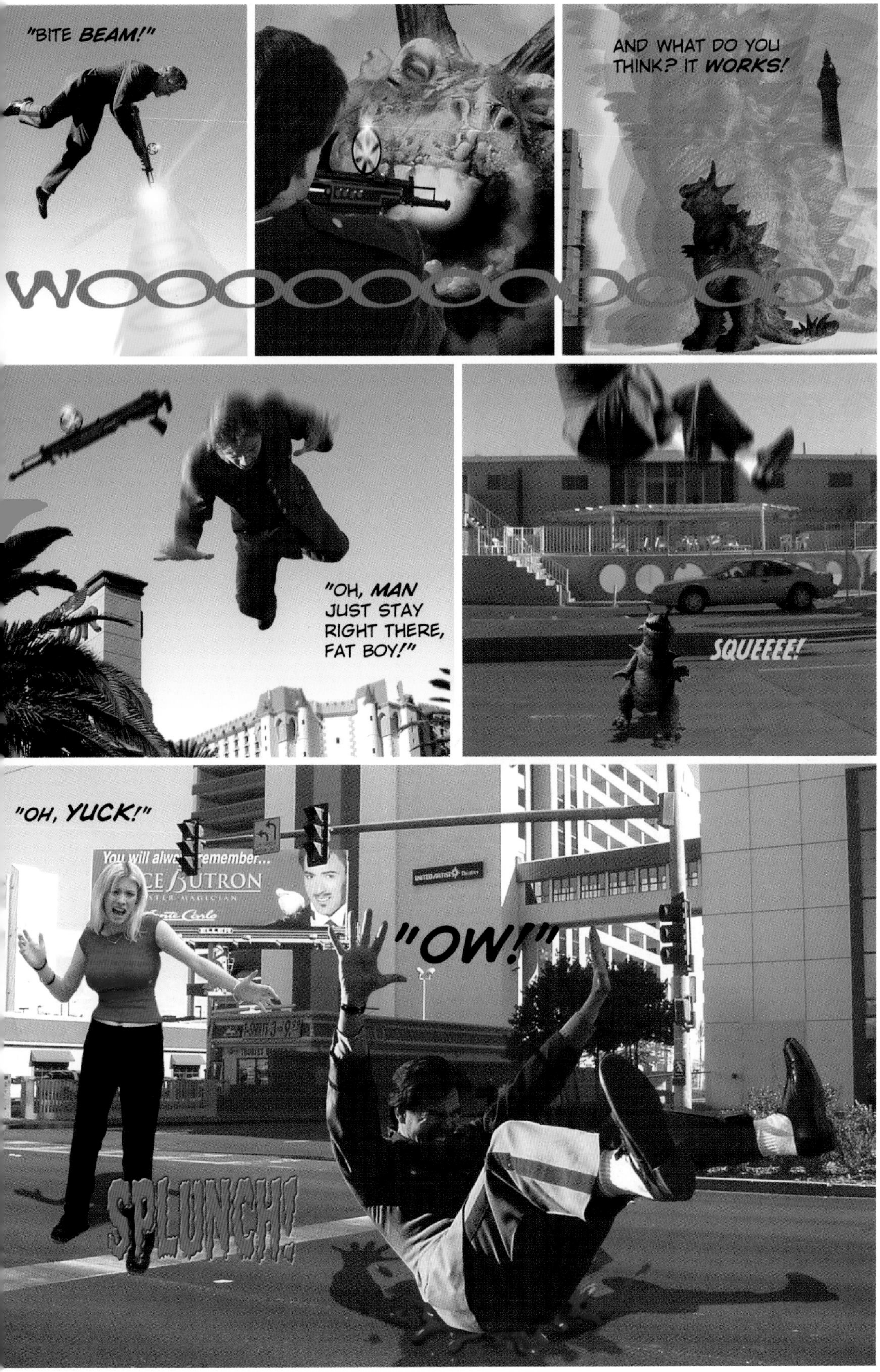
"BITE BEAM!"
WOOOOOOOOOOO!
AND WHAT DO YOU THINK? IT WORKS!
"OH, MAN JUST STAY RIGHT THERE, FAT BOY!"
SQUEEEE!
"OH, YUCK!"
"OW!"
SPLUNCH!

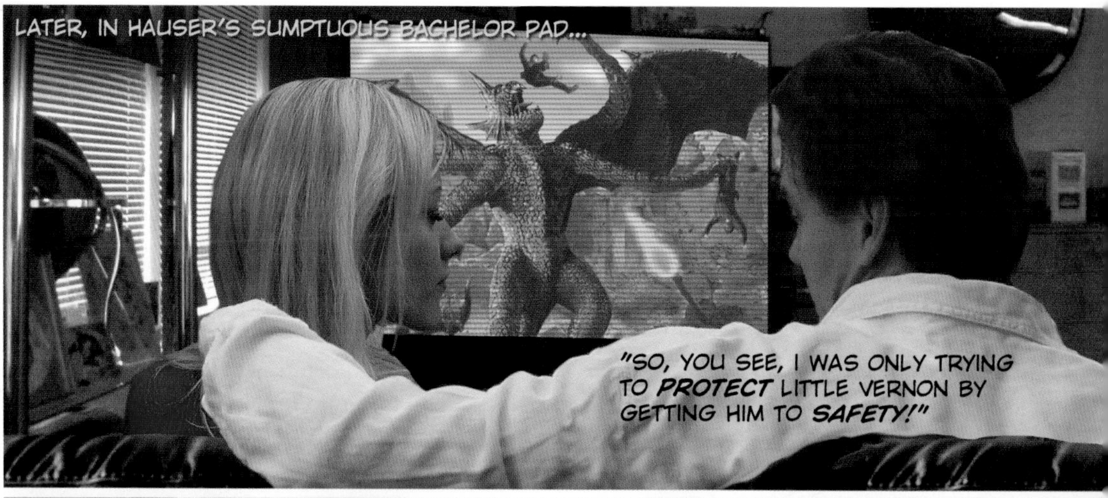
LATER, IN HAUSER'S SUMPTUOUS BACHELOR PAD...
"SO, YOU SEE, I WAS ONLY TRYING TO PROTECT LITTLE VERNON BY GETTING HIM TO SAFETY!"

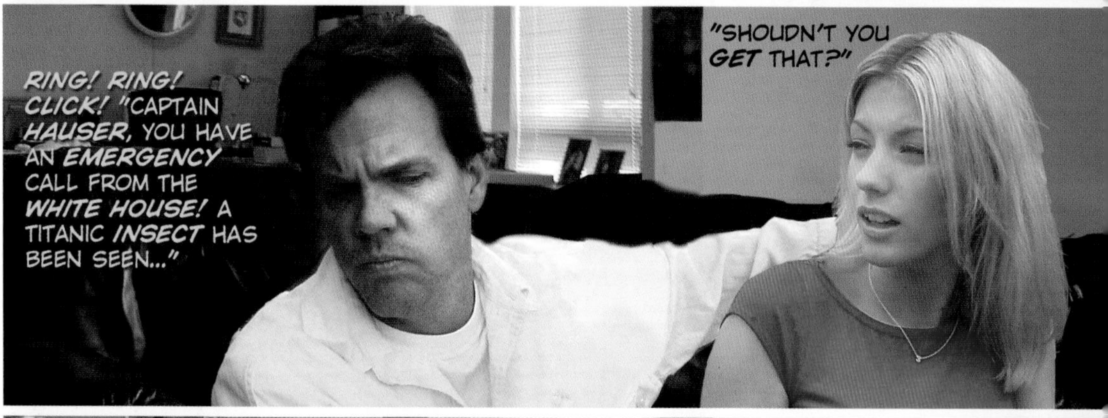
RING! RING! CLICK! "CAPTAIN HAUSER, YOU HAVE AN EMERGENCY CALL FROM THE WHITE HOUSE! A TITANIC INSECT HAS BEEN SEEN..."
"SHOUDN'T YOU GET THAT?"

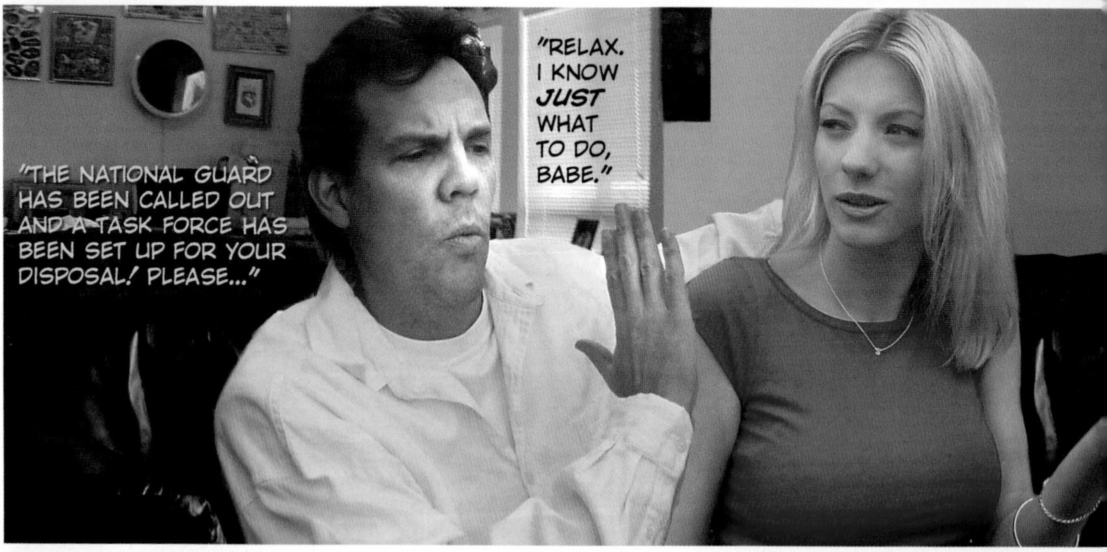
"THE NATIONAL GUARD HAS BEEN CALLED OUT AND A TASK FORCE HAS BEEN SET UP FOR YOUR DISPOSAL! PLEASE..."
"RELAX. I KNOW JUST WHAT TO DO, BABE."

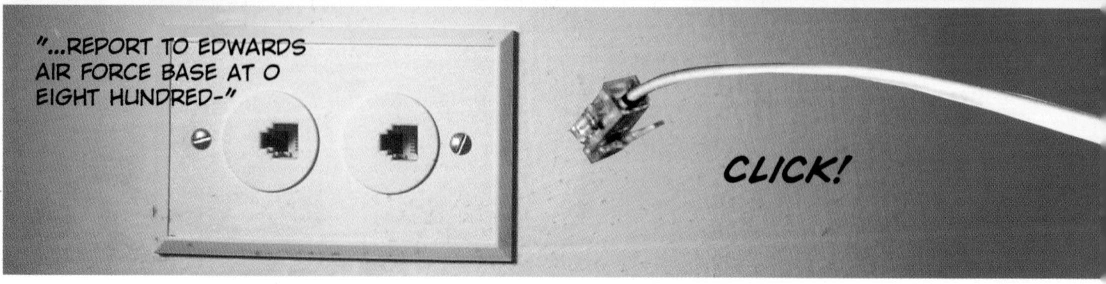
"...REPORT TO EDWARDS AIR FORCE BASE AT O EIGHT HUNDRED-"
CLICK!

KUNG FI

Thaaaat's right, tough guy. Kung Fi. It's the new GENRE that's sweeping the nation. It's like how they mix two succesful things assuming that a third succesful thing will result. So you take KUNG FU and cross it with SCI FI to get this new thing. Is it any good? Are Kung Fu and Sci Fi any good? Sometimes. Sometimes not. Right? Anyway, whatever it is, here it comes!

What is reality? Who's to say? Is it all an illusion? Who's asking? Who knows? And who cares? Who came first in the universe? Was it man or machine? Are you so sure? Did man create the machine in his own image or was it the other way around? What other way? And around what? Had enough? Shall we move on? Good.

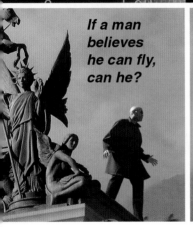

If a man believes he can fly, can he?

Maybe.

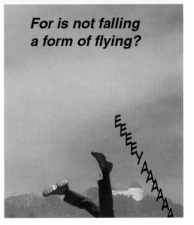

For is not falling a form of flying?

21

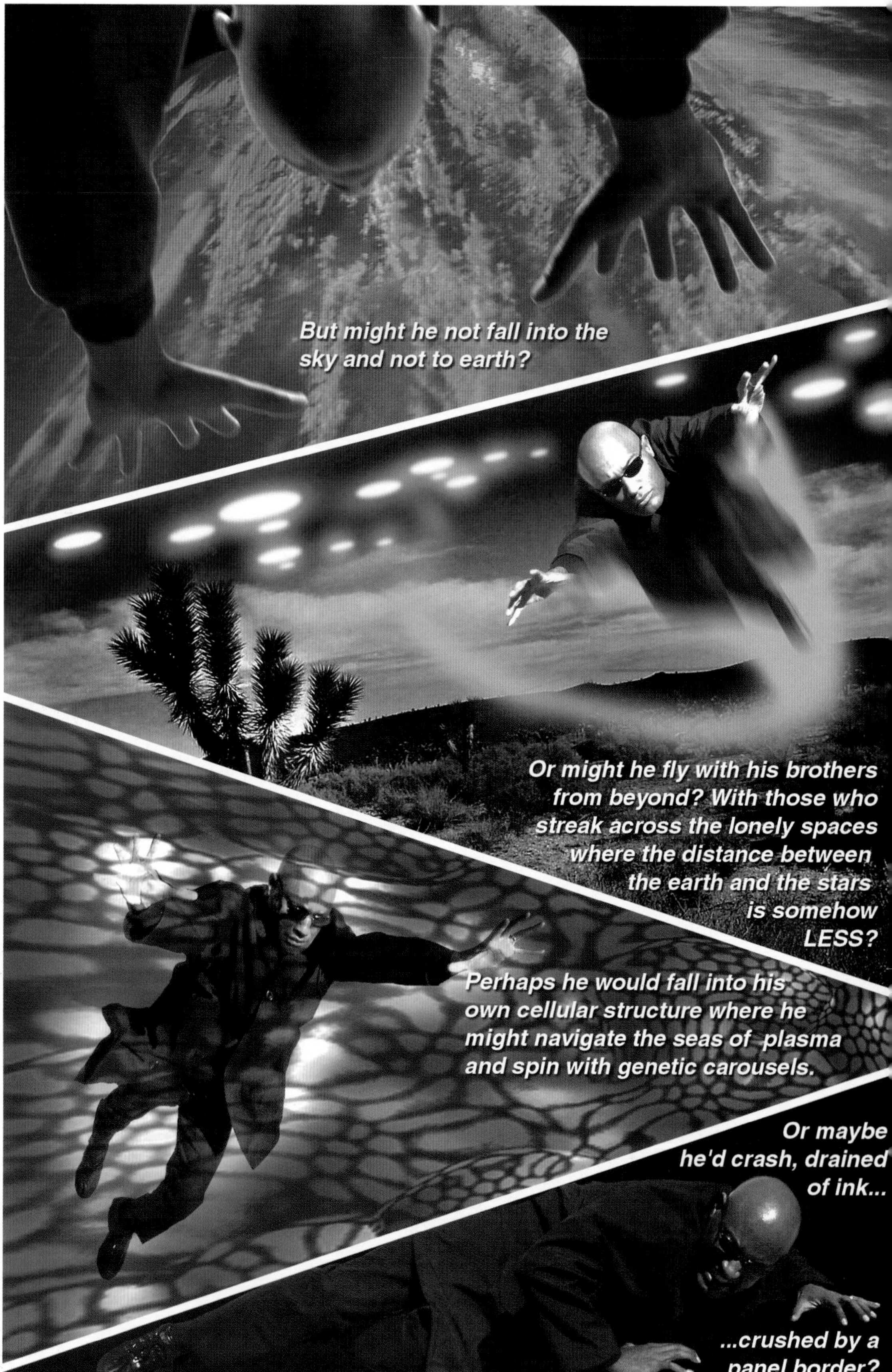

But might he not fall into the sky and not to earth?
Or might he fly with his brothers from beyond? With those who streak across the lonely spaces where the distance between the earth and the stars is somehow LESS?
Perhaps he would fall into his own cellular structure where he might navigate the seas of plasma and spin with genetic carousels.
Or maybe he'd crash, drained of ink...
...crushed by a panel border?

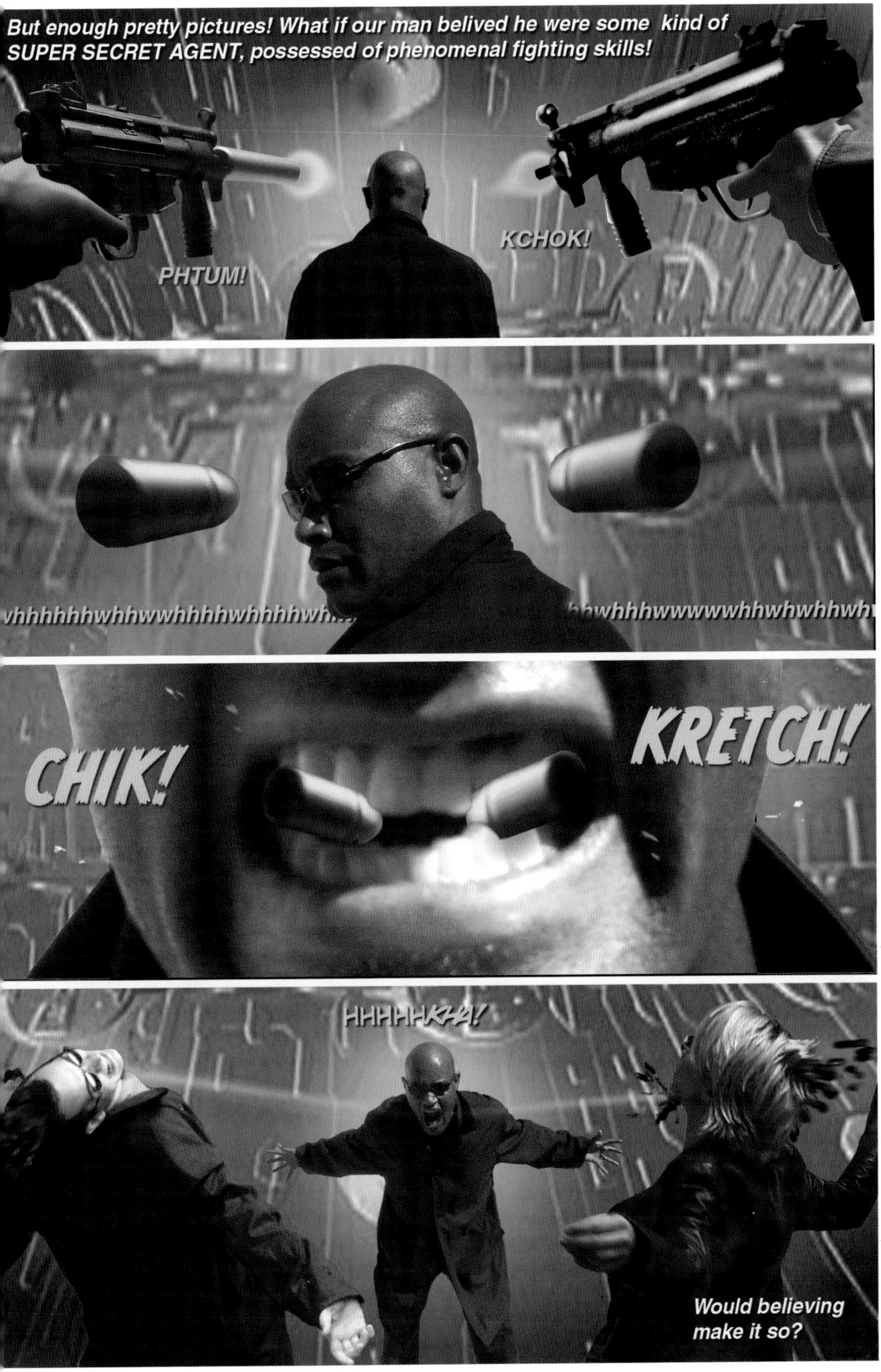
But enough pretty pictures! What if our man belived he were some kind of SUPER SECRET AGENT, possessed of phenomenal fighting skills!
PHTUM!
KCHOK!
vhhhhhhwhhwwhhhhwhhhhwh...
...hwhhhwwwwwhhwhwhhwh
CHIK!
KRETCH!
HHHHHKZA!
Would believing make it so?

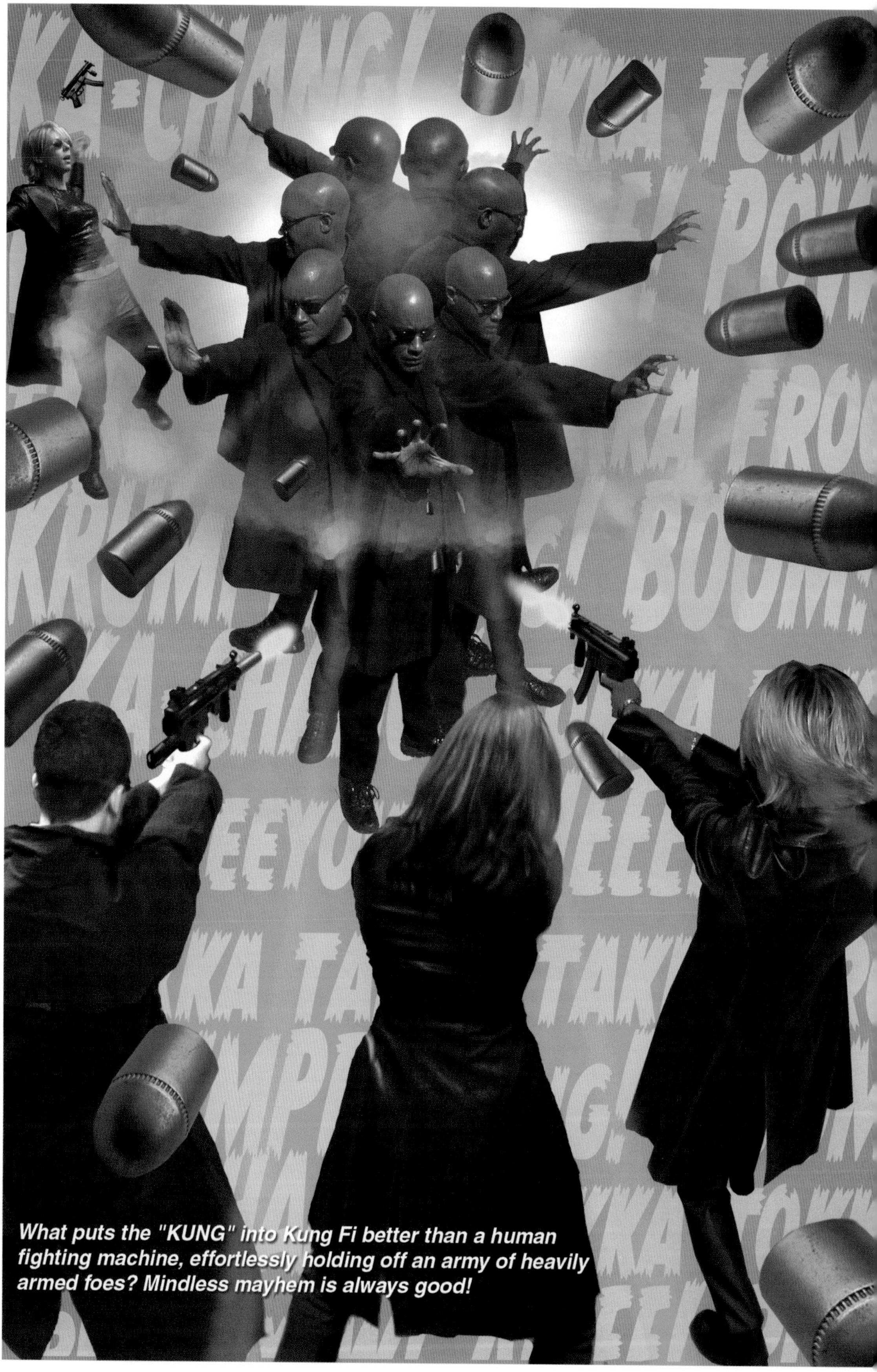

What puts the "KUNG" into Kung Fi better than a human fighting machine, effortlessly holding off an army of heavily armed foes? Mindless mayhem is always good!

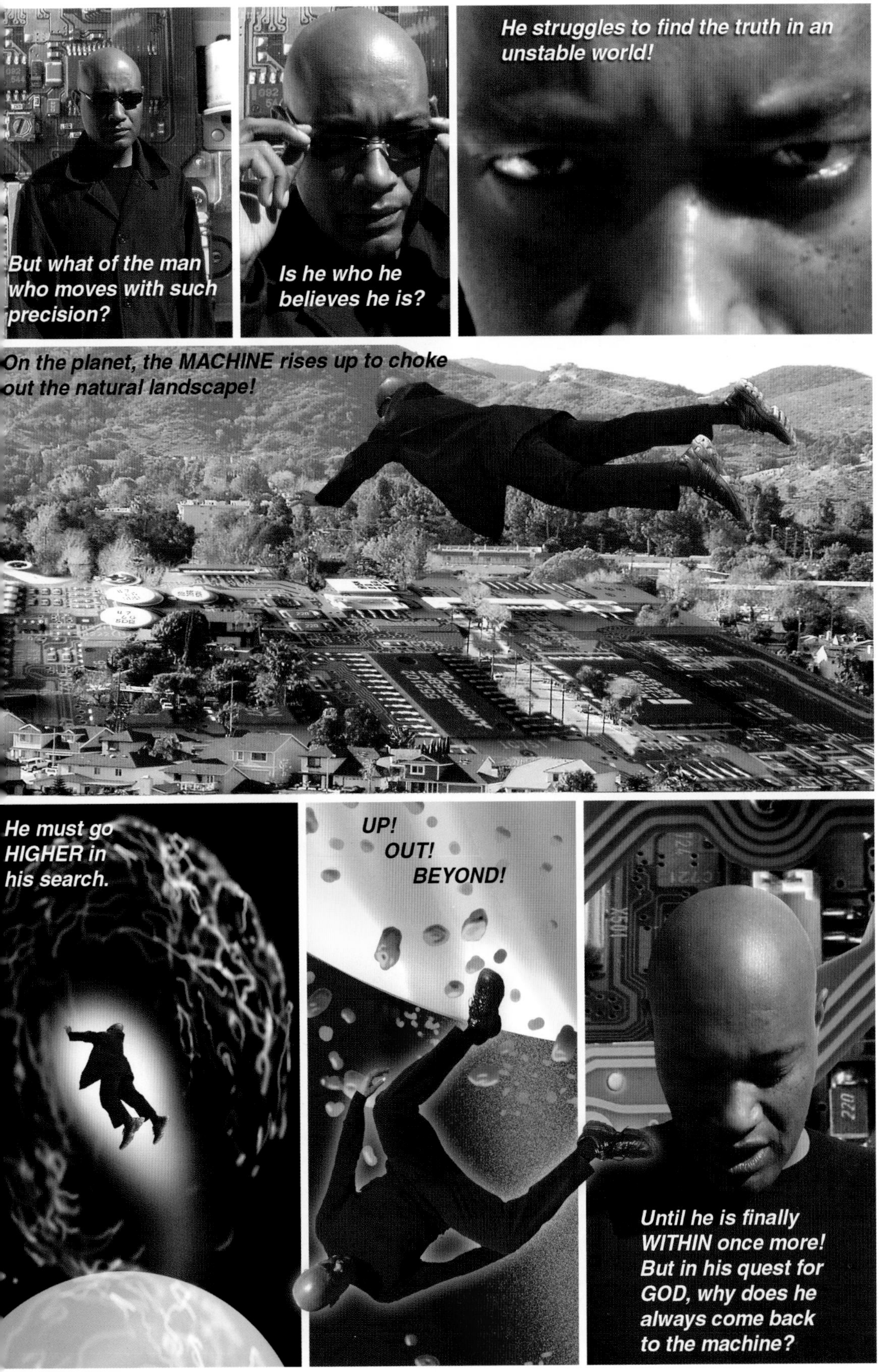

But what of the man who moves with such precision?
Is he who he believes he is?
He struggles to find the truth in an unstable world!
On the planet, the MACHINE rises up to choke out the natural landscape!
He must go HIGHER in his search.
UP!
OUT!
BEYOND!
Until he is finally WITHIN once more! But in his quest for GOD, why does he always come back to the machine?

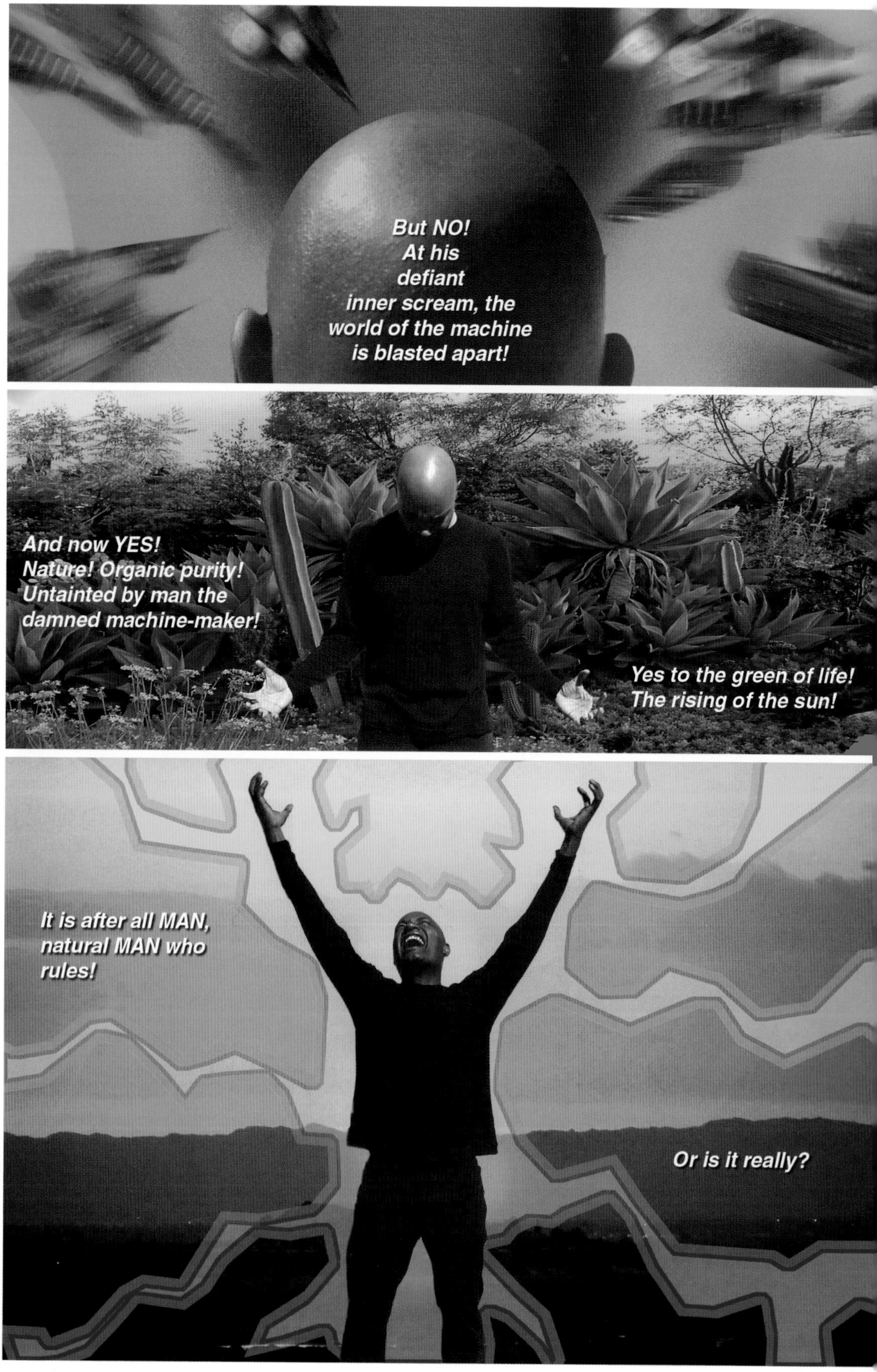
But NO!
At his
defiant
inner scream, the
world of the machine
is blasted apart!
And now YES!
Nature! Organic purity!
Untainted by man the
damned machine-maker!
Yes to the green of life!
The rising of the sun!
It is after all MAN,
natural MAN who
rules!
Or is it really?

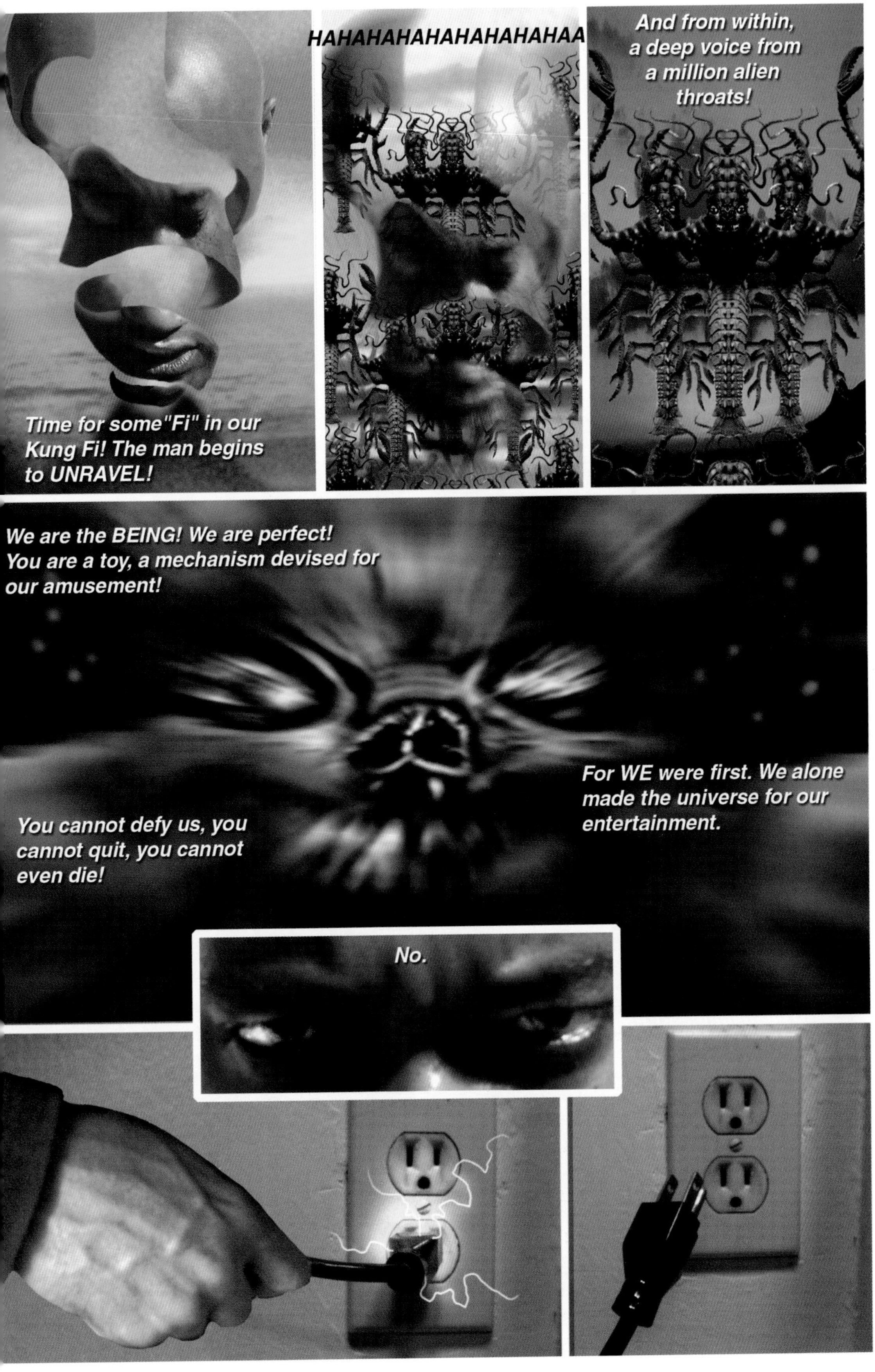
Time for some "Fi" in our Kung Fi! The man begins to UNRAVEL!
HAHAHAHAHAHAHAHAHAHAA
And from within, a deep voice from a million alien throats!
We are the BEING! We are perfect! You are a toy, a mechanism devised for our amusement!
For WE were first. We alone made the universe for our entertainment.
You cannot defy us, you cannot quit, you cannot even die!
No.

What is reality? Is man the maker of the machine?

Or is it the other way around after all?

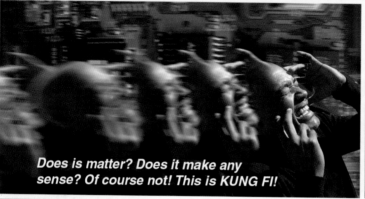

Does is matter? Does it make any sense? Of course not! This is KUNG FI!

It just has to be confusing and look cool.

The machine plugs itself back in.

Aaahhh, that's better.

The machine turns the man off.

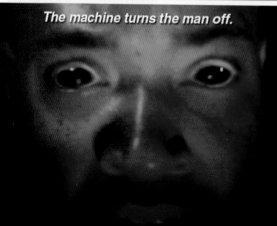

It is bored with him for now.

SHUT DOWN

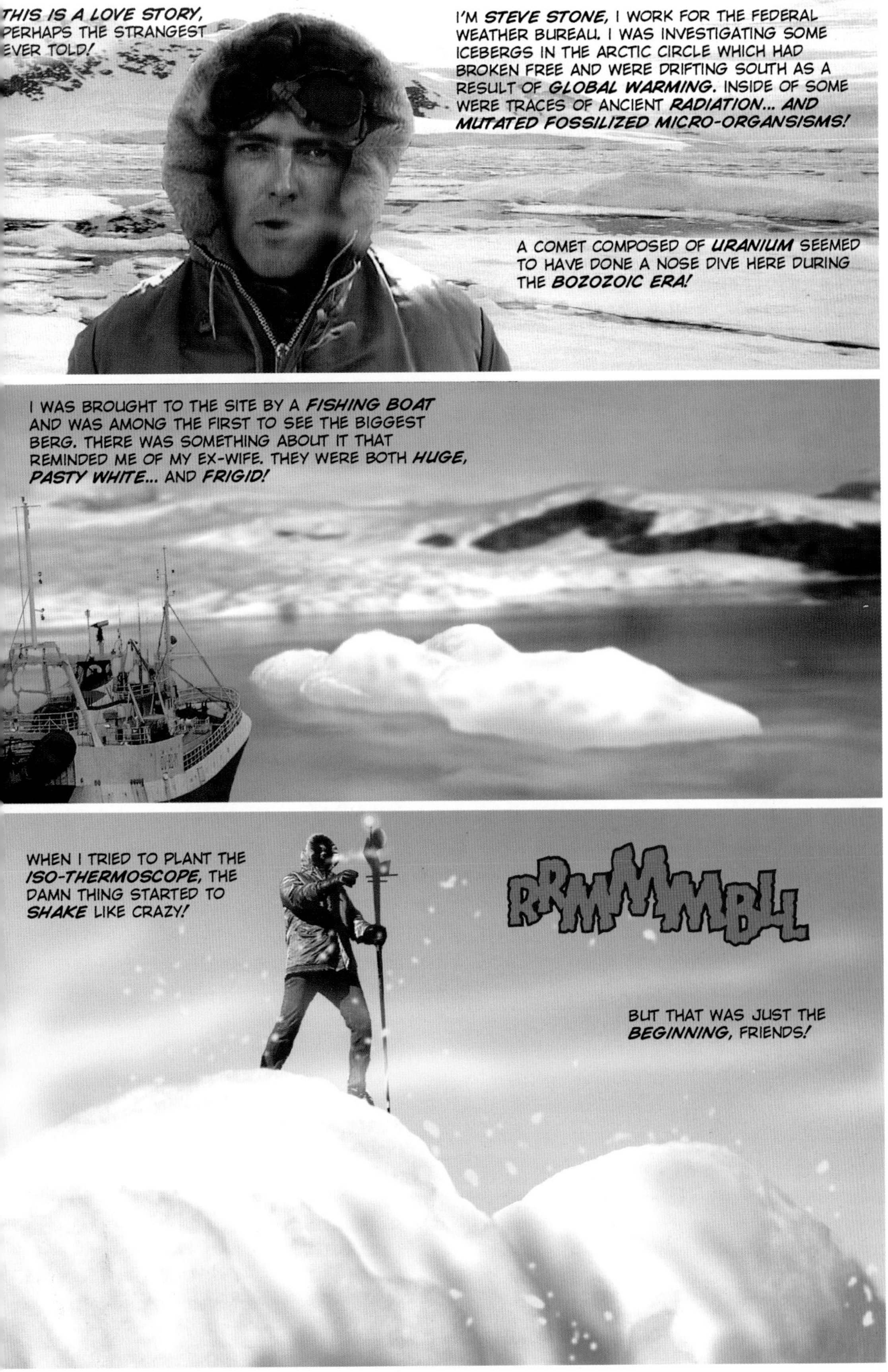
THIS IS A LOVE STORY, PERHAPS THE STRANGEST EVER TOLD!
I'M STEVE STONE, I WORK FOR THE FEDERAL WEATHER BUREAU. I WAS INVESTIGATING SOME ICEBERGS IN THE ARCTIC CIRCLE WHICH HAD BROKEN FREE AND WERE DRIFTING SOUTH AS A RESULT OF GLOBAL WARMING. INSIDE OF SOME WERE TRACES OF ANCIENT RADIATION... AND MUTATED FOSSILIZED MICRO-ORGANSISMS!
A COMET COMPOSED OF URANIUM SEEMED TO HAVE DONE A NOSE DIVE HERE DURING THE BOZOZOIC ERA!
I WAS BROUGHT TO THE SITE BY A FISHING BOAT AND WAS AMONG THE FIRST TO SEE THE BIGGEST BERG. THERE WAS SOMETHING ABOUT IT THAT REMINDED ME OF MY EX-WIFE. THEY WERE BOTH HUGE, PASTY WHITE... AND FRIGID!
WHEN I TRIED TO PLANT THE ISO-THERMOSCOPE, THE DAMN THING STARTED TO SHAKE LIKE CRAZY!
RRMMMMBLL
BUT THAT WAS JUST THE BEGINNING, FRIENDS!

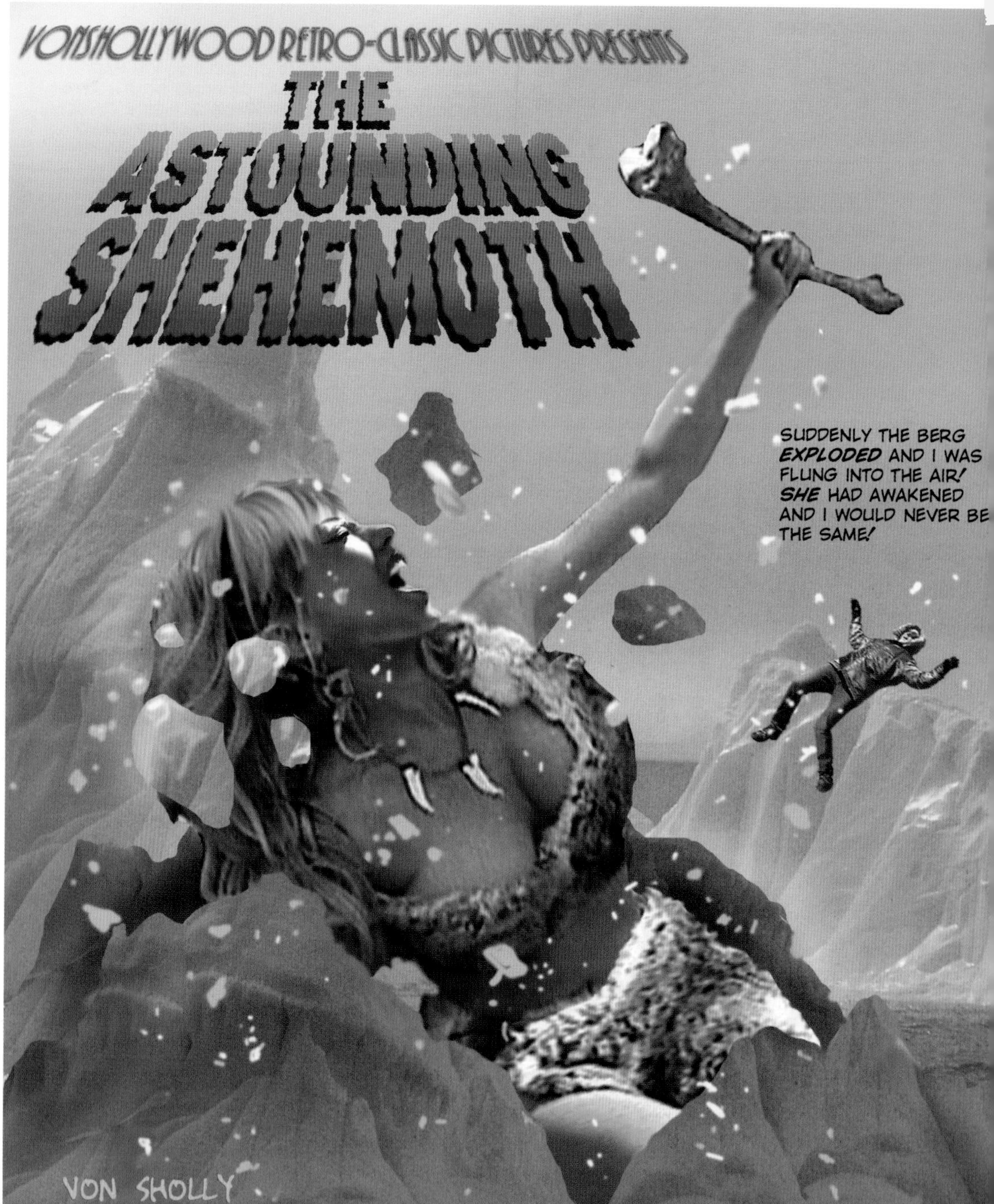
VONSHOLLYWOOD RETRO-CLASSIC PICTURES PRESENTS
THE ASTOUNDING SHEHEMOTH
SUDDENLY THE BERG EXPLODED AND I WAS FLUNG INTO THE AIR! SHE HAD AWAKENED AND I WOULD NEVER BE THE SAME!
VON SHOLLY 99/00

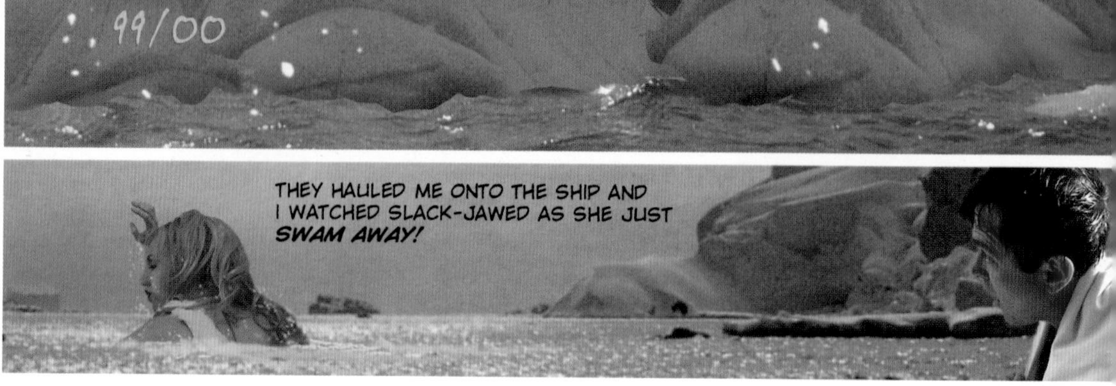
THEY HAULED ME ONTO THE SHIP AND I WATCHED SLACK-JAWED AS SHE JUST SWAM AWAY!

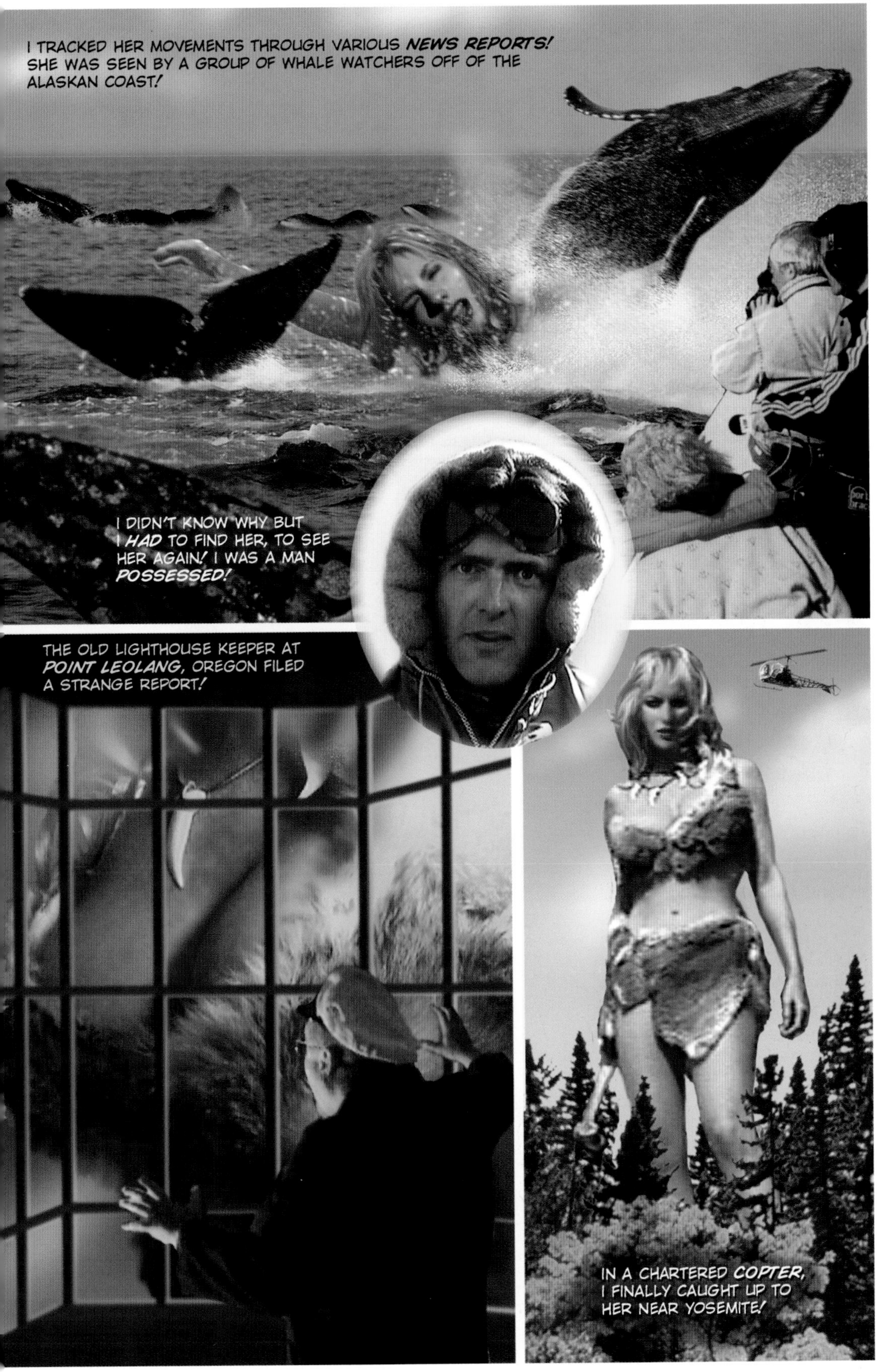
I TRACKED HER MOVEMENTS THROUGH VARIOUS NEWS REPORTS! SHE WAS SEEN BY A GROUP OF WHALE WATCHERS OFF OF THE ALASKAN COAST!
I DIDN'T KNOW WHY BUT I HAD TO FIND HER, TO SEE HER AGAIN! I WAS A MAN POSSESSED!
THE OLD LIGHTHOUSE KEEPER AT POINT LEOLANG, OREGON FILED A STRANGE REPORT!
IN A CHARTERED COPTER, I FINALLY CAUGHT UP TO HER NEAR YOSEMITE!

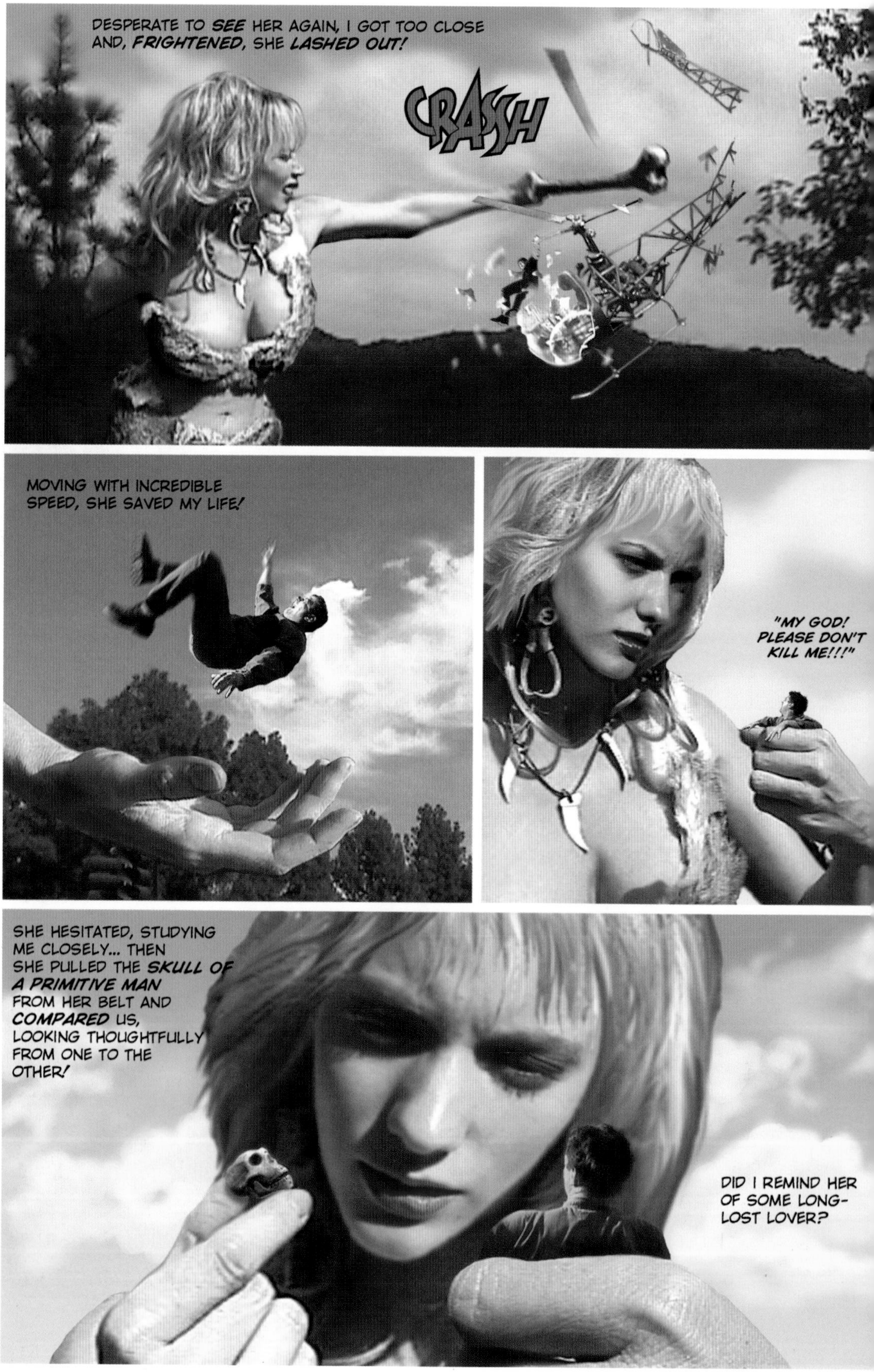
DESPERATE TO SEE HER AGAIN, I GOT TOO CLOSE AND, FRIGHTENED, SHE LASHED OUT!
CRASSH
MOVING WITH INCREDIBLE SPEED, SHE SAVED MY LIFE!
"MY GOD! PLEASE DON'T KILL ME!!!"
SHE HESITATED, STUDYING ME CLOSELY... THEN SHE PULLED THE SKULL OF A PRIMITIVE MAN FROM HER BELT AND COMPARED US, LOOKING THOUGHTFULLY FROM ONE TO THE OTHER!
DID I REMIND HER OF SOME LONG-LOST LOVER?

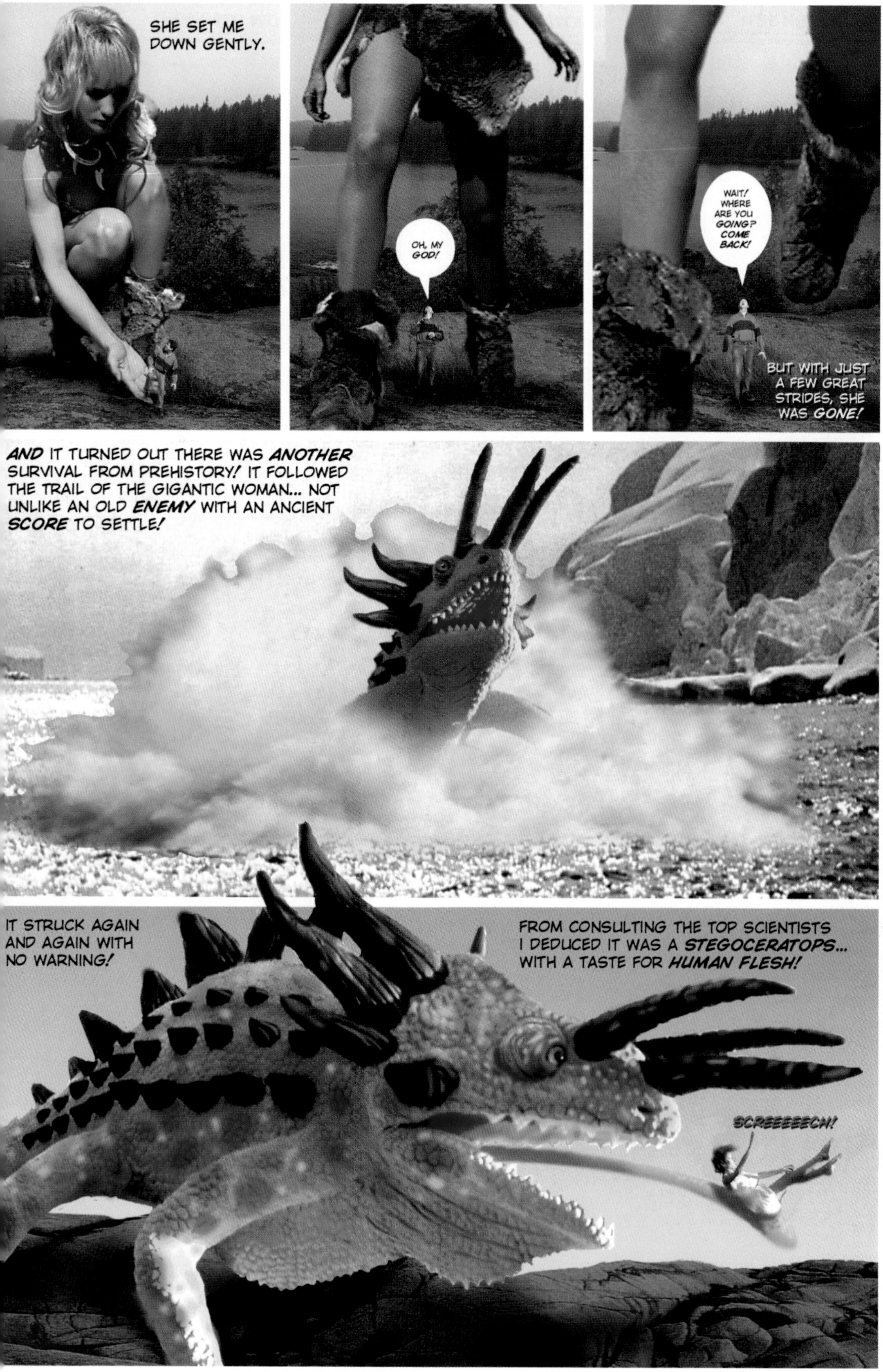
SHE SET ME DOWN GENTLY.
OH, MY GOD!
WAIT! WHERE ARE YOU GOING? COME BACK!
BUT WITH JUST A FEW GREAT STRIDES, SHE WAS GONE!
AND IT TURNED OUT THERE WAS ANOTHER SURVIVAL FROM PREHISTORY! IT FOLLOWED THE TRAIL OF THE GIGANTIC WOMAN... NOT UNLIKE AN OLD ENEMY WITH AN ANCIENT SCORE TO SETTLE!
IT STRUCK AGAIN AND AGAIN WITH NO WARNING!
FROM CONSULTING THE TOP SCIENTISTS I DEDUCED IT WAS A STEGOCERATOPS... WITH A TASTE FOR HUMAN FLESH!
SCREEEEEEECH!

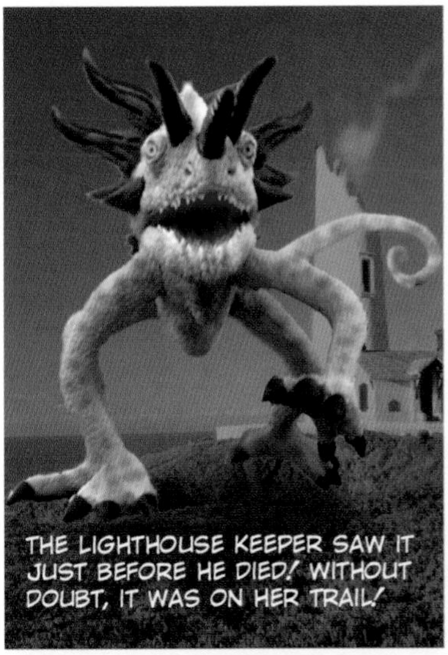
THE LIGHTHOUSE KEEPER SAW IT JUST BEFORE HE DIED! WITHOUT DOUBT, IT WAS ON HER TRAIL!

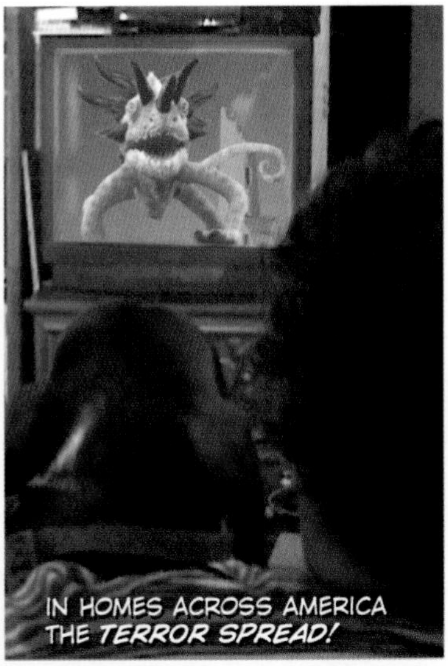
IN HOMES ACROSS AMERICA THE TERROR SPREAD!

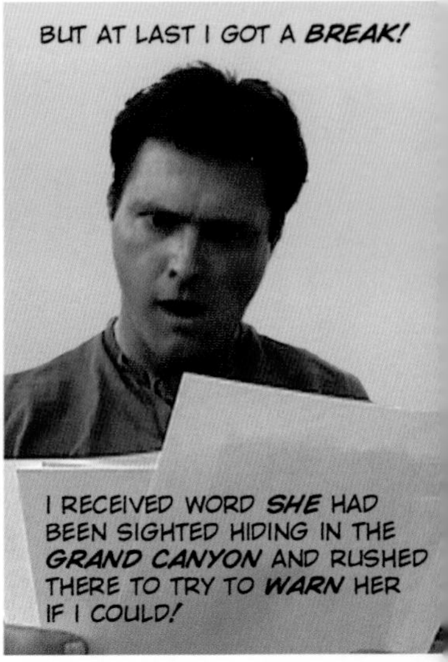
BUT AT LAST I GOT A BREAK!
I RECEIVED WORD SHE HAD BEEN SIGHTED HIDING IN THE GRAND CANYON AND RUSHED THERE TO TRY TO WARN HER IF I COULD!

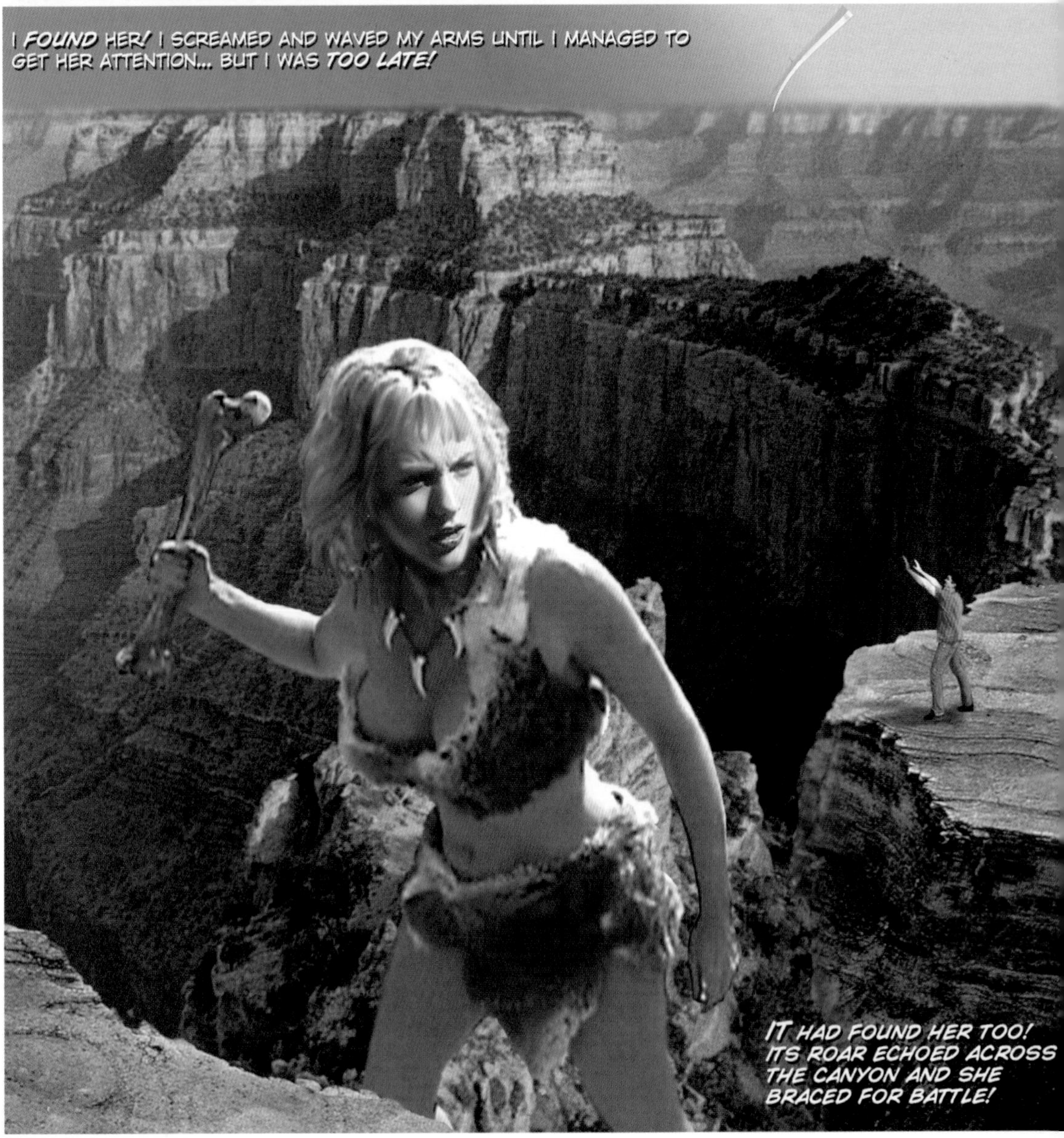
I FOUND HER! I SCREAMED AND WAVED MY ARMS UNTIL I MANAGED TO GET HER ATTENTION... BUT I WAS TOO LATE!
IT HAD FOUND HER TOO! ITS ROAR ECHOED ACROSS THE CANYON AND SHE BRACED FOR BATTLE!

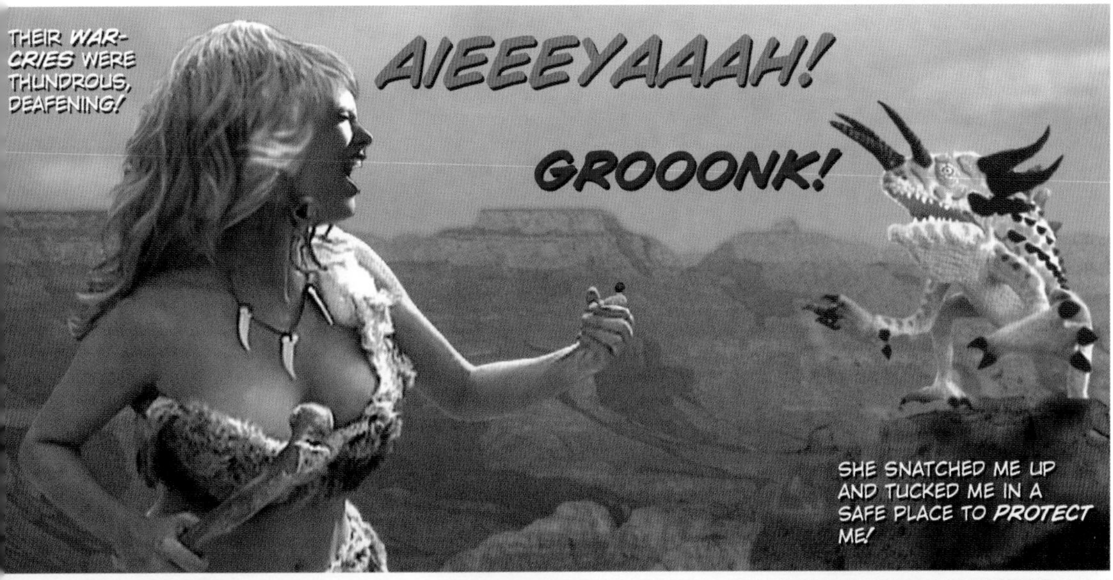
THEIR *WAR-CRIES* WERE THUNDROUS, DEAFENING!
AIEEEYAAAH!
GROOONK!
SHE SNATCHED ME UP AND TUCKED ME IN A SAFE PLACE TO *PROTECT* ME!

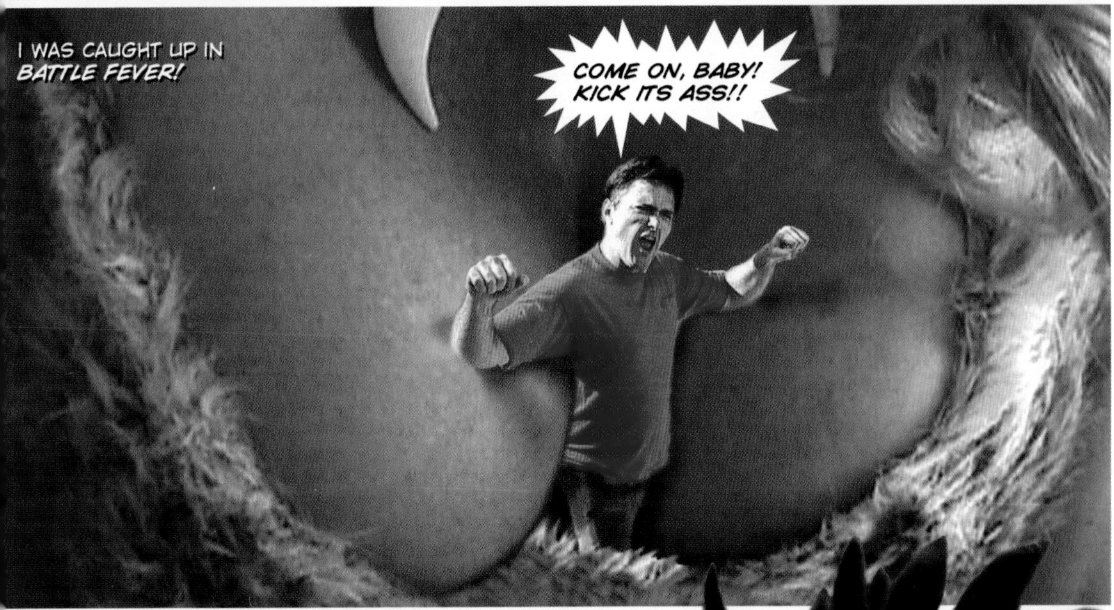
I WAS CAUGHT UP IN *BATTLE FEVER!*
COME ON, BABY! KICK ITS ASS!!

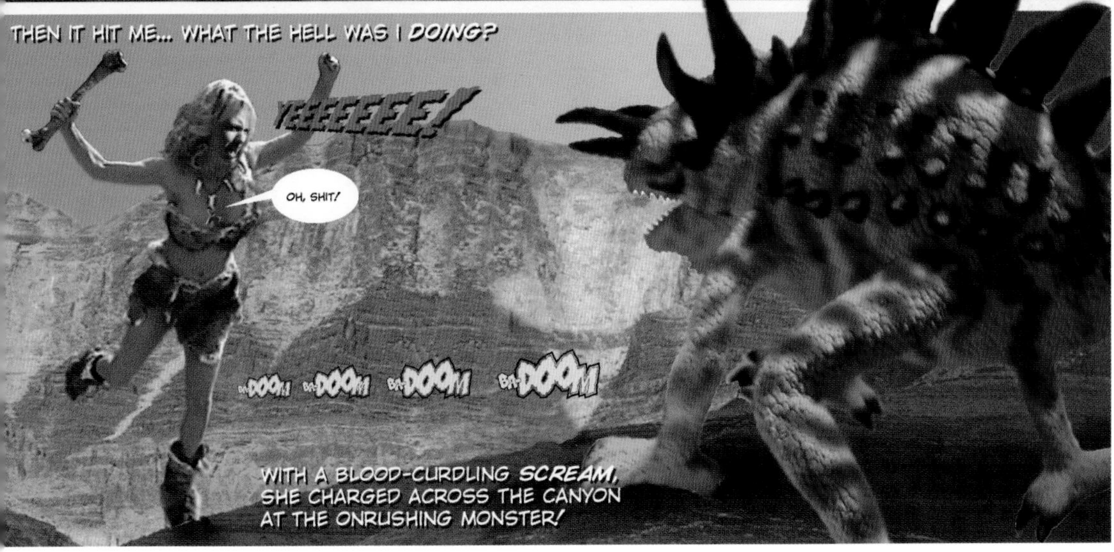
THEN IT HIT ME... WHAT THE HELL WAS I *DOING?*
YEEEEEEE!
OH, SHIT!
BA-DOOM BA-DOOM BA-DOOM BA-DOOM
WITH A BLOOD-CURDLING *SCREAM,* SHE CHARGED ACROSS THE CANYON AT THE ONRUSHING MONSTER!

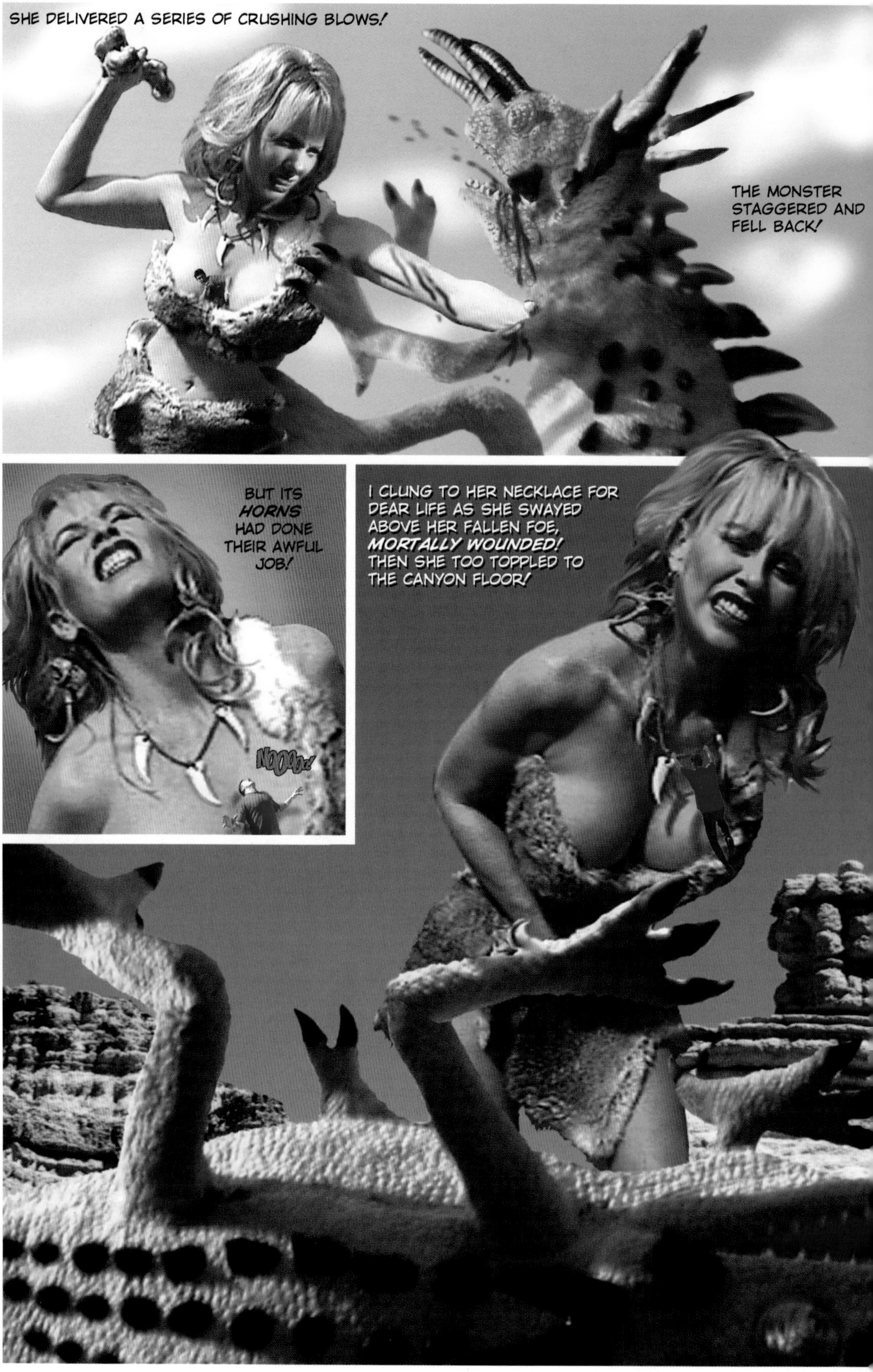
SHE DELIVERED A SERIES OF CRUSHING BLOWS!
THE MONSTER STAGGERED AND FELL BACK!
BUT ITS HORNS HAD DONE THEIR AWFUL JOB!
NOOOOO!
I CLUNG TO HER NECKLACE FOR DEAR LIFE AS SHE SWAYED ABOVE HER FALLEN FOE, MORTALLY WOUNDED! THEN SHE TOO TOPPLED TO THE CANYON FLOOR!

SHE WAS PROBABLY *MUTATED* BY THE RADIOACTIVE COMET AND BECAME A *GIANT*...
MOST LIKELY THE ONLY ONE OF HER KIND... HAD SHE SURVIVED THE AGES JUST FOR *THIS?*

BABY? *BABY?* CAN YOU HEAR ME?

I DON'T KNOW IF SHE KNEW WHAT A *KISS* WAS, BUT WHEN I LAID ONE ON HER, SHE *KISSED BACK* WITH THE LAST OF HER STRENGTH!

AND THAT WAS THE END...

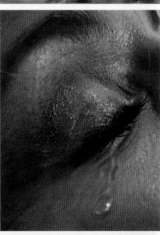

PART OF ME WENT WITH HER!

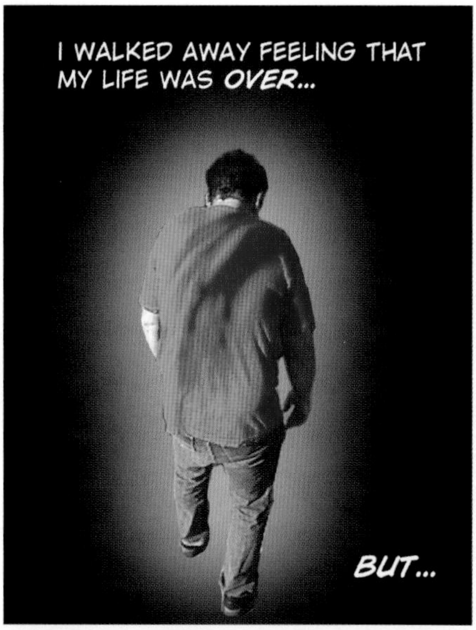
I WALKED AWAY FEELING THAT MY LIFE WAS *OVER...*
BUT...

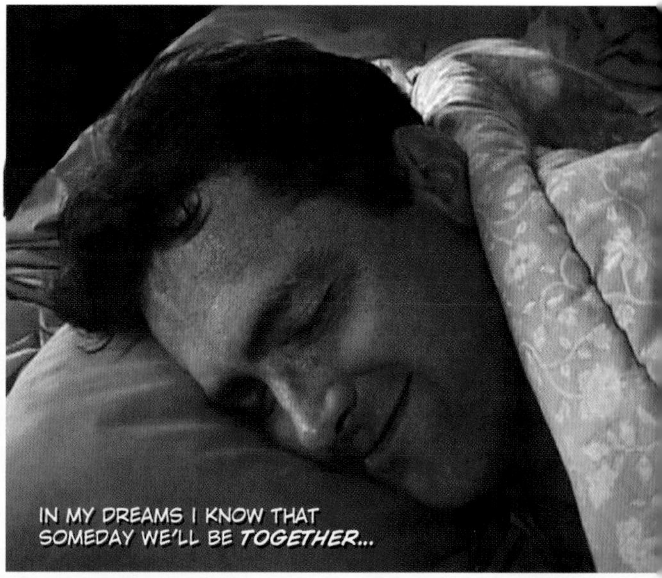
IN MY DREAMS I KNOW THAT SOMEDAY WE'LL BE *TOGETHER...*

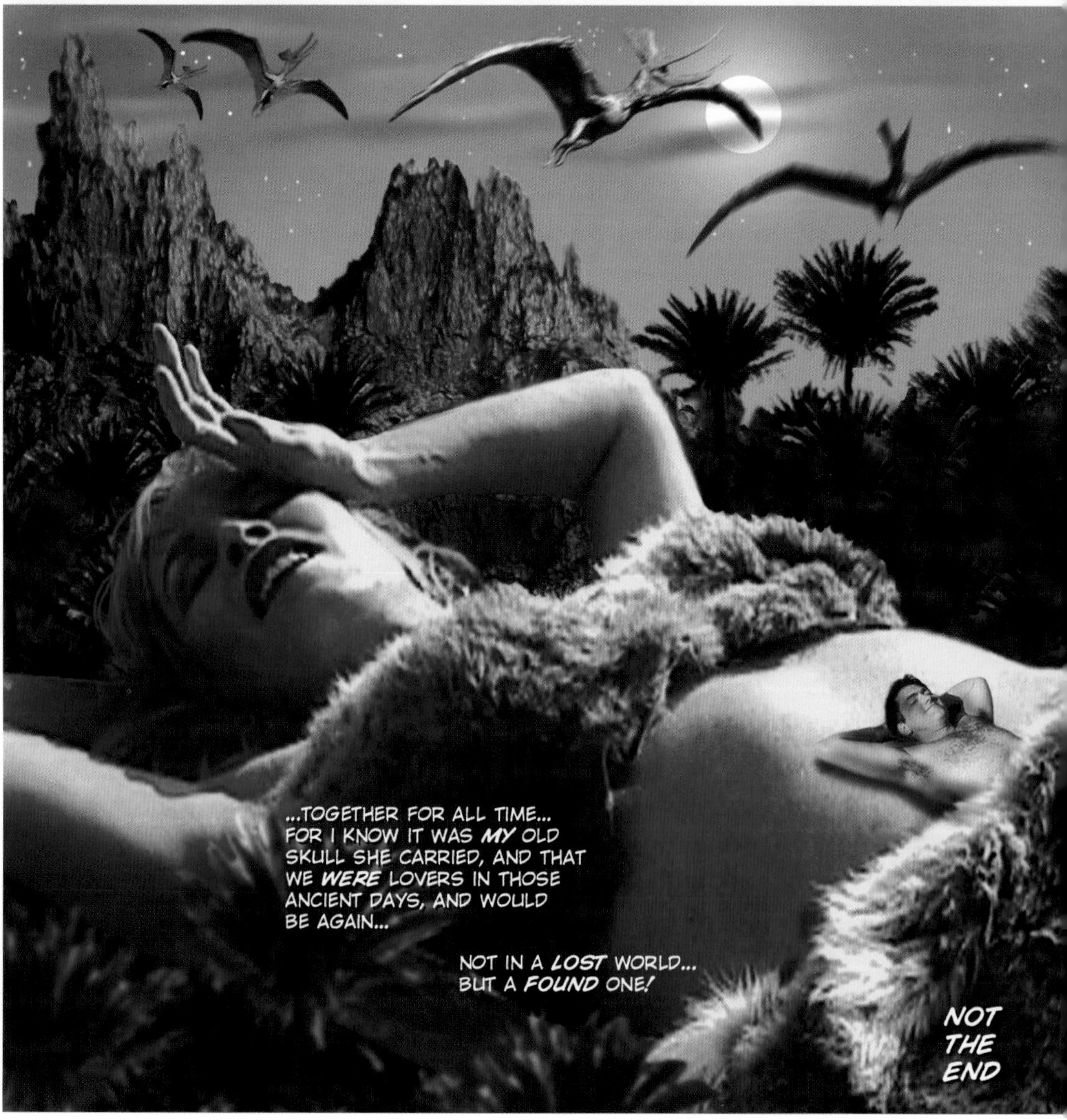
...TOGETHER FOR ALL TIME... FOR I KNOW IT WAS *MY* OLD SKULL SHE CARRIED, AND THAT WE *WERE* LOVERS IN THOSE ANCIENT DAYS, AND WOULD BE AGAIN...
NOT IN A *LOST* WORLD... BUT A *FOUND* ONE!
NOT THE END

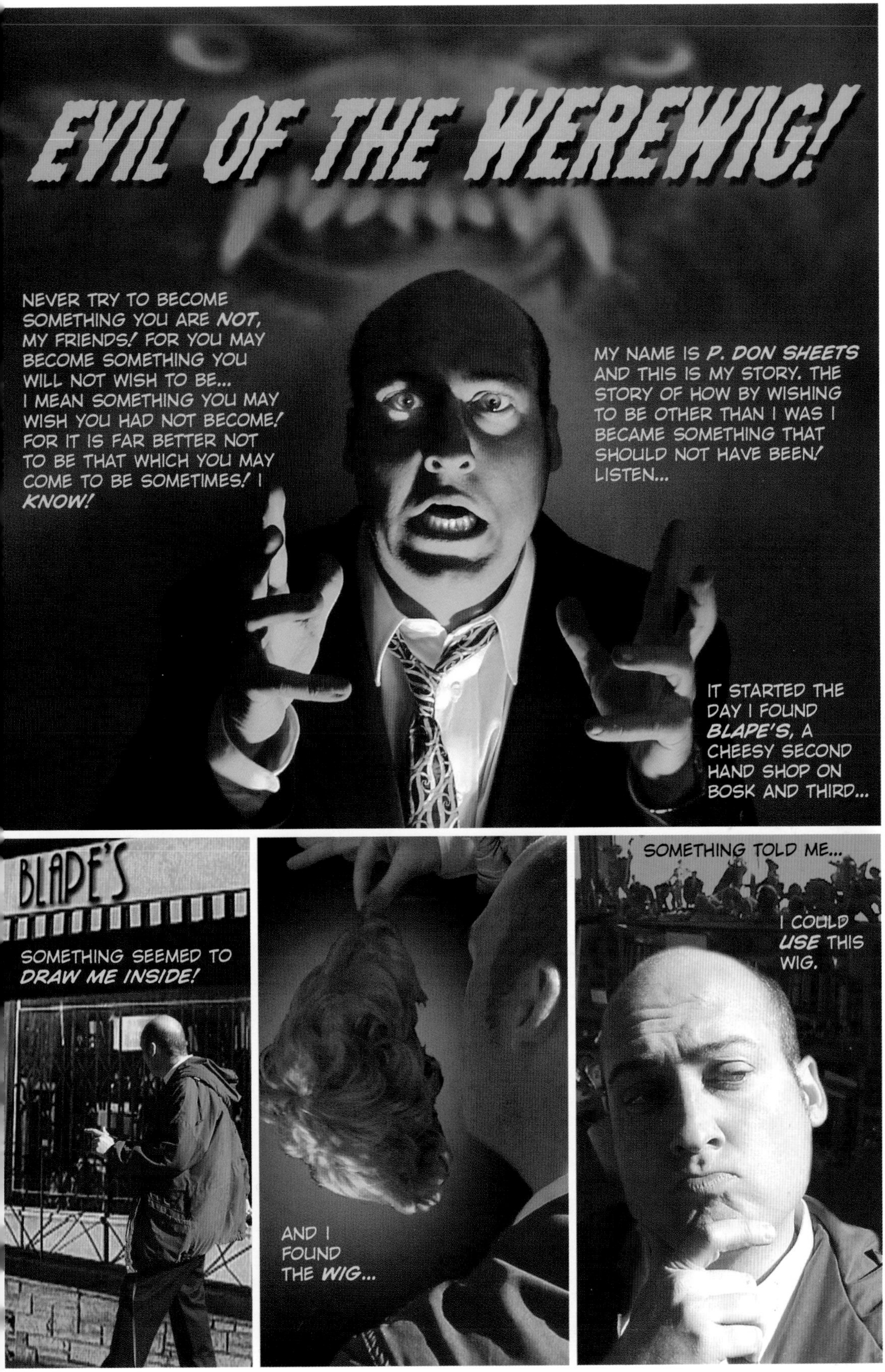
EVIL OF THE WEREWIG!
NEVER TRY TO BECOME SOMETHING YOU ARE NOT, MY FRIENDS! FOR YOU MAY BECOME SOMETHING YOU WILL NOT WISH TO BE... I MEAN SOMETHING YOU MAY WISH YOU HAD NOT BECOME! FOR IT IS FAR BETTER NOT TO BE THAT WHICH YOU MAY COME TO BE SOMETIMES! I KNOW!
MY NAME IS P. DON SHEETS AND THIS IS MY STORY. THE STORY OF HOW BY WISHING TO BE OTHER THAN I WAS I BECAME SOMETHING THAT SHOULD NOT HAVE BEEN! LISTEN...
IT STARTED THE DAY I FOUND BLAPE'S, A CHEESY SECOND HAND SHOP ON BOSK AND THIRD...
BLAPE'S
SOMETHING SEEMED TO DRAW ME INSIDE!
AND I FOUND THE WIG...
SOMETHING TOLD ME...
I COULD USE THIS WIG.

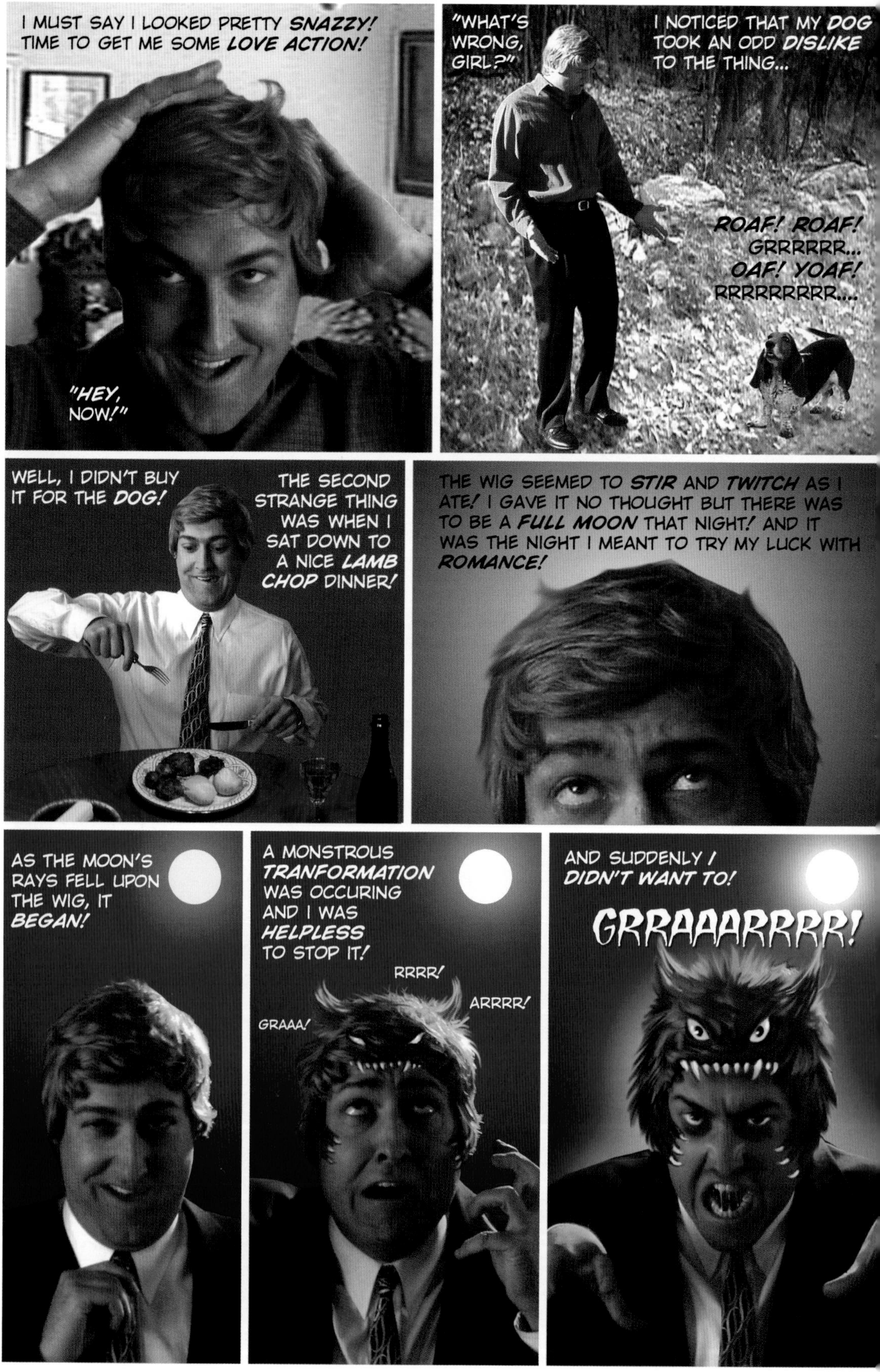
I MUST SAY I LOOKED PRETTY SNAZZY! TIME TO GET ME SOME LOVE ACTION!
"HEY, NOW!"
"WHAT'S WRONG, GIRL?"
I NOTICED THAT MY DOG TOOK AN ODD DISLIKE TO THE THING...
ROAF! ROAF! GRRRRRR... OAF! YOAF! RRRRRRRRR....
WELL, I DIDN'T BUY IT FOR THE DOG!
THE SECOND STRANGE THING WAS WHEN I SAT DOWN TO A NICE LAMB CHOP DINNER!
THE WIG SEEMED TO STIR AND TWITCH AS I ATE! I GAVE IT NO THOUGHT BUT THERE WAS TO BE A FULL MOON THAT NIGHT! AND IT WAS THE NIGHT I MEANT TO TRY MY LUCK WITH ROMANCE!
AS THE MOON'S RAYS FELL UPON THE WIG, IT BEGAN!
A MONSTROUS TRANFORMATION WAS OCCURING AND I WAS HELPLESS TO STOP IT!
RRRR!
ARRRR!
GRAAA!
AND SUDDENLY I DIDN'T WANT TO!
GRRAAARRRR!

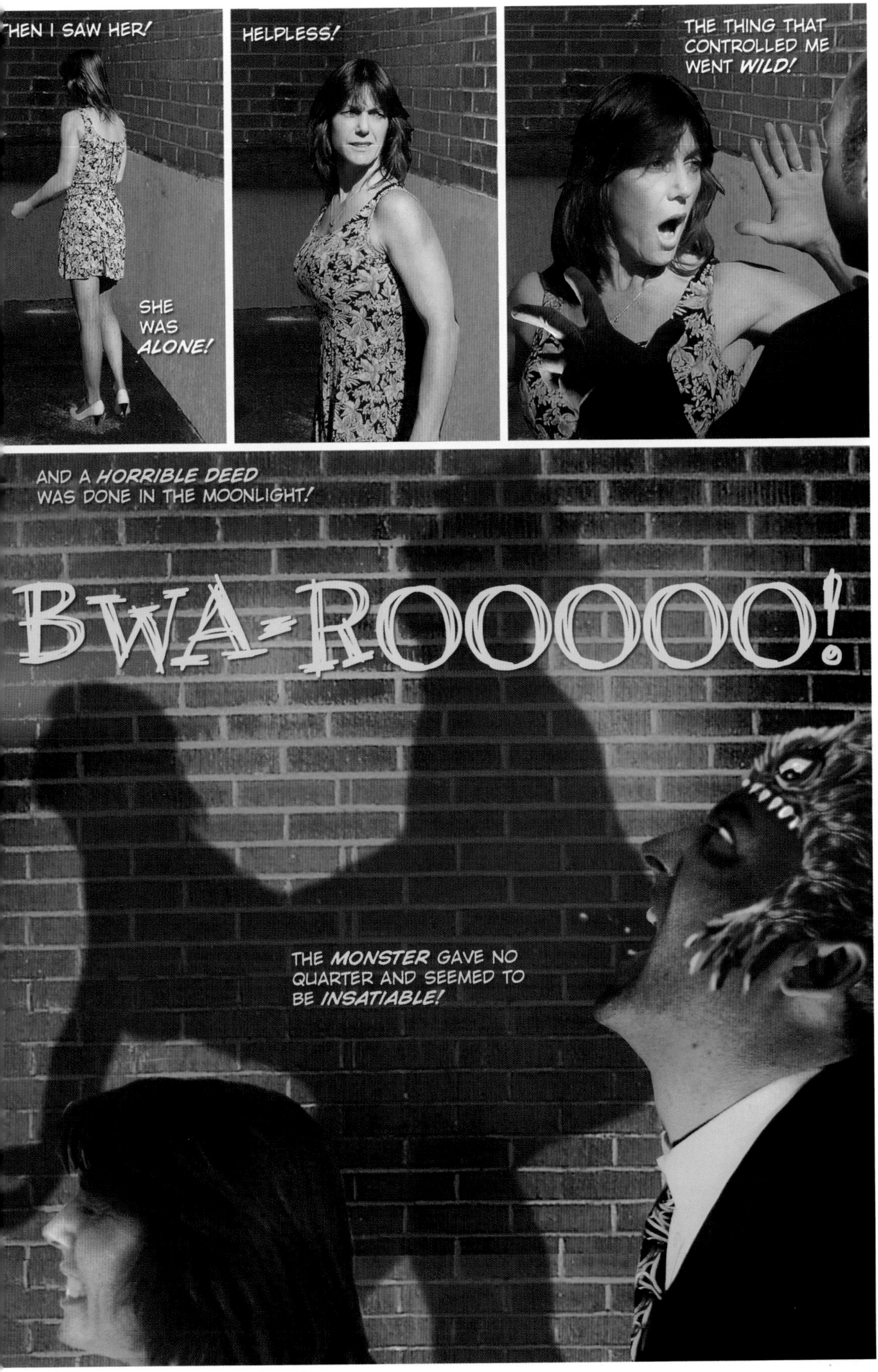
HEN I SAW HER!
SHE WAS ALONE!
HELPLESS!
THE THING THAT CONTROLLED ME WENT WILD!
AND A HORRIBLE DEED WAS DONE IN THE MOONLIGHT!
BWA-ROOOOOO!
THE MONSTER GAVE NO QUARTER AND SEEMED TO BE INSATIABLE!

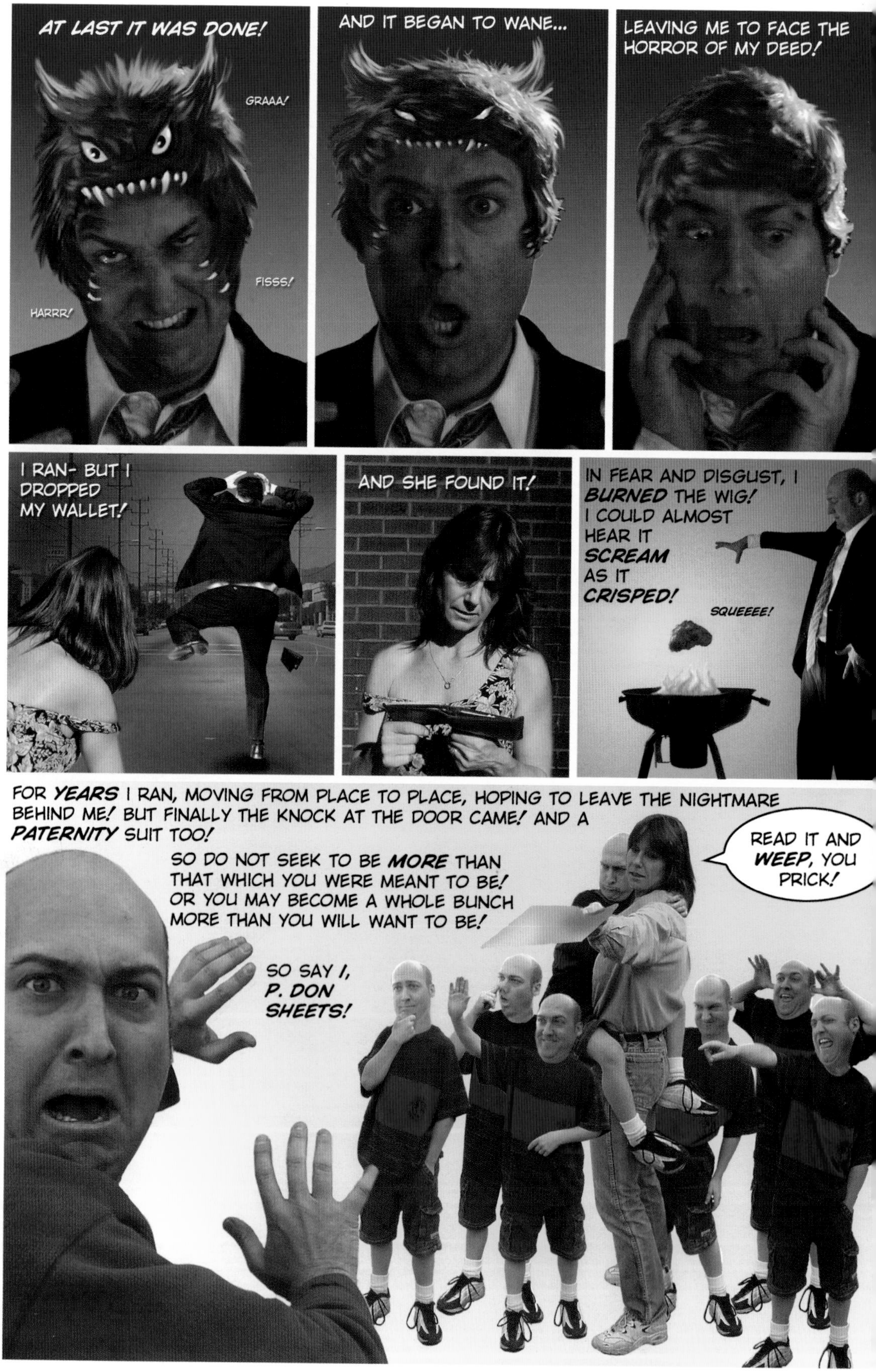

AT LAST IT WAS DONE!
GRAAA!
FISSS!
HARRR!
AND IT BEGAN TO WANE...
LEAVING ME TO FACE THE HORROR OF MY DEED!
I RAN- BUT I DROPPED MY WALLET!
AND SHE FOUND IT!
IN FEAR AND DISGUST, I BURNED THE WIG! I COULD ALMOST HEAR IT SCREAM AS IT CRISPED!
SQUEEEE!
FOR YEARS I RAN, MOVING FROM PLACE TO PLACE, HOPING TO LEAVE THE NIGHTMARE BEHIND ME! BUT FINALLY THE KNOCK AT THE DOOR CAME! AND A PATERNITY SUIT TOO!
SO DO NOT SEEK TO BE MORE THAN THAT WHICH YOU WERE MEANT TO BE! OR YOU MAY BECOME A WHOLE BUNCH MORE THAN YOU WILL WANT TO BE!
READ IT AND WEEP, YOU PRICK!
SO SAY I, P. DON SHEETS!

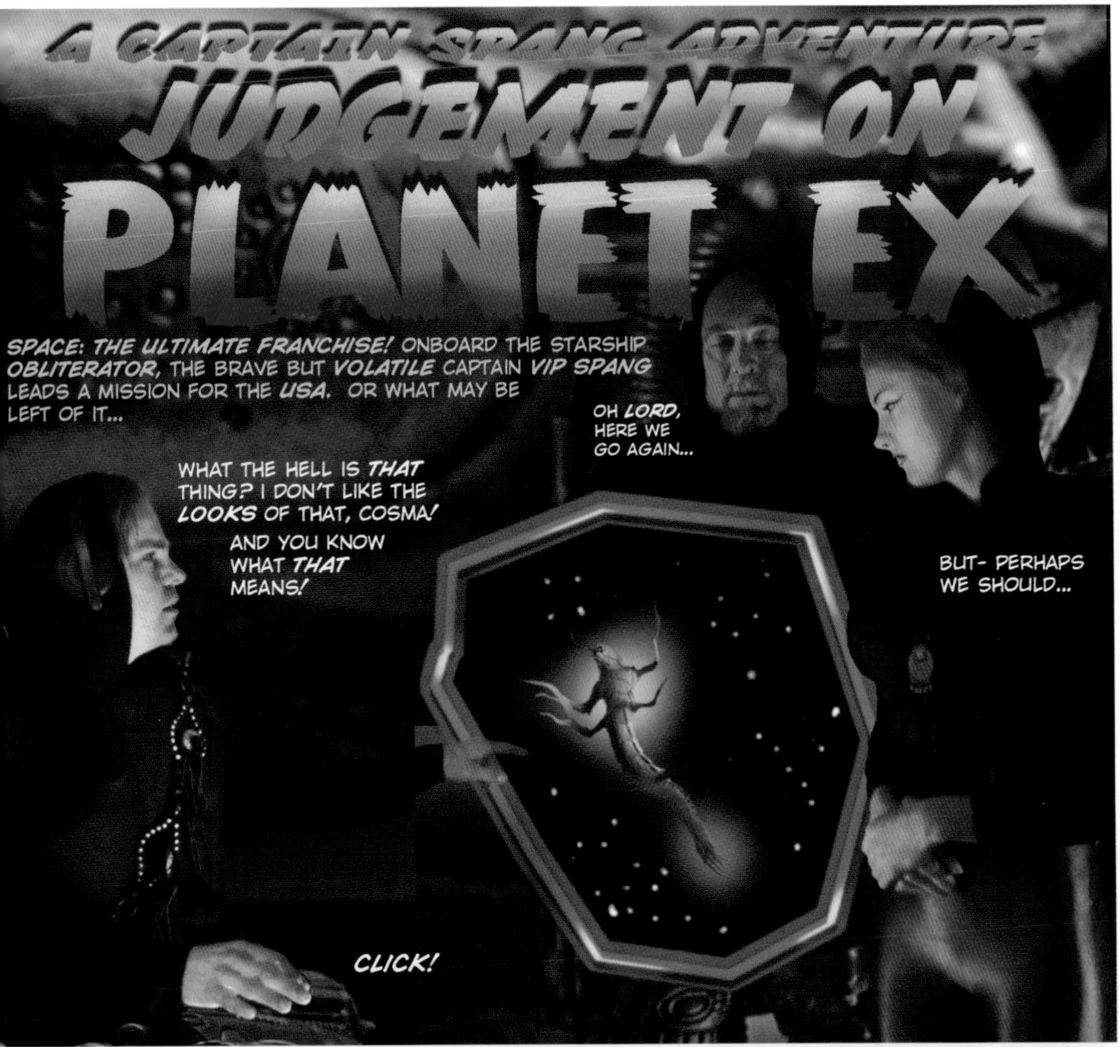
A CAPTAIN SPANG ADVENTURE
JUDGEMENT ON
PLANET EX
SPACE: THE ULTIMATE FRANCHISE! ONBOARD THE STARSHIP OBLITERATOR, THE BRAVE BUT VOLATILE CAPTAIN VIP SPANG LEADS A MISSION FOR THE USA. OR WHAT MAY BE LEFT OF IT...
WHAT THE HELL IS THAT THING? I DON'T LIKE THE LOOKS OF THAT, COSMA!
AND YOU KNOW WHAT THAT MEANS!
OH LORD, HERE WE GO AGAIN...
BUT- PERHAPS WE SHOULD...
CLICK!

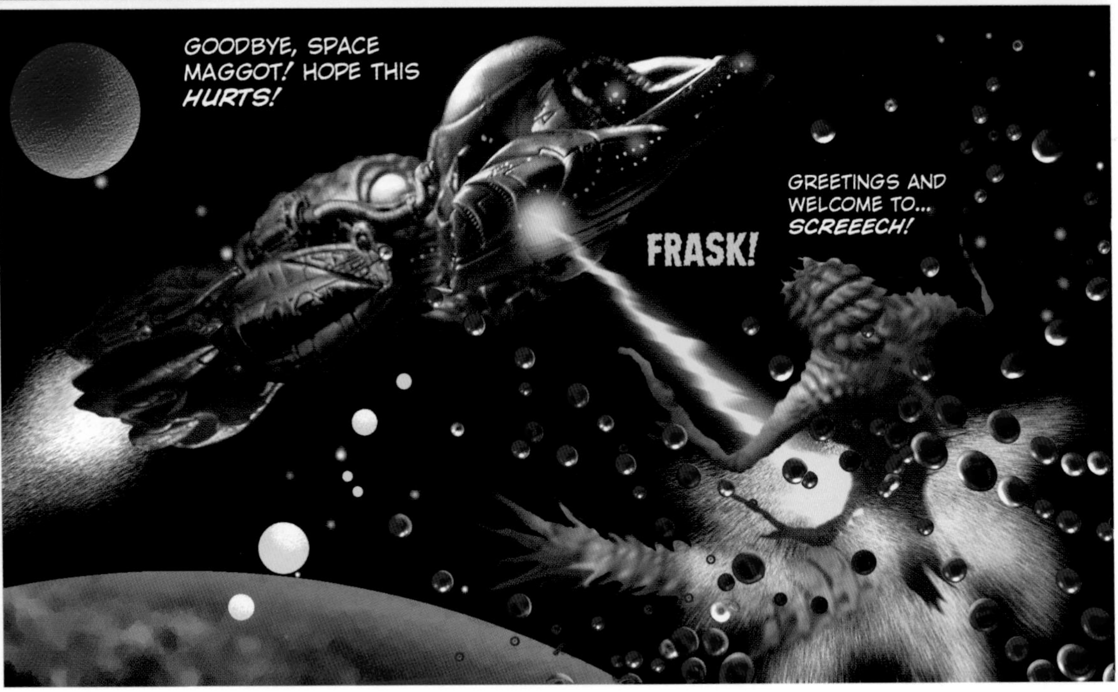
GOODBYE, SPACE MAGGOT! HOPE THIS HURTS!
FRASK!
GREETINGS AND WELCOME TO... SCREEECH!

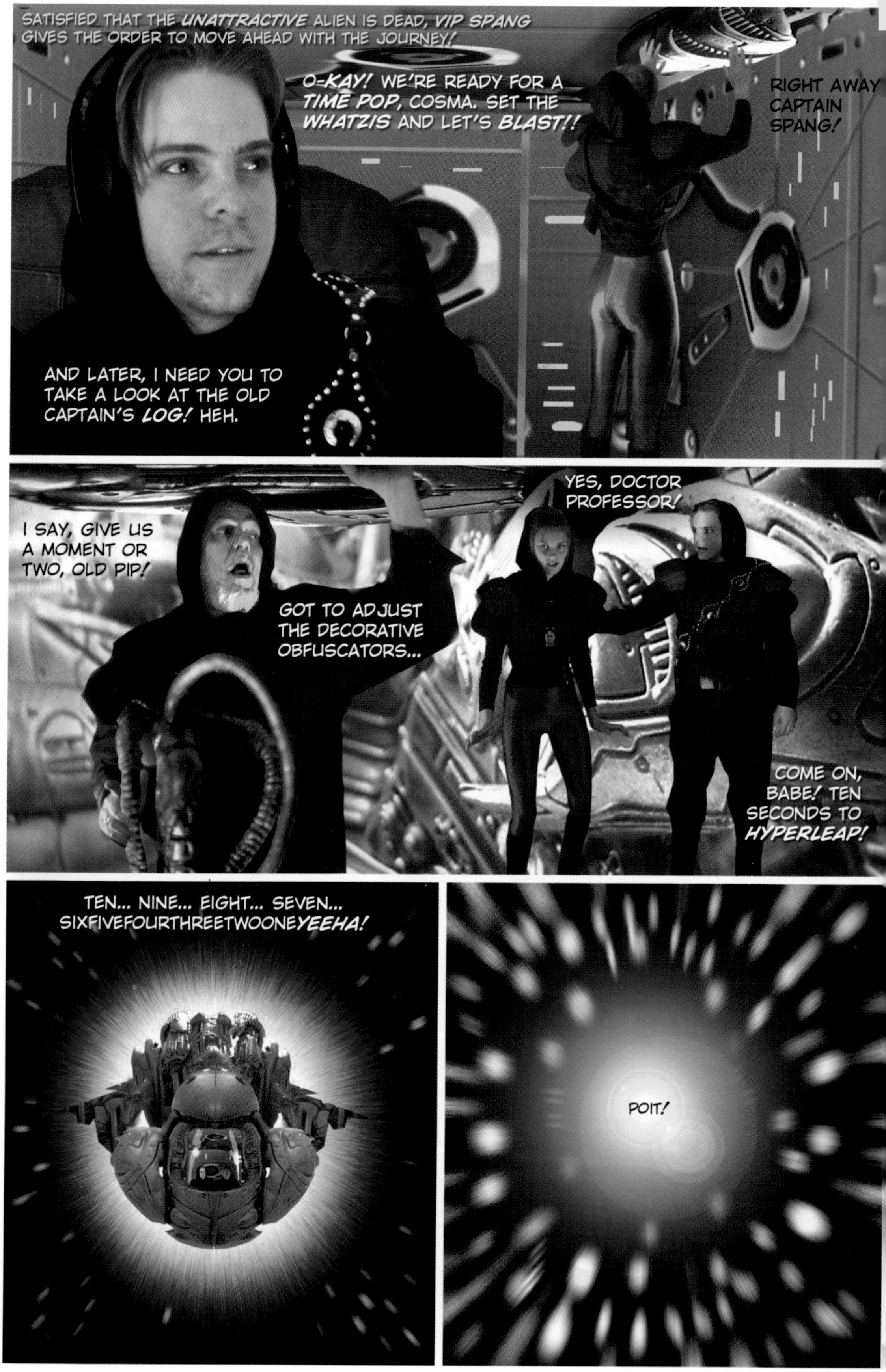
SATISFIED THAT THE UNATTRACTIVE ALIEN IS DEAD, VIP SPANG GIVES THE ORDER TO MOVE AHEAD WITH THE JOURNEY!
O-KAY! WE'RE READY FOR A TIME POP, COSMA. SET THE WHATZIS AND LET'S BLAST!!
RIGHT AWAY CAPTAIN SPANG!
AND LATER, I NEED YOU TO TAKE A LOOK AT THE OLD CAPTAIN'S LOG! HEH.
I SAY, GIVE US A MOMENT OR TWO, OLD PIP!
GOT TO ADJUST THE DECORATIVE OBFUSCATORS...
YES, DOCTOR PROFESSOR!
COME ON, BABE! TEN SECONDS TO HYPERLEAP!
TEN... NINE... EIGHT... SEVEN... SIXFIVEFOURTHREETWOONEYEEHA!
POIT!

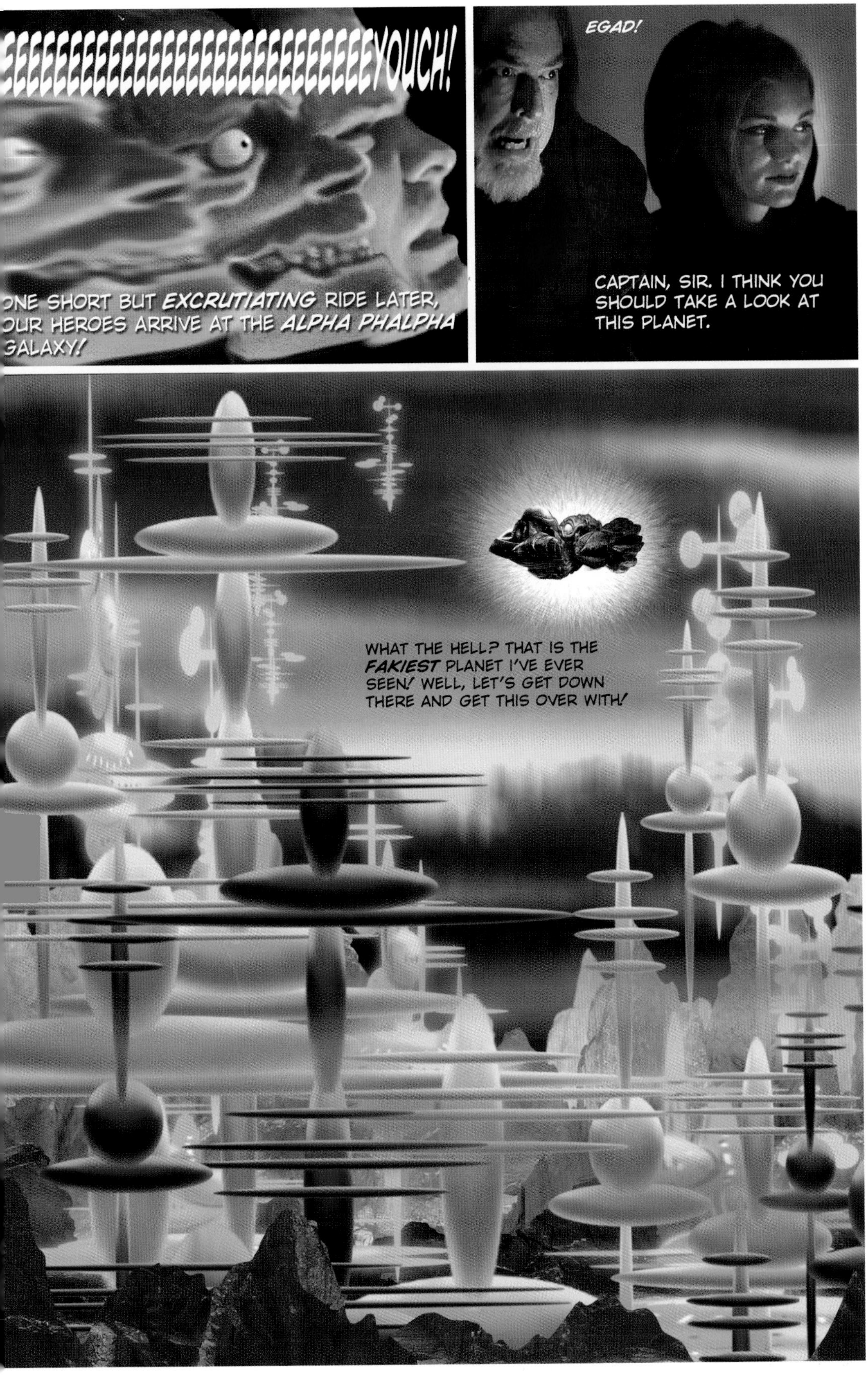
EEEEEEEEEEEEEEEEEEEEEEEEEEEEEEEYOUCH!
ONE SHORT BUT EXCRUTIATING RIDE LATER, OUR HEROES ARRIVE AT THE ALPHA PHALPHA GALAXY!
EGAD!
CAPTAIN, SIR. I THINK YOU SHOULD TAKE A LOOK AT THIS PLANET.
WHAT THE HELL? THAT IS THE FAKIEST PLANET I'VE EVER SEEN! WELL, LET'S GET DOWN THERE AND GET THIS OVER WITH!

NOW, THE *MANUAL* SAYS— EEEYAGH!

C'MON! PUT THAT SHIT DOWN AND LET'S *GO*, YOU OLD WEENIE!

BWEEYOOM!

ALIENS AND THEIR WAYS
A FEDERAL GALACTIC GUIDEBOOK

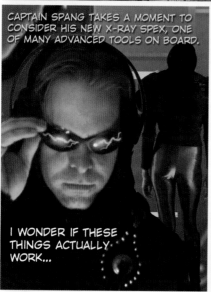

CAPTAIN SPANG TAKES A MOMENT TO CONSIDER HIS NEW X-RAY SPEX, ONE OF MANY ADVANCED TOOLS ON BOARD.

I WONDER IF THESE THINGS ACTUALLY WORK...

WHOOPS! HEY NOW!

THE FUTURE IS BITCHIN'!

ONE *BEAMDOWN* LATER, SPANG AND COSMA ARE MET BY A BIZARRE INHABITANT OF THE NEW PLANET.

GREEETINGS, O CITIZENS OF EARTH! I, *XIXOGG*, WELCOME YOU TO THE PLANET *XYXAX* IN THE SPIRIT OF INTERPLANETARY FELLOWSHIP AND GOOD WILL. *SQUEET!*

WHOA THERE, BLOBBO! TAKE IT NICE AND SLOW!

YOU TELL IT, CAPTAI SPANG!

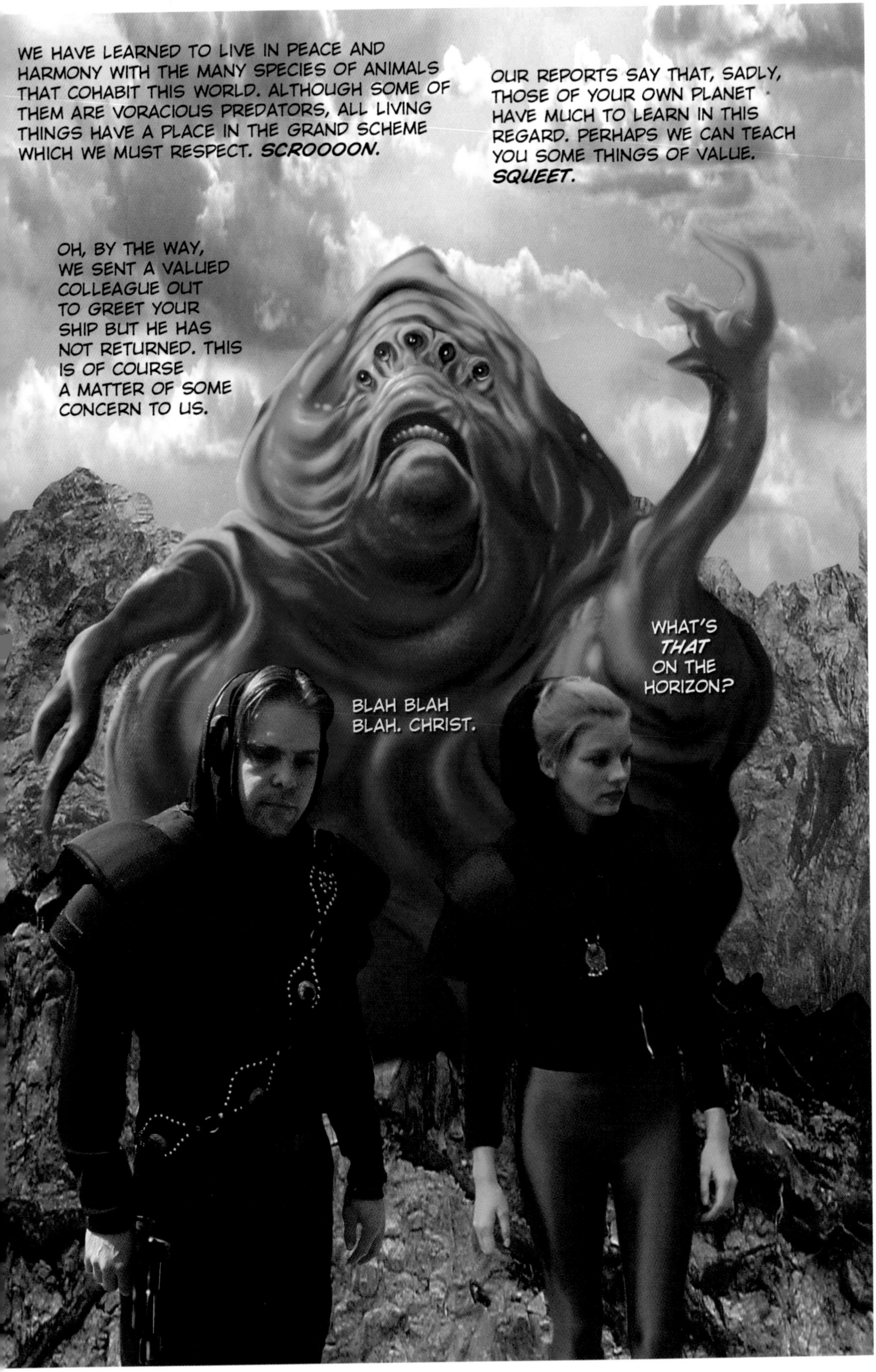
WE HAVE LEARNED TO LIVE IN PEACE AND HARMONY WITH THE MANY SPECIES OF ANIMALS THAT COHABIT THIS WORLD. ALTHOUGH SOME OF THEM ARE VORACIOUS PREDATORS, ALL LIVING THINGS HAVE A PLACE IN THE GRAND SCHEME WHICH WE MUST RESPECT. ***SCROOOON.***
OUR REPORTS SAY THAT, SADLY, THOSE OF YOUR OWN PLANET HAVE MUCH TO LEARN IN THIS REGARD. PERHAPS WE CAN TEACH YOU SOME THINGS OF VALUE. ***SQUEET***.
OH, BY THE WAY, WE SENT A VALUED COLLEAGUE OUT TO GREET YOUR SHIP BUT HE HAS NOT RETURNED. THIS IS OF COURSE A MATTER OF SOME CONCERN TO US.
BLAH BLAH BLAH. CHRIST.
WHAT'S *THAT* ON THE HORIZON?

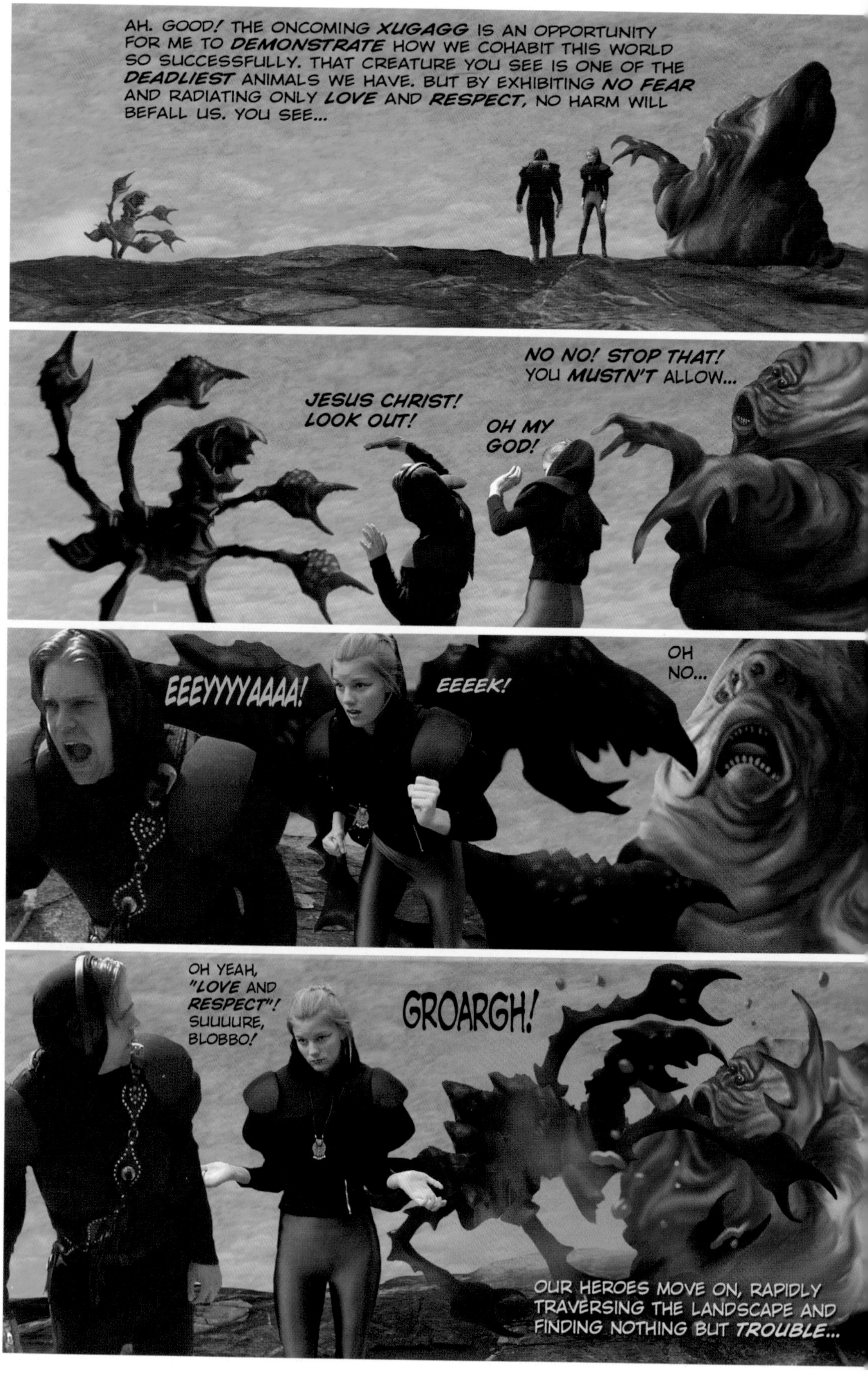
AH. GOOD! THE ONCOMING XUGAGG IS AN OPPORTUNITY FOR ME TO DEMONSTRATE HOW WE COHABIT THIS WORLD SO SUCCESSFULLY. THAT CREATURE YOU SEE IS ONE OF THE DEADLIEST ANIMALS WE HAVE. BUT BY EXHIBITING NO FEAR AND RADIATING ONLY LOVE AND RESPECT, NO HARM WILL BEFALL US. YOU SEE...
JESUS CHRIST! LOOK OUT!
OH MY GOD!
NO NO! STOP THAT! YOU MUSTN'T ALLOW...
EEEYYYYAAAA!
EEEEK!
OH NO...
OH YEAH, "LOVE AND RESPECT"! SUUUURE, BLOBBO!
GROARGH!
OUR HEROES MOVE ON, RAPIDLY TRAVERSING THE LANDSCAPE AND FINDING NOTHING BUT TROUBLE...

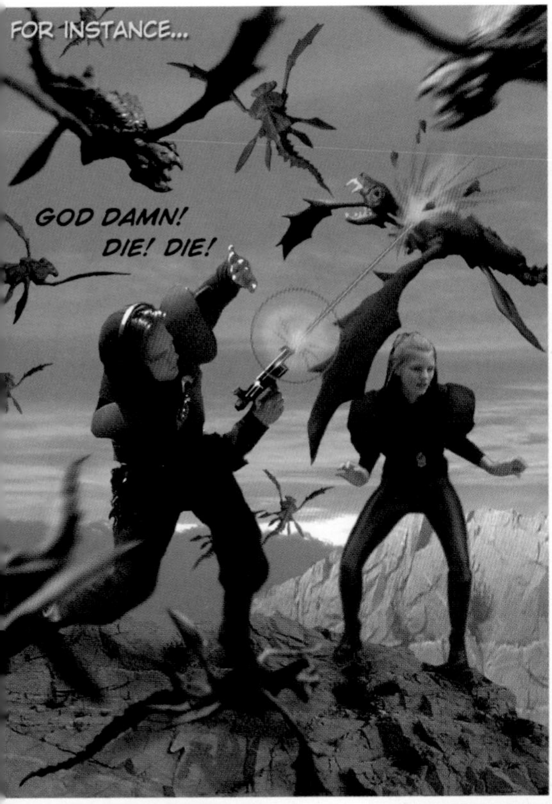
FOR INSTANCE...
GOD DAMN! DIE! DIE!

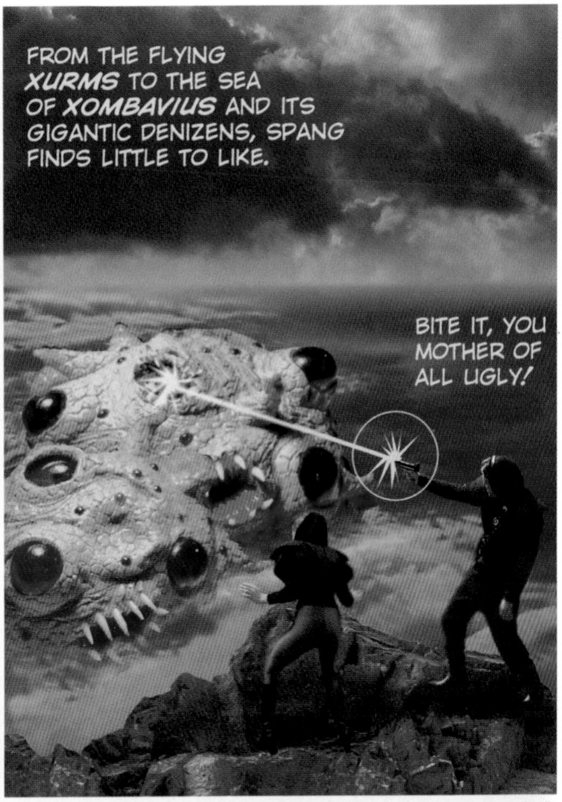
FROM THE FLYING *XURMS* TO THE SEA OF *XOMBAVIUS* AND ITS GIGANTIC DENIZENS, SPANG FINDS LITTLE TO LIKE.
BITE IT, YOU MOTHER OF ALL UGLY!

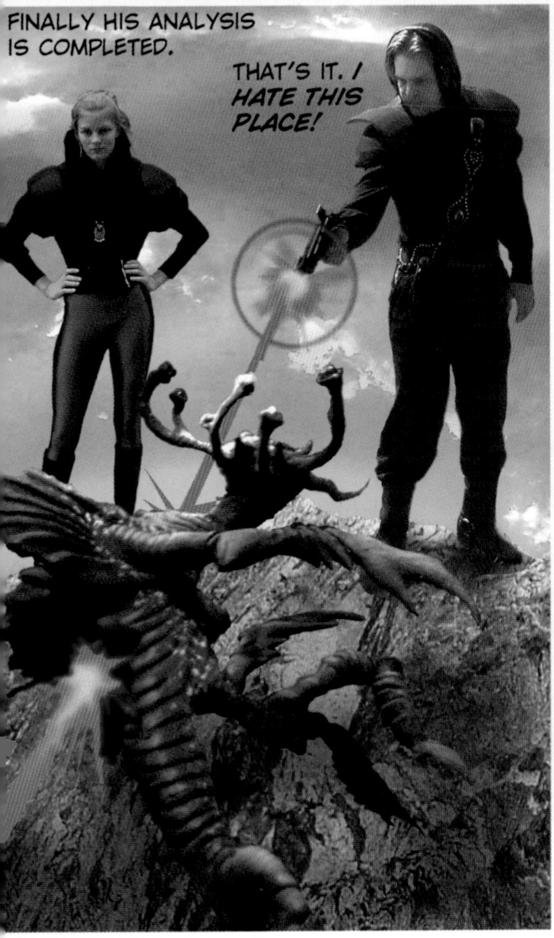
FINALLY HIS ANALYSIS IS COMPLETED.
THAT'S IT. *I HATE THIS PLACE!*

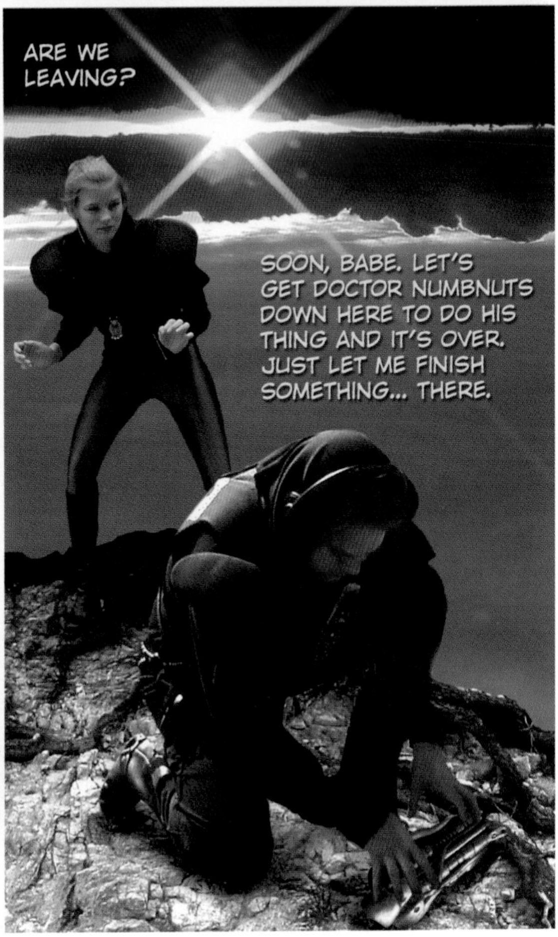
ARE WE LEAVING?
SOON, BABE. LET'S GET DOCTOR NUMBNUTS DOWN HERE TO DO HIS THING AND IT'S OVER. JUST LET ME FINISH SOMETHING... THERE.

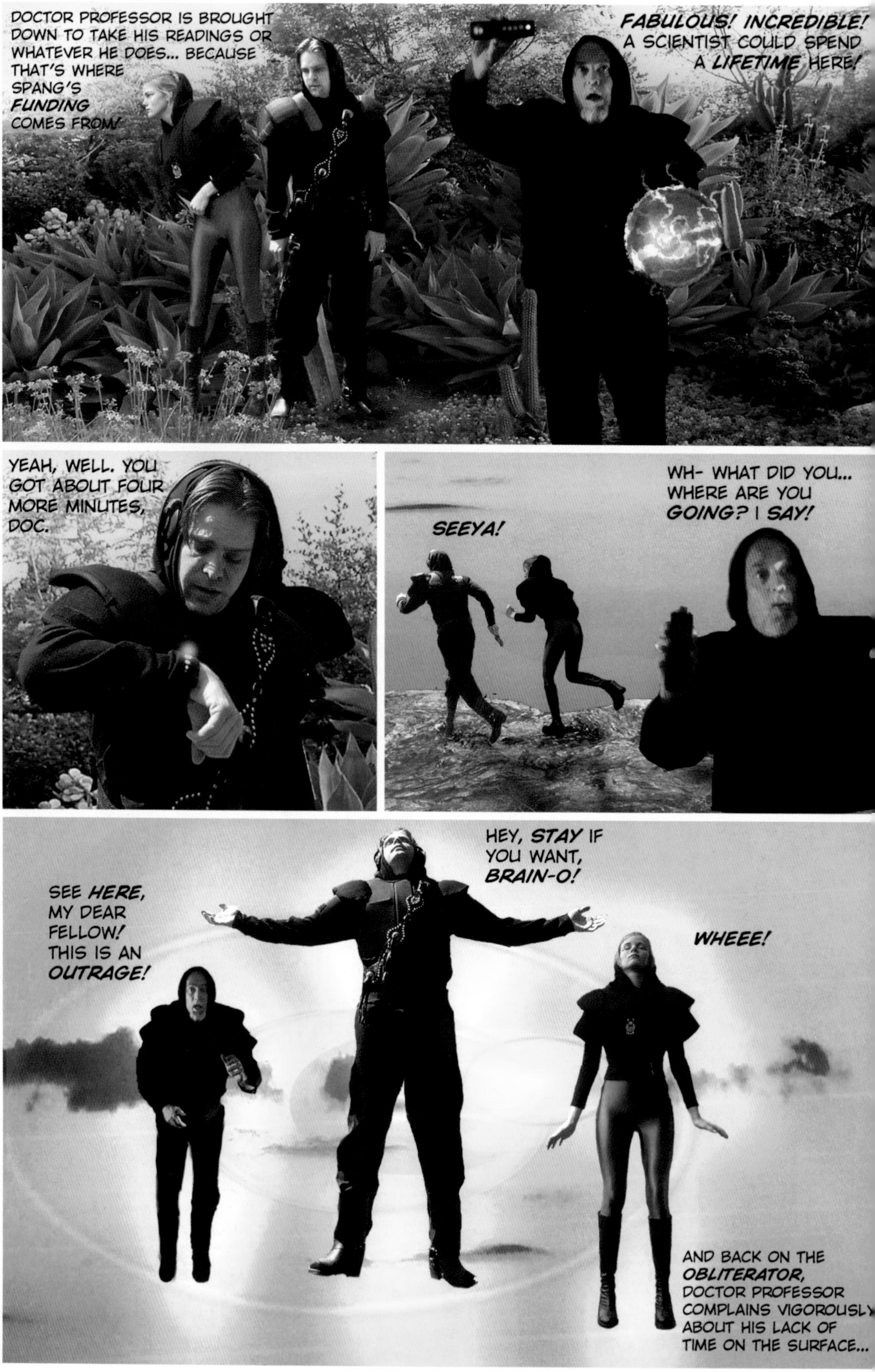
DOCTOR PROFESSOR IS BROUGHT DOWN TO TAKE HIS READINGS OR WHATEVER HE DOES... BECAUSE THAT'S WHERE SPANG'S FUNDING COMES FROM!
FABULOUS! INCREDIBLE! A SCIENTIST COULD SPEND A LIFETIME HERE!
YEAH, WELL. YOU GOT ABOUT FOUR MORE MINUTES, DOC.
SEEYA!
WH- WHAT DID YOU... WHERE ARE YOU GOING? I SAY!
HEY, STAY IF YOU WANT, BRAIN-O!
SEE HERE, MY DEAR FELLOW! THIS IS AN OUTRAGE!
WHEEE!
AND BACK ON THE OBLITERATOR, DOCTOR PROFESSOR COMPLAINS VIGOROUSLY ABOUT HIS LACK OF TIME ON THE SURFACE...

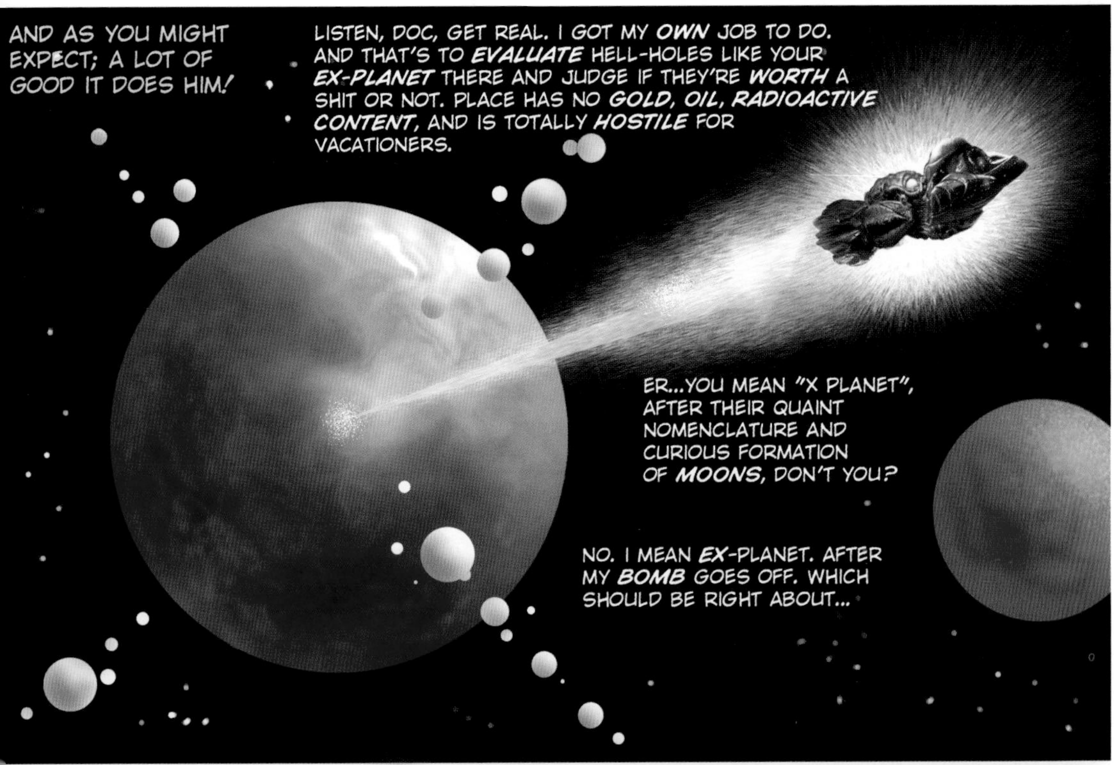
AND AS YOU MIGHT EXPECT; A LOT OF GOOD IT DOES HIM!
LISTEN, DOC, GET REAL. I GOT MY OWN JOB TO DO. AND THAT'S TO EVALUATE HELL-HOLES LIKE YOUR EX-PLANET THERE AND JUDGE IF THEY'RE WORTH A SHIT OR NOT. PLACE HAS NO GOLD, OIL, RADIOACTIVE CONTENT, AND IS TOTALLY HOSTILE FOR VACATIONERS.
ER...YOU MEAN "X PLANET", AFTER THEIR QUAINT NOMENCLATURE AND CURIOUS FORMATION OF MOONS, DON'T YOU?
NO. I MEAN EX-PLANET. AFTER MY BOMB GOES OFF. WHICH SHOULD BE RIGHT ABOUT...

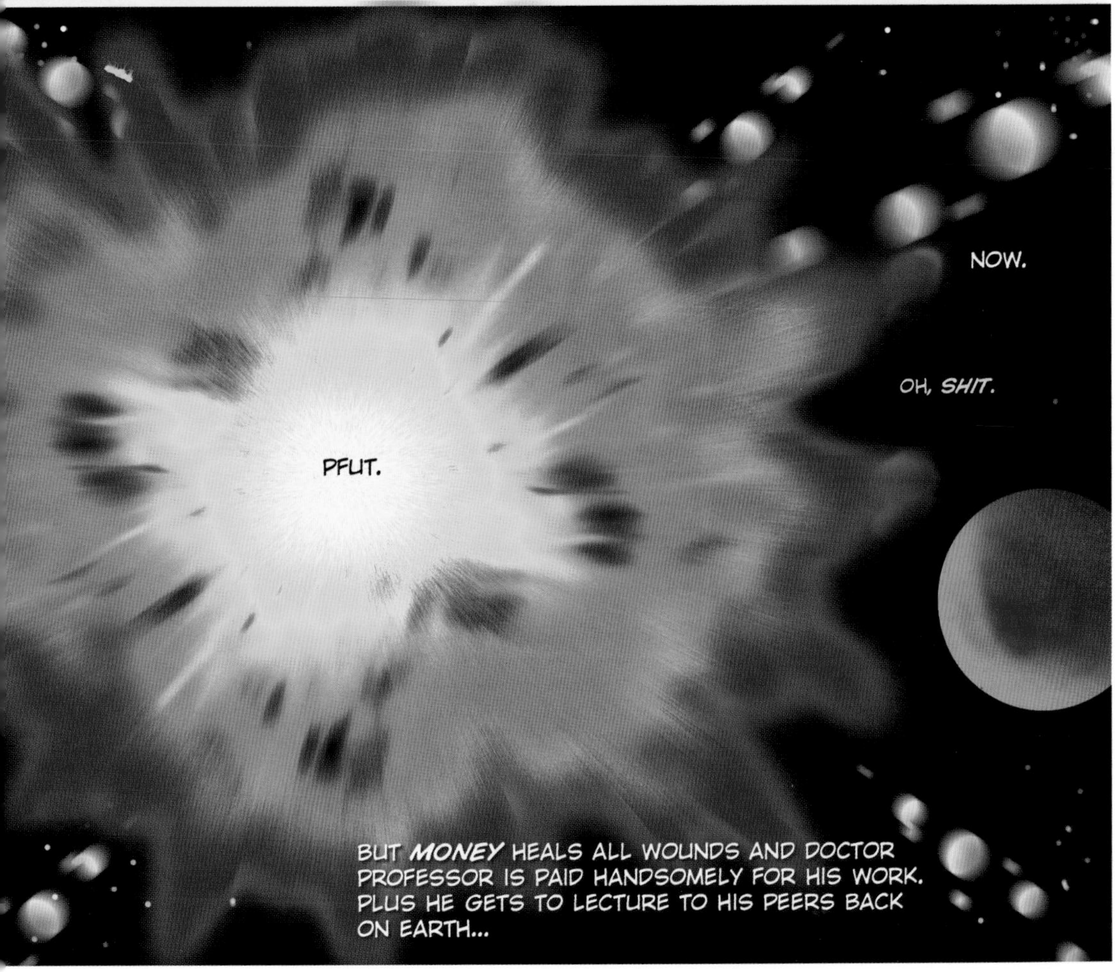
NOW.
OH, SHIT.
PFUT.
BUT MONEY HEALS ALL WOUNDS AND DOCTOR PROFESSOR IS PAID HANDSOMELY FOR HIS WORK. PLUS HE GETS TO LECTURE TO HIS PEERS BACK ON EARTH...

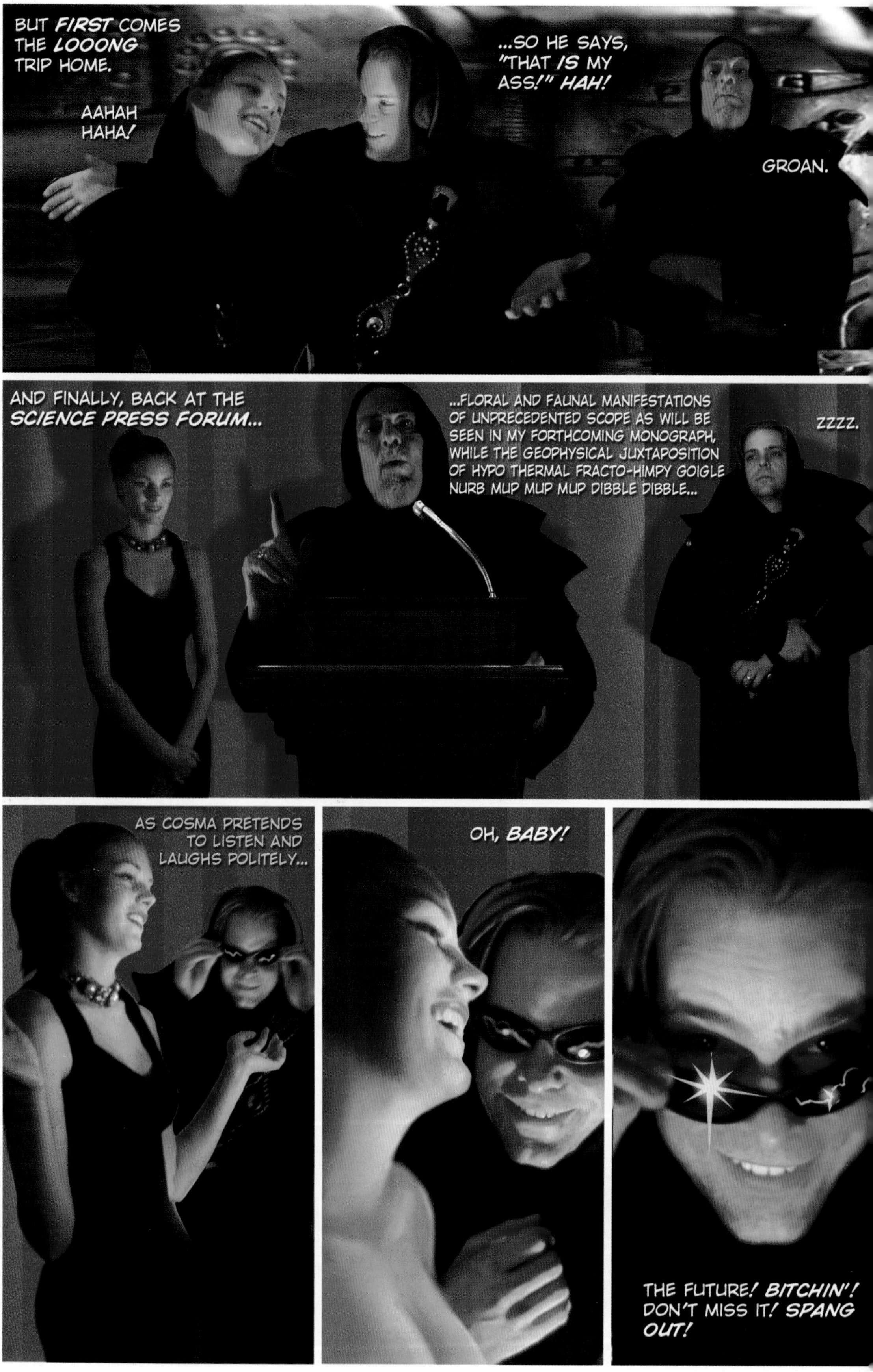
BUT FIRST COMES THE LOOONG TRIP HOME.
AAHAH HAHA!
...SO HE SAYS, "THAT IS MY ASS!" HAH!
GROAN.
AND FINALLY, BACK AT THE SCIENCE PRESS FORUM...
...FLORAL AND FAUNAL MANIFESTATIONS OF UNPRECEDENTED SCOPE AS WILL BE SEEN IN MY FORTHCOMING MONOGRAPH, WHILE THE GEOPHYSICAL JUXTAPOSITION OF HYPO THERMAL FRACTO-HIMPY GOIGLE NURB MUP MUP MUP DIBBLE DIBBLE...
ZZZZ.
AS COSMA PRETENDS TO LISTEN AND LAUGHS POLITELY...
OH, BABY!
THE FUTURE! BITCHIN'! DON'T MISS IT! SPANG OUT!

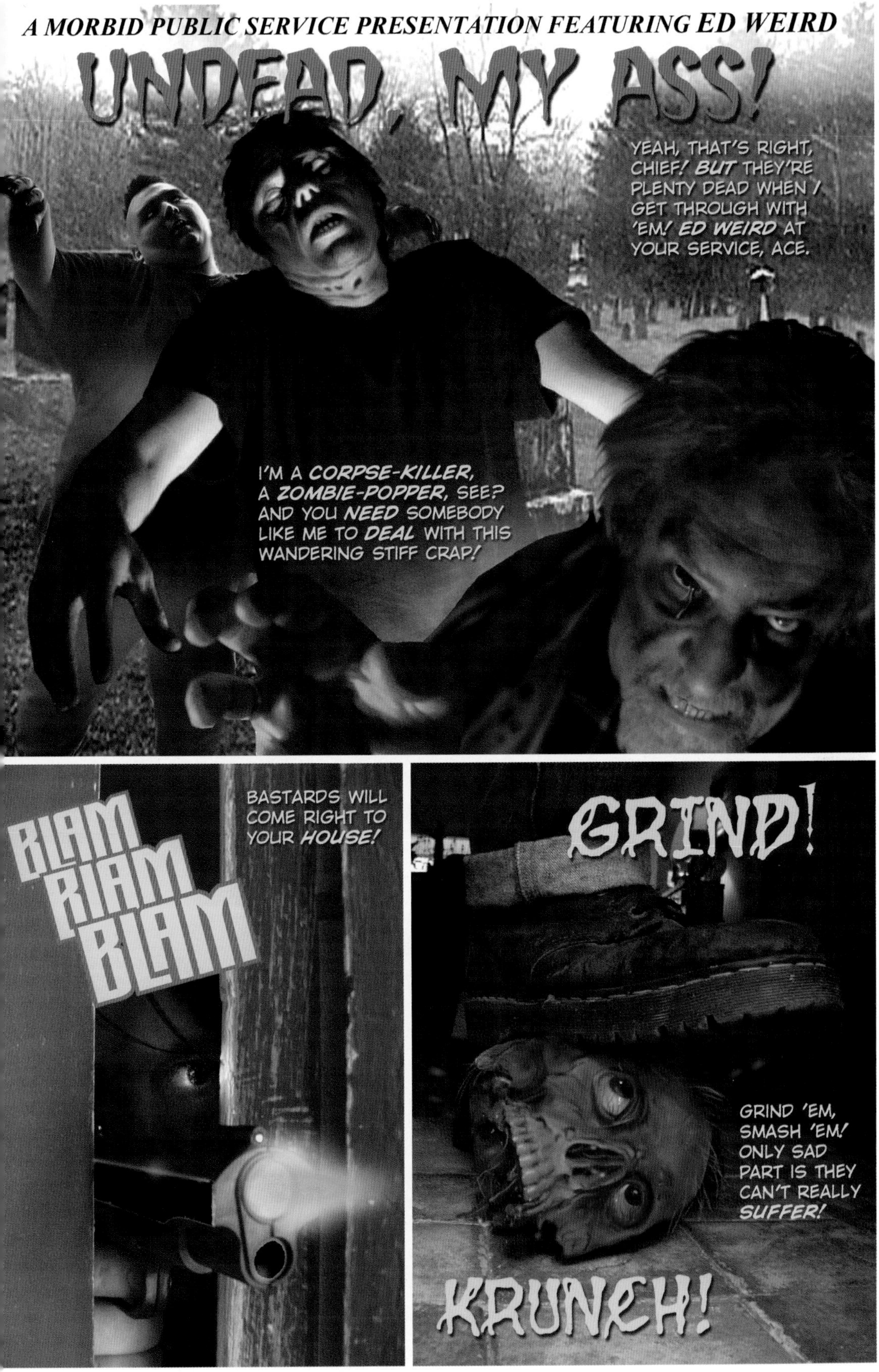
A MORBID PUBLIC SERVICE PRESENTATION FEATURING ED WEIRD
UNDEAD, MY ASS!
YEAH, THAT'S RIGHT, CHIEF! BUT THEY'RE PLENTY DEAD WHEN I GET THROUGH WITH 'EM! ED WEIRD AT YOUR SERVICE, ACE.
I'M A CORPSE-KILLER, A ZOMBIE-POPPER, SEE? AND YOU NEED SOMEBODY LIKE ME TO DEAL WITH THIS WANDERING STIFF CRAP!
BASTARDS WILL COME RIGHT TO YOUR HOUSE!
BLAM BLAM BLAM
GRIND!
GRIND 'EM, SMASH 'EM! ONLY SAD PART IS THEY CAN'T REALLY SUFFER!
KRUNCH!

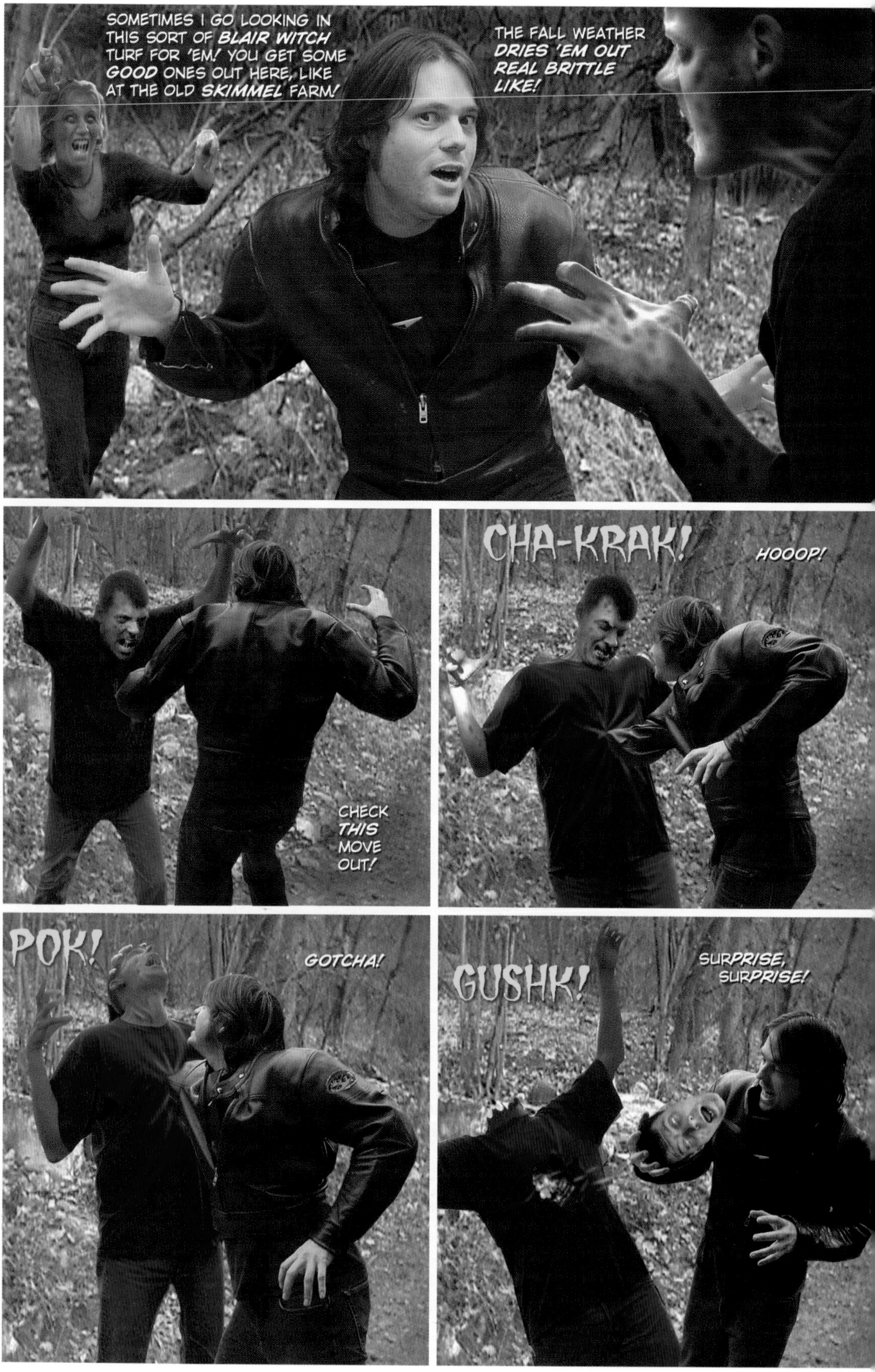
SOMETIMES I GO LOOKING IN THIS SORT OF BLAIR WITCH TURF FOR 'EM! YOU GET SOME GOOD ONES OUT HERE, LIKE AT THE OLD SKIMMEL FARM!
THE FALL WEATHER DRIES 'EM OUT REAL BRITTLE LIKE!
CHECK THIS MOVE OUT!
CHA-KRAK!
HOOOP!
POK!
GOTCHA!
GUSHK!
SURPRISE, SURPRISE!

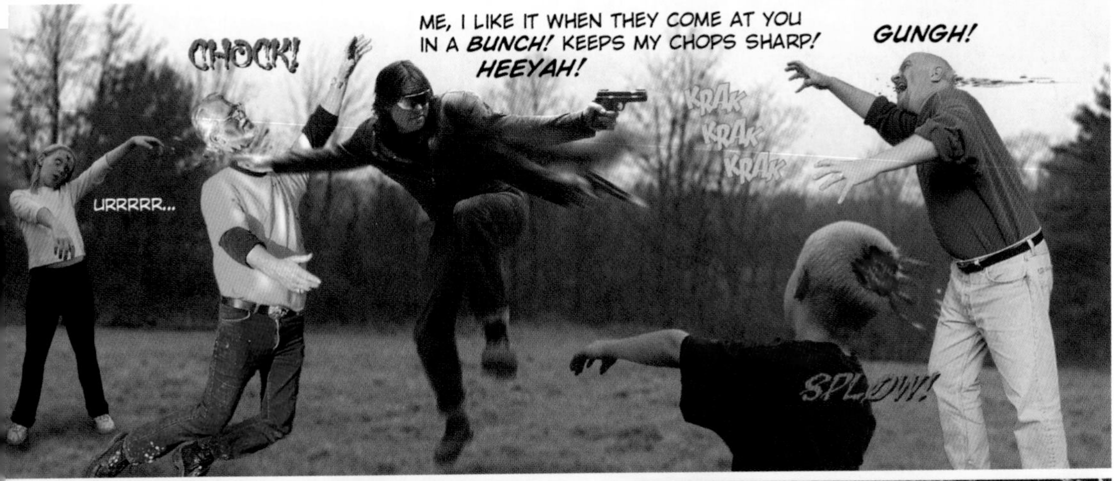
ME, I LIKE IT WHEN THEY COME AT YOU IN A *BUNCH!* KEEPS MY CHOPS SHARP! *HEEYAH!*
CHOCK!
GUNGH!
URRRRR...
KRAK KRAK KRAK
SPLOW!

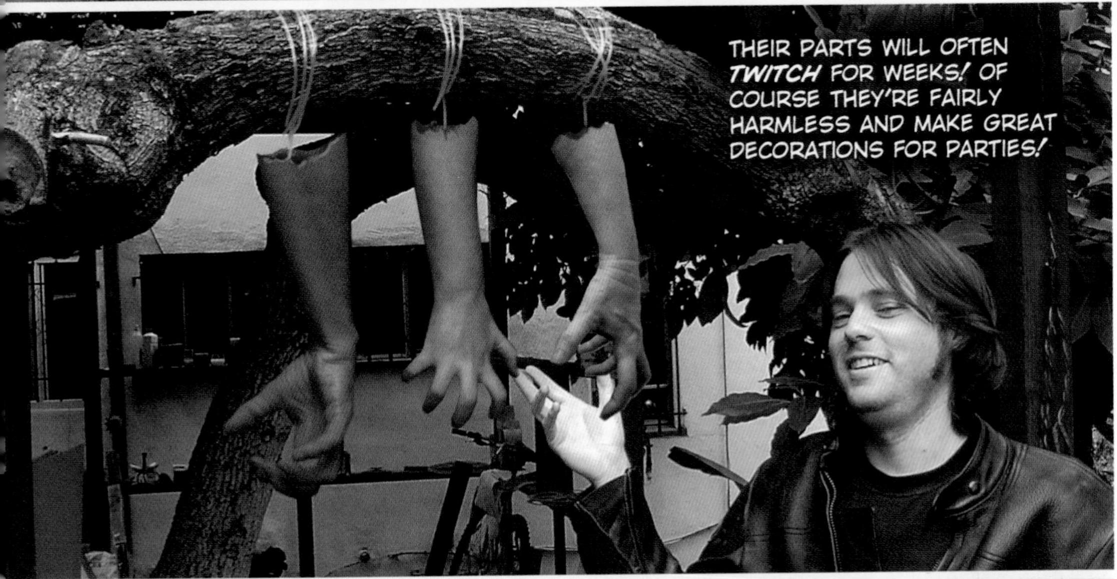
THEIR PARTS WILL OFTEN *TWITCH* FOR WEEKS! OF COURSE THEY'RE FAIRLY HARMLESS AND MAKE GREAT DECORATIONS FOR PARTIES!

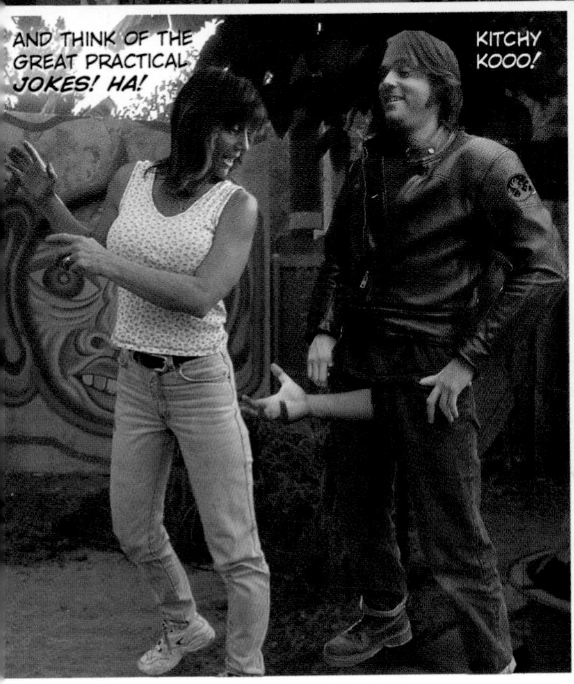
AND THINK OF THE GREAT PRACTICAL *JOKES! HA!*
KITCHY KOOO!

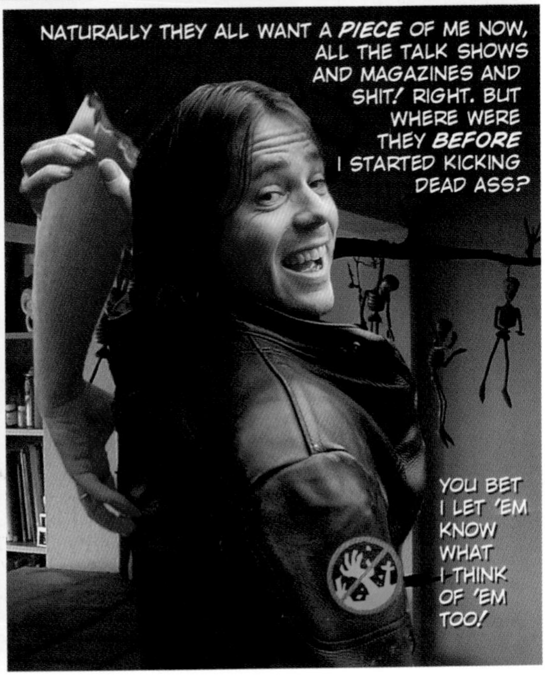
NATURALLY THEY ALL WANT A *PIECE* OF ME NOW, ALL THE TALK SHOWS AND MAGAZINES AND SHIT! RIGHT. BUT WHERE WERE THEY *BEFORE* I STARTED KICKING DEAD ASS?
YOU BET I LET 'EM KNOW WHAT I THINK OF 'EM TOO!

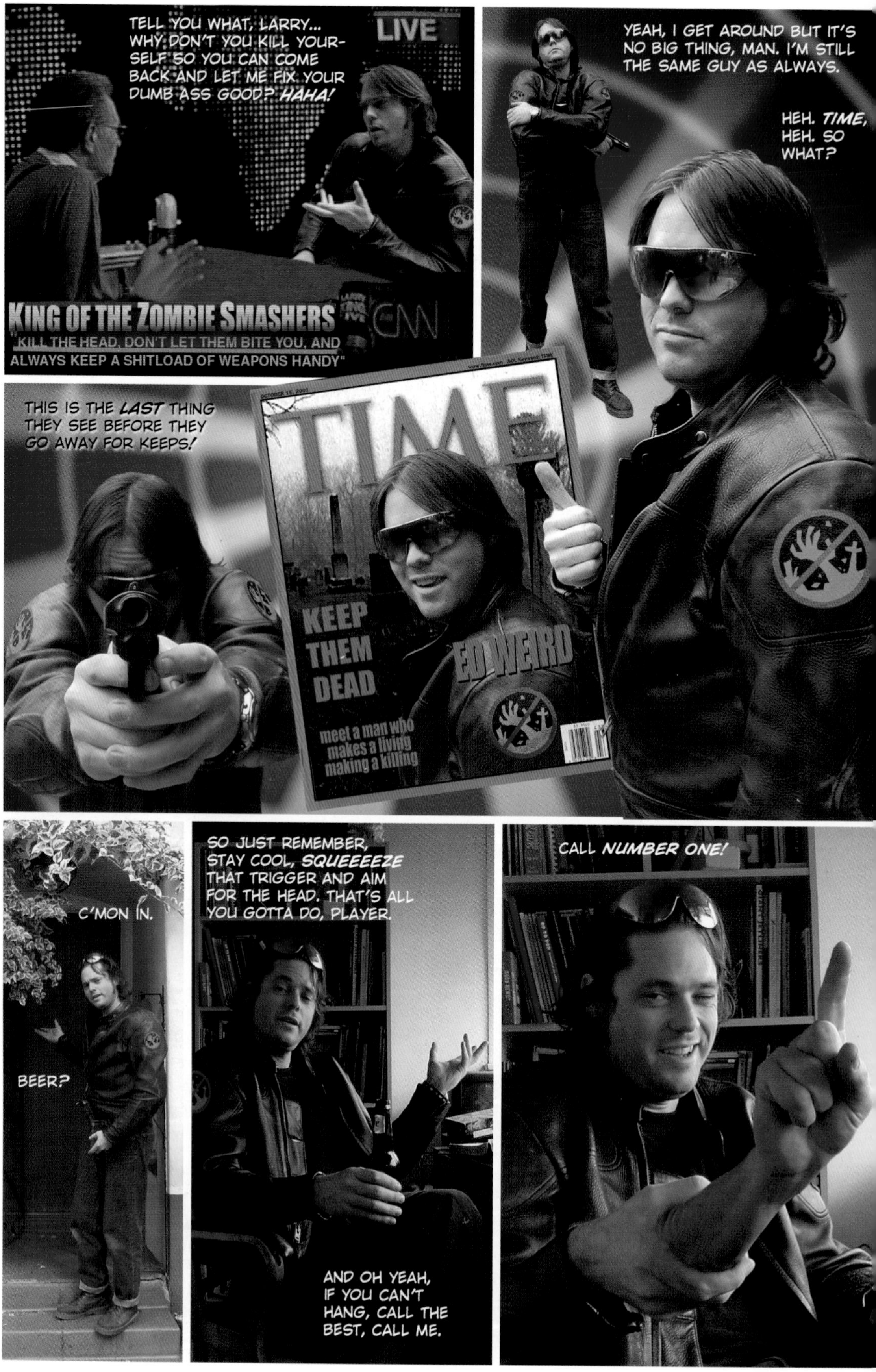
TELL YOU WHAT, LARRY... WHY DON'T YOU KILL YOURSELF SO YOU CAN COME BACK AND LET ME FIX YOUR DUMB ASS GOOD? HAHA!
LIVE
KING OF THE ZOMBIE SMASHERS
"KILL THE HEAD, DON'T LET THEM BITE YOU, AND ALWAYS KEEP A SHITLOAD OF WEAPONS HANDY"
CNN
YEAH, I GET AROUND BUT IT'S NO BIG THING, MAN. I'M STILL THE SAME GUY AS ALWAYS.
HEH. TIME, HEH. SO WHAT?
THIS IS THE LAST THING THEY SEE BEFORE THEY GO AWAY FOR KEEPS!
TIME
KEEP THEM DEAD
ED WEIRD
meet a man who makes a living making a killing
C'MON IN.
BEER?
SO JUST REMEMBER, STAY COOL, SQUEEEEZE THAT TRIGGER AND AIM FOR THE HEAD. THAT'S ALL YOU GOTTA DO, PLAYER.
AND OH YEAH, IF YOU CAN'T HANG, CALL THE BEST, CALL ME.
CALL NUMBER ONE!

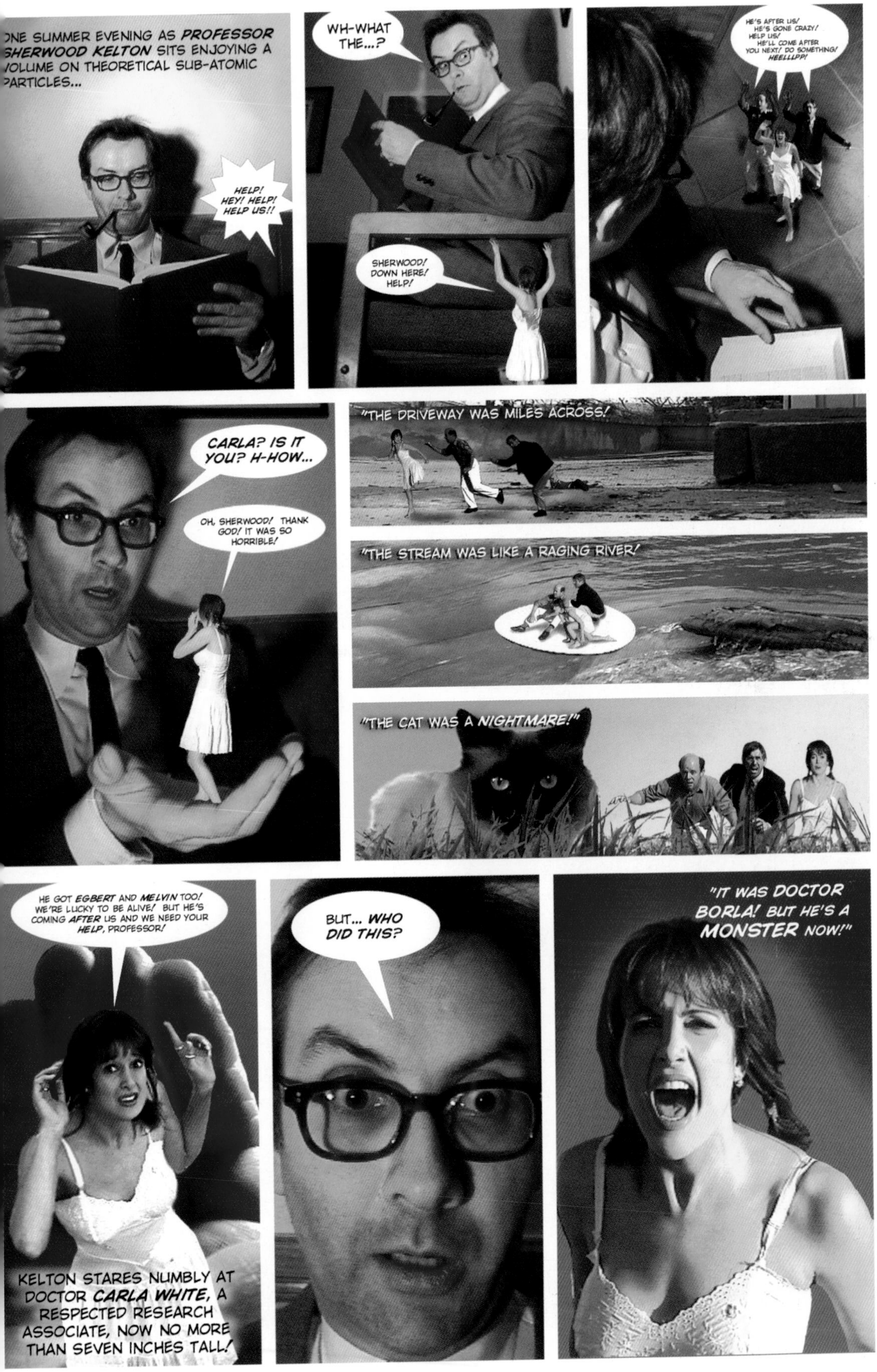

ONE SUMMER EVENING AS PROFESSOR SHERWOOD KELTON SITS ENJOYING A VOLUME ON THEORETICAL SUB-ATOMIC PARTICLES...
HELP! HEY! HELP! HELP US!!
WH-WHAT THE...?
SHERWOOD! DOWN HERE! HELP!
HE'S AFTER US! HE'S GONE CRAZY! HELP US! HE'LL COME AFTER YOU NEXT! DO SOMETHING! HEELLLPP!
CARLA? IS IT YOU? H-HOW...
OH, SHERWOOD! THANK GOD! IT WAS SO HORRIBLE!
"THE DRIVEWAY WAS MILES ACROSS!
"THE STREAM WAS LIKE A RAGING RIVER!
"THE CAT WAS A NIGHTMARE!"
HE GOT EGBERT AND MELVIN TOO! WE'RE LUCKY TO BE ALIVE! BUT HE'S COMING AFTER US AND WE NEED YOUR HELP, PROFESSOR!
KELTON STARES NUMBLY AT DOCTOR CARLA WHITE, A RESPECTED RESEARCH ASSOCIATE, NOW NO MORE THAN SEVEN INCHES TALL!
BUT... WHO DID THIS?
"IT WAS DOCTOR BORLA! BUT HE'S A MONSTER NOW!"

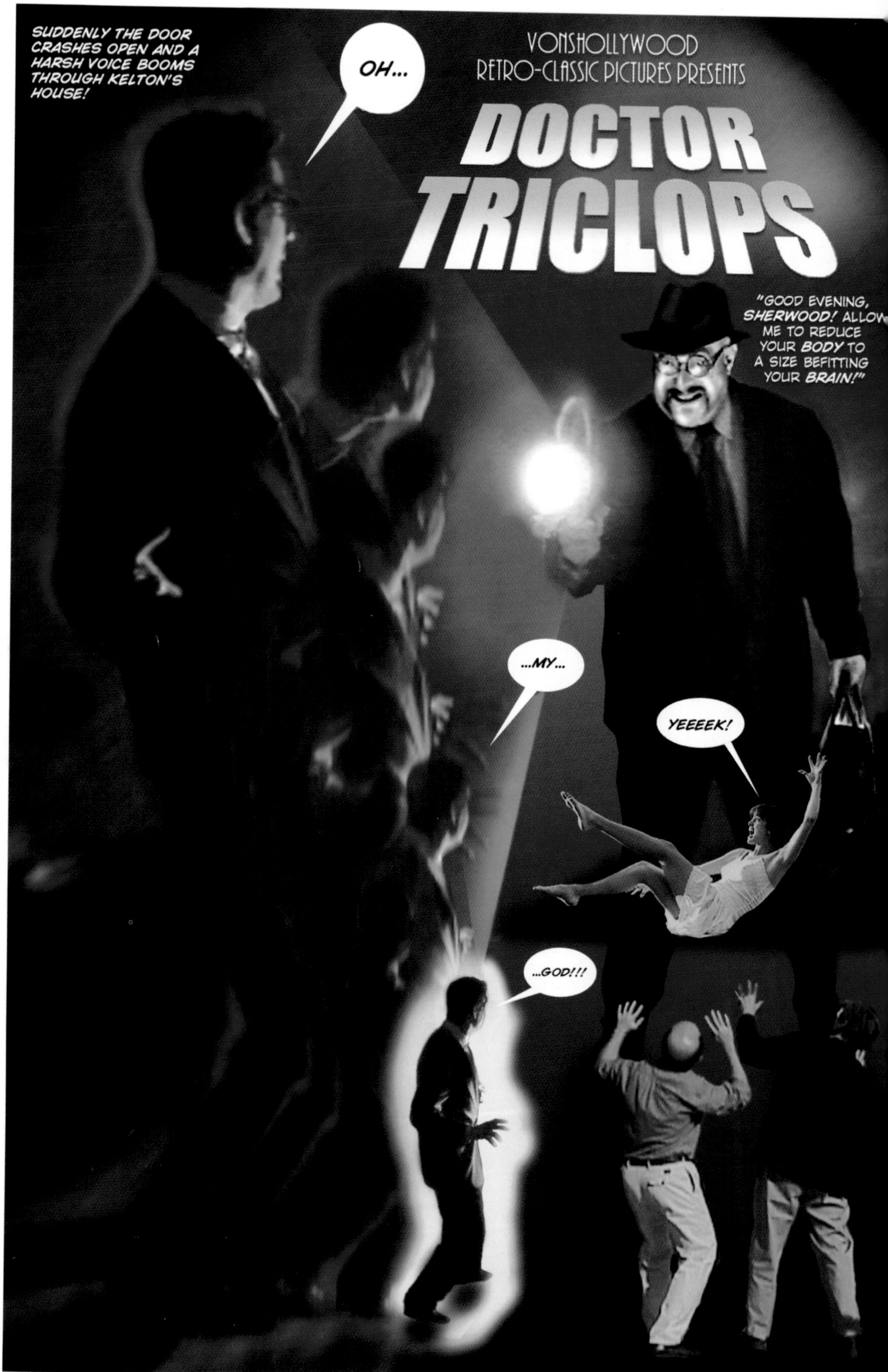
SUDDENLY THE DOOR CRASHES OPEN AND A HARSH VOICE BOOMS THROUGH KELTON'S HOUSE!
OH...
VONSHOLLYWOOD RETRO-CLASSIC PICTURES PRESENTS
DOCTOR TRICLOPS
"GOOD EVENING, SHERWOOD! ALLOW ME TO REDUCE YOUR BODY TO A SIZE BEFITTING YOUR BRAIN!"
...MY...
YEEEEK!
...GOD!!!

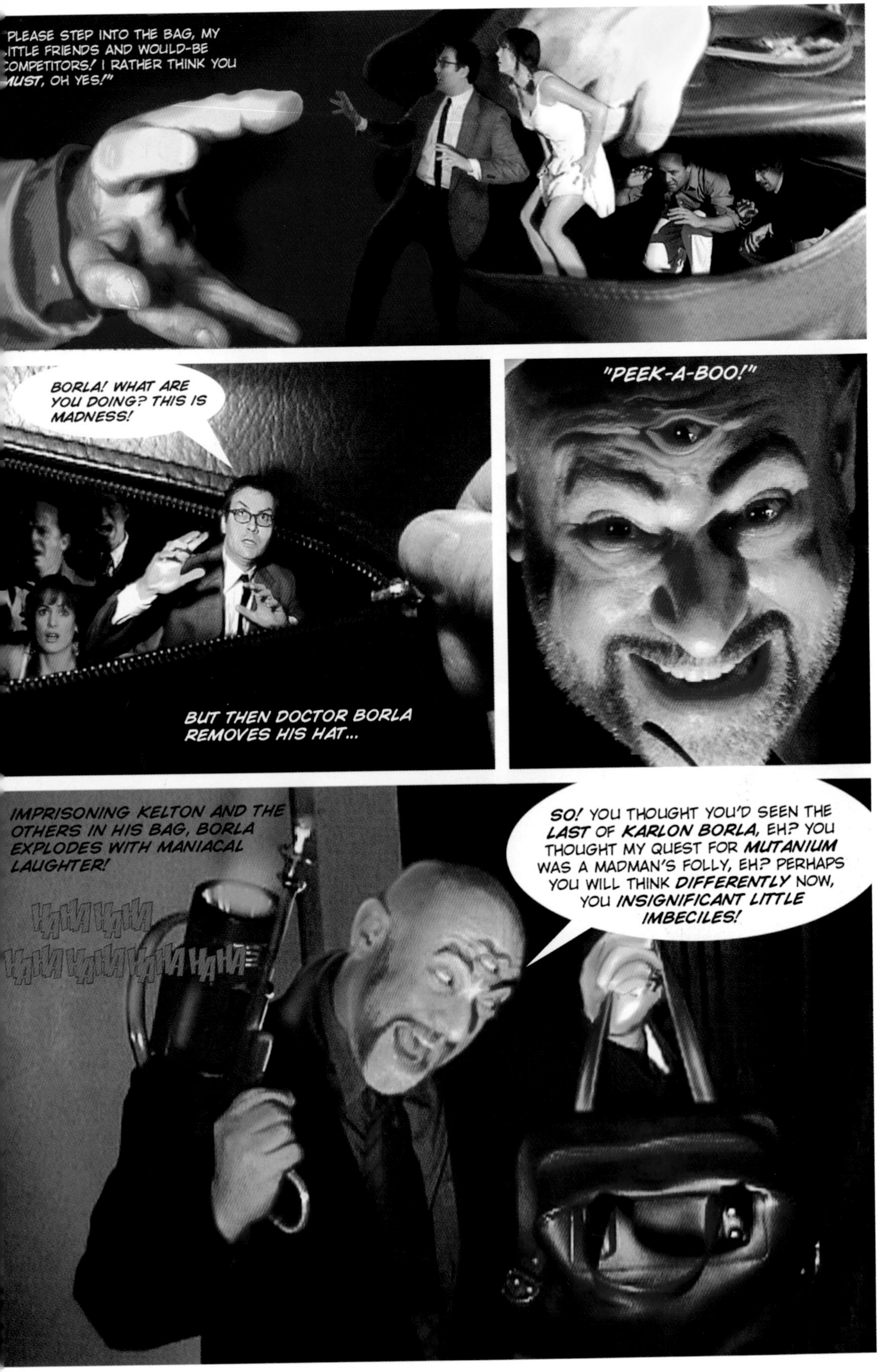
"PLEASE STEP INTO THE BAG, MY ITTLE FRIENDS AND WOULD-BE OMPETITORS! I RATHER THINK YOU MUST, OH YES!"
BORLA! WHAT ARE YOU DOING? THIS IS MADNESS!
BUT THEN DOCTOR BORLA REMOVES HIS HAT...
"PEEK-A-BOO!"
IMPRISONING KELTON AND THE OTHERS IN HIS BAG, BORLA EXPLODES WITH MANIACAL LAUGHTER!
HAHA HAHA
HAHA HAHA HAHA HAHA
SO! YOU THOUGHT YOU'D SEEN THE LAST OF KARLON BORLA, EH? YOU THOUGHT MY QUEST FOR MUTANIUM WAS A MADMAN'S FOLLY, EH? PERHAPS YOU WILL THINK DIFFERENTLY NOW, YOU INSIGNIFICANT LITTLE IMBECILES!

BACK IN BORLA'S LAB...

I HAD POSTULATED THE EXISTENCE OF A *THEORETICAL ELEMENT* WHICH WOULD DICTATE THE *SCALE* OF *MATTER* AT THE *MOLECULAR LEVEL* BY CHANGING THE *SPACE* BETWEEN ITS *ATOMIC COMPONENTS*.

"I ADMIT THAT THE *SOURCE* WAS A SURPRISE! I FOUND IT IN A METEORITE WHILE IN *BRAZIL!*

"BUT *PROLONGED EXPOSURE* HAD *MORE* UNEXPECTED RESULTS!

"THE *PAIN* WAS INCREDIBLE!

"I BECAME *HIGHLY SENSITIZED TO ITS RAYS*, HENCE MY TERM, *MUTANIUM!* BUT WITH MY... *CHANGE* HAD COME INCREASED INTELLIGENCE, AWARENESS AND *VISION*, IN MORE WAYS THAN *ONE!*

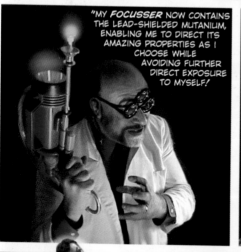

"MY *FOCUSSER* NOW CONTAINS THE LEAD-SHIELDED MUTANIUM, ENABLING ME TO DIRECT ITS AMAZING PROPERTIES AS I CHOOSE WHILE AVOIDING FURTHER DIRECT EXPOSURE TO MYSELF!

"AND WITH IT I SHALL DWARF THIS ENTIRE *PLANET* AND ALL THOSE WHO WOULD DARE TO OPPOSE ME!

"YOU FOUR MEMBERS OF THE ALLEGED *SCIENTIFIC COMMUNITY* WILL BE MY FIRST DEMONSTRATION OF *POWER!*"

WHILE BORLA RANTS, KELTON AND HIS FELLOW PRISONERS MAKE THEIR DESPERATE *ESCAPE*...

...BUT UNFORTUNATELY, THEY ARE *OBSERVED!*

GOING SOMEWHERE?

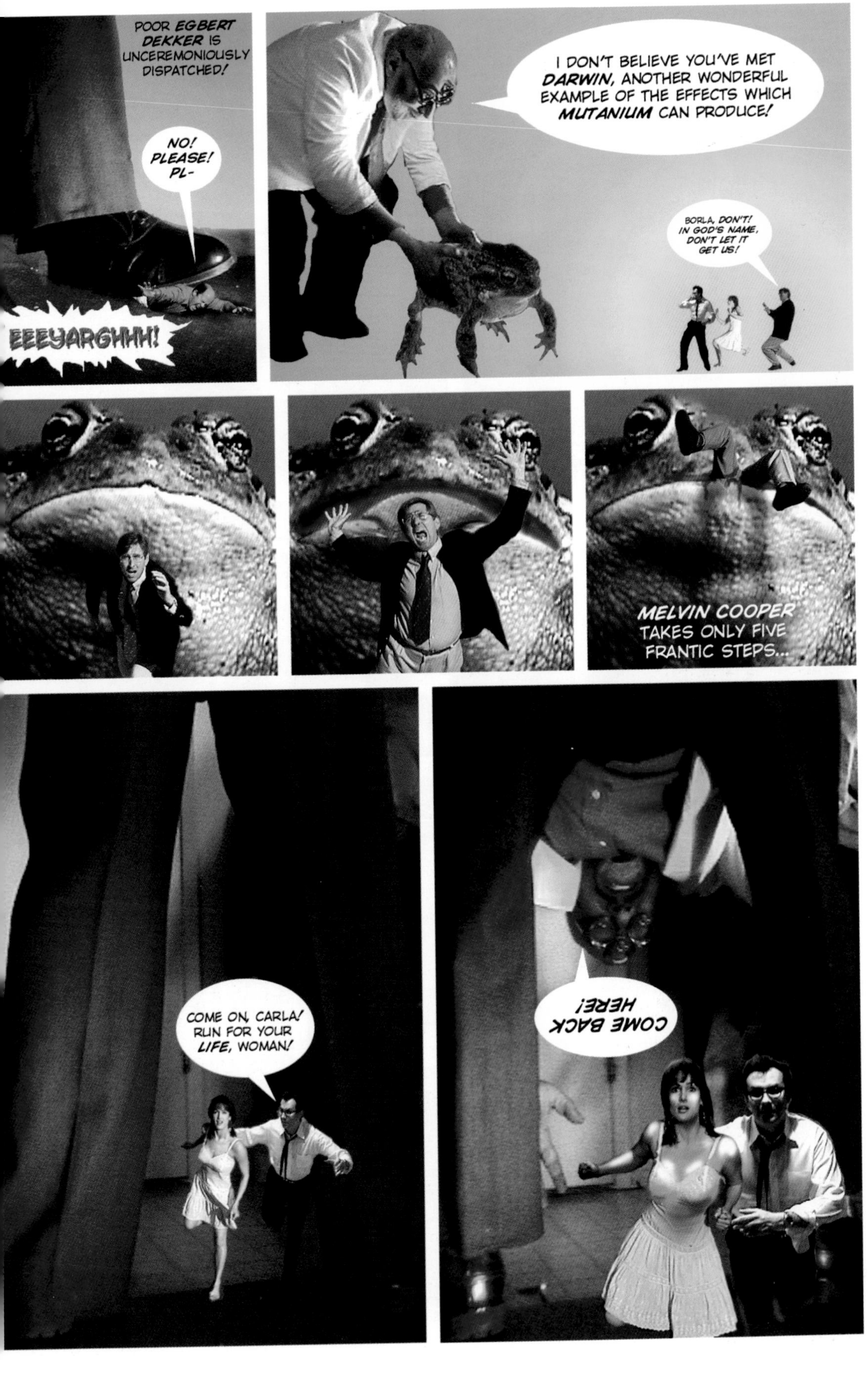
POOR EGBERT DEKKER IS UNCEREMONIOUSLY DISPATCHED!
NO! PLEASE! PL-
EEEYARGHHH!
I DON'T BELIEVE YOU'VE MET DARWIN, ANOTHER WONDERFUL EXAMPLE OF THE EFFECTS WHICH MUTANIUM CAN PRODUCE!
BORLA, DON'T! IN GOD'S NAME, DON'T LET IT GET US!
MELVIN COOPER TAKES ONLY FIVE FRANTIC STEPS...
COME ON, CARLA! RUN FOR YOUR LIFE, WOMAN!
COME BACK HERE!

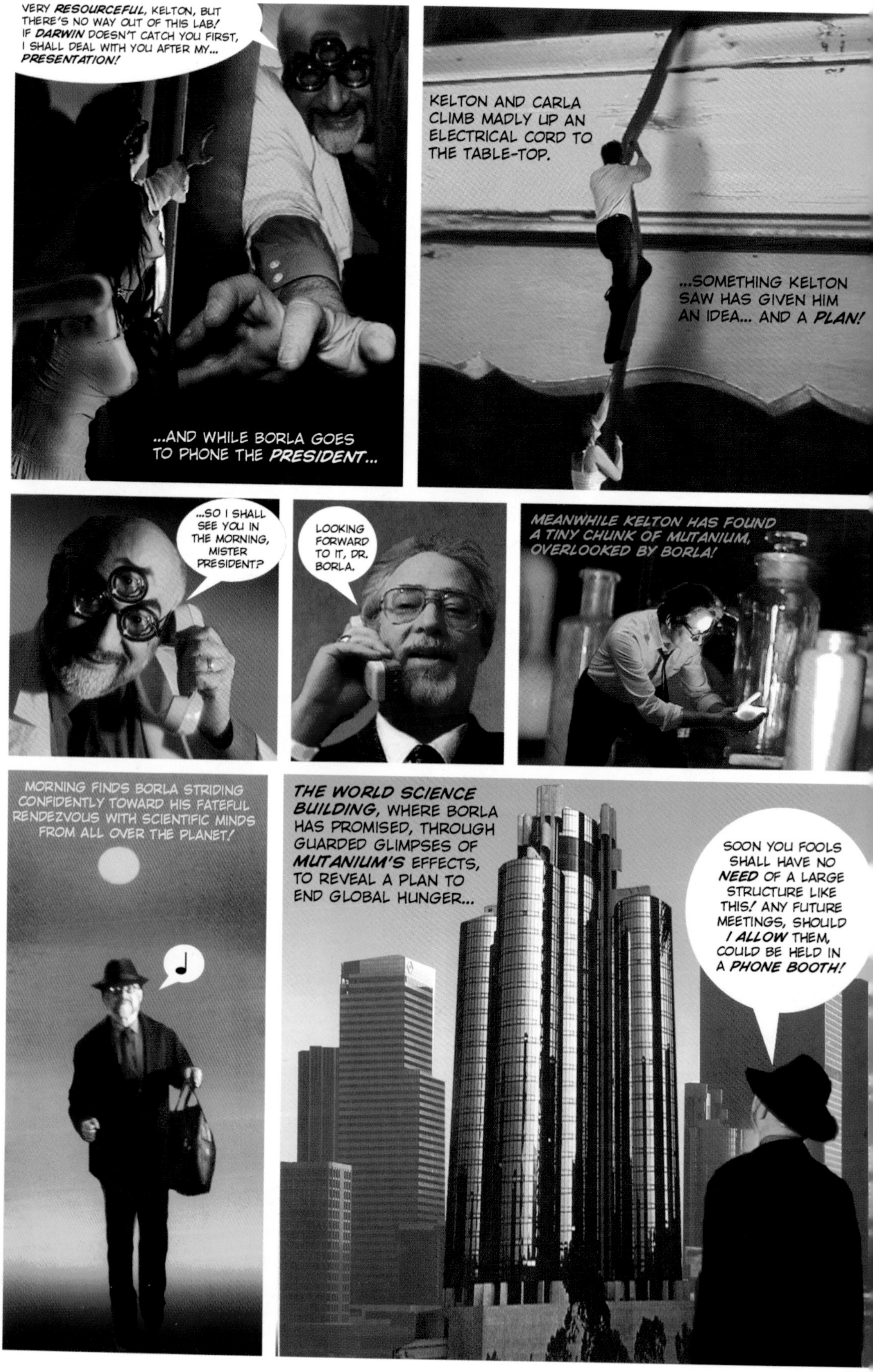
VERY RESOURCEFUL, KELTON, BUT THERE'S NO WAY OUT OF THIS LAB! IF DARWIN DOESN'T CATCH YOU FIRST, I SHALL DEAL WITH YOU AFTER MY... PRESENTATION!
...AND WHILE BORLA GOES TO PHONE THE PRESIDENT...
KELTON AND CARLA CLIMB MADLY UP AN ELECTRICAL CORD TO THE TABLE-TOP.
...SOMETHING KELTON SAW HAS GIVEN HIM AN IDEA... AND A PLAN!
...SO I SHALL SEE YOU IN THE MORNING, MISTER PRESIDENT?
LOOKING FORWARD TO IT, DR. BORLA.
MEANWHILE KELTON HAS FOUND A TINY CHUNK OF MUTANIUM, OVERLOOKED BY BORLA!
MORNING FINDS BORLA STRIDING CONFIDENTLY TOWARD HIS FATEFUL RENDEZVOUS WITH SCIENTIFIC MINDS FROM ALL OVER THE PLANET!
♩
THE WORLD SCIENCE BUILDING, WHERE BORLA HAS PROMISED, THROUGH GUARDED GLIMPSES OF MUTANIUM'S EFFECTS, TO REVEAL A PLAN TO END GLOBAL HUNGER...
SOON YOU FOOLS SHALL HAVE NO NEED OF A LARGE STRUCTURE LIKE THIS! ANY FUTURE MEETINGS, SHOULD I ALLOW THEM, COULD BE HELD IN A PHONE BOOTH!

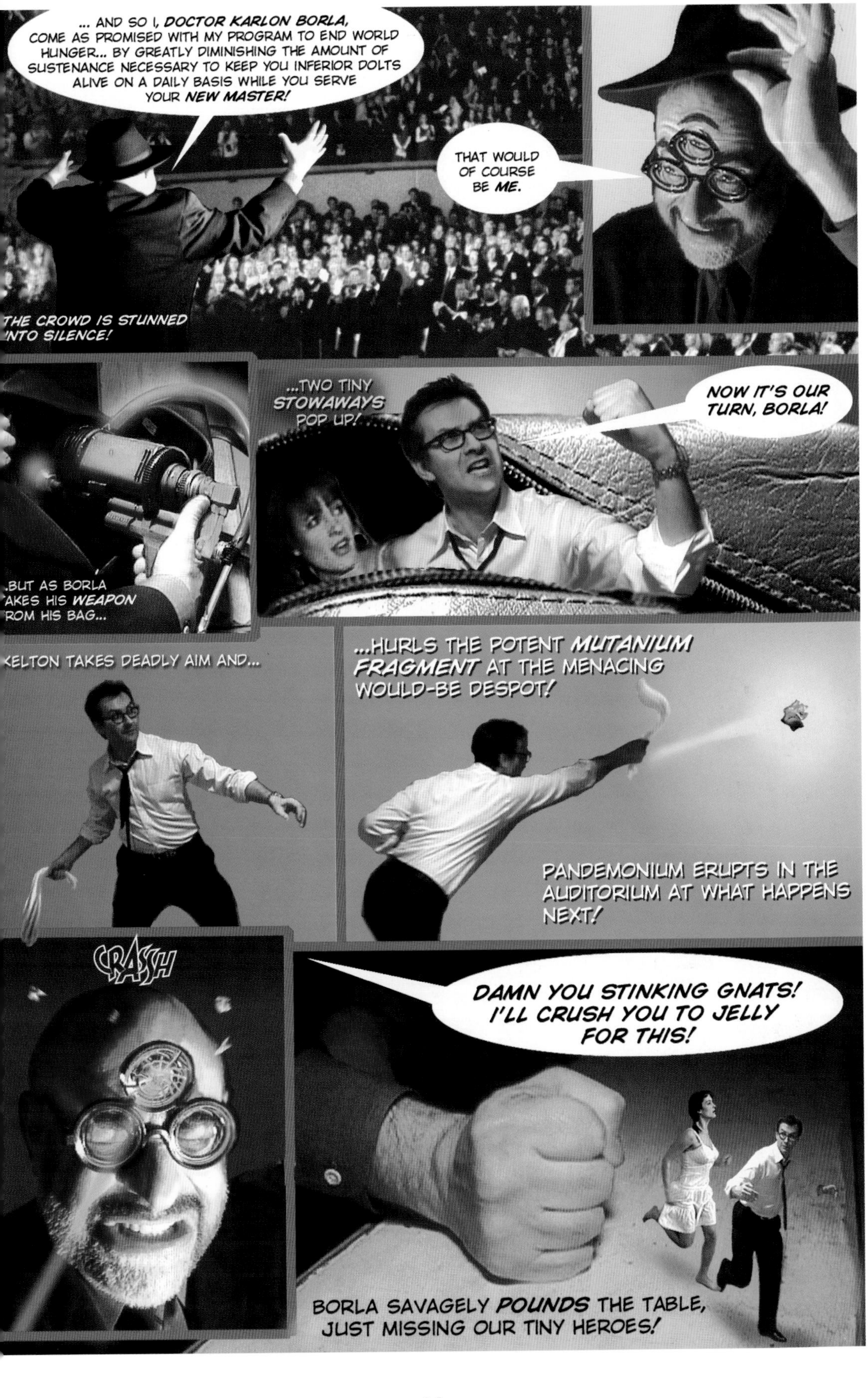
... AND SO I, DOCTOR KARLON BORLA, COME AS PROMISED WITH MY PROGRAM TO END WORLD HUNGER... BY GREATLY DIMINISHING THE AMOUNT OF SUSTENANCE NECESSARY TO KEEP YOU INFERIOR DOLTS ALIVE ON A DAILY BASIS WHILE YOU SERVE YOUR NEW MASTER!
THAT WOULD OF COURSE BE ME.
THE CROWD IS STUNNED INTO SILENCE!
.BUT AS BORLA AKES HIS WEAPON ROM HIS BAG...
...TWO TINY STOWAWAYS POP UP!
NOW IT'S OUR TURN, BORLA!
KELTON TAKES DEADLY AIM AND...
...HURLS THE POTENT MUTANIUM FRAGMENT AT THE MENACING WOULD-BE DESPOT!
PANDEMONIUM ERUPTS IN THE AUDITORIUM AT WHAT HAPPENS NEXT!
CRASH
DAMN YOU STINKING GNATS! I'LL CRUSH YOU TO JELLY FOR THIS!
BORLA SAVAGELY POUNDS THE TABLE, JUST MISSING OUR TINY HEROES!

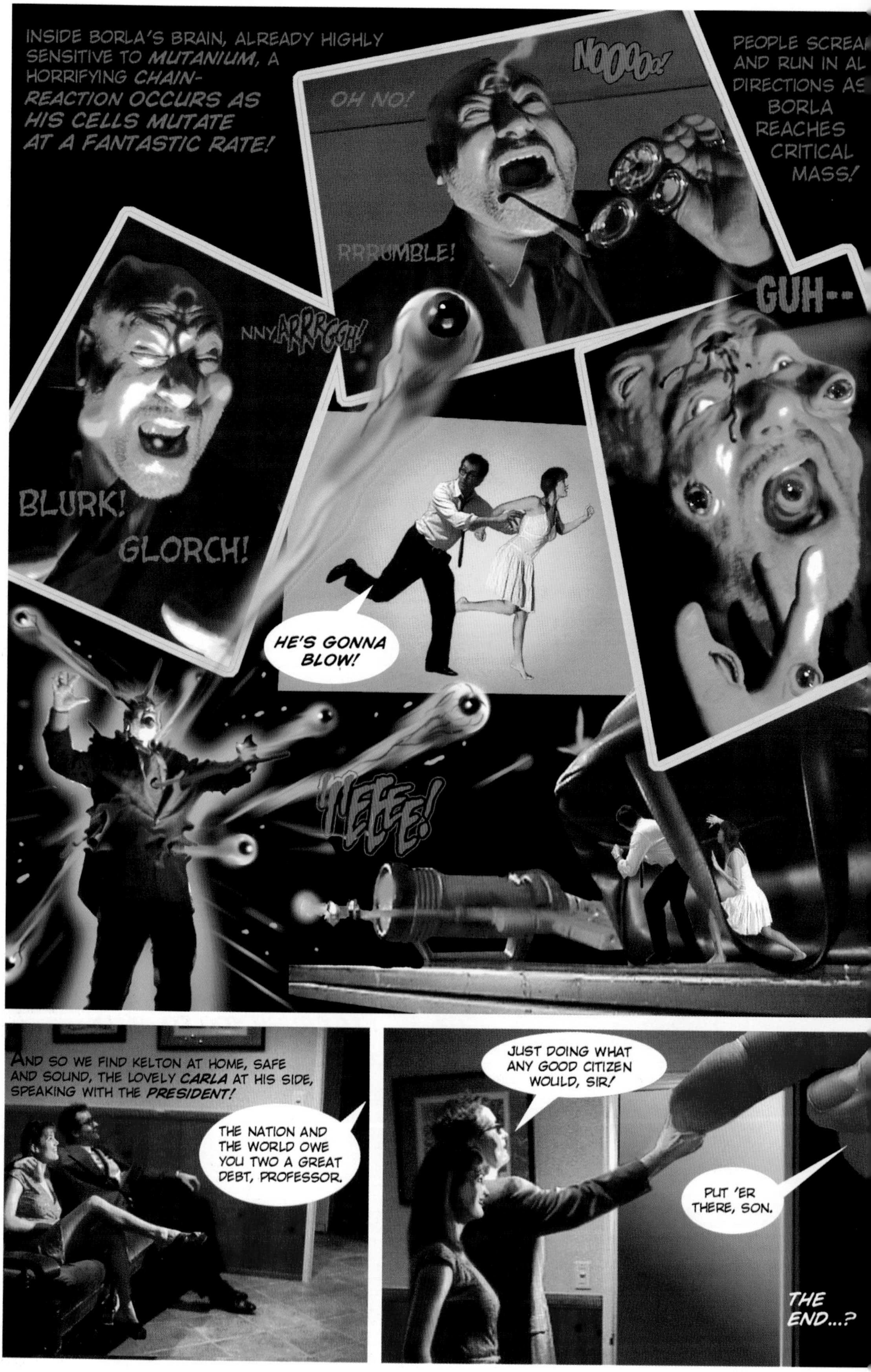

INSIDE BORLA'S BRAIN, ALREADY HIGHLY SENSITIVE TO MUTANIUM, A HORRIFYING CHAIN-REACTION OCCURS AS HIS CELLS MUTATE AT A FANTASTIC RATE!
NOOOOO!
OH NO!
RRRUMBLE!
PEOPLE SCREA AND RUN IN AL DIRECTIONS AS BORLA REACHES CRITICAL MASS!
GUH--
NNYARRRGGH!
BLURK!
GLORCH!
HE'S GONNA BLOW!
EEEEE!
AND SO WE FIND KELTON AT HOME, SAFE AND SOUND, THE LOVELY CARLA AT HIS SIDE, SPEAKING WITH THE PRESIDENT!
THE NATION AND THE WORLD OWE YOU TWO A GREAT DEBT, PROFESSOR.
JUST DOING WHAT ANY GOOD CITIZEN WOULD, SIR!
PUT 'ER THERE, SON.
THE END...?

T'WAS *ELDRITCH* AND THE NOISOME GUGS DID SHAMBLE AND GIBBER IN THE VALE. ALL FETID WERE THE FARNOTH FLIES AS MEPHITIC GHASTS DID WAIL. BEWARE THE CTHULHU SPAWN, MY SON, THEIR ICTHYIC HORROR SO APPALLING, READ *NOT* THE NECRONOMICON NOR *ANSWER* IF IT'S

YUGGOTH CALLING

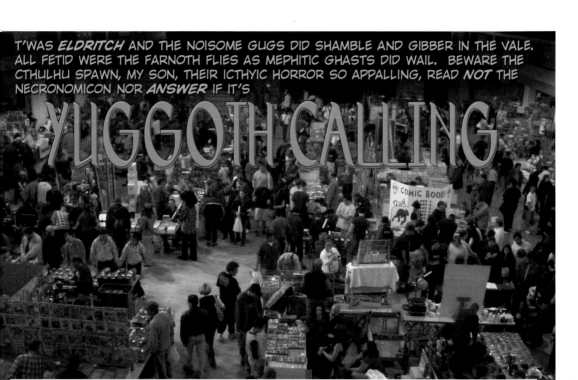

THE ROOM ECHOES WITH HUNDREDS OF INDISTINGUISHABLE VOICES AND THE SHUFFLE OF THOUSANDS OF FEET AS YOU WANDER AIMLESSLY INTO THE CROWD. NOBODY SEEMS TO NOTICE YOU; EVERYONE IS *BUSY* SEEKING HIS PARTICULAR PAPER TREASURES AMONG THE BOXES AND BAGS OF *COMIC BOOKS*. THEIR DRY BRITTLE PAGES RUSTLE SOFTLY AS EAGER FINGERS GINGERLY TURN THEM, ONE BY ONE. YOU LIKE THE SOUND, DON'T YOU?

YOU MOVE SILENTLY DOWN THROUGH THE SHIFTING, MUMBLING FIGURES, SEARCHING FOR SOMETHING.

BUT YOU DON'T KNOW *WHAT*.

SOMETHING SEEMS TO BECKON NOW... NOT EXACTLY A SOUND OR A VOICE, MORE LIKE A MEMORY.

A MEMORY OF A *DREAM*. AND STILL YOU SEEM UTTERLY ALONE AMONG THESE BUSY FELLOW SEEKERS.

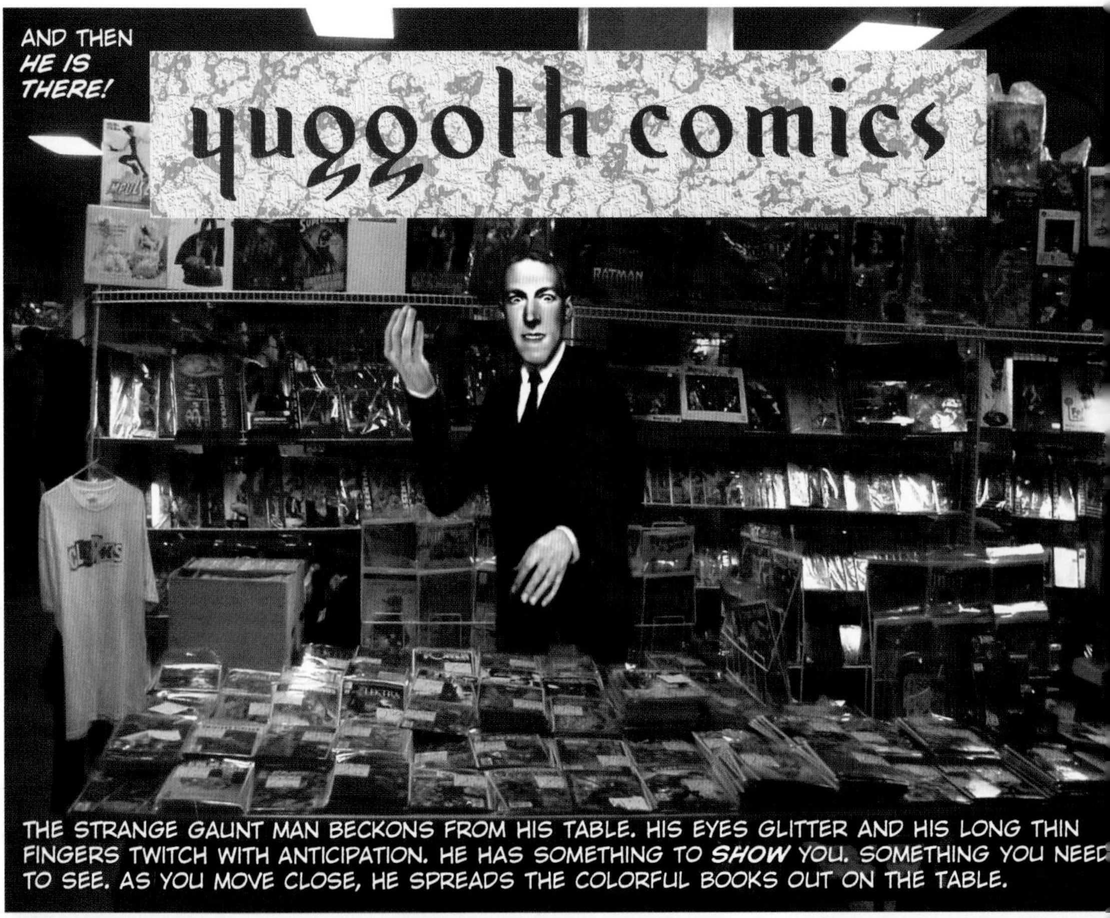
AND THEN *HE IS THERE!*
yuggoth comics
BATMAN
THE STRANGE GAUNT MAN BECKONS FROM HIS TABLE. HIS EYES GLITTER AND HIS LONG THIN FINGERS TWITCH WITH ANTICIPATION. HE HAS SOMETHING TO ***SHOW*** YOU. SOMETHING YOU NEED TO SEE. AS YOU MOVE CLOSE, HE SPREADS THE COLORFUL BOOKS OUT ON THE TABLE.

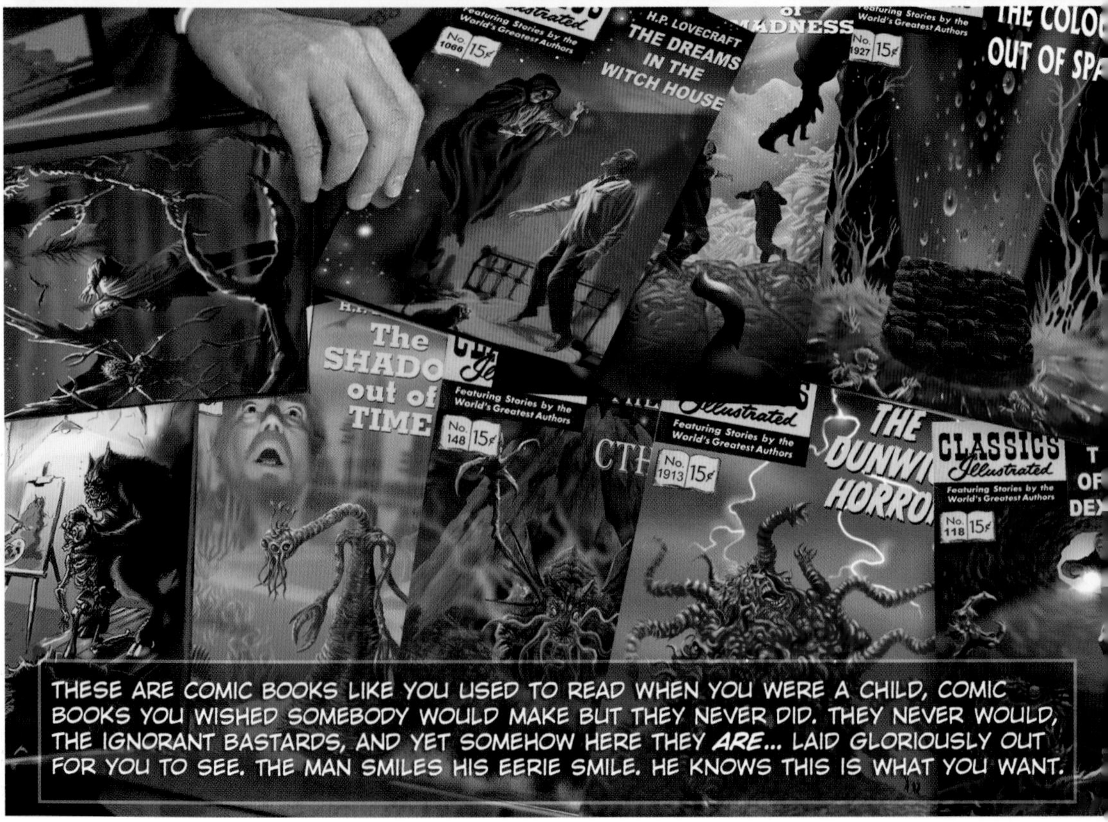
Featuring Stories by the World's Greatest Authors
No. 1066 15¢
H.P. LOVECRAFT
THE DREAMS IN THE WITCH HOUSE
Featuring Stories by the World's Greatest Authors
No. 1927 15¢
The SHADO out of TIME
Featuring Stories by the World's Greatest Authors
No. 148 15¢
Illustrated
Featuring Stories by the World's Greatest Authors
No. 1913 15¢
CLASSICS Illustrated
Featuring Stories by the World's Greatest Authors
No. 118 15¢
THESE ARE COMIC BOOKS LIKE YOU USED TO READ WHEN YOU WERE A CHILD, COMIC BOOKS YOU WISHED SOMEBODY WOULD MAKE BUT THEY NEVER DID. THEY NEVER WOULD, THE IGNORANT BASTARDS, AND YET SOMEHOW HERE THEY ***ARE***... LAID GLORIOUSLY OUT FOR YOU TO SEE. THE MAN SMILES HIS EERIE SMILE. HE KNOWS THIS IS WHAT YOU WANT.

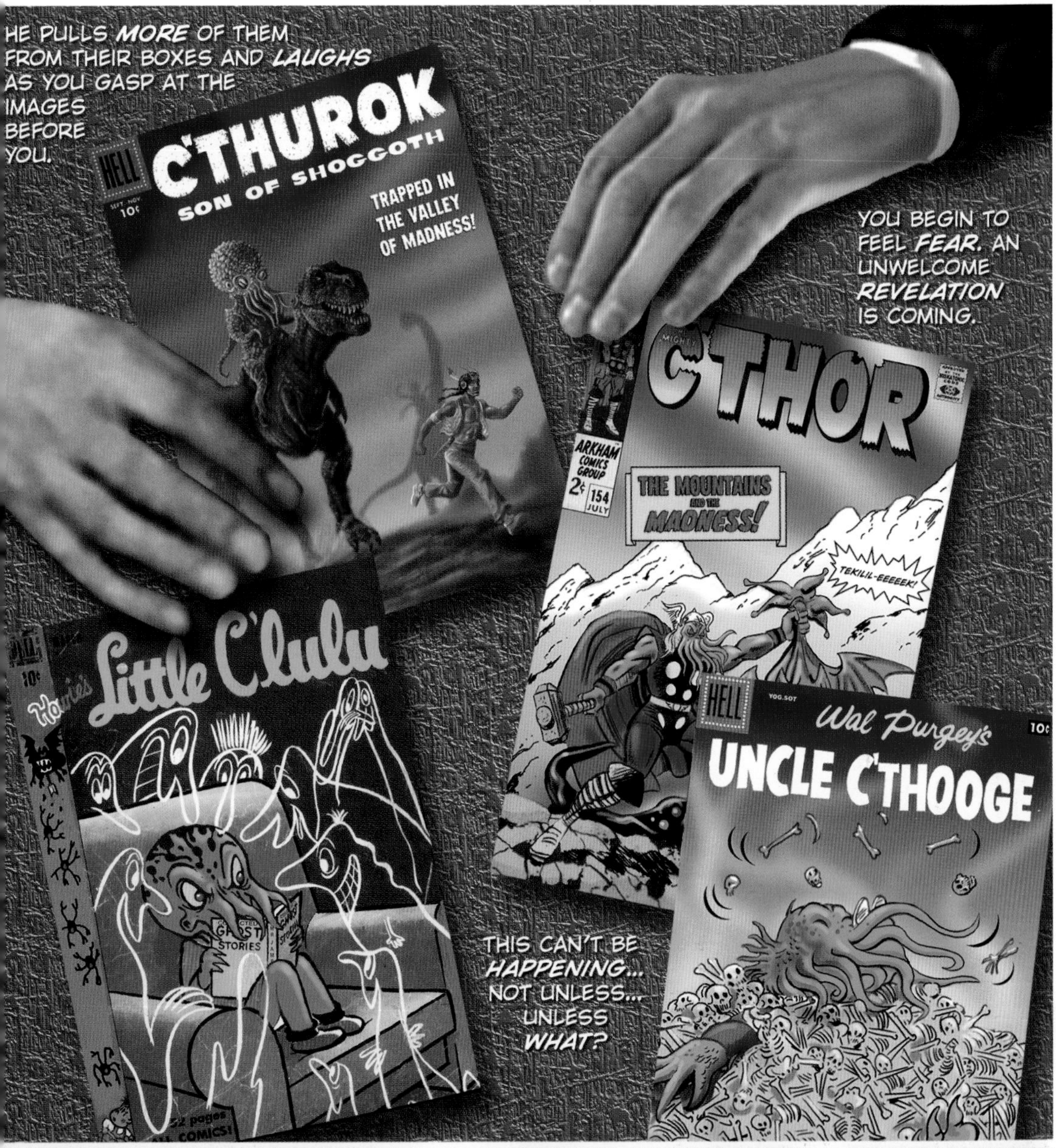
HE PULLS MORE OF THEM FROM THEIR BOXES AND LAUGHS AS YOU GASP AT THE IMAGES BEFORE YOU.
HELL
C'THUROK
SON OF SHOGGOTH
10¢
TRAPPED IN THE VALLEY OF MADNESS!
YOU BEGIN TO FEEL FEAR. AN UNWELCOME REVELATION IS COMING.
C'THOR
ARKHAM COMICS GROUP
2¢
154
JULY
THE MOUNTAINS AND THE MADNESS!
TEKILIL-EEEEEK!
Little C'lulu
10¢
GHOST STORIES
HELL
Wal Purgey's
UNCLE C'THOOGE
10¢
THIS CAN'T BE HAPPENING... NOT UNLESS... UNLESS WHAT?

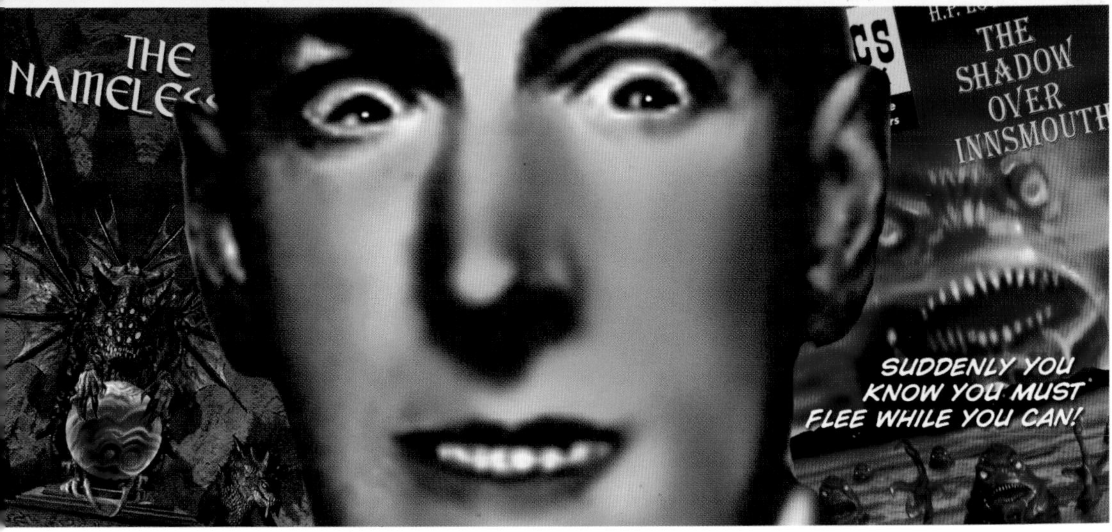
THE NAMELES
THE SHADOW OVER INNSMOUTH
SUDDENLY YOU KNOW YOU MUST FLEE WHILE YOU CAN!

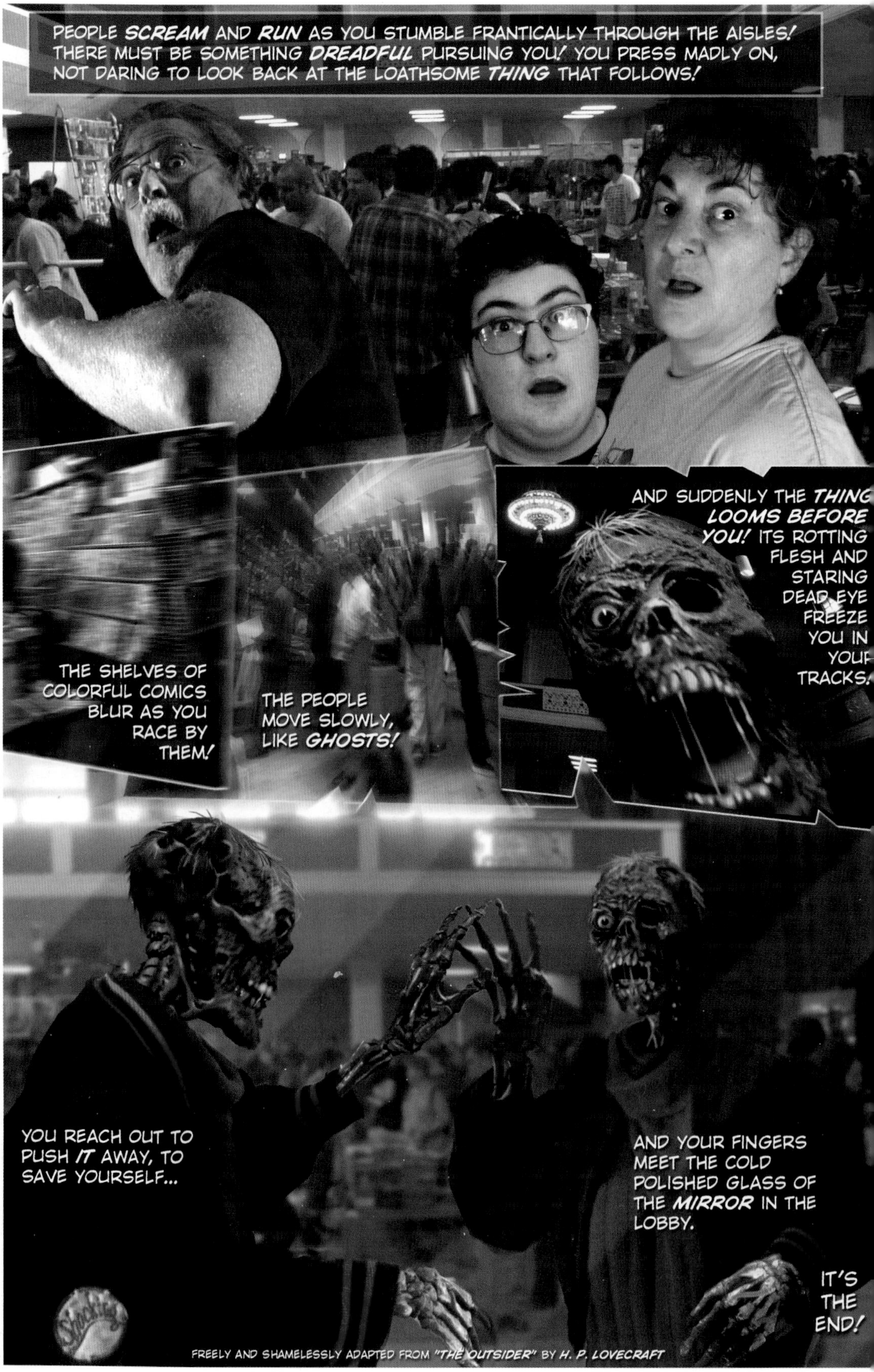
PEOPLE SCREAM AND RUN AS YOU STUMBLE FRANTICALLY THROUGH THE AISLES! THERE MUST BE SOMETHING DREADFUL PURSUING YOU! YOU PRESS MADLY ON, NOT DARING TO LOOK BACK AT THE LOATHSOME THING THAT FOLLOWS!
THE SHELVES OF COLORFUL COMICS BLUR AS YOU RACE BY THEM!
THE PEOPLE MOVE SLOWLY, LIKE GHOSTS!
AND SUDDENLY THE THING LOOMS BEFORE YOU! ITS ROTTING FLESH AND STARING DEAD EYE FREEZE YOU IN YOUR TRACKS!
YOU REACH OUT TO PUSH IT AWAY, TO SAVE YOURSELF...
AND YOUR FINGERS MEET THE COLD POLISHED GLASS OF THE MIRROR IN THE LOBBY.
IT'S THE END!
FREELY AND SHAMELESSLY ADAPTED FROM "THE OUTSIDER" BY H. P. LOVECRAFT

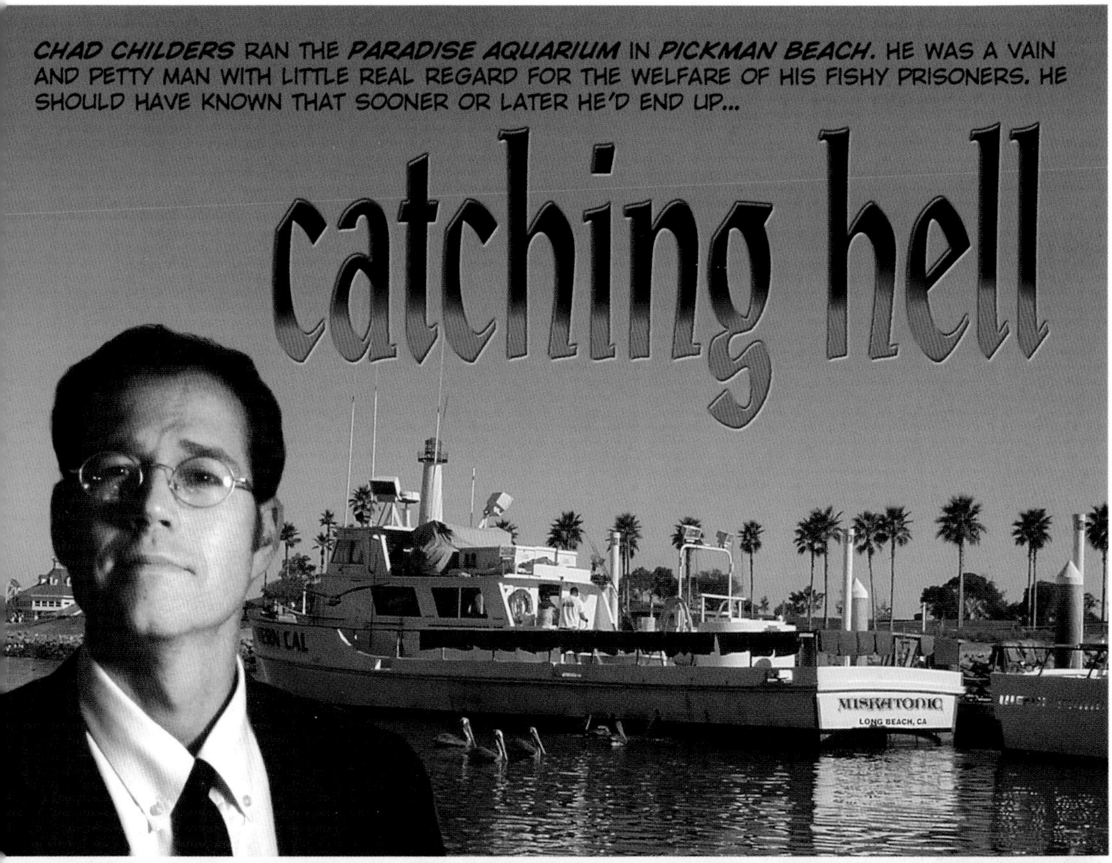
CHAD CHILDERS RAN THE PARADISE AQUARIUM IN PICKMAN BEACH. HE WAS A VAIN AND PETTY MAN WITH LITTLE REAL REGARD FOR THE WELFARE OF HIS FISHY PRISONERS. HE SHOULD HAVE KNOWN THAT SOONER OR LATER HE'D END UP...
catching hell
MISKATONIC
LONG BEACH, CA

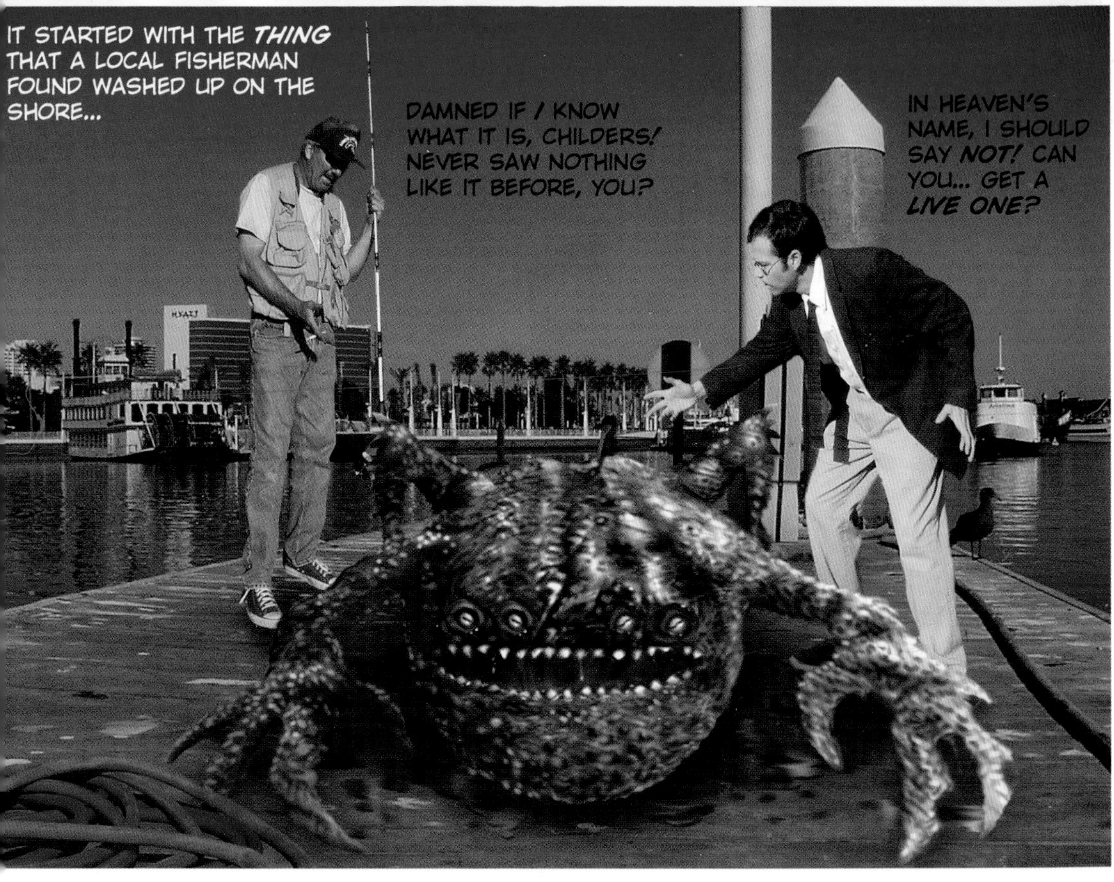
IT STARTED WITH THE THING THAT A LOCAL FISHERMAN FOUND WASHED UP ON THE SHORE...
DAMNED IF I KNOW WHAT IT IS, CHILDERS! NEVER SAW NOTHING LIKE IT BEFORE, YOU?
IN HEAVEN'S NAME, I SHOULD SAY NOT! CAN YOU... GET A LIVE ONE?

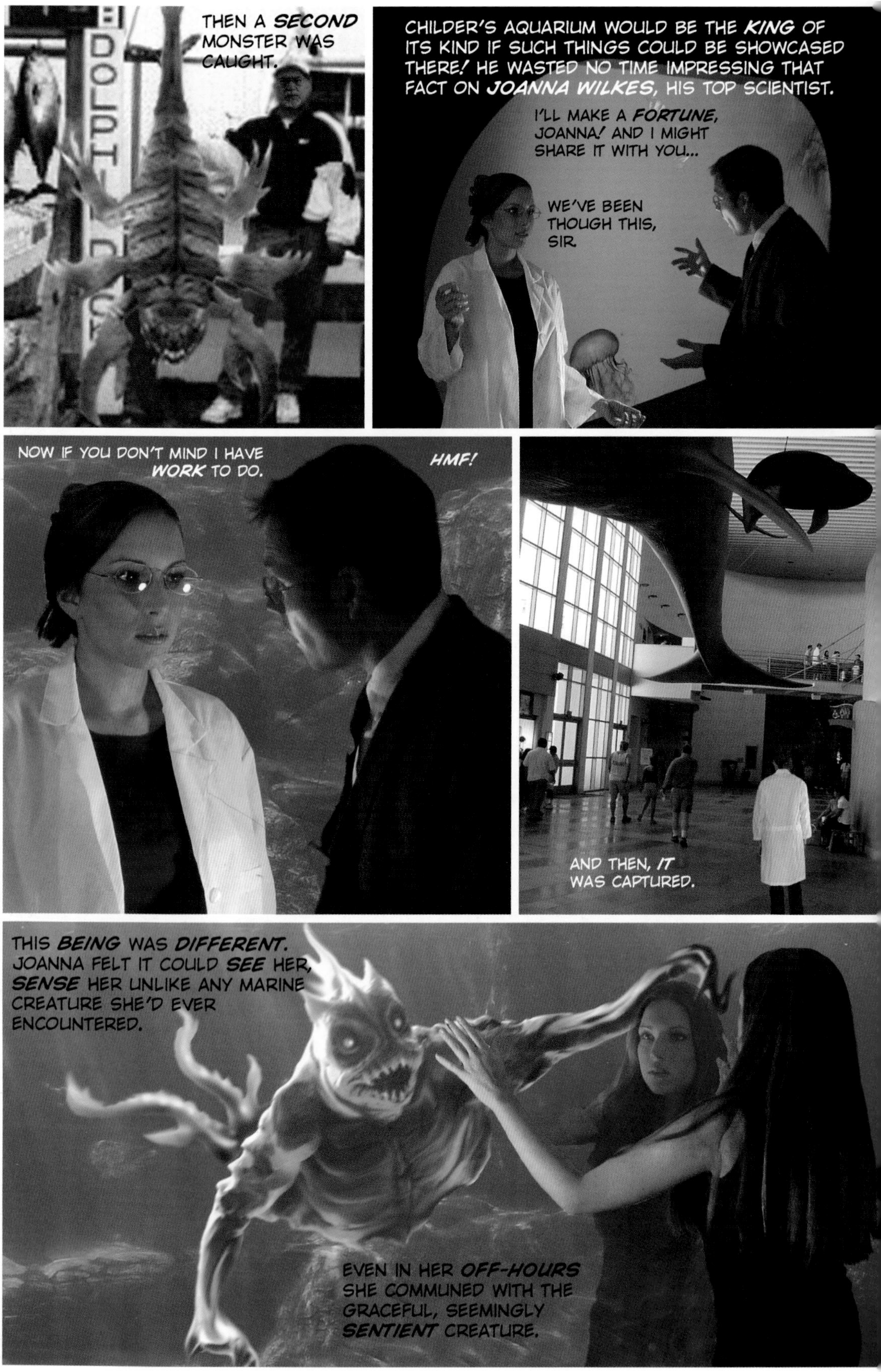
THEN A SECOND MONSTER WAS CAUGHT.
CHILDER'S AQUARIUM WOULD BE THE KING OF ITS KIND IF SUCH THINGS COULD BE SHOWCASED THERE! HE WASTED NO TIME IMPRESSING THAT FACT ON JOANNA WILKES, HIS TOP SCIENTIST.
I'LL MAKE A FORTUNE, JOANNA! AND I MIGHT SHARE IT WITH YOU...
WE'VE BEEN THOUGH THIS, SIR.
NOW IF YOU DON'T MIND I HAVE WORK TO DO.
HMF!
AND THEN, IT WAS CAPTURED.
THIS BEING WAS DIFFERENT. JOANNA FELT IT COULD SEE HER, SENSE HER UNLIKE ANY MARINE CREATURE SHE'D EVER ENCOUNTERED.
EVEN IN HER OFF-HOURS SHE COMMUNED WITH THE GRACEFUL, SEEMINGLY SENTIENT CREATURE.

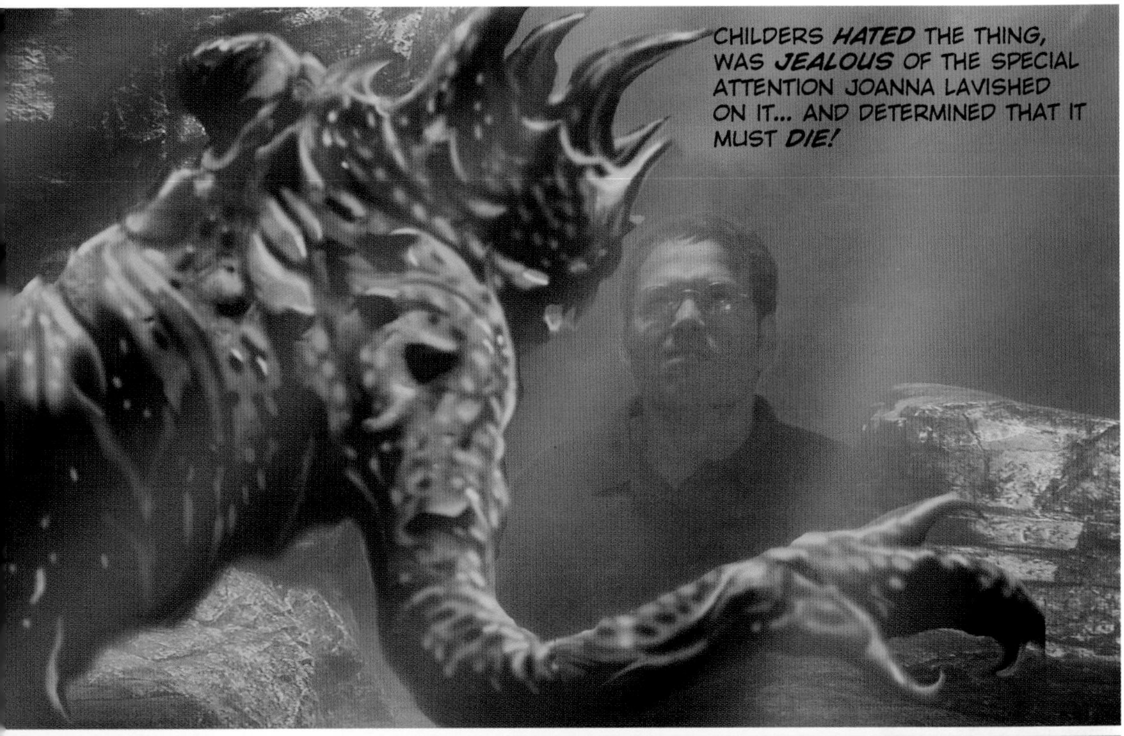
CHILDERS *HATED* THE THING, WAS *JEALOUS* OF THE SPECIAL ATTENTION JOANNA LAVISHED ON IT... AND DETERMINED THAT IT MUST *DIE!*

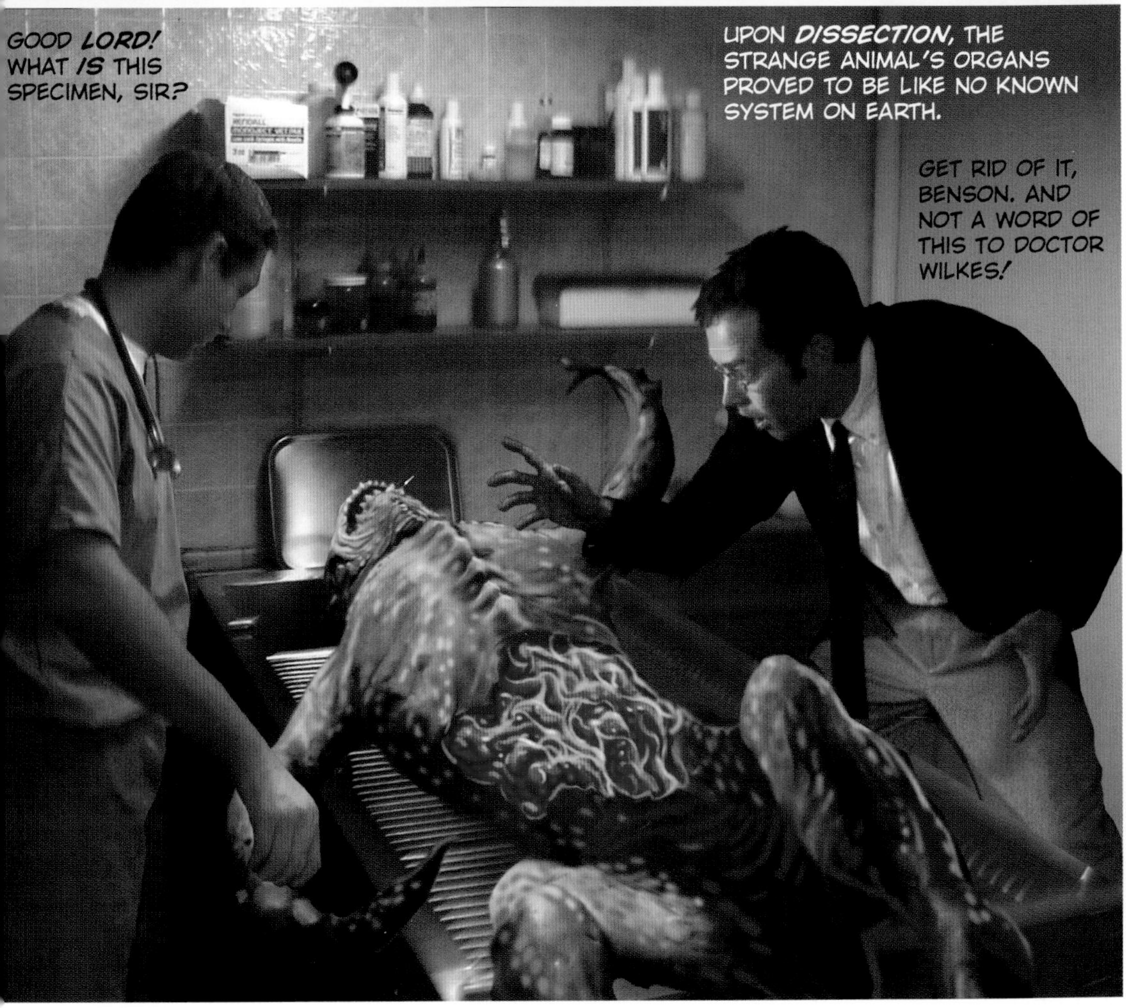
GOOD *LORD!* WHAT *IS* THIS SPECIMEN, SIR?
UPON *DISSECTION*, THE STRANGE ANIMAL'S ORGANS PROVED TO BE LIKE NO KNOWN SYSTEM ON EARTH.
GET RID OF IT, BENSON. AND NOT A WORD OF THIS TO DOCTOR WILKES!

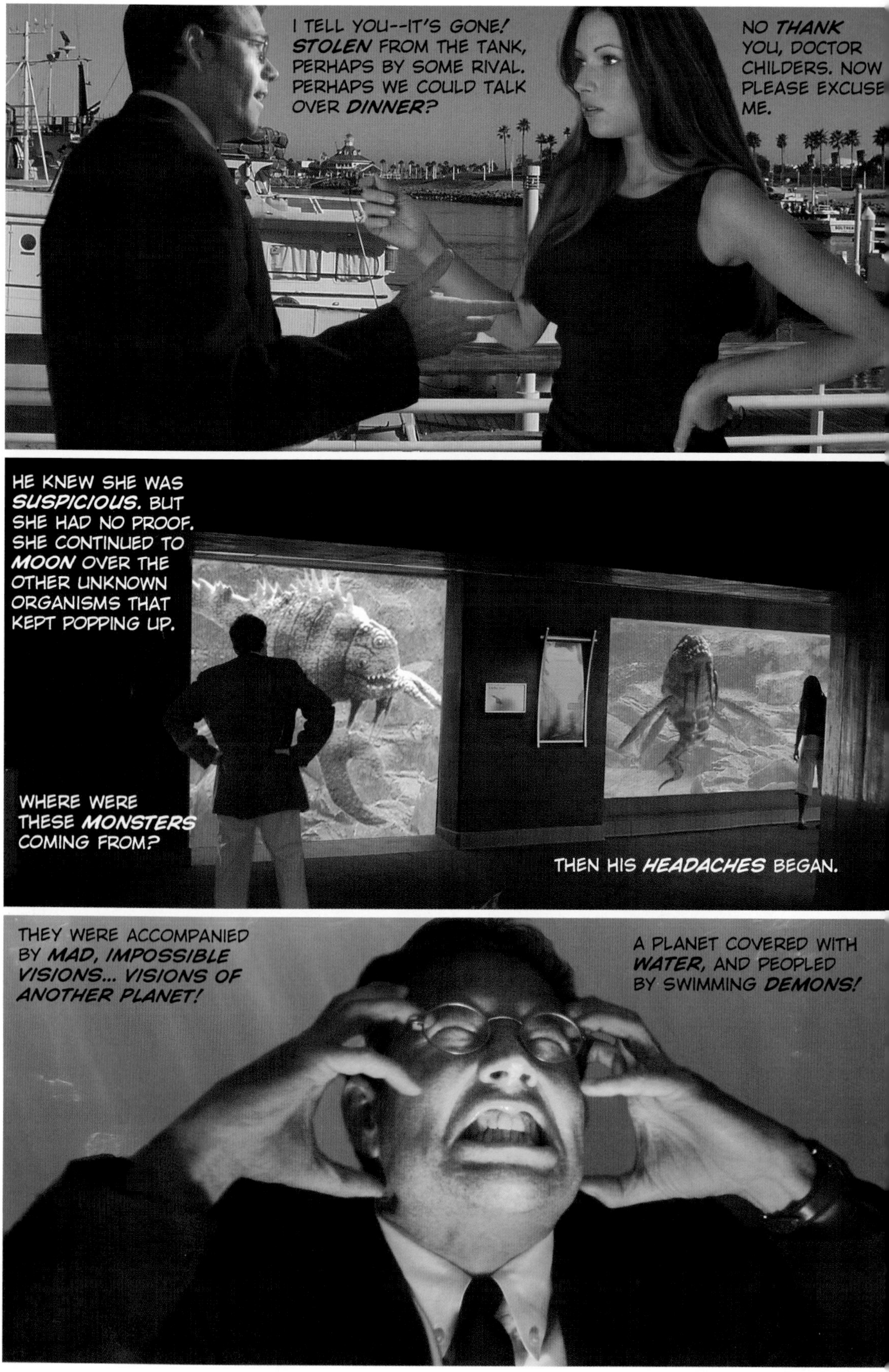
I TELL YOU--IT'S GONE! STOLEN FROM THE TANK, PERHAPS BY SOME RIVAL. PERHAPS WE COULD TALK OVER DINNER?
NO THANK YOU, DOCTOR CHILDERS. NOW PLEASE EXCUSE ME.
HE KNEW SHE WAS SUSPICIOUS. BUT SHE HAD NO PROOF. SHE CONTINUED TO MOON OVER THE OTHER UNKNOWN ORGANISMS THAT KEPT POPPING UP.
WHERE WERE THESE MONSTERS COMING FROM?
THEN HIS HEADACHES BEGAN.
THEY WERE ACCOMPANIED BY MAD, IMPOSSIBLE VISIONS... VISIONS OF ANOTHER PLANET!
A PLANET COVERED WITH WATER, AND PEOPLED BY SWIMMING DEMONS!

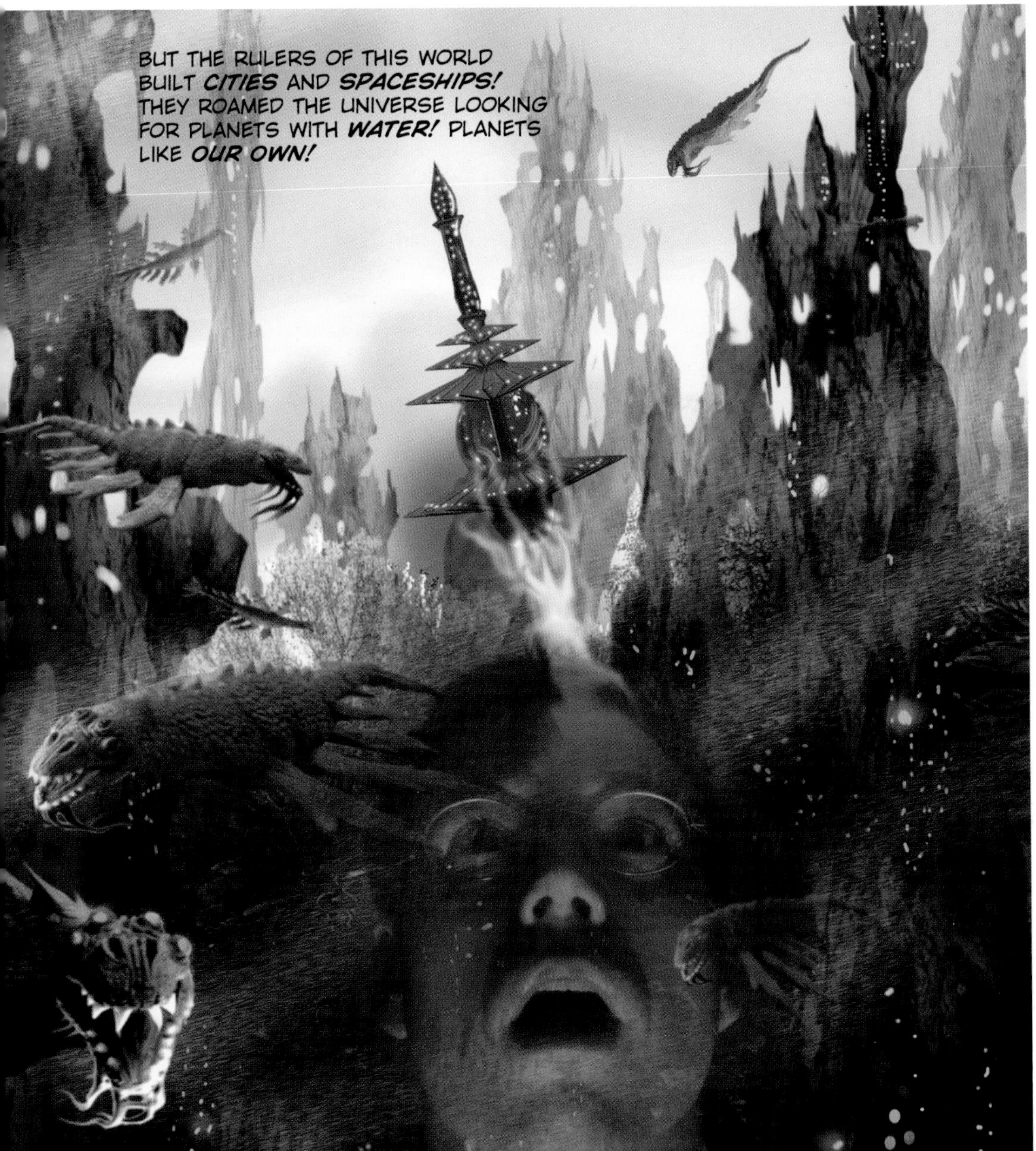
BUT THE RULERS OF THIS WORLD BUILT CITIES AND SPACESHIPS! THEY ROAMED THE UNIVERSE LOOKING FOR PLANETS WITH WATER! PLANETS LIKE OUR OWN!

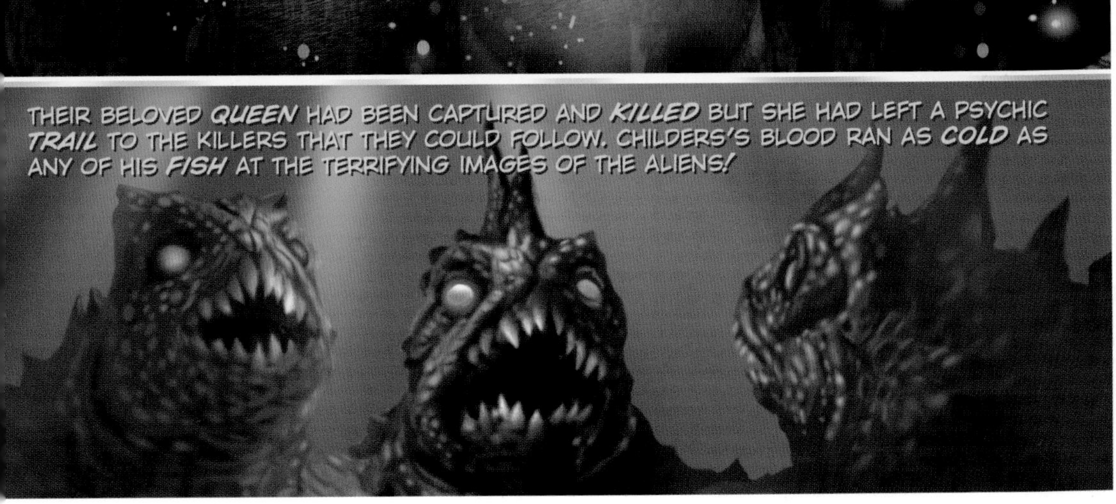
THEIR BELOVED QUEEN HAD BEEN CAPTURED AND KILLED BUT SHE HAD LEFT A PSYCHIC TRAIL TO THE KILLERS THAT THEY COULD FOLLOW. CHILDERS'S BLOOD RAN AS COLD AS ANY OF HIS FISH AT THE TERRIFYING IMAGES OF THE ALIENS!

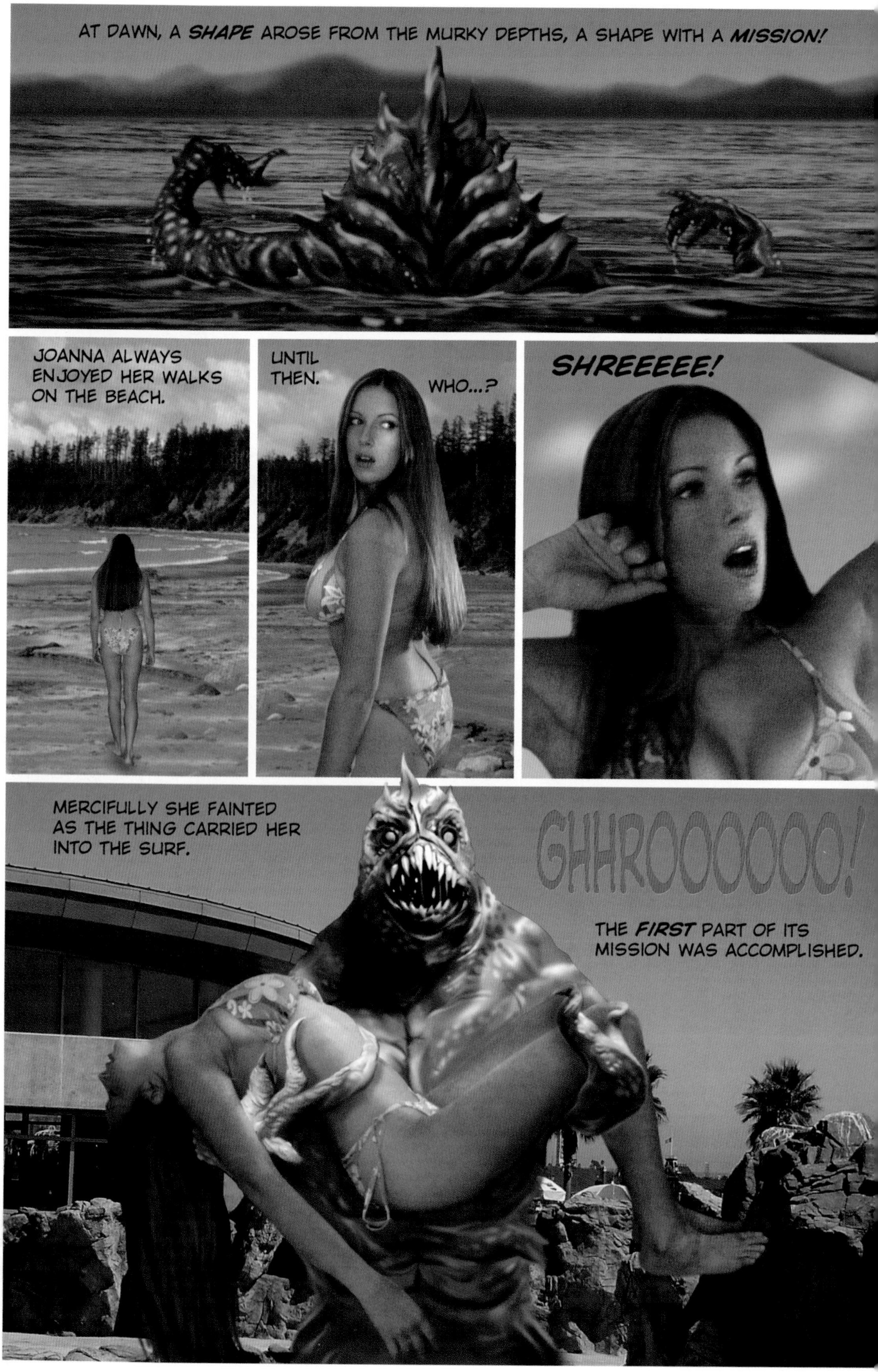
AT DAWN, A SHAPE AROSE FROM THE MURKY DEPTHS, A SHAPE WITH A MISSION!
JOANNA ALWAYS ENJOYED HER WALKS ON THE BEACH.
UNTIL THEN.
WHO...?
SHREEEEE!
MERCIFULLY SHE FAINTED AS THE THING CARRIED HER INTO THE SURF.
GHHROOOOOO!
THE FIRST PART OF ITS MISSION WAS ACCOMPLISHED.

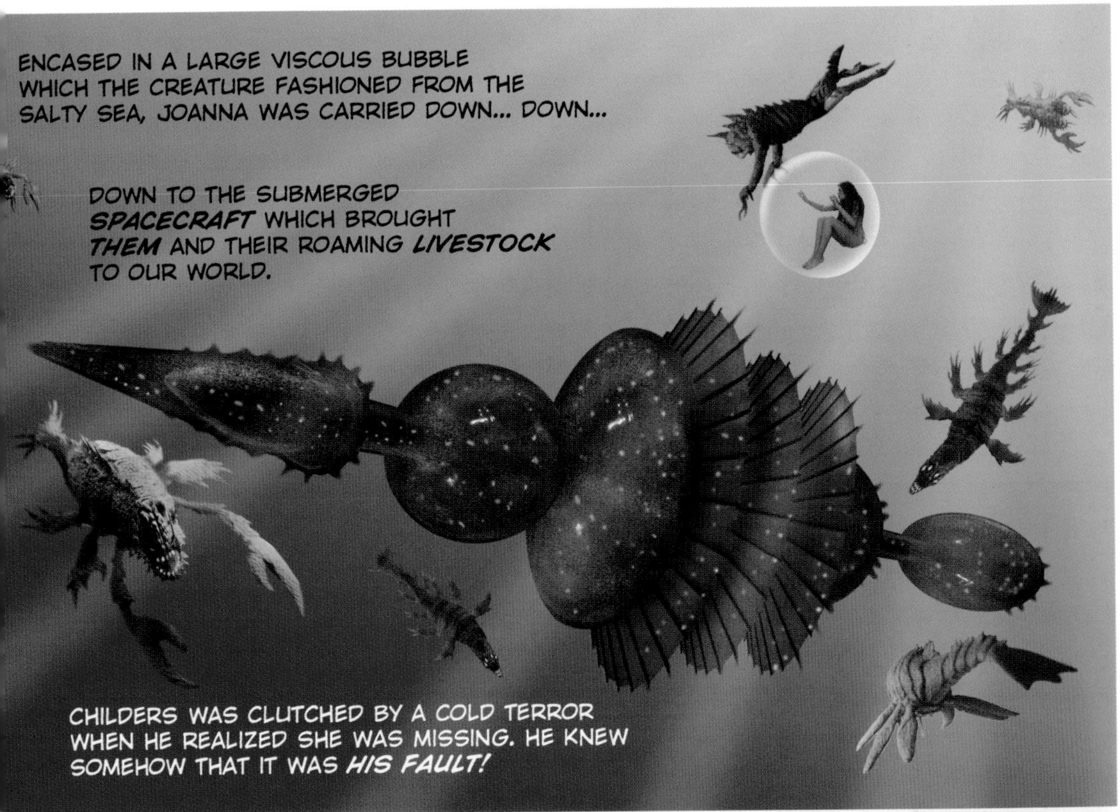
ENCASED IN A LARGE VISCOUS BUBBLE WHICH THE CREATURE FASHIONED FROM THE SALTY SEA, JOANNA WAS CARRIED DOWN... DOWN...
DOWN TO THE SUBMERGED SPACECRAFT WHICH BROUGHT THEM AND THEIR ROAMING LIVESTOCK TO OUR WORLD.
CHILDERS WAS CLUTCHED BY A COLD TERROR WHEN HE REALIZED SHE WAS MISSING. HE KNEW SOMEHOW THAT IT WAS HIS FAULT!

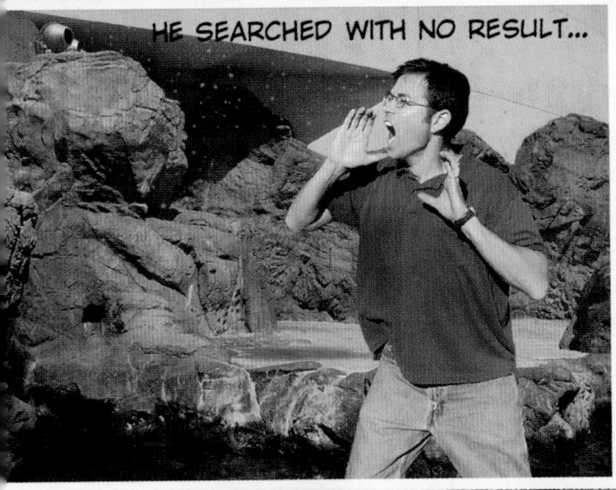
HE SEARCHED WITH NO RESULT...

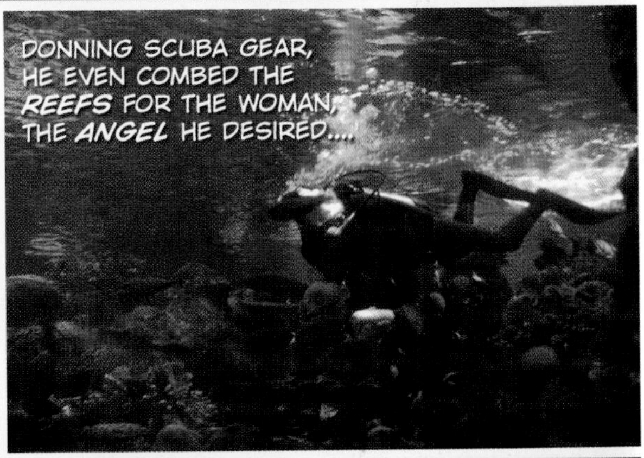
DONNING SCUBA GEAR, HE EVEN COMBED THE REEFS FOR THE WOMAN, THE ANGEL HE DESIRED....

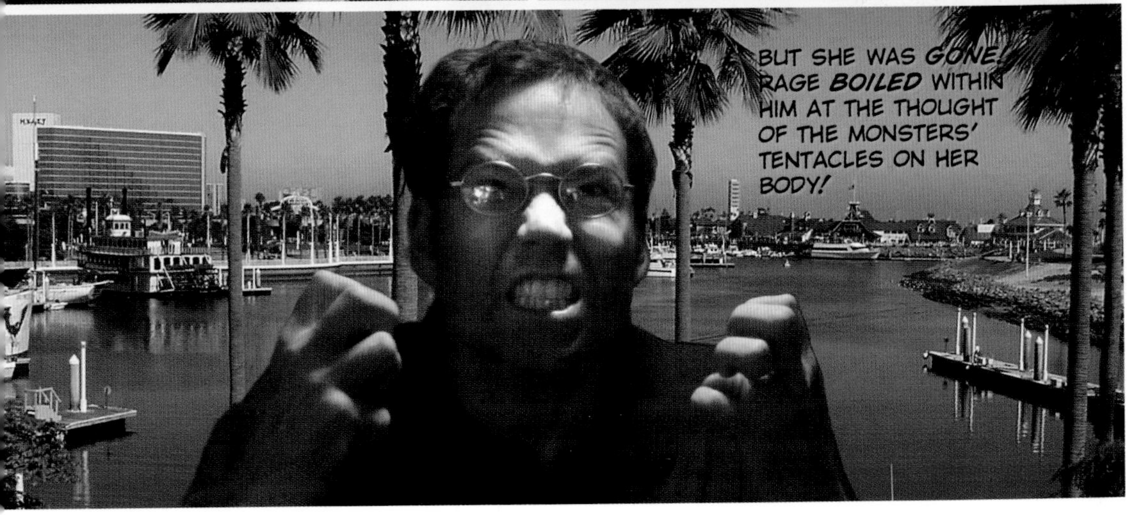
BUT SHE WAS GONE! RAGE BOILED WITHIN HIM AT THE THOUGHT OF THE MONSTERS' TENTACLES ON HER BODY!

ROAMING THE BEACH THAT NIGHT, HE SUDDENLY SEEMED TO HEAR HER *CALLING* TO HIM!

JOANNA? JOANNA, IS THAT YOU?

HERE I AM, CHADWICK. AT LAST I'M ALL YOURS!

OH, MY *DARLING!* *THANK GOD* YOU'RE ALRIGHT!

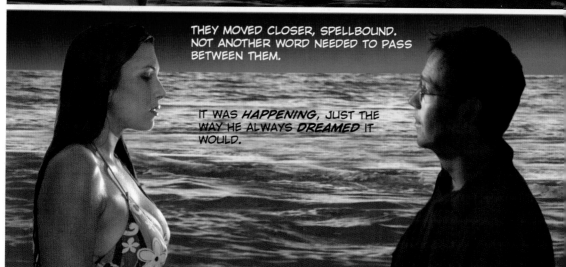

THEY MOVED CLOSER, SPELLBOUND. NOT ANOTHER WORD NEEDED TO PASS BETWEEN THEM.

IT WAS *HAPPENING*, JUST THE WAY HE ALWAYS *DREAMED* IT WOULD.

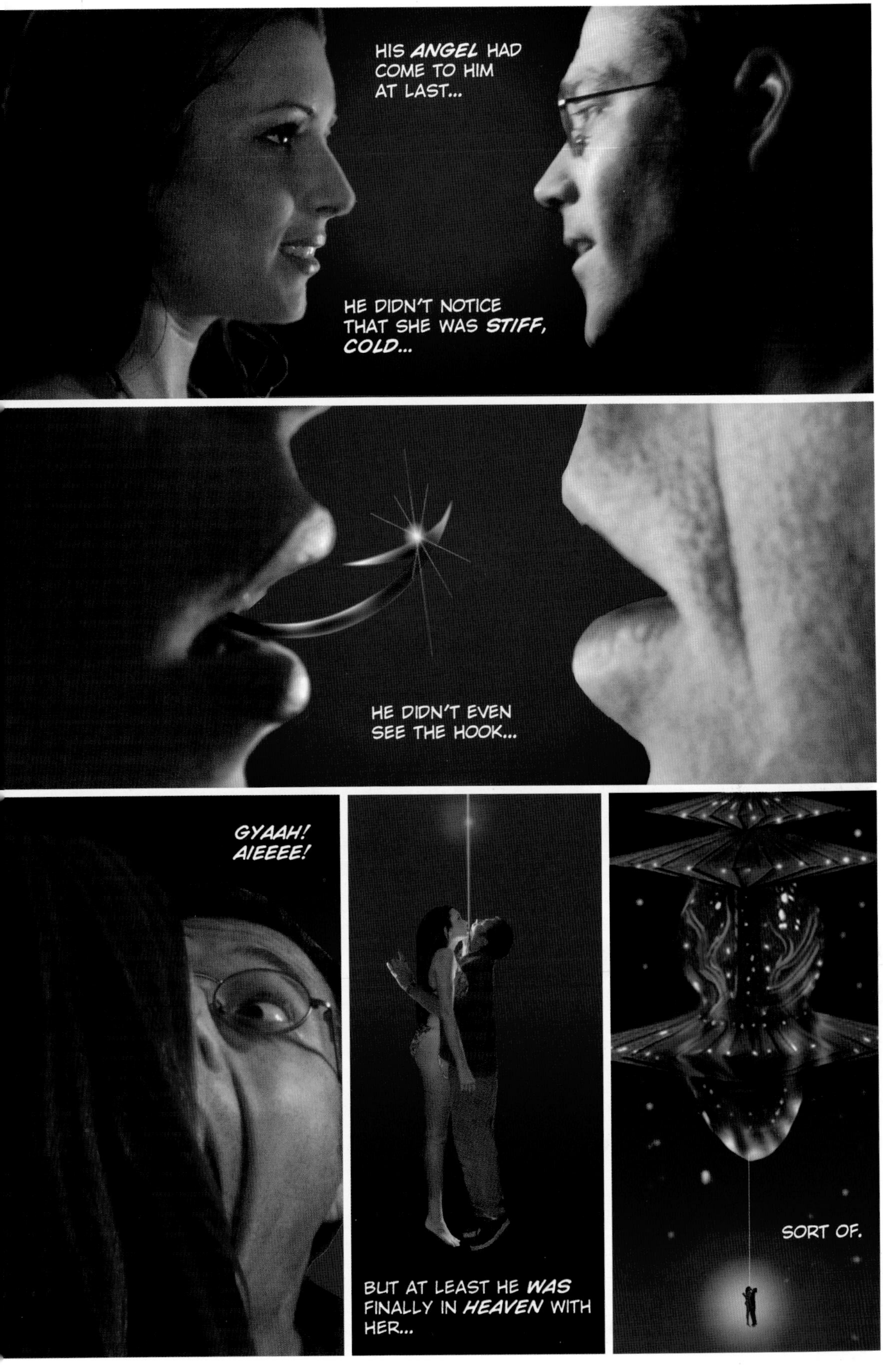
HIS ANGEL HAD COME TO HIM AT LAST...
HE DIDN'T NOTICE THAT SHE WAS STIFF, COLD...
HE DIDN'T EVEN SEE THE HOOK...
GYAAH! AIEEEE!
BUT AT LEAST HE WAS FINALLY IN HEAVEN WITH HER...
SORT OF.

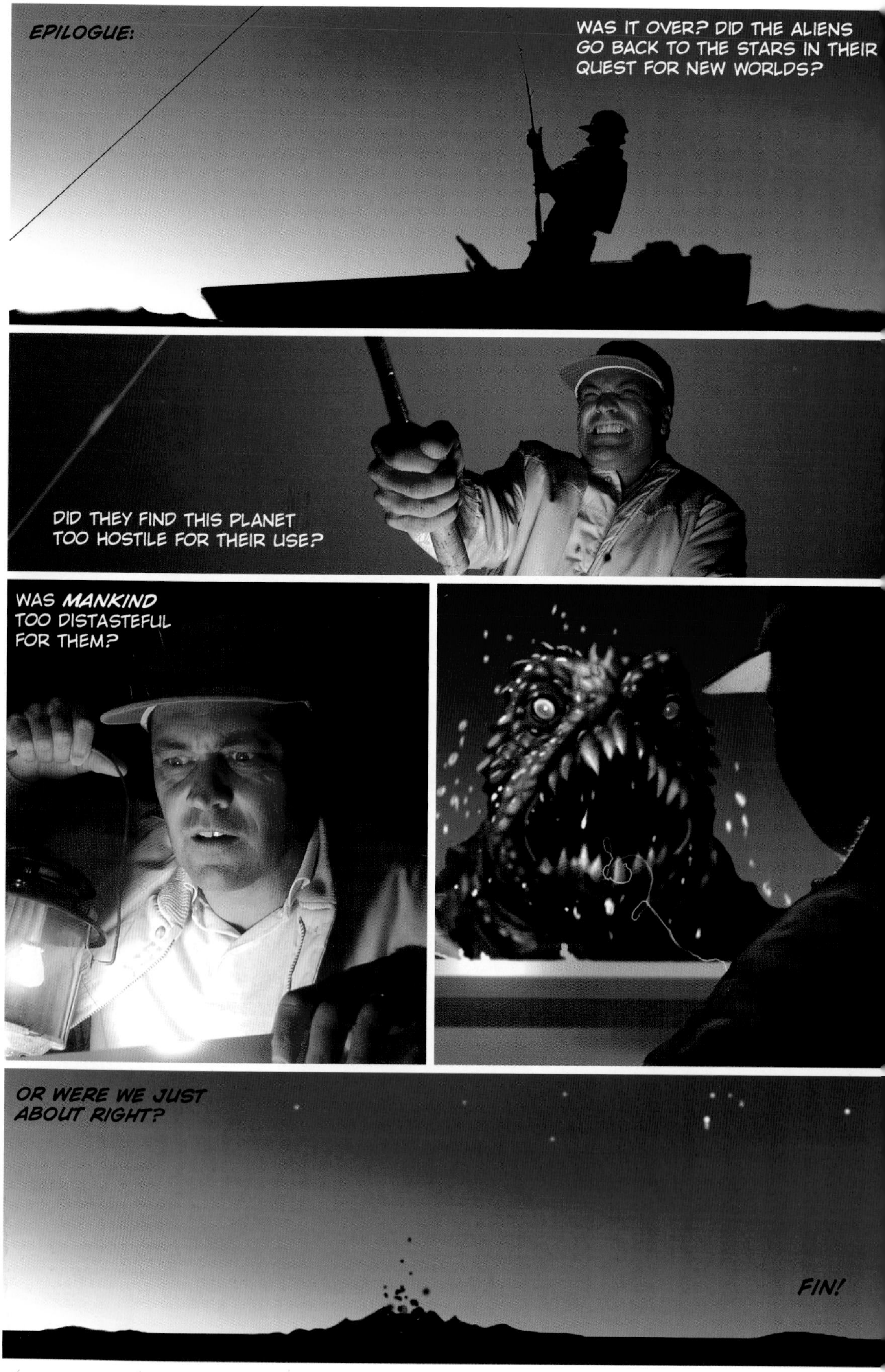
EPILOGUE:
WAS IT OVER? DID THE ALIENS GO BACK TO THE STARS IN THEIR QUEST FOR NEW WORLDS?
DID THEY FIND THIS PLANET TOO HOSTILE FOR THEIR USE?
WAS MANKIND TOO DISTASTEFUL FOR THEM?
OR WERE WE JUST ABOUT RIGHT?
FIN!

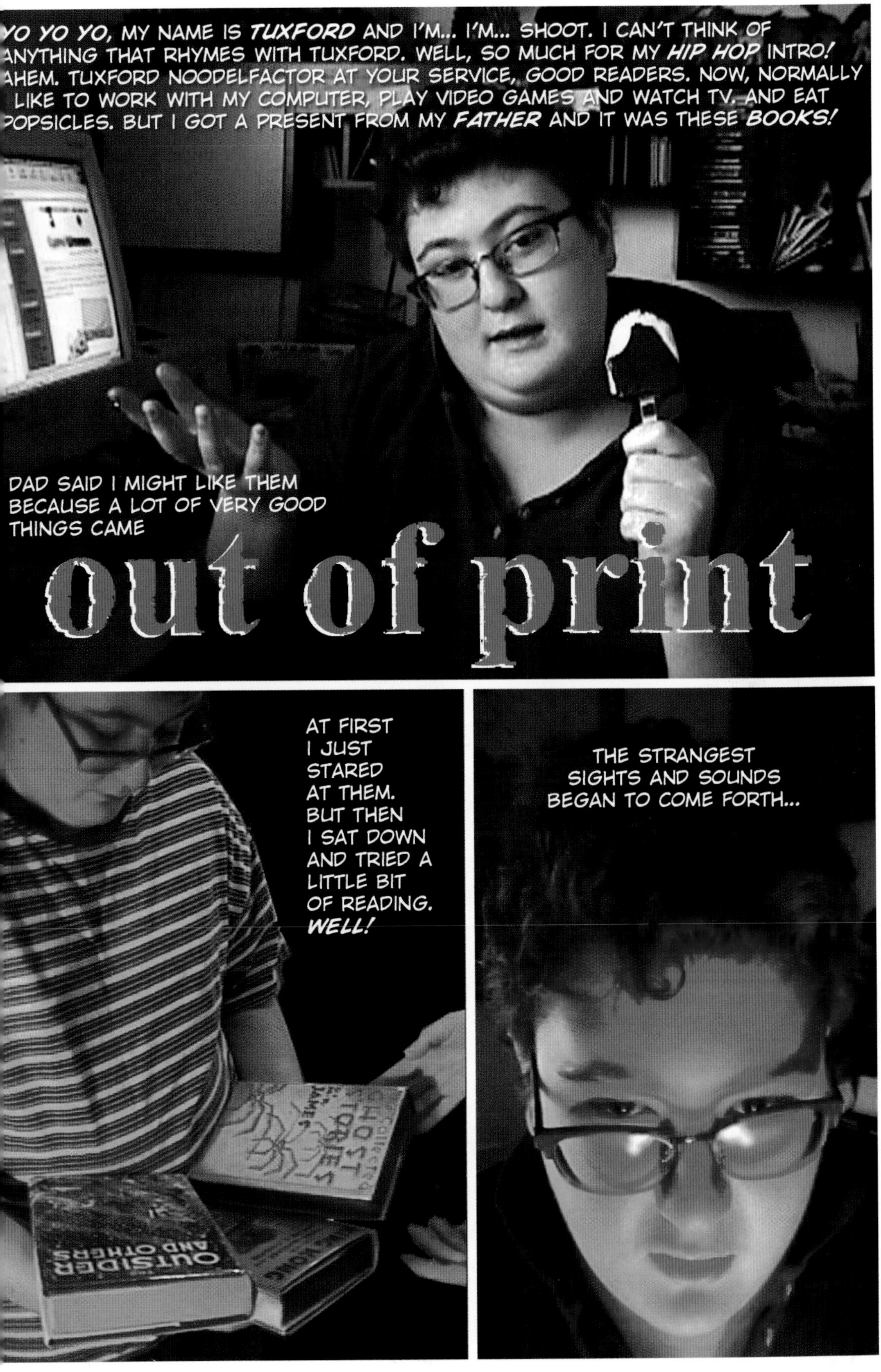
YO YO YO, MY NAME IS TUXFORD AND I'M... I'M... SHOOT. I CAN'T THINK OF ANYTHING THAT RHYMES WITH TUXFORD. WELL, SO MUCH FOR MY HIP HOP INTRO! AHEM. TUXFORD NOODELFACTOR AT YOUR SERVICE, GOOD READERS. NOW, NORMALLY I LIKE TO WORK WITH MY COMPUTER, PLAY VIDEO GAMES AND WATCH TV. AND EAT POPSICLES. BUT I GOT A PRESENT FROM MY FATHER AND IT WAS THESE BOOKS!
DAD SAID I MIGHT LIKE THEM BECAUSE A LOT OF VERY GOOD THINGS CAME
out of print
AT FIRST I JUST STARED AT THEM. BUT THEN I SAT DOWN AND TRIED A LITTLE BIT OF READING. WELL!
OUTSIDER AND OTHERS
THE STRANGEST SIGHTS AND SOUNDS BEGAN TO COME FORTH...

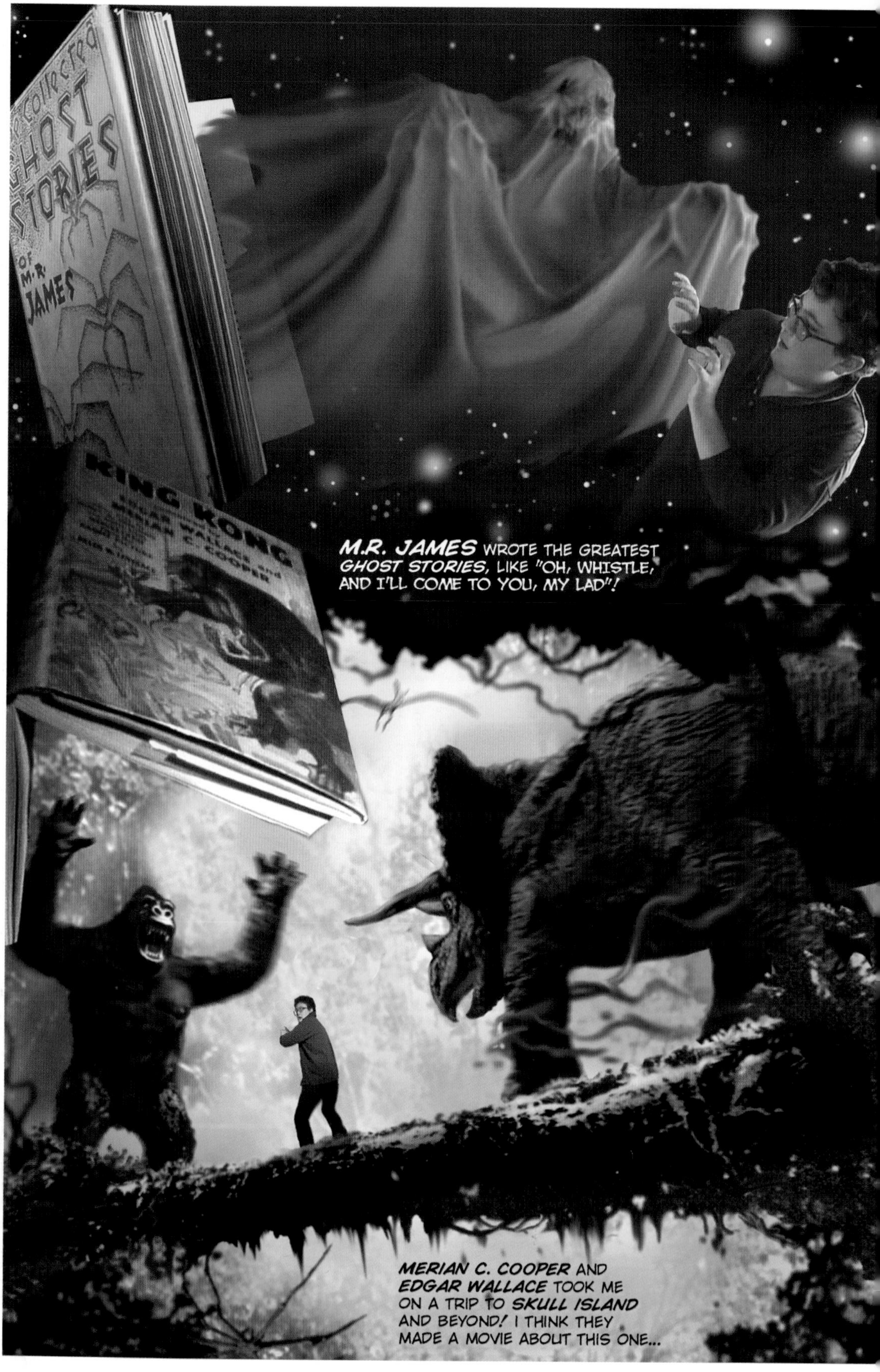

COLLECTED GHOST STORIES OF M.R. JAMES
KING KONG
M.R. JAMES WROTE THE GREATEST GHOST STORIES, LIKE "OH, WHISTLE, AND I'LL COME TO YOU, MY LAD"!
MERIAN C. COOPER AND EDGAR WALLACE TOOK ME ON A TRIP TO SKULL ISLAND AND BEYOND! I THINK THEY MADE A MOVIE ABOUT THIS ONE...

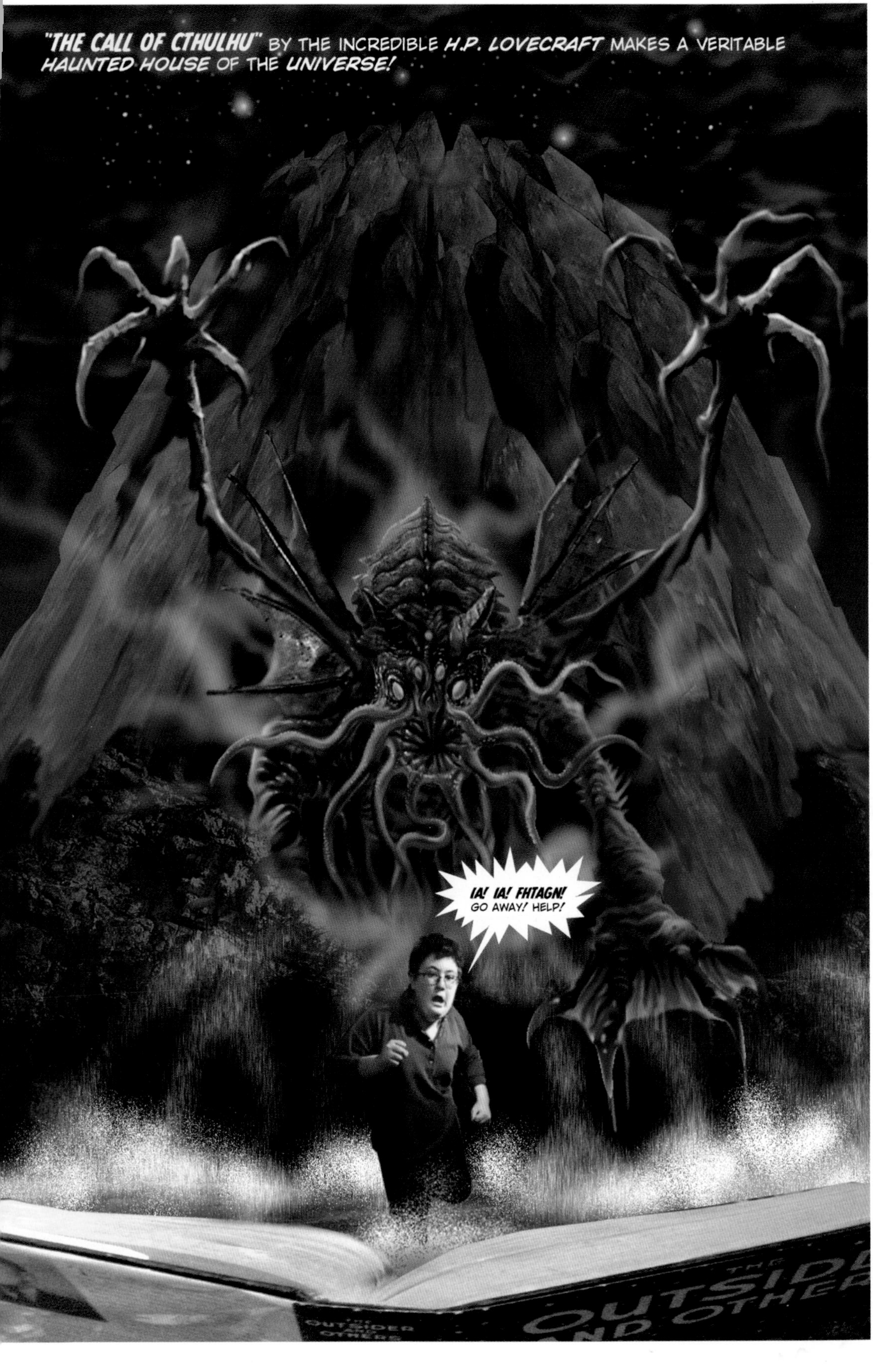
"THE CALL OF CTHULHU" BY THE INCREDIBLE H.P. LOVECRAFT MAKES A VERITABLE HAUNTED HOUSE OF THE UNIVERSE!
IA! IA! FHTAGN! GO AWAY! HELP!

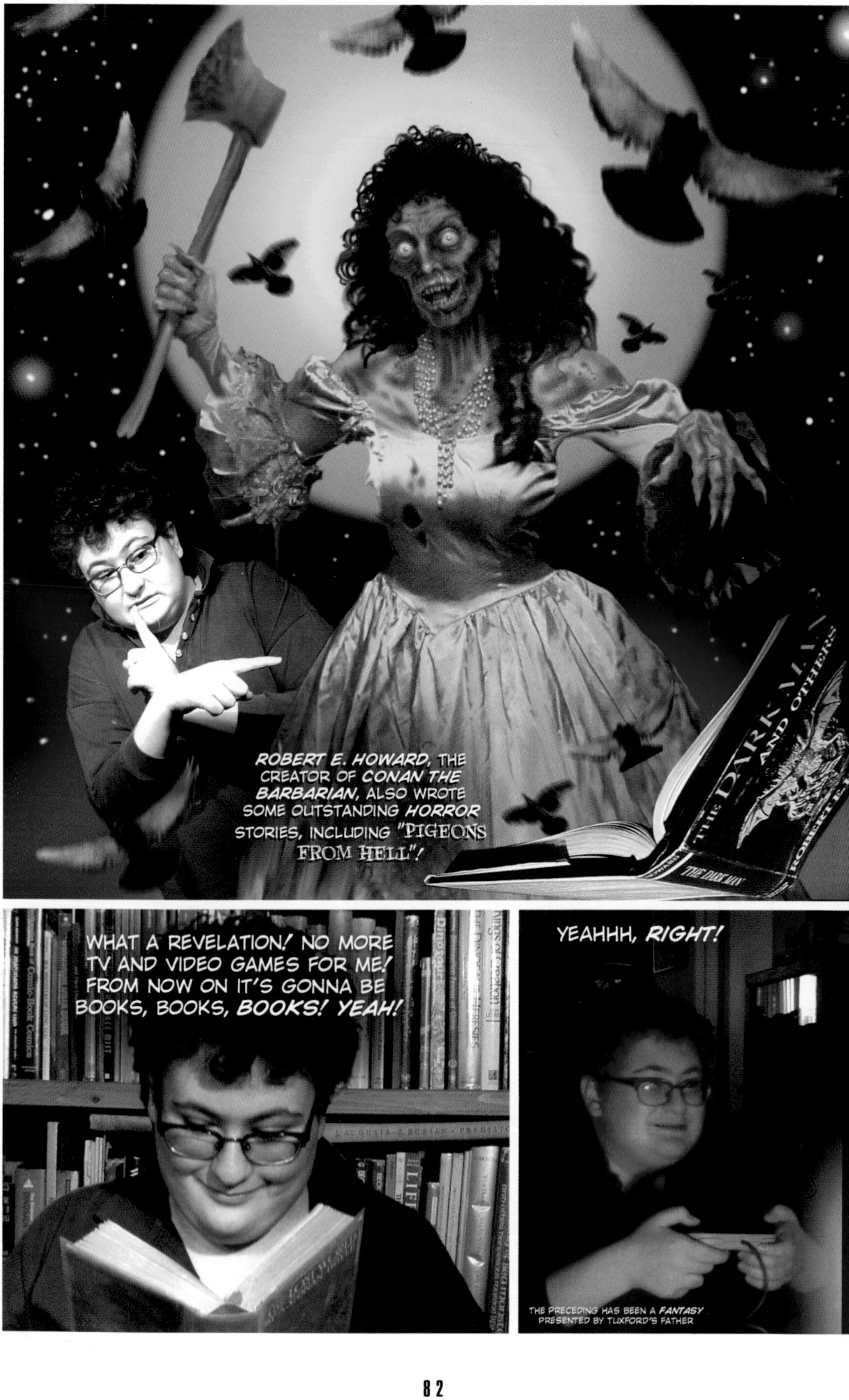

ROBERT E. HOWARD, THE CREATOR OF CONAN THE BARBARIAN, ALSO WROTE SOME OUTSTANDING HORROR STORIES, INCLUDING "PIGEONS FROM HELL"!
THE DARK MAN AND OTHERS
WHAT A REVELATION! NO MORE TV AND VIDEO GAMES FOR ME! FROM NOW ON IT'S GONNA BE BOOKS, BOOKS, BOOKS! YEAH!
YEAHHH, RIGHT!
THE PRECEDING HAS BEEN A FANTASY PRESENTED BY TUXFORD'S FATHER

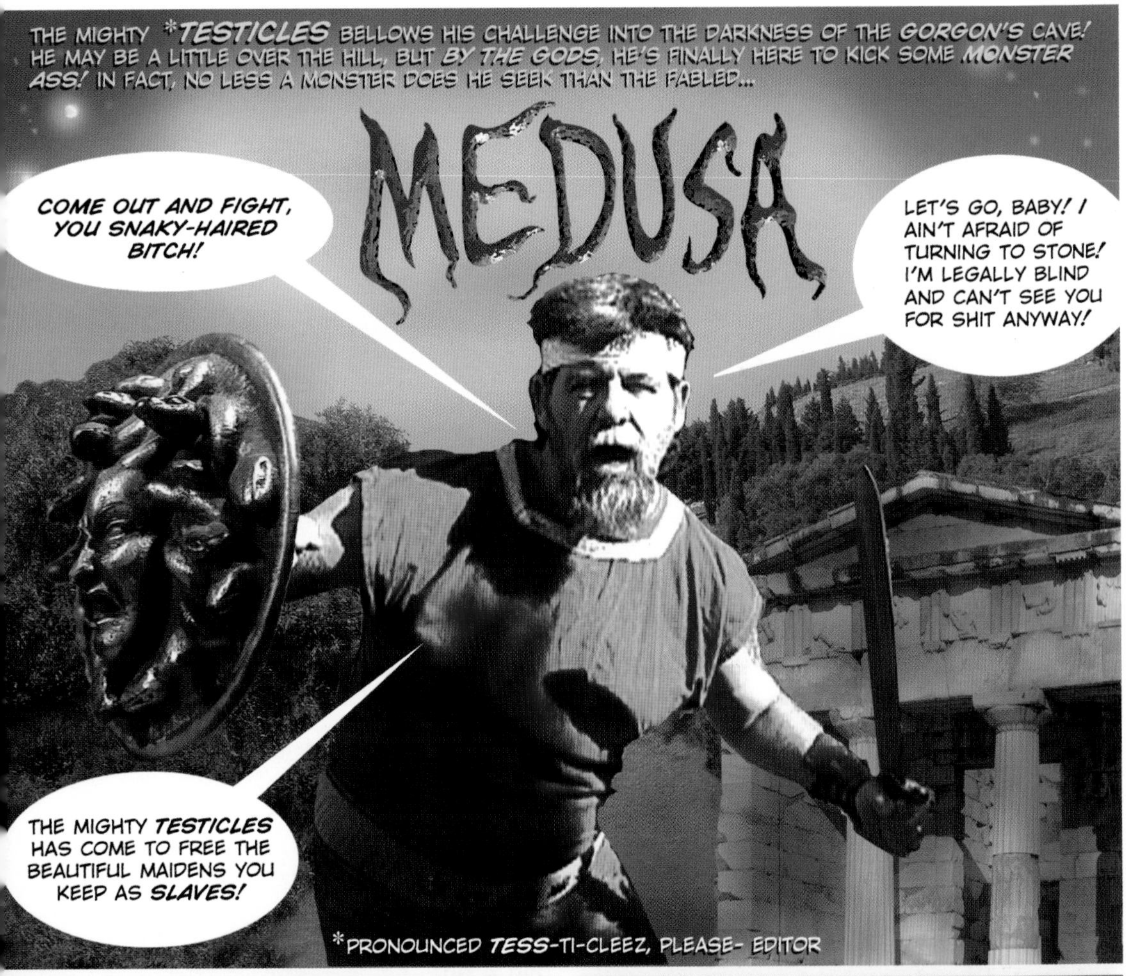
THE MIGHTY *TESTICLES BELLOWS HIS CHALLENGE INTO THE DARKNESS OF THE GORGON'S CAVE! HE MAY BE A LITTLE OVER THE HILL, BUT BY THE GODS, HE'S FINALLY HERE TO KICK SOME MONSTER ASS! IN FACT, NO LESS A MONSTER DOES HE SEEK THAN THE FABLED...
MEDUSA
COME OUT AND FIGHT, YOU SNAKY-HAIRED BITCH!
LET'S GO, BABY! I AIN'T AFRAID OF TURNING TO STONE! I'M LEGALLY BLIND AND CAN'T SEE YOU FOR SHIT ANYWAY!
THE MIGHTY TESTICLES HAS COME TO FREE THE BEAUTIFUL MAIDENS YOU KEEP AS SLAVES!
*PRONOUNCED TESS-TI-CLEEZ, PLEASE- EDITOR

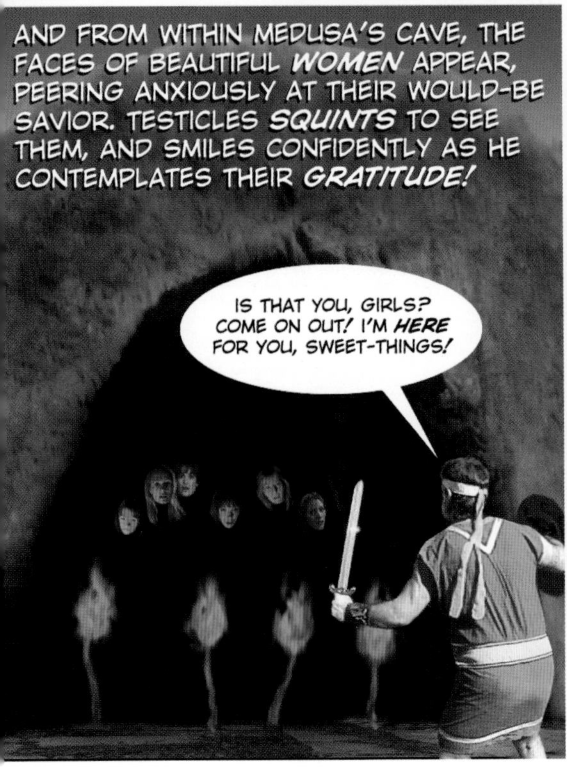
AND FROM WITHIN MEDUSA'S CAVE, THE FACES OF BEAUTIFUL WOMEN APPEAR, PEERING ANXIOUSLY AT THEIR WOULD-BE SAVIOR. TESTICLES SQUINTS TO SEE THEM, AND SMILES CONFIDENTLY AS HE CONTEMPLATES THEIR GRATITUDE!
IS THAT YOU, GIRLS? COME ON OUT! I'M HERE FOR YOU, SWEET-THINGS!

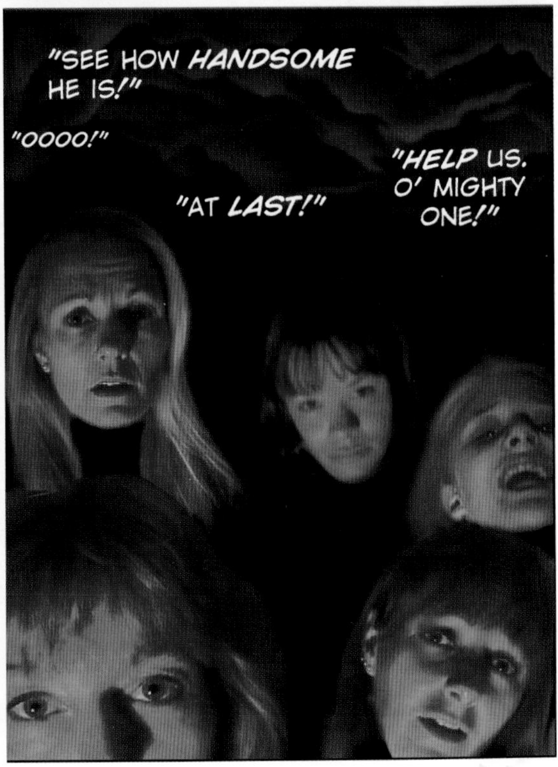
"SEE HOW HANDSOME HE IS!"
"OOOO!"
"AT LAST!"
"HELP US. O' MIGHTY ONE!"

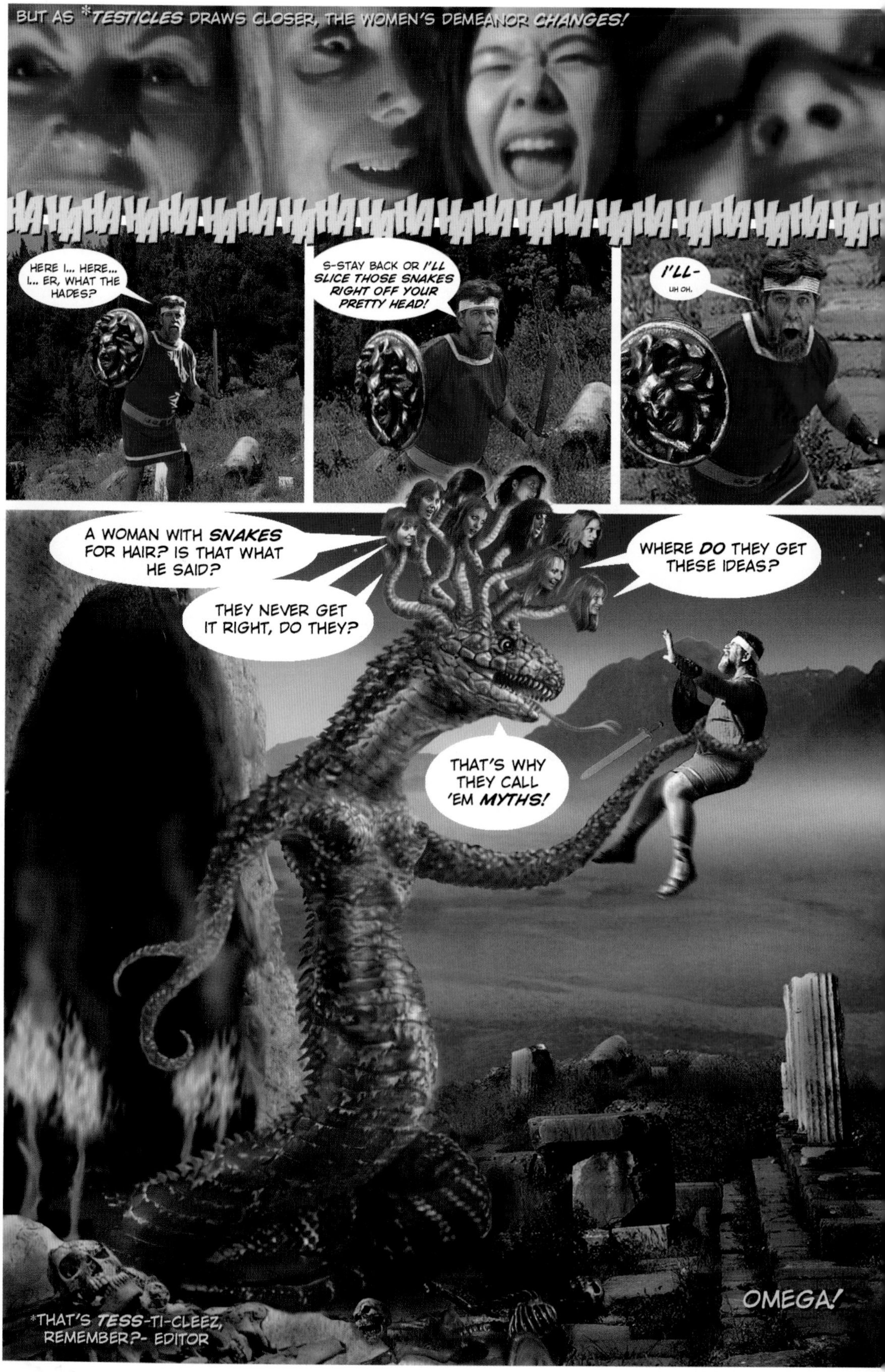
BUT AS *TESTICLES DRAWS CLOSER, THE WOMEN'S DEMEANOR CHANGES!
HAHAHAHAHAHAHAHAHAHAHAHAHAHAHAHAHAHAHAHAHAHAHAHAHAHAHAHAHAHAHA
HERE I... HERE... I... ER, WHAT THE HADES?
S-STAY BACK OR I'LL SLICE THOSE SNAKES RIGHT OFF YOUR PRETTY HEAD!
I'LL-
UH OH.
A WOMAN WITH SNAKES FOR HAIR? IS THAT WHAT HE SAID?
THEY NEVER GET IT RIGHT, DO THEY?
WHERE DO THEY GET THESE IDEAS?
THAT'S WHY THEY CALL 'EM MYTHS!
OMEGA!
*THAT'S TESS-TI-CLEEZ, REMEMBER?- EDITOR

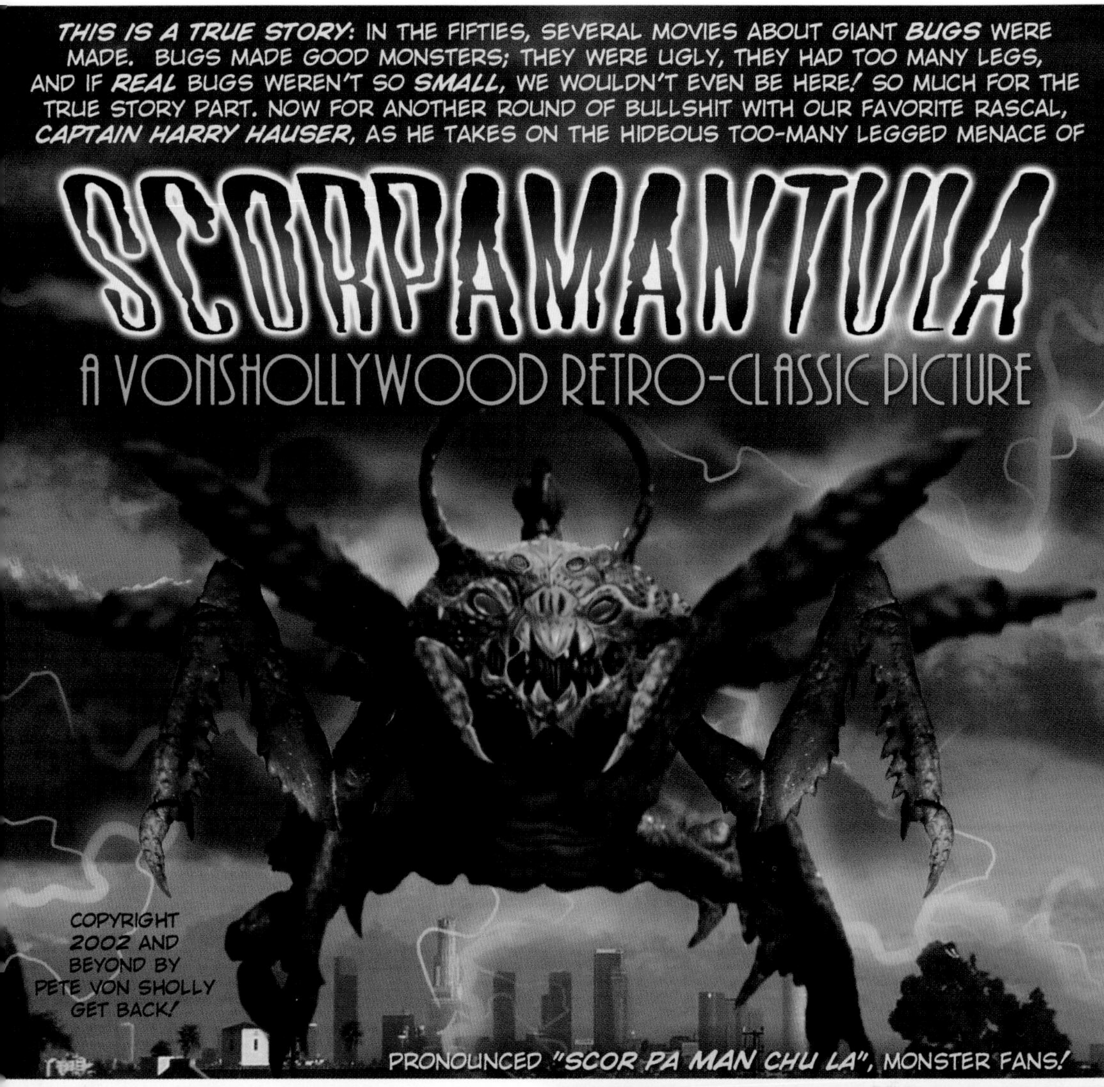
THIS IS A TRUE STORY: IN THE FIFTIES, SEVERAL MOVIES ABOUT GIANT BUGS WERE MADE. BUGS MADE GOOD MONSTERS; THEY WERE UGLY, THEY HAD TOO MANY LEGS, AND IF REAL BUGS WEREN'T SO SMALL, WE WOULDN'T EVEN BE HERE! SO MUCH FOR THE TRUE STORY PART. NOW FOR ANOTHER ROUND OF BULLSHIT WITH OUR FAVORITE RASCAL, CAPTAIN HARRY HAUSER, AS HE TAKES ON THE HIDEOUS TOO-MANY LEGGED MENACE OF
SCORPAMANTULA
A VONSHOLLYWOOD RETRO-CLASSIC PICTURE
COPYRIGHT 2002 AND BEYOND BY PETE VON SHOLLY GET BACK!
PRONOUNCED "SCOR PA MAN CHU LA", MONSTER FANS!

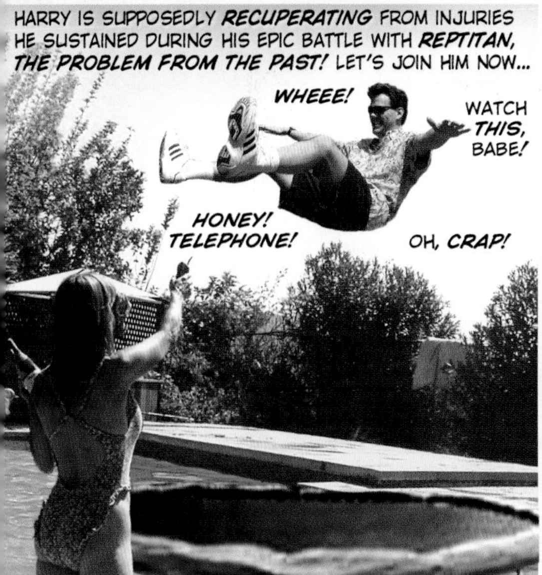
HARRY IS SUPPOSEDLY RECUPERATING FROM INJURIES HE SUSTAINED DURING HIS EPIC BATTLE WITH REPTITAN, THE PROBLEM FROM THE PAST! LET'S JOIN HIM NOW...
WHEEE!
WATCH THIS, BABE!
HONEY! TELEPHONE!
OH, CRAP!

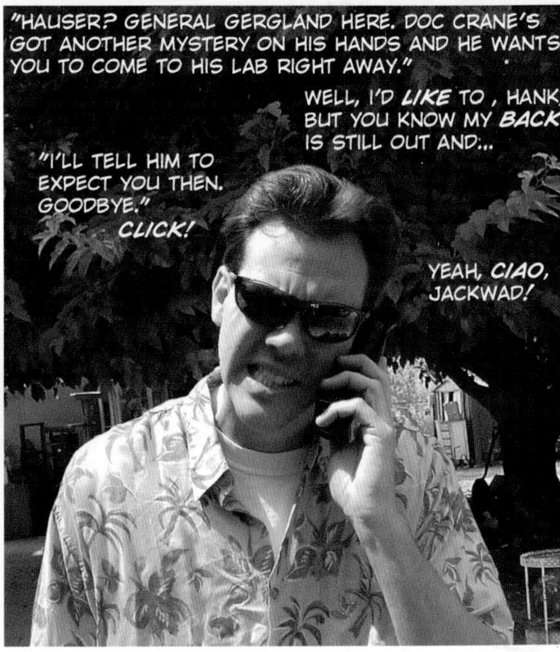
"HAUSER? GENERAL GERGLAND HERE. DOC CRANE'S GOT ANOTHER MYSTERY ON HIS HANDS AND HE WANTS YOU TO COME TO HIS LAB RIGHT AWAY."
WELL, I'D LIKE TO , HANK, BUT YOU KNOW MY BACK IS STILL OUT AND...
"I'LL TELL HIM TO EXPECT YOU THEN. GOODBYE."
CLICK!
YEAH, CIAO, JACKWAD!

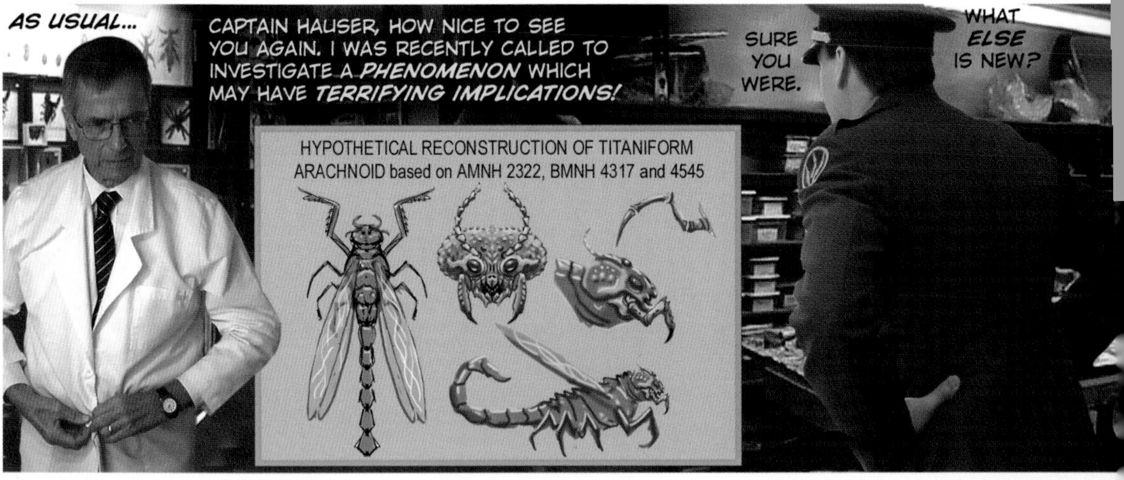
AS USUAL...
CAPTAIN HAUSER, HOW NICE TO SEE YOU AGAIN. I WAS RECENTLY CALLED TO INVESTIGATE A PHENOMENON WHICH MAY HAVE TERRIFYING IMPLICATIONS!
HYPOTHETICAL RECONSTRUCTION OF TITANIFORM ARACHNOID based on AMNH 2322, BMNH 4317 and 4545
SURE YOU WERE.
WHAT ELSE IS NEW?

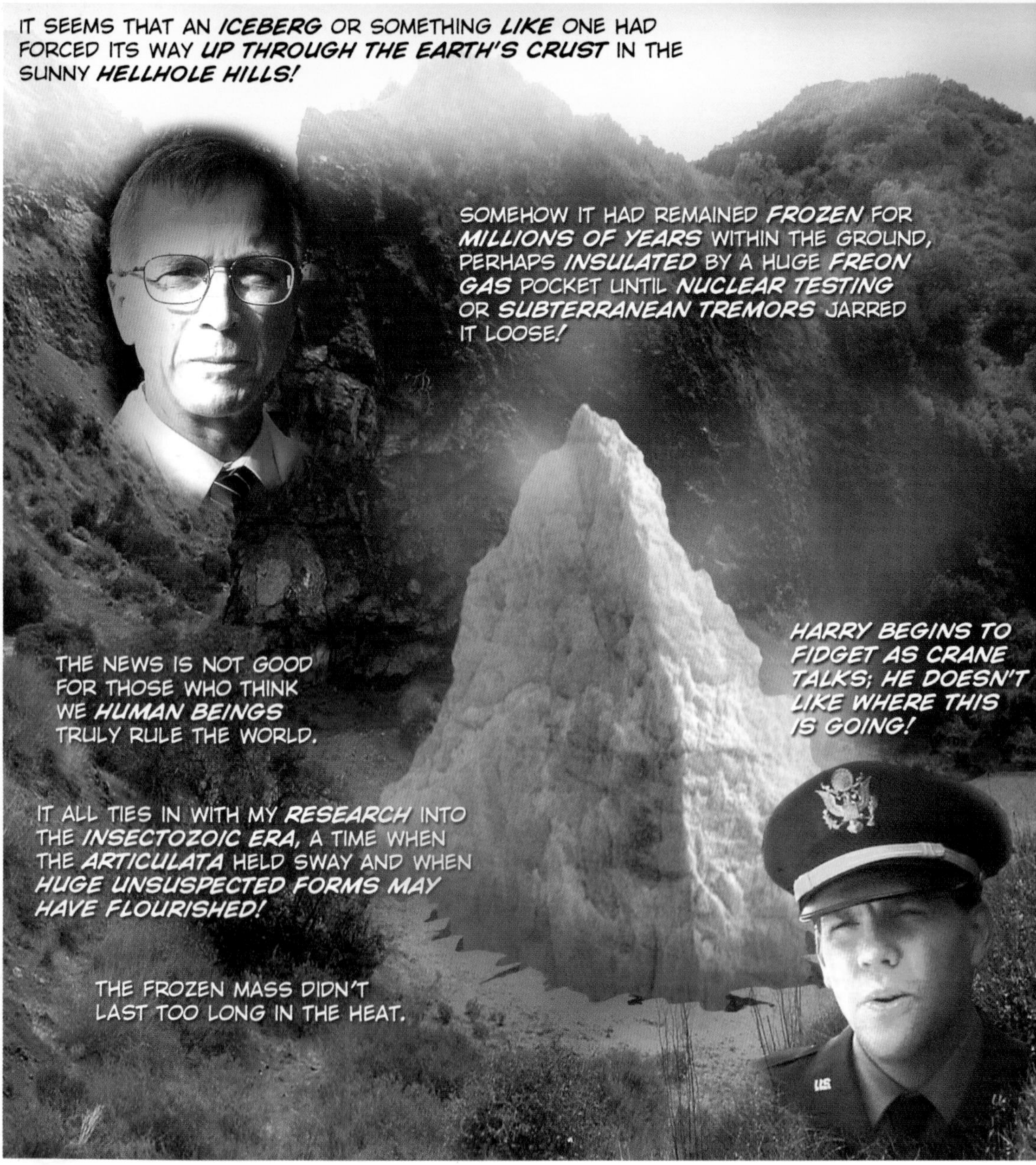
IT SEEMS THAT AN ICEBERG OR SOMETHING LIKE ONE HAD FORCED ITS WAY UP THROUGH THE EARTH'S CRUST IN THE SUNNY HELLHOLE HILLS!
SOMEHOW IT HAD REMAINED FROZEN FOR MILLIONS OF YEARS WITHIN THE GROUND, PERHAPS INSULATED BY A HUGE FREON GAS POCKET UNTIL NUCLEAR TESTING OR SUBTERRANEAN TREMORS JARRED IT LOOSE!
THE NEWS IS NOT GOOD FOR THOSE WHO THINK WE HUMAN BEINGS TRULY RULE THE WORLD.
HARRY BEGINS TO FIDGET AS CRANE TALKS; HE DOESN'T LIKE WHERE THIS IS GOING!
IT ALL TIES IN WITH MY RESEARCH INTO THE INSECTOZOIC ERA, A TIME WHEN THE ARTICULATA HELD SWAY AND WHEN HUGE UNSUSPECTED FORMS MAY HAVE FLOURISHED!
THE FROZEN MASS DIDN'T LAST TOO LONG IN THE HEAT.

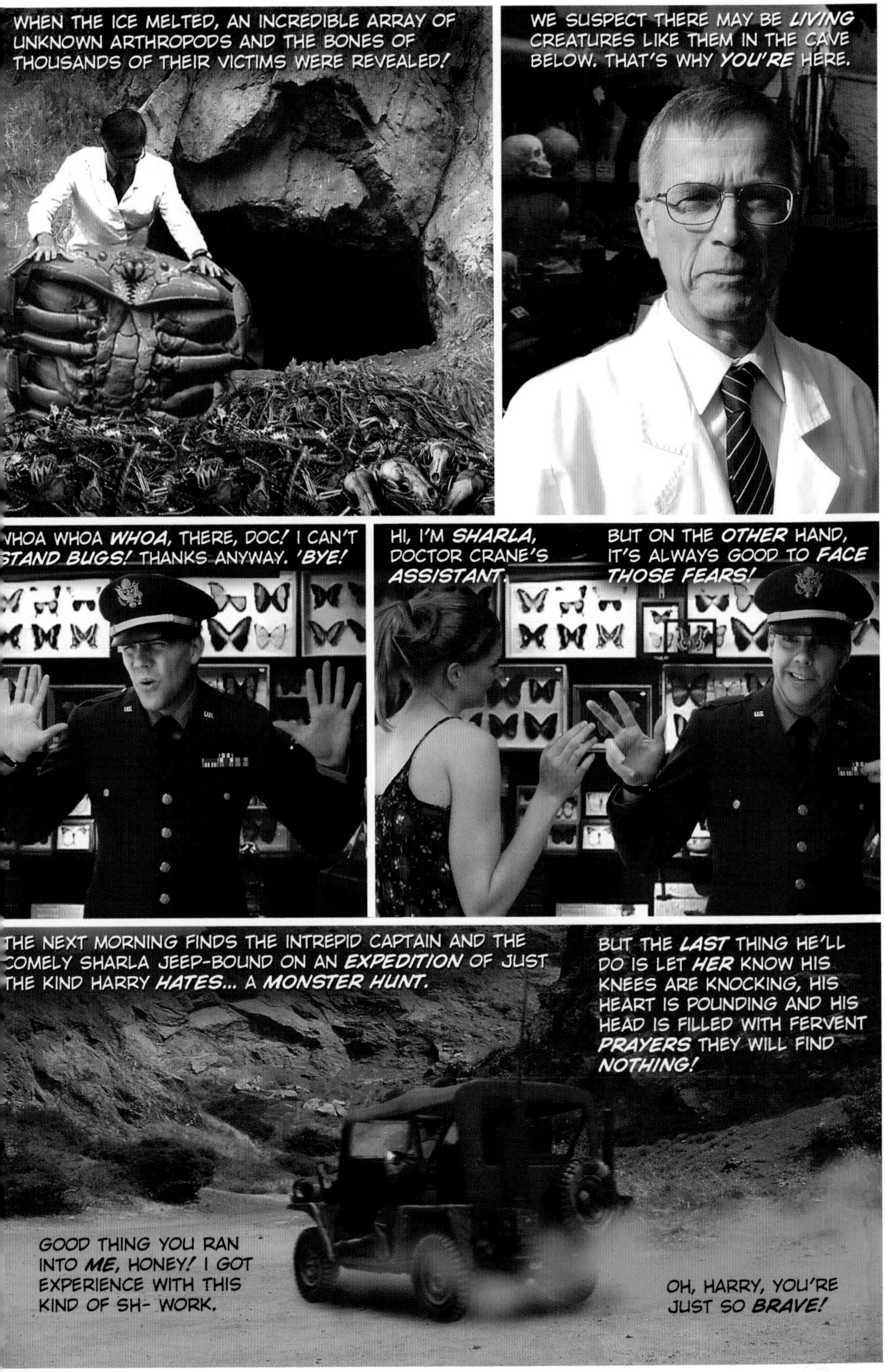
WHEN THE ICE MELTED, AN INCREDIBLE ARRAY OF UNKNOWN ARTHROPODS AND THE BONES OF THOUSANDS OF THEIR VICTIMS WERE REVEALED!
WE SUSPECT THERE MAY BE LIVING CREATURES LIKE THEM IN THE CAVE BELOW. THAT'S WHY YOU'RE HERE.
WHOA WHOA WHOA, THERE, DOC! I CAN'T STAND BUGS! THANKS ANYWAY. 'BYE!
HI, I'M SHARLA, DOCTOR CRANE'S ASSISTANT.
BUT ON THE OTHER HAND, IT'S ALWAYS GOOD TO FACE THOSE FEARS!
THE NEXT MORNING FINDS THE INTREPID CAPTAIN AND THE COMELY SHARLA JEEP-BOUND ON AN EXPEDITION OF JUST THE KIND HARRY HATES... A MONSTER HUNT.
BUT THE LAST THING HE'LL DO IS LET HER KNOW HIS KNEES ARE KNOCKING, HIS HEART IS POUNDING AND HIS HEAD IS FILLED WITH FERVENT PRAYERS THEY WILL FIND NOTHING!
GOOD THING YOU RAN INTO ME, HONEY! I GOT EXPERIENCE WITH THIS KIND OF SH- WORK.
OH, HARRY, YOU'RE JUST SO BRAVE!

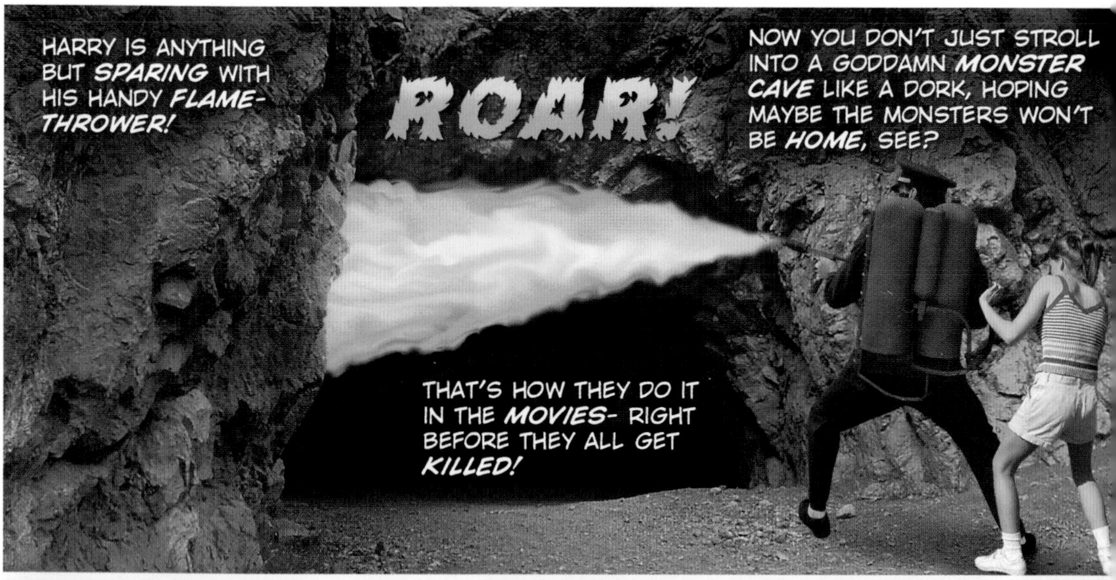

HARRY IS ANYTHING BUT SPARING WITH HIS HANDY FLAME-THROWER!
ROAR!
NOW YOU DON'T JUST STROLL INTO A GODDAMN MONSTER CAVE LIKE A DORK, HOPING MAYBE THE MONSTERS WON'T BE HOME, SEE?
THAT'S HOW THEY DO IT IN THE MOVIES- RIGHT BEFORE THEY ALL GET KILLED!

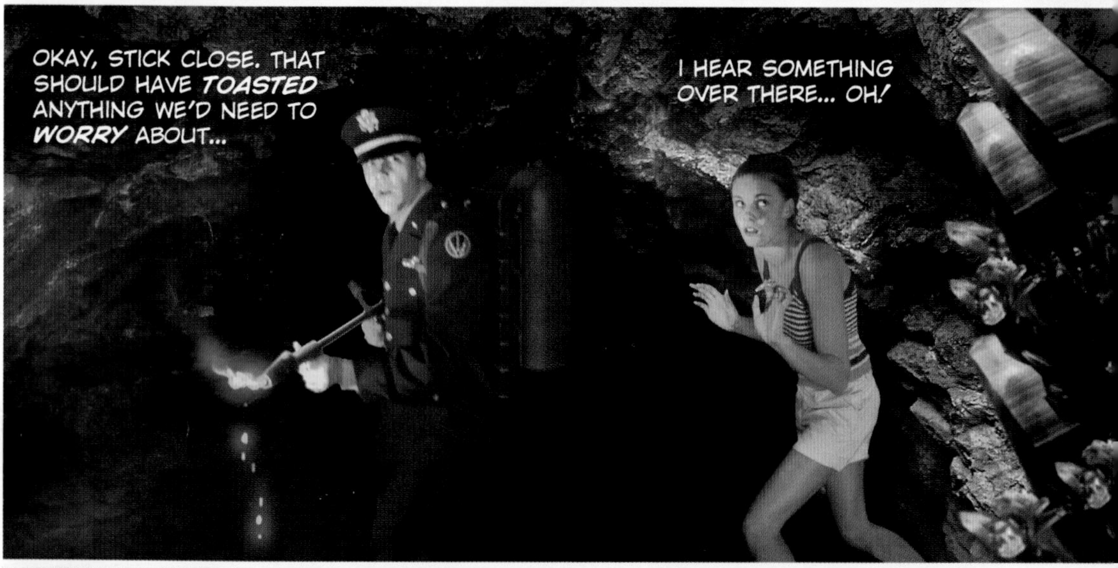

OKAY, STICK CLOSE. THAT SHOULD HAVE TOASTED ANYTHING WE'D NEED TO WORRY ABOUT...
I HEAR SOMETHING OVER THERE... OH!

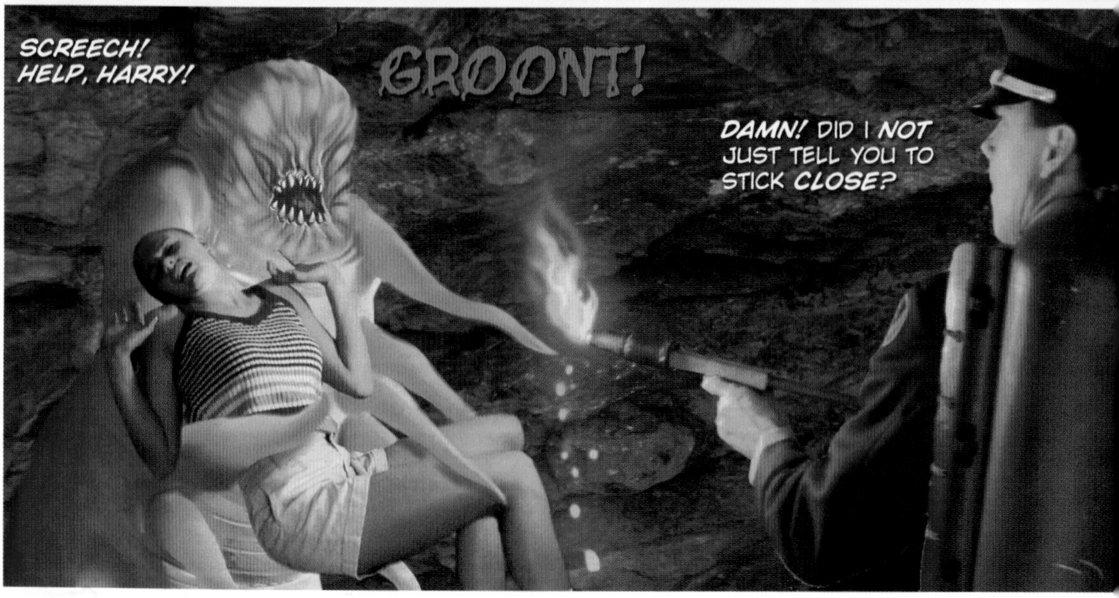

SCREECH! HELP, HARRY!
GROONT!
DAMN! DID I NOT JUST TELL YOU TO STICK CLOSE?

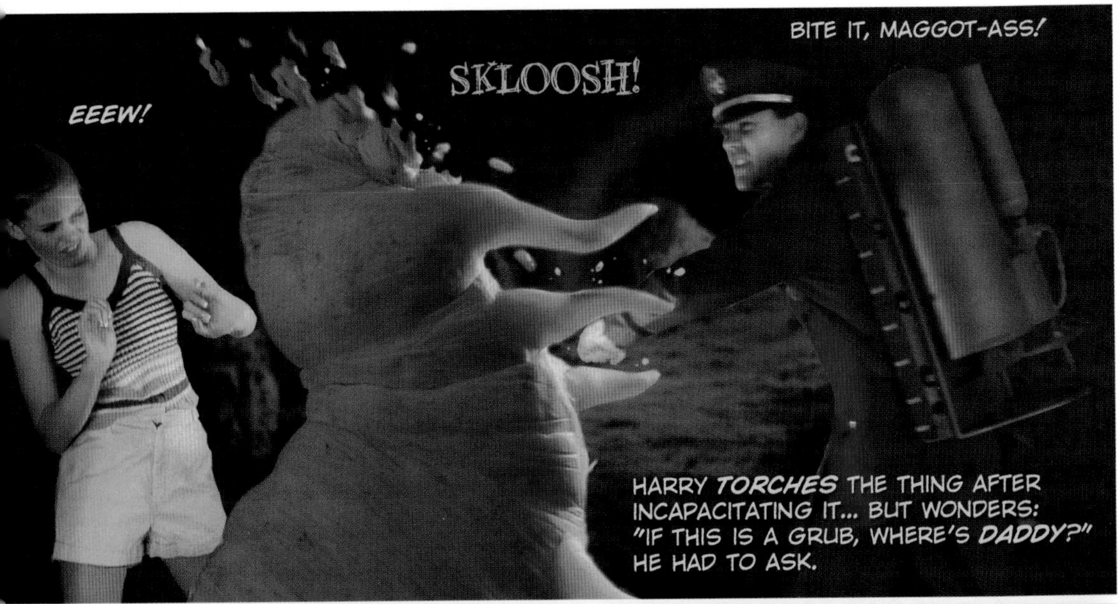
EEEW!
SKLOOSH!
BITE IT, MAGGOT-ASS!
HARRY TORCHES THE THING AFTER INCAPACITATING IT... BUT WONDERS: "IF THIS IS A GRUB, WHERE'S DADDY?" HE HAD TO ASK.

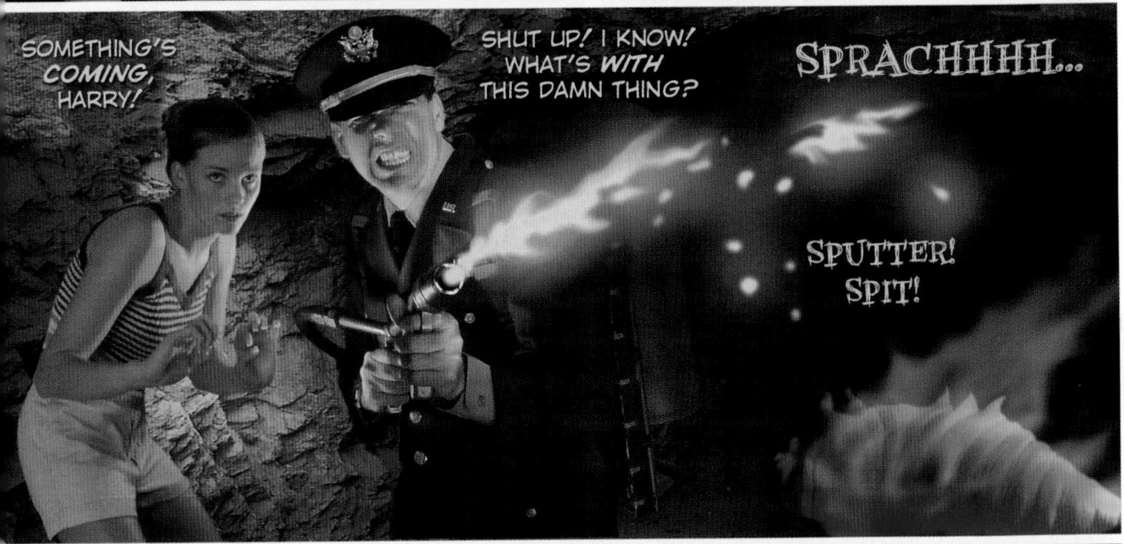
SOMETHING'S COMING, HARRY!
SHUT UP! I KNOW! WHAT'S WITH THIS DAMN THING?
SPRACHHHH...
SPUTTER! SPIT!

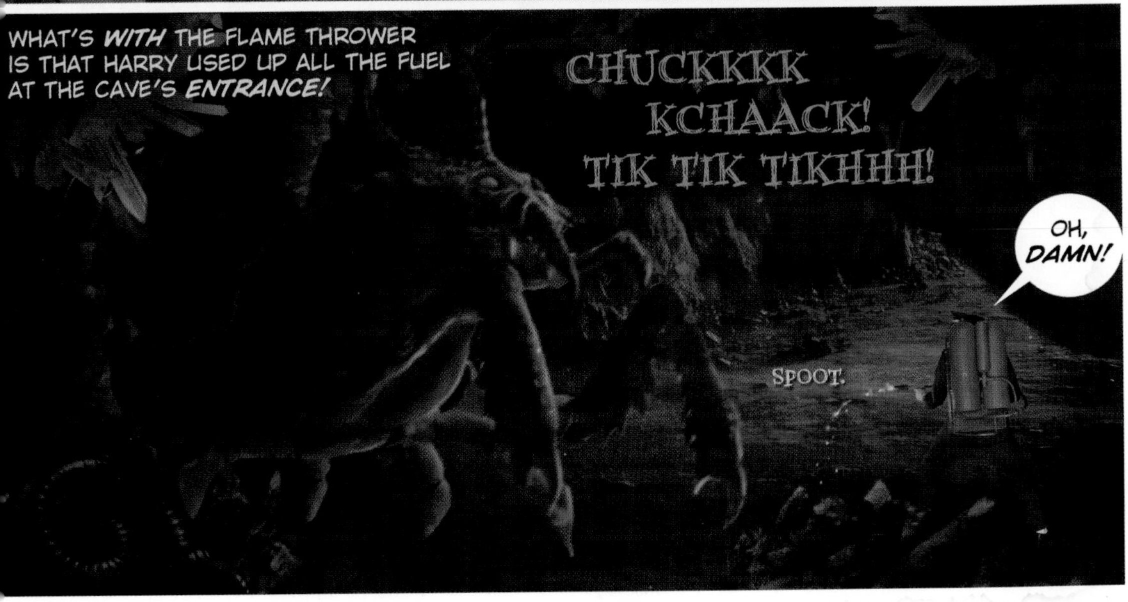
WHAT'S WITH THE FLAME THROWER IS THAT HARRY USED UP ALL THE FUEL AT THE CAVE'S ENTRANCE!
CHUCKKKK
KCHAACK!
TIK TIK TIKHHH!
OH, DAMN!
SPOOT.

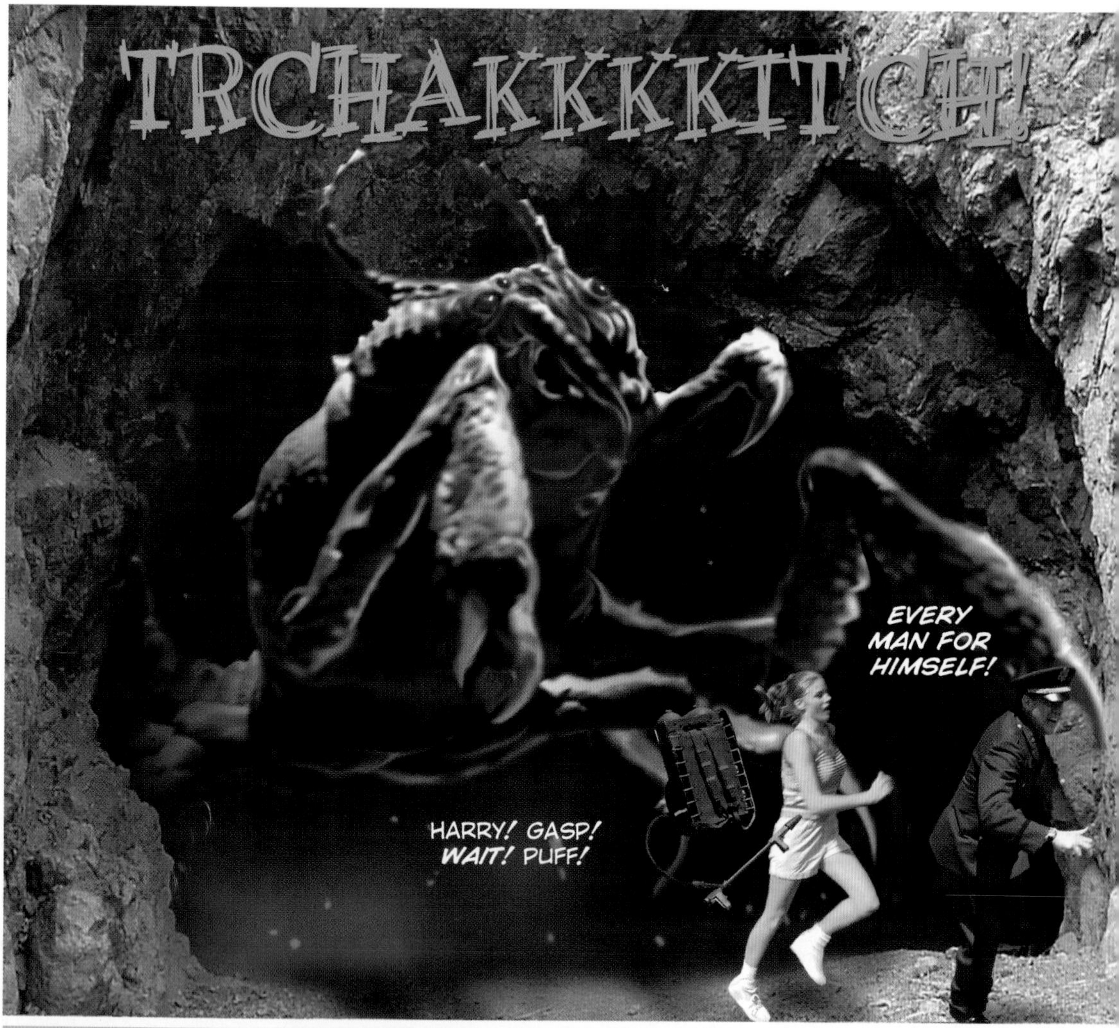
TRCHAKKKKITCH!
EVERY MAN FOR HIMSELF!
HARRY! GASP! WAIT! PUFF!

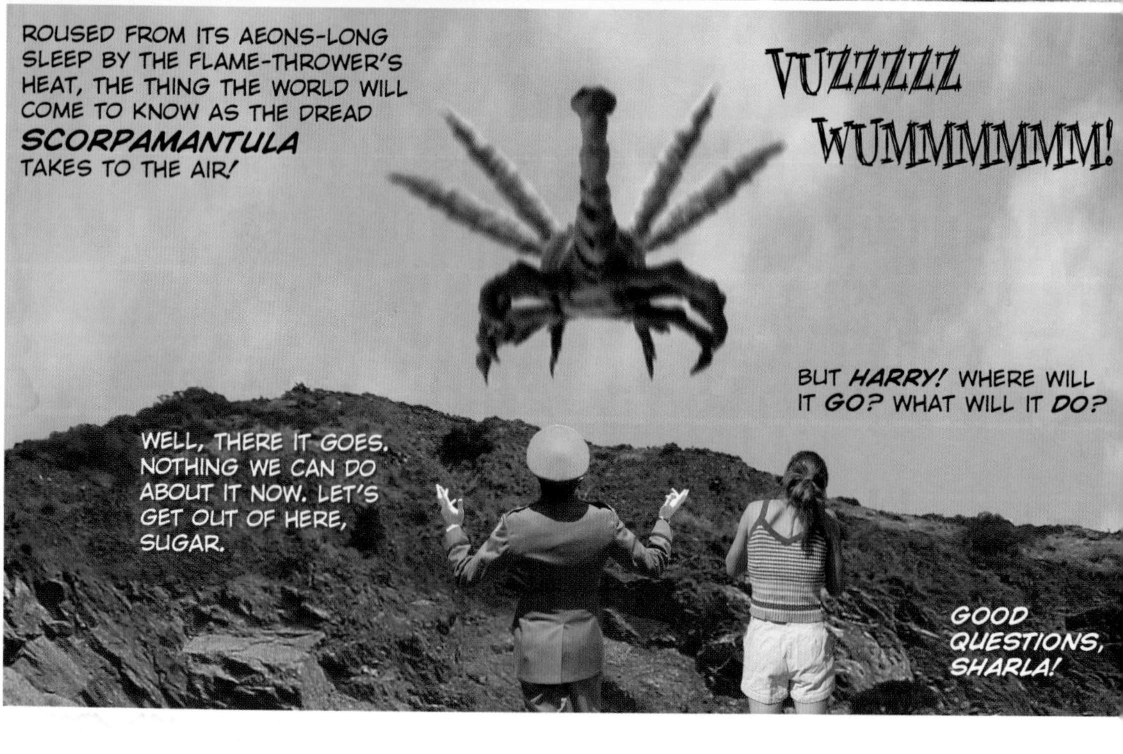
ROUSED FROM ITS AEONS-LONG SLEEP BY THE FLAME-THROWER'S HEAT, THE THING THE WORLD WILL COME TO KNOW AS THE DREAD SCORPAMANTULA TAKES TO THE AIR!
VUZZZZZ WUMMMMMMM!
BUT HARRY! WHERE WILL IT GO? WHAT WILL IT DO?
WELL, THERE IT GOES. NOTHING WE CAN DO ABOUT IT NOW. LET'S GET OUT OF HERE, SUGAR.
GOOD QUESTIONS, SHARLA!

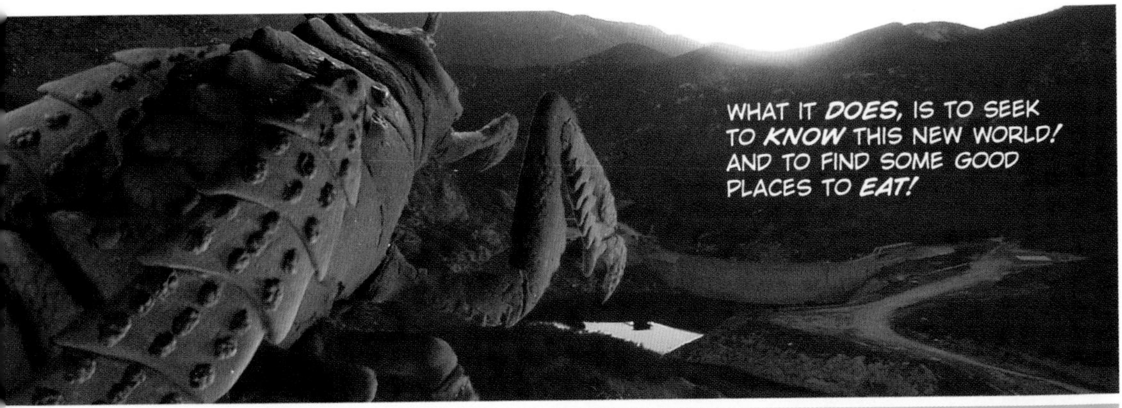
WHAT IT DOES, IS TO SEEK TO KNOW THIS NEW WORLD! AND TO FIND SOME GOOD PLACES TO EAT!

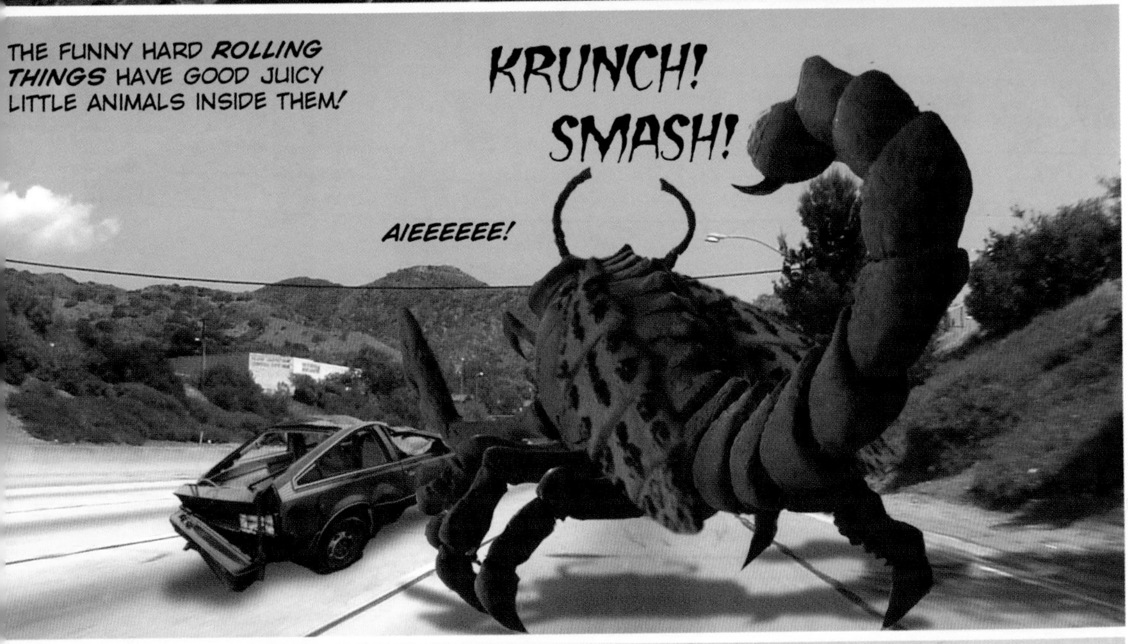
THE FUNNY HARD ROLLING THINGS HAVE GOOD JUICY LITTLE ANIMALS INSIDE THEM!
KRUNCH!
SMASH!
AIEEEEEE!

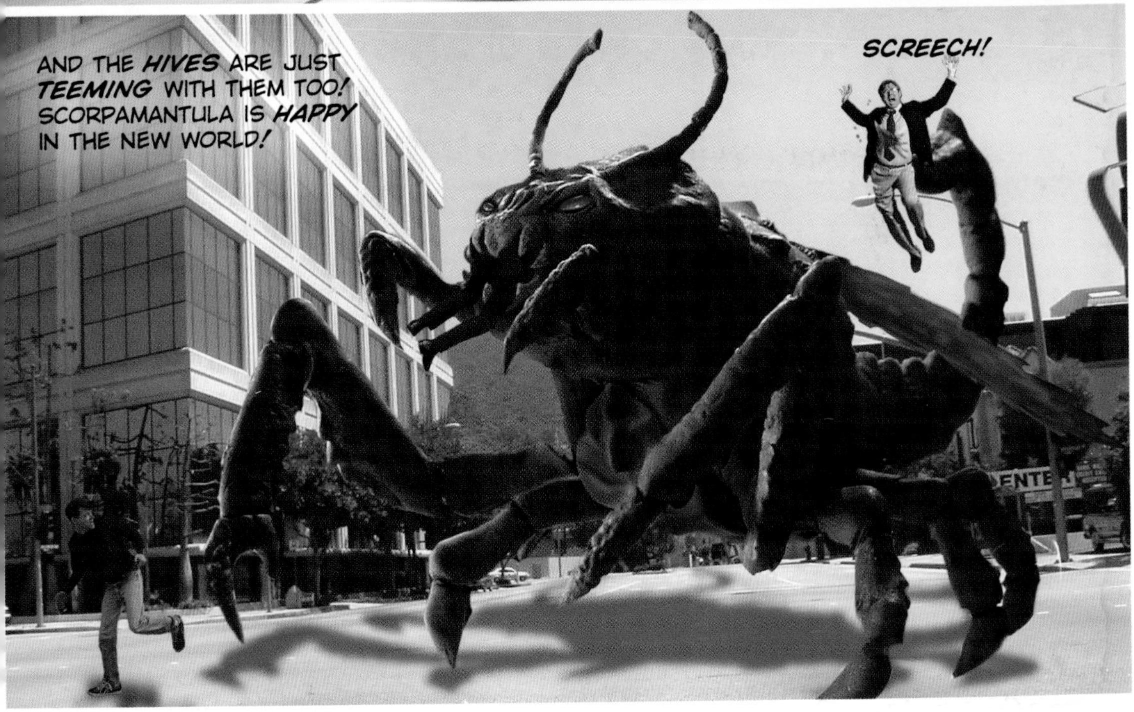
AND THE HIVES ARE JUST TEEMING WITH THEM TOO! SCORPAMANTULA IS HAPPY IN THE NEW WORLD!
SCREECH!

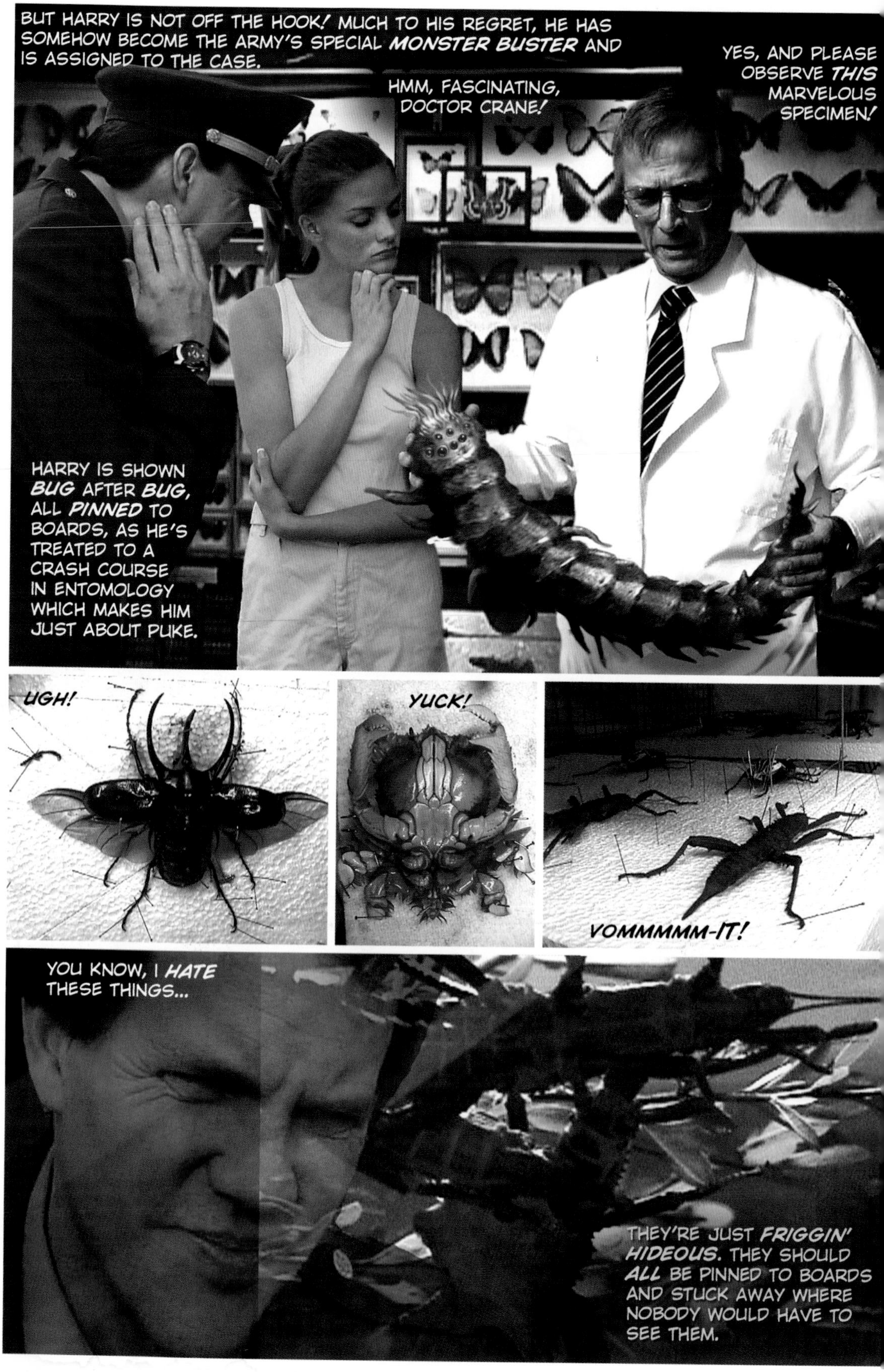
BUT HARRY IS NOT OFF THE HOOK! MUCH TO HIS REGRET, HE HAS SOMEHOW BECOME THE ARMY'S SPECIAL MONSTER BUSTER AND IS ASSIGNED TO THE CASE.
HMM, FASCINATING, DOCTOR CRANE!
YES, AND PLEASE OBSERVE THIS MARVELOUS SPECIMEN!
HARRY IS SHOWN BUG AFTER BUG, ALL PINNED TO BOARDS, AS HE'S TREATED TO A CRASH COURSE IN ENTOMOLOGY WHICH MAKES HIM JUST ABOUT PUKE.
UGH!
YUCK!
VOMMMMM-IT!
YOU KNOW, I HATE THESE THINGS...
THEY'RE JUST FRIGGIN' HIDEOUS. THEY SHOULD ALL BE PINNED TO BOARDS AND STUCK AWAY WHERE NOBODY WOULD HAVE TO SEE THEM.

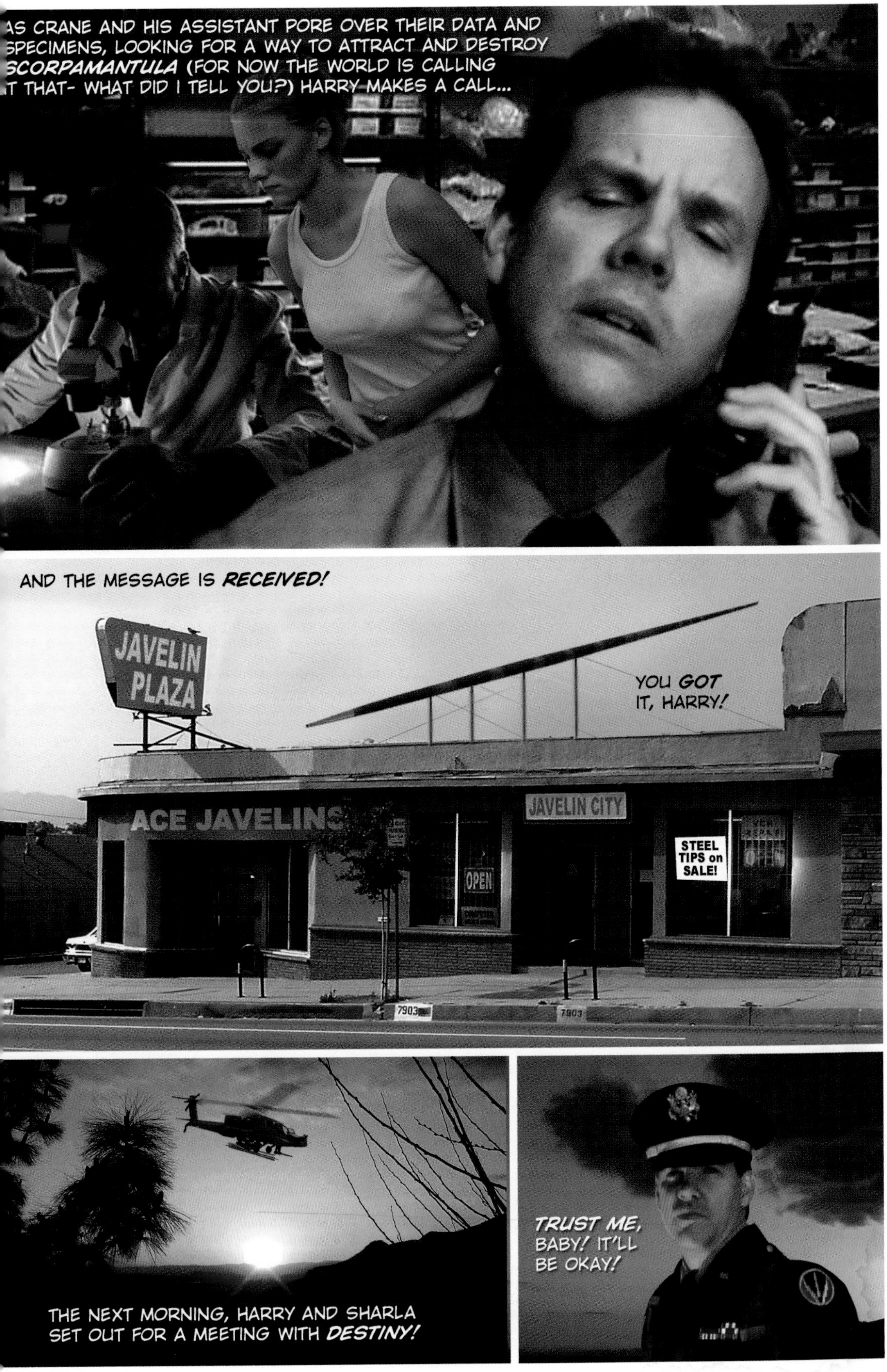
AS CRANE AND HIS ASSISTANT PORE OVER THEIR DATA AND SPECIMENS, LOOKING FOR A WAY TO ATTRACT AND DESTROY SCORPAMANTULA (FOR NOW THE WORLD IS CALLING IT THAT- WHAT DID I TELL YOU?) HARRY MAKES A CALL...
AND THE MESSAGE IS RECEIVED!
JAVELIN PLAZA
YOU GOT IT, HARRY!
ACE JAVELINS
JAVELIN CITY
OPEN
STEEL TIPS on SALE!
7903
7903
THE NEXT MORNING, HARRY AND SHARLA SET OUT FOR A MEETING WITH DESTINY!
TRUST ME, BABY! IT'LL BE OKAY!

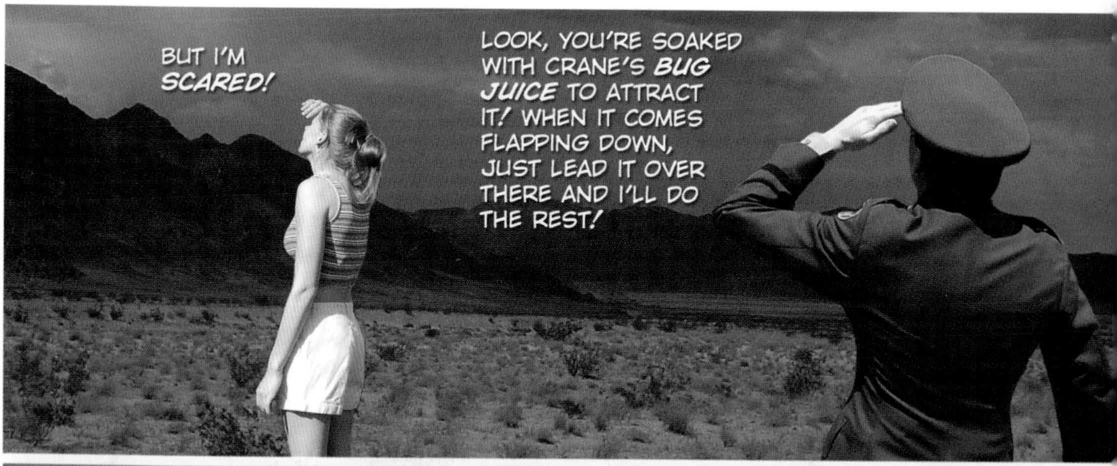
BUT I'M SCARED!
LOOK, YOU'RE SOAKED WITH CRANE'S BUG JUICE TO ATTRACT IT! WHEN IT COMES FLAPPING DOWN, JUST LEAD IT OVER THERE AND I'LL DO THE REST!

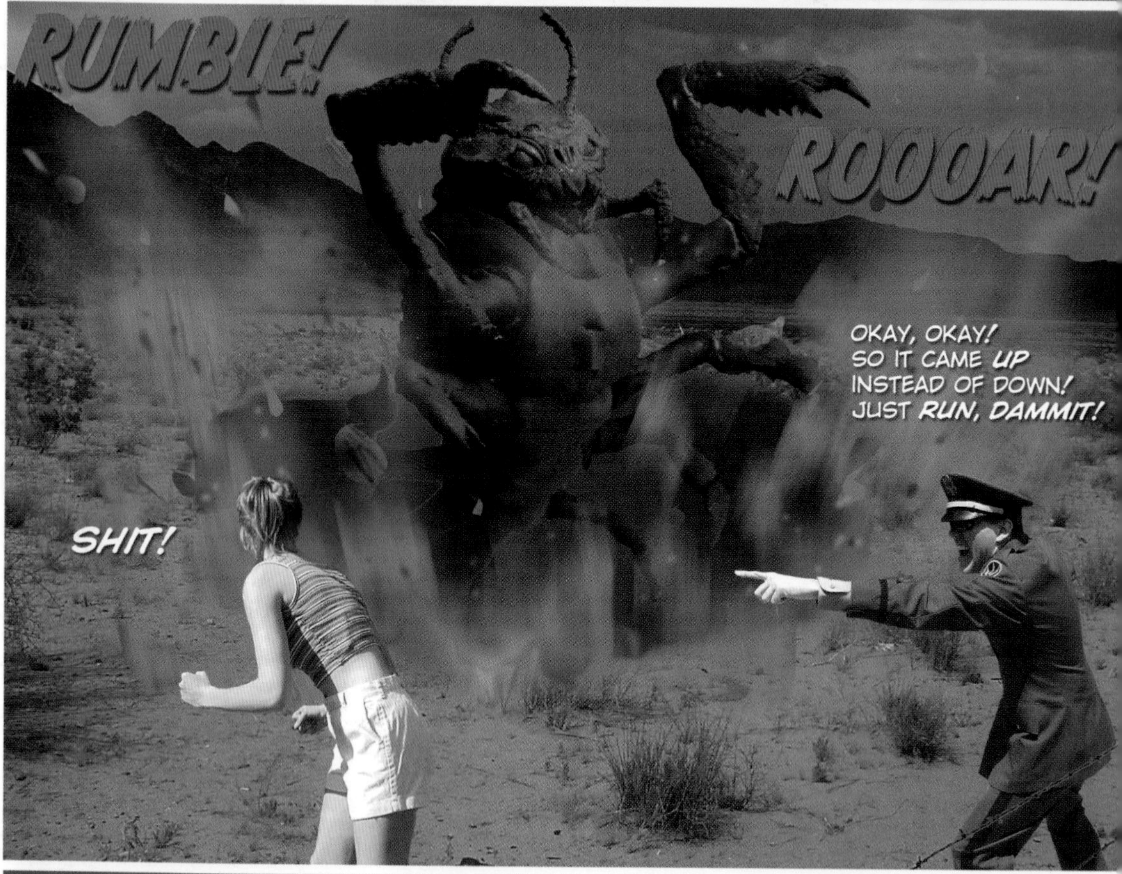
RUMBLE!
ROOOAR!
OKAY, OKAY! SO IT CAME UP INSTEAD OF DOWN! JUST RUN, DAMMIT!
SHIT!

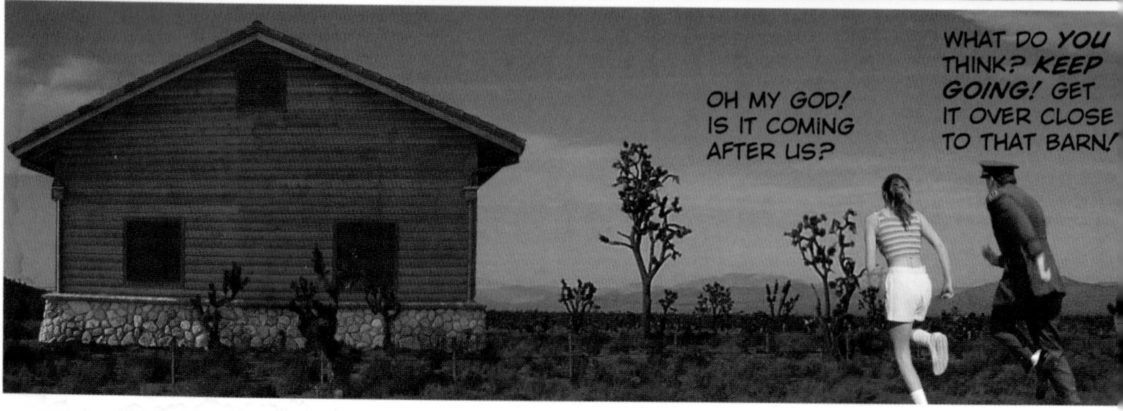
OH MY GOD! IS IT COMING AFTER US?
WHAT DO YOU THINK? KEEP GOING! GET IT OVER CLOSE TO THAT BARN!

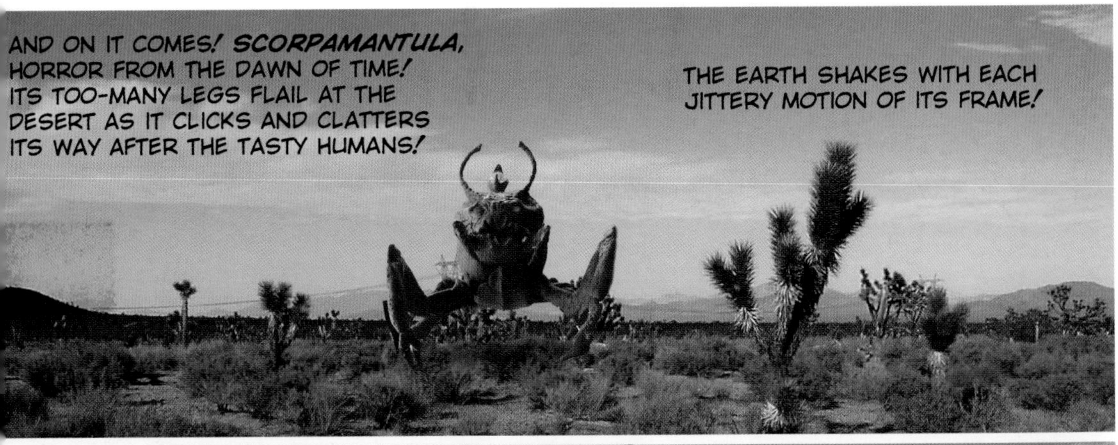
AND ON IT COMES! SCORPAMANTULA, HORROR FROM THE DAWN OF TIME! ITS TOO-MANY LEGS FLAIL AT THE DESERT AS IT CLICKS AND CLATTERS ITS WAY AFTER THE TASTY HUMANS!
THE EARTH SHAKES WITH EACH JITTERY MOTION OF ITS FRAME!

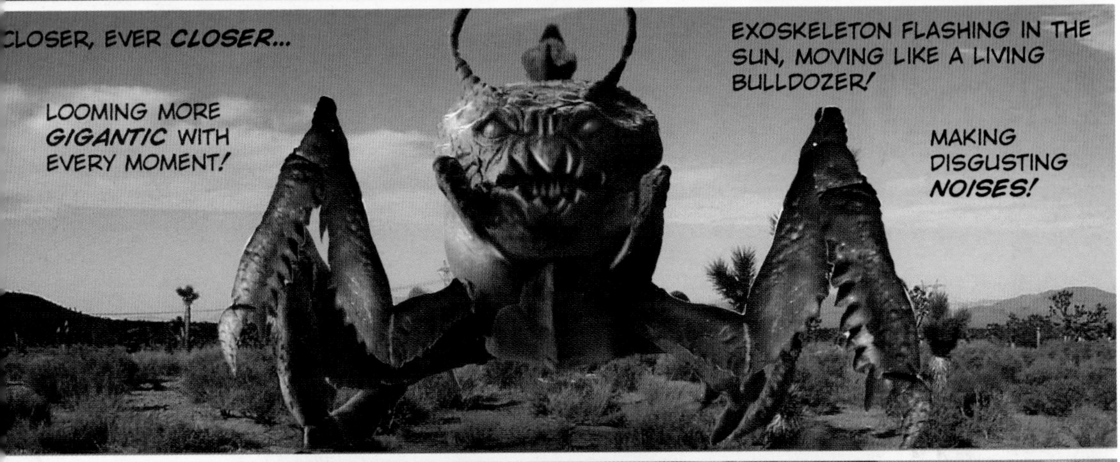
CLOSER, EVER CLOSER...
LOOMING MORE GIGANTIC WITH EVERY MOMENT!
EXOSKELETON FLASHING IN THE SUN, MOVING LIKE A LIVING BULLDOZER!
MAKING DISGUSTING NOISES!

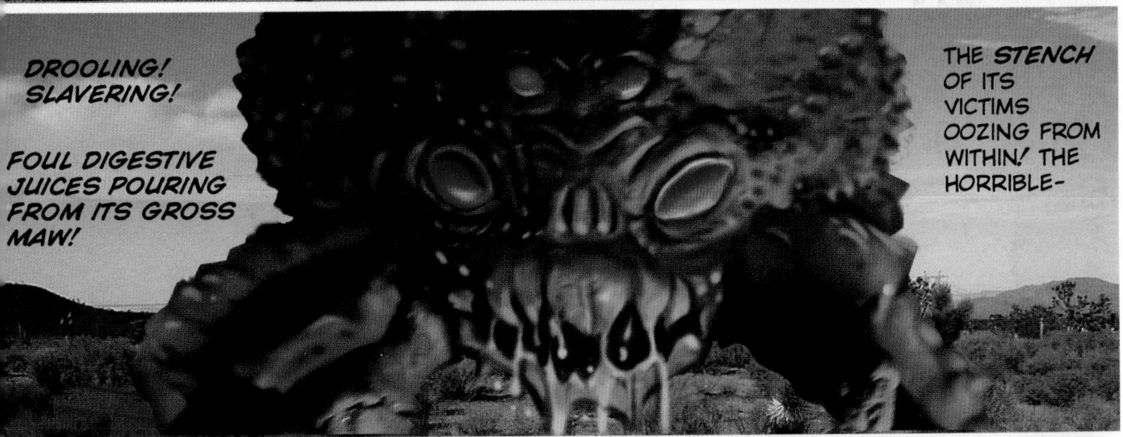
DROOLING! SLAVERING!
FOUL DIGESTIVE JUICES POURING FROM ITS GROSS MAW!
THE STENCH OF ITS VICTIMS OOZING FROM WITHIN! THE HORRIBLE-

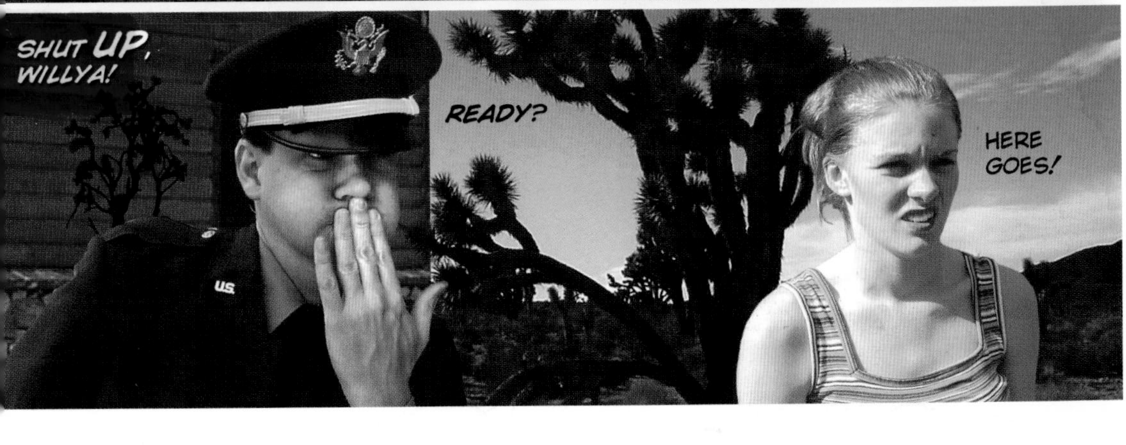
SHUT UP, WILLYA!
READY?
HERE GOES!

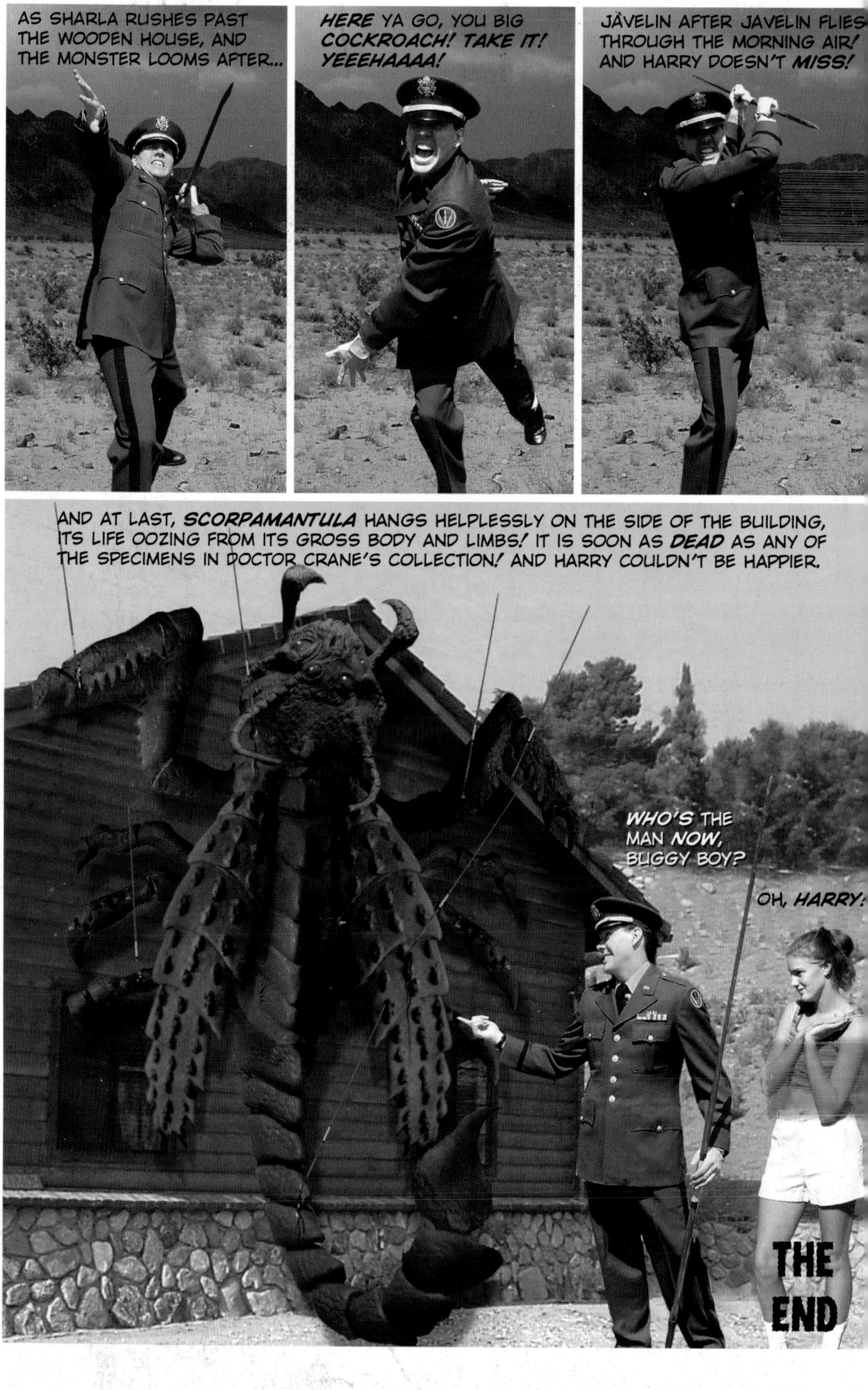
AS SHARLA RUSHES PAST THE WOODEN HOUSE, AND THE MONSTER LOOMS AFTER...
HERE YA GO, YOU BIG COCKROACH! TAKE IT! YEEEHAAAA!
JÄVELIN AFTER JAVELIN FLIES THROUGH THE MORNING AIR! AND HARRY DOESN'T MISS!
AND AT LAST, SCORPAMANTULA HANGS HELPLESSLY ON THE SIDE OF THE BUILDING, ITS LIFE OOZING FROM ITS GROSS BODY AND LIMBS! IT IS SOON AS DEAD AS ANY OF THE SPECIMENS IN DOCTOR CRANE'S COLLECTION! AND HARRY COULDN'T BE HAPPIER.
WHO'S THE MAN NOW, BUGGY BOY?
OH, HARRY!
THE END